THE QUEST TO UNITE US

BOOK I
of the
MARCUS SANTANA
TIME TRAVEL
CHRONICLES

WILLIAM de RHAM

Cover design by Liana Moisescu

Interior design by Ebook Launch

First Printing: July, 2020

Printed and bound in the United States of America.

ISBNs: 978-1-7352393-0-9 (paperback); 978-1-7352393-1-6 (ebook)

Library of Congress Control Number:

For Eugenie

CHAPTER 1

January 1, 2098
Philadelphia, Pennsylvania.

I am a very old man, now—a *Viejo* my grandparents from Spain and Cuba would have called me.

And yet, I feel so young! As if my whole life still lies before me.

It is the meteorite they have uncovered just next door, underneath Franklin Court, where Benjamin Franklin and his family once lived.

I can see it now from the window of the third floor bedroom I once shared with my brother Gus, God rest his soul. A massive cuboid, it is bigger than an old-time locomotive, and as ashen and scarred as the body of Moby Dick.

Once or twice each week, like any good neighbor, I bring *café Cubanos* and guava *pastelitos*—pastries I learned from my mother—to the scientists studying the meteorite. I act the friendly old man: not very sophisticated, but politely interested in their work. I dare not reveal what I know. They would think me a lunatic.

They tell me all their tests have been inconclusive. X-rays, spectrometers, Geiger counters, and every other diagnostic tool they can think of, none register anything whatsoever! As such, they cannot explain why the meteorite sometimes seems to glow. Nor why its surface is so pitted and gouged, even though it cannot be split, cracked, chiseled, or chipped by the hardest substances known to man. Nor why it radiates an energy that makes the skin tingle, an energy that grows stronger as storm clouds gather. Nor why metal objects are sometimes attracted to it and sometimes repelled, often at the same time.

All the scientists can do is guess. They have tested the soil, rocks, and fossils that surrounded the meteorite deep below the surface. From those tests, they speculate that it fell to earth billions of years ago, well before anyone was alive to see it. Some think it came from the farthest reaches of space, passing through galaxy after galaxy, acquiring its unique electro-magnetic properties before streaking into the molten soup that was the beginning of our planet. Then, through the ages, as the earth's crust cooled and volcanoes erupted and tectonic plates shifted and the oceans and continents formed, as our planet heaved up its mountains and carved its rivers, the meteorite slowly migrated to its resting place and sat for ages, underneath where Benjamin Franklin would one day live.

And wouldn't he, great scientist that he was, have been fascinated by it?

As I am fascinated by the experiences it afforded me. I can see them so clearly, as if they are movies running in the theater of my mind—as if they are happening now. And as they play out, I write them down so that, when the meteorite's true nature is revealed, there will be a record of what began some 80 years ago, on my 17th birthday.

***

On that Saturday, I wake early to rain drumming against my window and a cold, March draft blowing through the loose panes. The sky is so gray that the white-painted steel beams forming the skeleton of what had been Benjamin Franklin's home shine neon-bright, as if somehow super-charged.

I remember: today is my special day! I scramble out of bed, eager for it to begin. I flash on last year's celebration: everyone—even Gus, home on leave before deploying to Afghanistan!—gathered at our old, yellow-Formica breakfast table piled with presents and the platter of *patatas fritas con huevos y jamon* Mom always makes for my birthday. Just the thought of those potatoes fried in olive oil and smothered in fried eggs and Spanish ham makes my mouth water.

But the image of Gus brings an empty feeling to my chest, like I've got no breath.

I look to the *MarsScapes* wall calendar above my desk with its rover-taken photos of Martian pink skies and red deserts. Inside today's square,

I've written the number 241, which follows yesterday's 240 and comes before tomorrow's 242. It's been 241 days since a Taliban rocket blew the Army chopper carrying Gus and his fellow Green Berets out of the sky.

The ache in my chest deepens, but I'm determined not to ruin the chance of a good day. Over the last eight months, there haven't been many. And I'm hopeful. Today, rehearsals begin for our high school's production of Arthur Miller's *The Crucible.* Because I'm big and lanky and look like I could be a farmer, I've been cast as John Proctor, the lead. If it's anything I've got a passion for these days, its acting. It's all I "want to be when I grow up."

I throw on old jeans, a flannel shirt, and a hoodie for rehearsal. Since farmers wear boots and my clumsy feet need to get used to the weight, I grab Gus's old ones from basic training. In socks, carrying the boots, I pad down the two flights of stairs to the open kitchen/living room that's the whole first floor of our small row house. Halfway down the last flight, as I clear the second floor, I see Mom, Pop, and my 12 year-old sister Penny at the Formica table.

There's no present, or platter of food, or smell of cooking, or excited talk, and I'm so disappointed that everything in me sags. But then I really see my family: three silent people—looking as sad as I feel inside—spooning up Grape Nuts, staring out the sliding glass door at the rain pelting the bricks of our tiny back patio. Right then, I want to break into song, or prat-fall down the stairs, or even dump one of those bowls of soggy cereal over my head—anything to get everyone laughing together, like we used to.

Even though it's Saturday, Mom and Pop are both dressed for work in their dark business suits, which means she's going to her law office and he's headed for the Philadelphia Historical Society where he's the Librarian. Penny wears pink tights and a black leotard for gymnastics class. I think how everyone's going off to do their own thing and that it's good I have rehearsal.

And how I gotta do something to lighten this mood.

"Hey, yo, yo, yo! *Mamacita! Papcita! Pennycita!* Check me out!" I say, holding the boots to my ear like a boom box, sway-swaggering down the stairs, doing my best John Leguizamo. "Who's everybody's favorite *caballero* this beautiful Philly morning?"

Penny giggles. Her small, dark face—"the jewel of Somalia" Mom's called it ever since adopting her as a toddler—beams one of her I'm-so-happy-to-see-you smiles; and that makes everything just a little bit better.

"Happy Birthday, Marcus!" she cries.

But then Mom looks at me. For some reason, she's furious. I can tell by the way she's got her jaw clenched. And her mane of dark-chocolate hair is pulled back from her widow's peak in a bun so tight it looks like it hurts. Always a bad sign.

"Hush, Penny!" she scolds. "What did I just say about Marcus being in big trouble?"

"Huh? What?" I say. "What'd I do?"

"This!" Mom says, waving typed pages that look like one of her legal memos. And she's got her prosecutor's face on—the one she learned during her 20 years with the Philadelphia D.A.'s office.

"What? What's that?"

"Your paper on Washington and Lincoln? The one you said you finished so I'd sign the permission slip for you to do *The Crucible*?"

"You printed it off the computer without asking? Yo, *Mami!* You *spied* on me?"

"*Don't* even begin down that road, Marcus!" she says, pointing an accusing finger. "The only issue here is this paper, which is terrible."

"Why? What's wrong with it?"

"*Hijo*," Pop says softly, using his pet name for me. "Better to ask: what is right with it?"

"Great! That tells me a lot!" I snap before I can stop myself. I know better than to back-sass, but I'm stung, especially since, with a Ph.D. in American History, Pop knows the difference between a good paper and a bad one, which is why I was never going to show it to him.

"Lose the attitude, Marcus, and hold that temper of yours," Mom warns. "And, both of you, stop with the "*Mami*"s and the "*Hijo*"s! In this house, we speak proper English!"

So much for John Leguizamo, I mourn as Pop begins his lecture.

"Your task, as I understood it, was to analyze which President—Washington or Lincoln—was more important to the development of our nation. Your paper begins by reciting some of the events of Washington's and Lincoln's lives and then goes on to say … absolutely nothing! There's no thesis, no argument, no analysis. Nothing to tell us who you think these men were, or why they were important, much less who made the bigger contribution. It is as if you simply went to Wikipedia, summarized what you found there, and stopped. Did you even read the biographies I brought home from the historical society?"

"Yeah ... but see—"

"So, no!" Mom says, slapping the table top.

Actually, I *had* plowed my way through a lot of what Pop brought home. But then, to save time, I'd pretty much copied from Wikipedia, which I'm disappointed Pop sussed out, since, if he did it, my history teacher probably will too.

"Marcus, what has happened to you?" Pop asks in his gentle way. "You used to be such an excellent student. But ever since Gus—"

"No excuses, Fernando!" Mom says.

"No, you are right, Marguerite, no excuses." He turns back to me. "Marcus, how do you expect to go to a decent college with a report card full of pig tracks?"

"I don't," I say, my temper rising, as it always seems to do whenever school or college comes up. I don't understand why, but it's how I feel.

"*What?*" Mom says. "What's that supposed to mean?"

"It means: I'm not going to college. There's nothing there for me. So it's a waste. Anyways, we can't afford it."

"Where'd you get that idea?" Mom says hotly, like I just ratted out some dark secret.

"From you! You're the one always saying how much we owe: mortgage and keeping up the house and Catholic school tuition for Gus, me, and Penny, your and Pop's old school loans, plus the loan you took so you could start your own practice—"

"Yes, so that I would make more money—"

"Yeah? And how's that working out for you? Found anyone to share the lease on that fancy office you rented across the street from Independence Hall—"

"Young man, that is *none* of your concern!"

I don't go any further. I know I've already gone too far.

"Marguerite, Marcus, please," Pop tries to interrupt.

But Mom rides right over him.

"Your only concern," she says, pointing that finger at me again, "is making the grades you need to get yourself into a good college. And you *are* going to a good college, even if I have to make you repeat your junior year to do it."

"Oh no, I ain't, *Mami!* And *you* can't make me," I say. "Especially since it isn't what I want to do."

"And what is it that you want to do, *hijo?*" Pop asks.

"Move to New York and be an actor. Do plays and movies and be a star—"

"An actor?" Mom splutters. "Have you lost your mind?"

"Why? What's wrong with being an actor?"

"Oh, I don't know," she says in that sarcastic way of hers. "How about … starvation? Do you know the odds—"

"Oh, Mom! Nobody's going to *starve.*"

"No, *hijo?*" Pop asks. "Then how will you make your living while you await your big break? Assuming a break comes your way and you have the talent, skill, knowledge, and experience to take advantage."

"I figured I'd do what everyone else does. Wait tables."

"Be a waiter," Mom repeats flatly. "Is that why you think my parents risked their lives to cross from Cuba in that leaky boat? Or why your father and I worked as hard as we've worked to educate ourselves and become respected professionals and make a home for you and send you to a good Catholic school? For you to be a waiter?"

"Why? What's wrong with it? It's good, honorable work."

"Yes, Marcus, you're right," Pop says. "It is good, honorable work. But it is also far less than what you are capable of. And I suspect that if you come to the end of your life and a waiter is all you have ever been, you will be very disappointed."

"No one's saying that's all I'll ever be," I snap. "All I'm saying is that waiting's what I'll do to make the rent while looking for acting work."

"And what happens, *hijo*, if you never find such work? What will you do with no college and no other skills? And has it occurred to you that college might just teach you some of the things and afford you some of the experiences you'll need to become a successful actor? Do you really want to so narrow your options? And what happened to your plan of becoming a lawyer and joining your mother in her practice?"

6

"That was never my plan!" I lie. "That was Gus's. He's the one who loved all that history and government and political stuff, just like you guys. Not me. Theater's what I want."

And it is, because the stage is the only place where I really feel like I know what I'm doing; where I don't feel scared or embarrassed or geeky or like some big fool. It's the one place where I'm totally focused on what I'm doing and able to forget about the bad stuff going on.

"And what about science?" Pop says. "What has happened to your love of science? Even my father and mother say you have a talent for that. Having both devoted their lives to research, they should know."

"Enough!" Mom says, slapping the table. "There's no more time. 'Nando, call the Uber now or we'll be late. I'll drop Penny at ballet and you at the historical society before going to the office to prepare the clients for trial. We start Monday, so don't expect to see me until late."

She turns to me.

"As for you, Marcus, you will spend the rest of this weekend re-writing that history paper."

"Sorry. Can't. Got rehearsal for the play—"

"There is no play," Mom says. "I've already called Father Mike and told him we're revoking our permission because of your grades."

"You *what???*"

"And he agreed. Wholeheartedly!"

"But it's the lead!" I say, hating the whine in my voice.

"Too bad. There's eight weeks left to the school year. Father Mike has been talking with your teachers and the feeling is that if you buckle down now, they'll work with you in terms of your final grades, the ones the colleges will see. But you must do the work. Which means no extracurricular activities: no debate team, no science club, no play."

"I can't believe you're doing this! This is *so* unfair!"

"*Hijo*, it is for your own good."

"No, it's not! It's got nothing to do with what I want. It only matters so you can brag how "our boy" is going to Harvard or Yale or MIT, like you did with Gus being a Green Beret—"

"What?" Mom says, looking like she's just been punched.

"Marcus, please," my father says, his eyes filling.

But I don't care. First they forget my birthday? Then they spy on me? And then cut me off from the one thing I really love? All for some stupid paper about two dead guys?

"You're not going to let me do the play?" I say. "Fine! How's about I just get on a bus and move to New York today?"

All of a sudden, Mom doesn't look so wounded. Standing straight with her shoulders squared, she raises an eyebrow.

"Very well, Marcus. If that's what you want. By all means, go."

"Marguerite—" Pop says, alarmed.

But she cuts him off with a chop of her hand; and as she does, outside a car honks three times.

"No," she says, gathering her coat. "If Marcus wishes to run away, that's his choice."

"Run away?" I say. "Ever occur to you I might be running *to* something, like my future?"

"Oh, please!" Mom says. "The only place you're running is away from your responsibility."

"What responsibility?"

"To yourself. To be the best Marcus Santana you can be."

"What are you talking about?"

"Perhaps that's something you can think about while you're down in that basement working on that paper. That's if you have the guts to stick around," she says over her shoulder as she pushes Pop and Penny out the door.

"Guts?" I splutter, like I've just been punched. "I'll show you guts—"

The door slams shut and I am alone.

At that moment I'm so angry and torn I don't know what to do. Part of me wants to run after them and keep arguing, especially since she's hit me in my courage, which I've always worried about. Part just wants to say "Screw it," rush upstairs, pack a bag, and split.

Frozen by indecision, I look out to the patio. The rain's pounding the brickwork, hissing like steam.

Over the back wall, the white-painted steel beams of Ben Franklin's "ghost house" loom. Mom and Pop love that we live next to Franklin Court with its museum dedicated to all things Franklin. Even Gus thought it was "awesome." Me? I couldn't care less.

"History!" I growl. "Give me a freakin' break! And I will so go to New York!" I yell at no one except the sky.

A huge bolt of lightning strikes the top-most beam of the steel skeleton, shooting off sparks and turning the whole world white. Sky-ripping thunder shakes the house. Wind hurls rain and leaves from

Franklin Court's big mulberry tree over the patio wall and into the glass door. Another jolt of lightning hits; and all the power dies.

"Great!" I fume. "Just effing GREAT!"

Pulling on Gus's boots without tying them, I grab the flashlight from the kitchen drawer to go to the basement and see if it's a fuse. After that lightning strike, I'm pretty sure it's not. But just in case.

I open the basement door, expecting nothing but darkness since there aren't any windows down there. Instead, everything's bathed in this strange blue light. Drawn by it, I go down the stairs in wonder. Our furnace, the hot water heater, the washer-dryer and the old table with the family computer all seem now to glow, as if they were made of sapphires.

I reach the bottom step. The light looks to be coming from the back of the cellar. So I turn; and completely stop breathing.

Our back wall of old brick and crumbling mortar is gone. In its place is something looking like it belongs in the Camden Aquarium: a wall of blue liquid, as blue as the Atlantic Ocean on a hot and sunny summer day down at the Jersey Shore.

Dazed, I approach it, squeezing past all our old junk: toys, games, and sports stuff we've stopped using, broken furniture Pop swears he'll fix, boxes of books and paperwork, Gus's footlocker and Dad's ornate old trunk, brought by his parents when they came from Spain.

The closer I get, the brighter the wall dazzles, sparkling and shimmering, casting its sapphire sheen onto everything. Through the "water," way off in the distance, I see a bright yellow disc. I wonder: *Is that a sun? Is this ocean? It can't be. There aren't any fish. And what's holding the water back? There's no glass! The basement should be flooded to the ceiling. But it isn't. Everything up to the wall is bone-dry.*

I reach out to touch the shimmering, radiant, blue surface.

Big mistake.

CHAPTER 2

A current shoots up my arm, filling my body, paralyzing me. It feels like millions of ants are racing through my veins.

I'm pulled forward, into the "water," which isn't wet at all. I can still breathe, but everything feels desert-dry and very still. What had seemed a cool blue from the outside is now all hot, yellow light. I try to move: an arm, a leg, a hand, a toe—anything! But I'm frozen.

Then, suddenly, I'm flying through the air. The ants are gone and I can move. Good thing, too, because I'm about to slam into the ground face first. I reach out, push off, and land flat on my back, staring up at a ceiling, the breath knocked out of me.

Everything's still glowing blue. But from the ceiling I can tell I'm definitely not in our basement. Made of broad planks of light-colored wood supported by dark-wood beams, it has no pipes or wires or ductwork hanging from it. It's just a bare wood ceiling. And this doesn't smell like our basement, all musty and dusty. This smells of earth and pine and smoke and … cornbread?

I look at the walls. One is still completely taken up by the blue, shimmering surface. The others are made from gray, irregular stones and mortar. A smoky, weak-flamed lantern hangs from each. *What is this? Some kind of dungeon?* I wonder groggily.

Groaning, I roll on my side. The floor isn't cement. It's packed earth, dark and damp and cool.

Two scuffed, buckled shoes appear, and stocky legs in mud-brown stockings bagging at the ankles. I follow those stockings up to a pair of knee britches and a leather apron.

"As I live and breathe, he has returned," a man says.

"*Qu—Qui?*" asks a woman in a trembling voice.

"English, please, Elise. English. It is the only way you will improve."

"Who?" she whispers.

"Marcus. Marcus Santana. He said this would happen. But it's been so long—eleven years—and so much has happened, I'd almost forgotten."

Lying back, I look up into the faces of an old white man and a young black woman. She is so pretty. Her short Afro—jet black and looking so very soft—frames a high forehead and cheekbones, a delicately flared nose, and a jaw and chin shaped like the bottom of a heart. Her skin is smooth and clear and the color of dark cacao. She stares at me with warm, brown eyes open wide with concern. Or is it fear?

The man? He isn't pretty at all. His high, pale forehead looms dome-like and alien. *Pretty big brain stuffed in there*, is all I can think as his yellow-ish, bloodshot eyes study me. I wonder why I can see every detail of those eyes so clearly. Then I realize I'm looking at them through the man's glasses: round, thick lenses with horizontal lines through the middle, set in heavy, gray-metal frames.

"No need to be frightened," he says soothingly, smiling. His teeth are stained, some almost black; and his breath smells like milk past its sell-by date. "You are among friends. Elise, help me raise him."

Their hands reach for me. His are gnarled and dirty, the nails full of grime. Hers are cleaner, pink-palmed and blunt-fingered. Both sets of hands grip my upper arms and set me on my feet, but never let go.

That makes me feel trapped. I try moving away. Their grips tighten. I look at the black woman. Now her eyes seem suspicious, hostile.

In that moment, I just know these two mean me harm. *RUN!* a voice in my head yells.

I jerk, twist, pull, and shove. Their hands let go and I bolt for a wooden staircase leading up to an open door.

"Stop! Wait!" the man cries.

"Monsieur, arrêtez!" the woman shouts.

I take the stairs two at a time and come to a long, broad-planked hall with a high ceiling and what looks like a front door at the end. Through narrow windows along the sides, I see lightning flash.

I hear ringing above—a little like an alarm clock or the period bell at school, but varying in speed, from fast and loud to slow and soft—and I wonder what it is. But I'm not stopping to investigate—especially not after another crash of thunder shakes the air.

Yanking open the door, I run down a brick walkway. Wind-driven rain stings my face and soaks my clothes.

I look all around, but can't recognize a thing. I'm in what looks like a large courtyard, paved with cobblestones, bounded on all sides by squat, wood or brick buildings, none more than two or three stories, all with chimneys pouring gray smoke. Where the heck am I?

To my right, at the end of the courtyard, I see what looks like a very short tunnel. There's something familiar about its low arch. I run for it.

"Monsieur, attendez! Arrêtez!"

I look back to see the black woman I've just escaped. I have no idea what she's saying, and I don't care. Reaching the tunnel, I run the several yards through it, only to stop short and gasp, "What the …?"

Everything I've ever known is gone: all the tall office buildings, the concrete sidewalks and asphalt streets, the cars, the busses, the trucks, the traffic lights and electric signs, the sirens, the horns, the blaring radios—all just … gone!

I stand on the brick sidewalk to a wide, cobblestoned avenue. A long building, divided into open stalls and covered by a steep-pitched roof runs down the middle. It is a market, but not like any I've ever seen. And the storm is wrecking it! Baskets of fruits and vegetables lay scattered. Sides of beef, strings of sausage, chickens, geese, and ducks—headless but with all their feathers—swing wildly in the wind. Tables and trays lie upended. Dead fish, eels, and oysters glisten on the cobbles amidst piles of horse manure.

People run in all directions. Some snatch up food. Others shove looters away. Some wrestle with saddled horses, or mules or oxen hitched to wagons, while others duck for cover.

And the clothes they wear! Three-cornered hats, knee britches, stockings, and buckled shoes or boots for the men; long dresses with aprons, shawls, and bonnets or mob caps for the women. It's like I've stumbled onto the set of a movie about the Revolution.

Another flash of lightning, another crash of thunder, and one of the horses pulling a wagon rears, only to slip on the smooth, wet stones, and fall, tipping over the wagon, throwing the driver and dumping barrels. One bursts and the smell of beer fills the air—which is better than the rest of the smells. The whole place stinks, like it's a stable and a pig sty and a garbage dump all rolled into one.

A hand clasps my elbow. A woman's voice—low and musical and very French—whispers warmly in my ear: "*Monsieur* Marcus, you must come away."

It is the woman from the house. Her eyes don't seem hostile now, but urgent.

"How … how do you know my name?" I stammer. Her whisper has filled my head and her hand on my arm is the gentlest yet most electrifying touch I've ever known. As long as I live, I will never forget that touch.

"*Monsieur le Docteur.* He says you must return. Otherwise, if the watchman sees you in those clothes, he will put you in jail."

* * *

Very suddenly, the rain stops.

Dazed, I let the woman bring me back to the large, three-story, red-brick house with several chimneys, windows with black shutters, and a pitched roof. On the way, we pass the smaller, neighboring house. A sign hanging outside the door reads:

B. Franklin
B. Bache
Printers

She leads me into the front hall. The plaster walls are white and clean and without pictures or other adornment, except for a plain, mounted coat rack of pegs. The broad-plank floor is gray-brown with age and has not been stained or varnished. A white-painted, wooden staircase with brown-painted risers and banisters leads upstairs.

The old man in the leather apron stands near the door to the cellar, leaning on a walking stick. The top of his head is completely bald, but fringed by long, white hair growing down the back and sides all the way to his shoulders. He studies me through those clunky glasses of his.

"Where am I?" I say. "And how come you know my name?"

"How come? Whatever do you mean?"

"You know, 'How come?'"

His confused look says he still isn't getting it.

"*Why?*" I say, like he's a five year-old. "Why do you know my name?"

"Ah! Of course." He peers at me again. "You have no recollection of me?"

"*Hombre!* I never met you before in my whole freakin' life!"

Except, that doesn't seem right. I know I don't know him; but somehow, I think I recognize him. Except … it's impossible.

From above, I hear the single tinkle of a bell.

"According to my lightning signal," he says, pointing upward with a finger, "it would seem that the storm is over." Then he looks at me. "So, this is your first journey. Helpful to know. It means there is not much I can tell you, for reasons I will explain. But I can say: it is not so much *where* you are, as *when*—at least I think that is correct. Of course, it could be that my lightning experiment opened something other than time. If that is the case, well then I'm afraid I can't really say where you are. At least, not in relation to where you were."

"Dude! Could you stop with the mumbo jumbo and tell me—"

"Mumbo Jumbo! How is it that you have come to learn of the great African idol, Mumbo Jumbo? Is he worshipped in your time?"

"What? No. What are you talking about?"

"The great idol of the Mundingoes in Africa—"

"STOP!"

I shake my head to reset.

"C'mon dude, I need you to focus. I need you to tell me who you are and where I am and how I get back to Philly."

"Philly?" he repeats in confusion.

"Phil-a-del-phia? Pennsylvania?"

"Ah, yes. Well, no need to fear on that score. You are certainly in Philadelphia. But you are not in your time. In fact, today is May 25th, in the year of our lord 1787. You have come here through some sort of portal, apparently opened by an electrical experiment I was conducting. As to who I am? Doctor Benjamin Franklin, at your service."

All of a sudden, it feels like the floor is tilting and everything's sliding away. There's a straw-bottomed, ladder-backed chair against the wall, and I sit—fall into it, would be more accurate.

"That's just not possible," I say.

"Oh, but it is, I assure you."

"How?"

"That I cannot say. Partly because I don't know. And partly because you cannot know your future. Just as I cannot know mine. Now, allow me to introduce our housekeeper, and my friend, Elise du Maurier."

"Bonjour, Monsieur," she says. As she looks at me with those warm, brown eyes my stomach does a different kind of flip.

"Wh … what do you mean, 'first journey?'" I ask Franklin, as much to avoid her gaze as to get an answer from him.

"Forget I said that. As I was about to say, Elise comes to us from Port-au-Prince on the island of Saint-Domingue, by way of Paris, France. She looked after me at my house in the village of Passy, just outside Paris."

"Forget, nothing! You brought me here! I gotta right to know what's happening—I mean, happened—I mean, going to happen?"

"I dare not tell you specifics," Franklin says, his face worried. "That might lead you to do, or not do, something you might otherwise have done, or not done; and thereby cause a disruption in forces I do not yet comprehend. I believe, however, that I can tell you we have met before, and even that we became friends. Nevertheless, while all that is in my past, apparently, since you have no recollection of it, it still lies in your future. The more I tell you about that future, the less likely you will be to allow it to unfold as it is meant to. Do you understand?"

"No! Not one freakin' word!"

Which is kind of a fib. I've seen and read enough science fiction to understand the concept: how a change to what *has* happened could cause a change to what *will* happen—how, for example, if Abraham Lincoln had lost the election of 1860 and never become President, the Civil War might never have been fought. But a discussion of theoretical physics isn't at the top of my "to-do" list. Getting home is. And right now! Before Mom and Pop find me gone and think I really have run away.

"Look," I say. "I gotta get back! You gotta send me back!"

Franklin looks towards the front door. Sunlight pours through the side windows, then is blocked by a passing cloud, then pours through again.

"I fear that will not be possible," he says. "But we can try. Come."

Turning, he opens the cellar door and slowly goes down, planting his walking stick and then each foot on each stair, grunting with pain at every step. I follow him. Elise follows me.

When we get to the bottom, we are in the cellar room I first landed in. The blue, shimmering wall is gone. In its place stands a fourth wall of gray stone and mortar with two small windows at the very top. Sunlight pours through the dirty, wavy glass of those windows, making the smoking lanterns unnecessary.

Firewood is stacked all along one wall. Nearby, an axe juts from a chopping block.

Across the room, a short set of stairs leads up to a hatch which I bet opens onto the street.

In one corner stands a large, cylindrical tank made of copper connected by wire to a series of large glass jars; all of which are wired to a thick metal bar running from the dirt floor up through the wood ceiling.

"I was afraid of that," Franklin says, his shoulders slumping. "It is too late."

"Too late?" My voice is trembling again.

"To return. The portal, or whatever, has closed."

"Well, open it back up again!"

"I can't!"

"Why NOT?"

"I don't know how it works."

CHAPTER 3

"You don't KNOW?" I just about shout, panicking. "You're the one who freakin' opened it!"

"So it would seem, although I cannot be sure. It has opened only twice before, so there is not enough evidence to draw that conclusion."

"What the hell am I supposed to do now?"

"Why, I should think that would be obvious. Remain here with us until I can devise a way to reopen the portal."

"Stay? Here? Are you *serious*? I've got things I gotta be doing! Places I'm supposed to be! You know, like home and school—"

"I am very sorry," Franklin says. "But there is nothing I can do right now. I simply do not know enough. The only thing I can be sure of is that you will return to your world ... someday."

"Yeah? And how do you know that?"

"I cannot say. I cannot tell you because—"

"Because I can't know my future. Yeah, yeah, yeah, I got that part already! *Pendejo,*" I say under my breath.

Angry, scared, searching for a way out of this mess, I start pacing, not really looking where I'm going. My big feet in Gus's untied boots trip over one of the wired glass jars on the floor and I go flying into the woodpile.

"Careful!" Franklin cries. "Those Leyden jars are expensive to make. As is the entire apparatus."

"Thanks. Appreciate your concern," I say, picking myself up and feeling the blood rush to my face as I watch Elise try not to laugh.

"I don't remember you being so clumsy," Franklin says.

"How's about I take this axe to all your little jars? Then we'll see how clumsy I am."

"That would be most unwise," Franklin says coolly. "Since they may be a key to opening the portal."

That gets my attention.

"Yeah? What's this whole thing for, anyway?" I ask, looking more closely at the round copper tank that reminds me of something, although I can't think of what.

"It is an experiment for heating water," Franklin says. "I am attempting to store and use electricity from lightning to heat water for my bath."

"Hot water heater," I mutter to myself and then take a very deep breath. "You mean I'm here because you want a hot bath? I don't *believe* this!"

"Now, let us not leap to conclusions—although it is … possible. Tell me: where were you when the portal opened?"

"In the basement of our house."

"Which is where, exactly?"

"In Philadelphia, on Third Street, between Market and Chestnut."

"This house is between Third and Fourth Streets, and between the market and Chestnut, which means our properties are close."

"Gee, ya think?"

He shoots me a look, but lets it go.

"Was there a storm over your Philadelphia?" he asks.

"Yup, a big one."

"So, you were in your basement, as you and your—uh … as you—"

"What? As me and who?"

"No one. Nothing," he says quickly. "I meant: as you were the last time. And there were electrical storms both here and at your home, as with the last time. From the two occurrences, we can theorize they share our cellars, my lightning rod and Leyden jars, and electrical storms of great power. Beyond that … ."

He falls quiet, seeming to go deep inside himself. A sharp rapping from upstairs brings him back.

"Well, certainly all this deserves more thought before we can come to any meaningful conclusion. I must see who is at the door."

Planting his walking stick, he turns and limps for the stairs.

"Wait!" I say. "That's all you're going to do? Think? What am I supposed to do in the meantime?"

Franklin stops and looks me up and down.

"Excellent question! First, you must have proper clothing. Elise, outfit him from our slop chest, please. Can't have him wandering Philadelphia like ... that."

"*Oui*, Doctor."

"You're gonna dress me in slop—like ... for a hog?" I say.

"No, no, you misunderstand!" Franklin laughs. "'Slop chest' is a nautical term for a ship's store. I'm fond of ships and the sea and so that is what I call our store of old clothes, all of which are quite serviceable. Although, no matter how you are dressed, I am not sure we can let you wander at all."

"How come?" I ask suspiciously, already knowing I'm not going to like the answer.

"Yet again you require an explanation of the obvious! Definitely not the Marcus I knew! Because," he says, like I'm the one who's five, "you are completely unfamiliar with our ways. You do not know how we dress, or talk, or greet each other, or anything of our laws or customs or traditions. I daresay you would not be able to purchase something as simple as an apple from the market without calling attention to yourself. Were people to see and hear you act as you have been acting, they would almost certainly think you a lunatic and demand you be locked in the asylum. And what if the portal opens again and you are not here?"

"So ... I'm a prisoner. That's what you're telling me?"

"No, not a prisoner—"

"Father?" a woman calls from the top of the stairs. "Are you down there?"

"Yes daughter? Don't come down. I'm coming up."

"James Wilson is here to see you," she says.

"I said, I'm coming—"

"No need, Dr. Franklin, no need. Save those gouty feet. I'll come to you," a man calls down. He sounds like Shrek or Scotty from *Star Trek*.

"Hush, Marcus, not a word!" Franklin says. "Your freedom—your very life—may depend on it!"

"My life?"

"Hush!" he hisses, slashing his hand across his throat.

I watch silently as a tall man in a long, black coat and knee britches comes down the stairs. Under the coat, he wears a gray vest and a shirt and cravat as white as his stockings. A curled, white wig frames his face. Heavy, round, metal specs magnify icy blue eyes that bore right into me and make me feel like he knows everything about me.

"James Wilson!" Franklin cries, like he's a long-lost friend. "So good of you to come after what must have been a tiring day."

"Aye, that it's been. But I said I would report on the convention's proceedings and I'm a man of my word."

"That you are. May I offer you cider? Ale?"

"A glass of ale would be most welcome," Wilson says, now smiling warmly.

"Elise, if you would," Franklin says. "Let us have it in the kitchen next door, it being so cool down here."

"Aye, it's turned warm after that storm," Wilson says, patting his forehead with a white handkerchief taken from his sleeve.

"Yes, Dr. Franklin," Elise says. "But first, I must split the wood."

Picking up the logs I'd knocked from the woodpile, she drops them next to the chopping block.

"Perhaps Marcus might do that," Franklin says, startling me. But what he says next floors me. "Mr. Wilson, this is Marcus Santana, just arrived from Paris to join our household. Unfortunately, a condition of his throat has left him unable to speak."

Like hell! I almost say, then remember his warning. But I stare at Franklin—very hard.

"Temporarily," he quickly adds. "Which is fortunate because he was very helpful during my days at Passy."

Wilson looks me up and down.

"Is tha' the fashion in Paris now?" he says with contempt, obviously offended by how I'm dressed. "And haven't I always said, ye canna' account for French taste?"

"Indeed not," Franklin says quickly. "Elise, show Marcus what to do. We'll be in the kitchen. Here, help me, James."

"Is the gout bad?" the Scotsman asks.

"It's been worse." Franklin leans on Wilson's arm and his own walking stick. "With the bladder stone, moving can be painful, especially when it rains. But I am … ."

Their voices fade as they move into the kitchen.

"Chop his wood!" I splutter. "Who the hell does he think I am? His slave?"

Elise's eyes turn cold and her jaw knots and I know I've just said the wrong thing.

"Do you even know how?" she asks.

"No."

She shakes her head and looks at me like I'm useless.

"What?" I say. "Where I come from, we don't need to chop wood."

"And where is that? Where you come from?"

"I'm not sure. It's … complicated."

"And how like that? From the wall? Through the wall?"

"The future … I think."

"*Où?*"

"Ooh? What do you mean, ooh?"

"*Where!* Where do you come from?"

"Like I said, it's complicated."

"*Mon dieu, c'est fou!*"

"Foo?"

"It is crazy, insane!" Shaking her head, she grabs the axe from the chopping block. "You watch."

She stands a log on the block, raises the axe above her head, and brings it down hard, splitting the wood in two.

"Now you try."

I do, and miss, hitting the edge of the log and sending it flying.

"*C'est impossible!* Give to me." She snatches the axe out of my hands and sets to work. Only minutes later, she has all the wood she wants, half of which she shoves into my arms.

"Now you follow!" She picks up her own armful. "Sit by the fire. Stir the soup. Turn the chicken. Say nothing."

She hurries off, leaving me half furious and half developing the most awesome crush.

CHAPTER 4

"*Vite! Vite! Rapidement!*" Elise hisses as I follow her into the kitchen.

Franklin and James Wilson sit with tankards of ale at a big, wooden table in the middle of the kitchen. Like the wood room, its walls are stone and its light comes from lanterns and the small, wavy-glass windows up high at the ceiling. And it has the biggest fireplace I've ever seen—so tall I could have stood inside without bending, so wide I could have lain down twice end to end. Franklin is right. Even though two small fires burn in that hearth, the kitchen is cool.

A pot of soup hangs from a hook over one fire. Elise picks up two chickens on a spit, sets them over the other fire, and shows me how she wants them turned. She's so harsh with me, I want to tell her to go jump. But she's so beautiful and I so want her to like me and to feel her touch again. And Franklin's warning still echoes in my head. So, I sit on that stool, and turn that spit, and keep my mouth shut, and listen.

"I'm sorry, Doctor Franklin," Wilson says. "I tried m'best, but I could no' persuade them."

Franklin shrugs, then sighs, then shakes his head. "Never mind grandson Temple. The important thing is the delegates have elected Washington president of our convention."

"Yer words convinced 'em," Wilson says. "That speech you gave me to read recommending they appoint Washington instead of you was greeted with great attention and respect."

Washington? I wonder. *Are they talking about George Washington?*

"I am most gratified and relieved," Franklin says. "I am too old to serve. And Washington really is the man to lead the convention—our one true national hero, admired by all, no matter what state they are from. Only Washington has the force and wisdom to unite and lead us."

22

Are they talking about the Constitutional Convention?

I'd read a little about Washington at the convention in one of the books Pop brought home for me to do my paper. The idea I got was that Washington hadn't said or done much—that he'd been more of a figurehead than leader. But according to Franklin, maybe that hadn't been—or wouldn't be?—the case.

"No, I couldn't be more pleased by Washington's selection," Franklin says. "I just wish the delegates had agreed to employ grandson Temple as secretary to the convention. For me, it would have solved a number of problems."

"They chose William Jackson, instead," Wilson says. "They felt Jackson's service on Washington's staff in the war entitled—"

"Let's not mince words! Temple has ruined his reputation with his carousing and foppery. I'd hoped this job as secretary might repair it. I'd also hoped to review his notes between sessions. My memory is failing. If I am to help find compromise, I must have the delegates' positions firmly in my mind. But, I will find another solution. Pity. Temple's presence might have allowed me to miss a session or two. I have so many irons in the fire, and some days, like today, my health seems … not all that it has been."

"I'd be willing to take notes for ye, Doctor."

"How kind, Mr. Wilson! How *very* kind! But no. You are one of our best lawyers. The delegates will need your knowledge of government and constitutional theory. You must remain focused on the issues, not my needs. I will manage. I do worry about Temple though—what will become of him." Franklin's voice has dropped almost to a whisper. Then it comes back strong. "But I waste your time. What else today?"

"General Washington appointed a three-man committee to write the convention's rules, including his fair-haired boy from New York, Alexander Hamilton."

"As is right and proper. After all, we wouldn't be having this convention without the work of Alexander Hamilton and James Madison to call us all together. And speaking of Mr. Madison, how fares his plan for a completely new government?"

"There's much resistance. Many o' the delegates believe we're here only to make modest adjustments to the existing Articles of Confederation."

"Reasonable, since that is the job our Congress up in New York gave to us."

"But Doctor Franklin, can you no' see those articles aren't worth the ink with which they were written? Our national government is a laughing stock—with only the Congress to run it and it having no power to compel any state to do anything, including pay any tax to fund it!"

"Yes, and since you served in Congress when we wrote those articles back in '76, you'll remember we did that intentionally. After all the years of tyranny from King George and his Parliament, no one wanted a strong central government. I am still not convinced we need one."

"Are ye daft, man? Our government's penniless! It canno' pay its debts here or abroad, which means it canno' borrow any more since no one trusts it. And it canno' pay to raise a national army or navy, which means it canno' defend us. It has no power to settle disputes between the states, which are many and which may lead to civil war. If that happens, England, France, and Spain will pick us apart like sharks at a bloody corpse. We'd be back to where we were before we broke with England— under a foreign thumb. All those years of war—all our dead—for naught."

All of a sudden, I'm not in Franklin's kitchen anymore. I'm back with Mom and Pop and Penny, watching as the horse-drawn caisson and Green Beret honor guard bear Gus's flag-draped coffin to his grave at Arlington.

Which is when Elise smacks my arm and points to the soup.

"Stir, boy! Before it burns!"

That gets me mad again. My hands clench into fists. Who is she to smack me and call me "boy?"

"You may be right," Franklin says to Wilson.

"I know I'm right. And I also know Mr. Madison's plan may well be the solution. It calls for a strong central government with power o'er the states. You've read it. What do *ye* think?"

"I think … that I am prepared to listen to all that the delegates have to say."

"Ah, keep'n yer cards close to yer vest, as always."

"Not at all. Just endeavoring to keep an open mind."

"Well, I must go. Clients await. And I've promised to bring Gouverneur Morris and Robert Morris to the Indian Queen to talk more with the Virginians about Madison's plan. Join us."

"Thank you, but I must rest. Tomorrow night, however, I am hosting the lads from the Union Fire Company for our monthly meeting. They are all likely men, mostly merchants, tradesman, and artisans. Perhaps you might bring some of the Pennsylvania and Virginia delegates? They might find the views of ordinary citizens helpful to their thinking."

"Aye, they might at that. And you always set a fine table."

"My Sally's doing. And Elise's, of course." Franklin points to my tormentor now rolling out dough. "I want the delegates to consider this home a place of respite during the convention. They will need a place to retreat to—away from the heat of debate—for refreshment and to join with each other as friends, no matter how their views differ. Might you spread word of my invitation?"

"Aye, it would be my honor, Doctor." He takes Franklin's hand.

When Wilson has gone, Franklin turns to Elise and me. "Do you hear? This house may have an important role in the repair of our government! Elise, do everything you can to make tomorrow's meal your best ever!"

"But of course, Doctor," Elise says.

He's as excited as a little kid going to his first Phillies game. Which means he isn't even thinking about how to get me home. My anger spikes.

"And Marcus, I commend you. Not a sound, just as I instructed," he says.

"As you *instructed*? Listen, old man, you and me better get something straight! I ain't here to do what you say!"

"I beg your pardon?" Franklin says, looking confused.

"I ain't here to be a prisoner in your house, or chop your wood, or stir your soup, or keep my mouth shut just 'cuz you say! Capisce?"

"Cap—whatever do you mean?"

"I *mean* you ain't the boss of me and I ain't your effing *slave*! You got me into this mess! Get me out! NOW!"

"Hey, boy, you watch your mouth!" Elise commands, smacking me again, this time in the chest.

"And quit hitting me, wouldja!"

Franklin's face has turned thin-lipped and cold. He fixes me with a hard-eyed stare.

"Clearly, Marcus, you do not appreciate your position. Let us review. You have arrived in a world you do not know, not its customs or manners or the ways in which its people speak and act. You have no money or possessions, except your clothes, which are strange and will call attention to you. You know no one, have no employment, and have no place to lay your head or eat at table, except *possibly* this house. Nor have you anyone to vouch for you or explain your presence here, except *possibly* me. At your age, you may very well be mistaken for a runaway apprentice or indentured servant and jailed or sold into bondage. That is your situation as I see it. Were we playing a game of whist, I would not want your cards. Of course, if you think differently, you are free to leave and make your own way."

So much for my anger. If I hadn't understood my "position" before, I certainly do now—including that whether Franklin will help me is entirely up to him.

"Now, I have no intention of exploiting you," he continues. "But in this house, everyone works, everyone contributes what they can. There is always plenty to do to keep food on our table and our home in good order.

"Also, I will have to explain you to my daughter Sally, her husband Richard, to young Benjamin—their son and my grandson—to their other small children, and to my other grandson, Temple, all of whom live here with me. It will look strange indeed if you refuse to contribute. You will stir resentment and make yourself disliked, which I cannot have."

"Look, Franklin—"

"Have you no manners?" Elise snaps, pinching the back of my hand. "He is Doctor Franklin!"

"Whatever! *Doctor* Franklin. Look, I just want to get home."

"I know you do," he says, softening. "And I want to send you. Far, far more than you can imagine. You do not belong here. You are not of this time—or, possibly, of this world. I don't know. Did I open a passage between our future and your past? Or do you come from a world that somehow parallels ours? Will your presence here change what is supposed to be? Will you change history in a way it is not supposed to be changed—somehow threaten or destroy the future? And what is your absence doing to wherever you come from? If I could, I'd put you to sleep until I'd found a way to return you. But that is impractical."

"Hey, you could always just shoot me dead."

"I could," he agrees, seeming to consider it. "But there's still the question of what that might do to where you come from. I wouldn't want the Great Creator blaming me for a cosmic imbalance."

I look at him closely. His eyes twinkle and he's biting his lip to keep from laughing.

"Thanks, Doc. You're all heart—"

"Pity, since it's my head that I've always relied upon."

CHAPTER 5

"Dinner is ready, Father!" the woman from before calls down. "The children await you in the garden."

"My favorite part of the day!" Franklin cries. "Especially when the weather is fine and we can all spend it together in the garden. Marcus, give me your arm. Help me up the stairs."

He loops his through mine and clutches tightly. He's heavy and we have to go slowly. I watch out carefully, so as not to trip over my clumsy feet.

"Now, I think we'll stick with the story I began for James Wilson: you have arrived from Paris—

"Why not Spain? That's where my Dad's folks are from."

"No, that won't do. First, because we need to have worked together before and I was never our representative to Spain. And second, because the Spanish are not very popular right now, having closed off our access to the Mississippi. No, it must be Paris, where you assisted me—doing what, we'll have to determine. Also, you cannot speak because of an injury to your throat. That will be temporary, of course, just until you learn how to talk as we do, and won't apply with family here inside the house. We shall tell everyone your purpose here is to … to … Ah, well done!" he says as we reach the top step. "Sally? SALLY?"

A solid looking woman in a long dress and apron bustles into the hallway. Curly blonde hair springs from under a mob cap. Her eyes take me in, then widen.

"Sally, I want you to meet—"

"Marcus!" she says, stopping still.

"You know this fellow?"

"Yes." Her cream-white skin turns pink at the cheeks.

"I don't understand," Franklin says. "I have no recollection of you two meeting. Sally, the last time Marcus was here, you, husband Richard, and the children were in New Jersey, looking after son William's farm while he languished in a Connecticut jail for his loyalty to the King.

"When Marcus and I met, you had left on your diplomatic mission to Paris, Father." She looks at me. "But how is it that so much time has passed and you seem … younger?"

Behind us, the front door slams. A thin young man with a high forehead and delicate features hurries down the hall, his silver-buckled shoes clacking angrily on the wood floor.

"Grandfather! Have you heard? The convention has rejected me."

"Yes, Temple," Franklin says wearily. "Do you not have the courtesy to greet your Aunt?"

"Aunt Sally." He makes an elaborate bow to her from the waist. "I am sorry. I did not mean to be rude. But that vote has me so distracted!"

Temple's green-velvet coat, pink-satin vest, buff-colored britches, and white stockings fit perfectly. A silk cravat swirls at his throat like a cloud. He gives me a glance, arches an eyebrow, and sniffs.

Stuck-up ass! I think.

"I am sorry, Temple," Franklin says. "I tried."

Two bright spots of red spread over the points of Temple's cheekbones.

"I cannot believe they selected Jackson! Jackson over me!" he says haughtily. "What am I to do now?"

"Well, you might remain here, as my secretary. There's plenty of work: my duties as President of Pennsylvania's Supreme Executive Council, my notes on the convention, correspondence, several scientific papers, the autobiography everyone wants me to finish. My wrist being what it is, writing is … difficult. We worked well together when you served as secretary to our diplomatic mission in France. I would enjoy working with you again."

"Oh, Grandfather, I couldn't possibly!" Temple waves dismissively "It would be so humiliating! Poor Temple, everyone will say, the only work he can get is clerking for his grandfather. No, it just won't do. I think I shall have to go to the farm and look after things there. Thank God you wrested it from Father, our erstwhile and exiled Royal Governor, wot? Yes, I think the farm is just the thing. Have cousin Benjy do your work."

"Your cousin is just beginning as a printer. I cannot distract him."

"Ah yes. 'Keep thy shop and thy shop will keep thee,' wot? Well, I'm sure you'll find someone. Plenty out there dying to work for the great Benjamin Franklin, wot?"

"Yes, dying," a sad-faced Franklin whispers; and I feel for him. Temple looks like he couldn't care less.

"That settles it. To the farm I go. I'll just pack a few things and be off, out of everyone's way. Aunt Sally? Of course, you and the children are welcome any time, should you like to escape the sicks and stinks of summer. Ha, ha! I say, Grandfather? I need cash. Say fifty pounds? To get me through until fall when rents are paid and crops go to market."

"Stop by my library before you go. I'll do what I can," Franklin says, resigned.

"Thank you very much, kind sir. Now, must dash."

He bows again and then just about runs back down the hall and upstairs.

"You know where that money will be spent," Sally says. "In the taverns of New York."

"What else can I do?" Franklin says. "I promised him that job, and I failed him. He has no one else to rely on—not with son William in England and likely never to return."

"And whose fault is that?" Sally asks. "William Franklin may be my half-brother, and I may love him like a full one, but even I can see he betrayed you. After you and Mama rescued him from whatever woman it was you consorted with—and I still want to hear that little secret—"

"Now, Sally—"

"And after you fed, clothed, and educated him and had him made Royal Governor of New Jersey, what does he do? Sides with the King and Parliament instead of you. Probably would have jailed you if he'd had the chance."

"Still, Temple is my grandson. I'll not forsake him for his father's sins."

As I listen, I'm embarrassed. This is private family business, like the arguments Mom and Pop sometimes have over money or how much "excellence" to demand from Gus, me, and Penny.

Sally changes the subject.

"What will you do for a clerk, Father? Ask Benjamin?"

"Absolutely not!" Franklin says, shaking his head so that his long, white hair brushes the shoulders of his linen shirt. "Benjy wants to be a printer and publisher, like his grandpapa. I've given him charge of the shop next door. He must have the chance to succeed. I will do for myself. Now, on to the garden. I want to see my grandchildren."

Walking through the house, we pass through a large room of dark blue walls and white trim and wainscoting. A brass chandelier of wax candles hangs from the ceiling. A polished mahogany table glows at the center. Twelve matching chairs line the walls.

"Our dining room, where we entertain company," Franklin says to me.

"Who's she?" I ask, pointing to the portrait of a proud woman above the fireplace.

"My dear wife Deborah, lost to me some twelve years ago. As fine a life partner as any man could ask for. She made this room."

His voice is soft when he says this, but then it strengthens.

"Sally, we will put it to good use this summer. I am opening our home to the delegates. I know it will create more work for everyone, especially you. But I think it essential they have a place to meet and come to know one another away from the State House. Your mother would be proud that a room she created is being used to help build our nation."

"As will I be proud to help in any way I can," Sally answers.

Franklin leads us into a small, sunny room with tall windows at the back of the house. A copper tub, shaped kind of like a shoe sits in the middle.

"My bathing closet, where I take the air and the water. Hot water does wonders for my stone and gout."

"Yeah, did wonders for me too," I say.

That draws a look and a small smile from Franklin. "Touché!" he says.

He goes to a small table where a bowl and pitcher sit. Pouring water into the bowl, he washes his hands.

"So ... this is where everyone takes a bath?" I ask doubtfully. It's just dawning on me that indoor plumbing, as I know it, is a thing of the future.

"Certainly not!" Franklin says. "Only I use this. Otherwise, we'd be all day boiling and hauling water up the stairs. Everyone else uses the pump downstairs or outside and a bucket. There's also the river. Know how to swim?"

"Uh … yeah?" I say, not knowing whether he means the Delaware or Schuylkill, where, in my Philadelphia, few people swim because of dangerous currents and pollution.

"Good. I swam the Delaware religiously in my youth. Most refreshing!"

"Oh boy! Can't wait!"

"You know, Marcus, you really are quite strong. All the time I leaned on you, I never felt unsteady."

Which makes me feel kind of good.

He takes a folding knife from his apron pocket and begins scraping the dirt from under his nails.

"Quite novel, actually," he says. "Sally here keeps me perpetually off-balance."

"I do not!"

"Especially if I'm tight with the purse strings." His eyes twinkle again.

"You'll watch your tales, if you know what's good for you," she says. "And if you want any of the cobbler Elise and I have been making."

"Apple or peach?"

"Neither, both, one or t'other. Wait and see."

"I shall look forward to it, daughter. Of all the things I missed in France, I missed your cobbler most."

He rinses his hands one last time. After drying them, he unties his apron and holds it out to me, saying, "Marcus, please be so kind as to exchange this for my weskit hanging on that coat tree by the door."

"That's what you call this?" I say, taking the long vest that matches his brown britches from the tree. "A weskit?"

"Indeed," he says.

I help him slip it on. He buttons it and then leads us outside.

We're in a big garden surrounded by a high, red-brick wall and filled with bright-flowered plants and bushes. Gravel paths cross each other. A large mulberry tree stands in the middle, offering cool shade in the hot sunshine. Underneath it, a teenaged boy and girl play chess.

"Welcome to my Eden," Franklin says. "We once grew our vegetables here. But with the market so close and abundant, I decided to make this into a formal garden, as I had in Passy. Not as large, but it is peaceful."

Peaceful? There's nothing peaceful about the children leapfrogging each other down the gravel paths. As soon as one of them sees us, they run for the old man, mobbing him.

"Careful of Grandpapa!" Sally warns. "You know not to jostle him."

"None of that, Sally!" Franklin is smiling, but his teeth are gritted and his next words hoarse. "I'm not so decrepit I can't play with my grandchildren. Who would like a peppermint?"

He digs into his weskit pocket and produces a small tin filled with crystal candies. "Remember your manners. One at a time. Louis, let your sister go first."

"Who are you?" a little girl asks me.

"A friend," Sally answers, surprising me.

"His name is Marcus," Franklin says. "He has come to us on a ship, all the way from France. Marcus, this is my granddaughter Deborah. She is six."

"Hi," I say, and get a curtsy and a sunny smile. She's missing her two front teeth and kind of reminds me of Penny at that age.

"And that's Eliza," Franklin continues. "She is ten. And Louis, who is eight. And this tyke is Richard. He is three."

"Hi," I say again.

"And those two over there at the chess board are William, who is fourteen, and Sarah who is twelve."

"Hey," I say, giving a brief wave.

Neither look over. Their eyes are glued to the board.

"Ah, the joys of chess," Franklin says. "My favorite pastime. So demanding of one's concentration. Do you play?"

"No."

"Pity," he says sadly, but then brightens. "Perhaps you will allow me to teach you?"

Elise comes through the door carrying a tray loaded with a soup tureen, bowls, and spoons. It is so heavy the muscles of her forearms stand out in cords.

"Here, let me help," I say, trying to get back on her good side.

She shakes her head curtly. "There are more trays downstairs with the chicken and other foods. Bring them, if you are so eager to help."

I hesitate. Who is she to refuse my help so rudely? And I'm damned if I'm going to let her keep ordering me around.

"Remember, Marcus," Franklin says softly. "Here, everyone helps. Everyone contributes what they can."

I look at Sally. She nods encouragingly.

I go downstairs and bring up the food.

CHAPTER 6

We sit at a long table, with Franklin at the head, me next to him, and Sally next to me. Elise doesn't sit with us. She serves—which is weird, since Franklin says she's a friend.

"Elise," Franklin says, "this fish chowder is better than any I ate growing up in Boston—and they are famous for their chowders. I commend you."

"Thank you, Doctor. It is the recipe of my *maman*. She taught it to me as a child in Saint-Domingue."

"Marcus certainly likes it," Franklin says. "Do you always eat so hoggishly? When was your last meal?"

"Yesterday," I say between gulps, having no idea, now, of just how long ago that was. All I know is that I'm hungrier than I've ever been.

"Was there no food on your ship?" little Deborah asks.

"Hush, child. It's not polite to ask guests such questions," Sally says.

I scrape up the last of the chowder.

"You can have mine if you are still hungry," Deborah offers.

"No, I'm good," I say, wanting not to be thought of as a pig. But I also don't want to hurt a little girl's feelings. Flashing the most grateful smile I can muster, I look her in the eye and say, "But thanks just the same."

"Good?" she asks, her expression confused. "What does being good or bad have to do with being hungry?"

"Er ... uh ... hmm," I babble, not knowing how to explain. I look to Franklin. He looks back at me with an expression that seems to say: *See? I told you so.*

"Granddaughter, I believe Marcus means his hunger has been satisfied."

"Yup ... yes, that's what I meant," I say, even though, I feel like I haven't begun to fill the hole in my belly. But what comes next— chicken, peas, potatoes, cornbread, and apple cobbler, all washed down with milk—leaves me stuffed.

"If this is lunch," I say, "what do you do for dinner?"

"Lunch?" Franklin says. "This is not lunch, which refers to a hunk of bread or cheese. This is dinner, our main meal of the day. Later, we will have supper, which is only a light repast. Unless we have guests."

As Elise clears the plates, the children ask to be excused. William and Sarah go back to their chess game while the others chase around the gravel paths. From outside the walls, I hear the clop of horse's hooves, church bells tolling the hour, the distant cries of sellers at the market, and underneath all that, a kind of quiet—from the absence of engines and electrics?—I have never experienced. And the air is so different. Yes there are smells, but none of them have anything to do with gasoline.

"Father, we must get Marcus proper clothes," Sally says.

"I've already asked Elise to dress him from the slop chest. Tomorrow, I will take him to a tailor I know and have him properly outfitted."

"As what?" Sally asks.

"Beg pardon?" Franklin's face is puzzled.

"As what? What will you outfit him as? A laborer? A seaman? An apprentice to an artisan or tradesman? A French aristocrat? They all dress differently. What is he to be?"

"Excellent question! Marcus, this is why Sally and her family live with me. She is as sound-minded and practical as her mother. I would be lost without her. Daughter, I have no idea."

"I might," Sally says. "Marcus, when I knew you, you had an ability ... oh, it was so long ago ... short-writing, I think you called it."

"Do you mean short-hand?" Franklin asks.

"Yes, that's it! Short-hand! Oh, you must see it, Father. It's wonderful. Someone will talk, and Marcus will jot all sorts of symbols, and then, tomorrow or the next day, he can copy out what was said, word for word."

"I am more than familiar with short-hand, daughter. My own Uncle Benjamin taught me one of his devising when I was a lad. Although, lacking the diligence to practice it, I forgot it long ago. Word for word, you say?"

"Word for word."

"Is this true, Marcus?"

"Um … yeah? I mean … I guess. Mom and Pop had me learn the Gregg method so I'd take better notes in class."

"Who are Mom and Pop?" little Deborah asks, but Franklin overrides her.

"How can it be that I did not learn of this during your last visit?" he asks.

"How'm I supposed to know? For me, the—"

"Visit hasn't happened yet." Franklin and I finish the sentence together.

"Never mind! Show me," he says, rising from the table.

"What?"

"Come to my library and show me. Here, both of you, help me upstairs."

But a kind of excitement has seized Franklin, so that he barely needs our help into the house and up the stairs to a large library where thousands of leather-bound volumes fill white-painted shelves reaching to the ceiling and small but bright-colored oriental rugs cover the broad-planked floor. A fireplace takes up one end of the room. Close by, a big desk and chair sit next to a window overlooking the garden. Next to the window, a framed drawing of a snake cut into eight pieces, and captioned "JOIN, or DIE." hangs on the wall.

Franklin's desk is crowded but neat. Piles of books and paper hide its leather top.

Moving some of it aside, he sits me down, puts paper and a small clay pot in front of me, and hands me a feather.

"Let us see if he can do as you claim," he says to Sally.

"What'm I supposed to do with this thing?" I ask.

"Write what I say."

"With a *feather*?"

"A turkey quill, to be precise. It is what is used by most. Simply dip the point in the ink; then write."

"But look at this thing! It's so thin I can hardly hold it. Don't you have any normal pens? Something with a metal point?"

"Well … I do have several instruments I acquired in France," Franklin admits doubtfully. "But they're very valuable. And some were gifts."

"You want me to show you or not?"

He opens a drawer and hands me a yellow metal pen with a point that glitters in the sunlight.

"Be careful," Franklin warns. "That nib is gold, and thus delicate. Now, let us begin: 'When in the course of human events, it becomes necessary for one people to dissolve—'"

"Whoa! Whoa! Whoa! Dude! Slow down."

"I shall not. Work faster!"

"You didn't even give me time to get the pen dipped!"

"Work *faster!* Or can you not? Perhaps your shorthand is no more than a myth, a canard, a bamboozle—"

"Oh I can! You just watch!" I stab the pen into the ink pot.

"Careful! Now write: 'When in the course of human events, it becomes necessary—'"

"STOP!"

"Now what is the matter?"

"Look what this thing made me do!" I hold up the page to show my first stroke has spilled a big blot. "Haven't you got something simple, like a pencil?"

"I have what is called a *porte-crayon*, which uses graphite, just like a pencil."

From the same drawer, he produces a slim, brass tube encasing a thin, round stick of graphite.

"Now, let us see what you can do. Ready?"

I practice a few strokes with the brass "pencil;" then nod.

"'When in the course of human events, it becomes necessary for one people to dissolve the political bands which have connected them with another and to assume among the powers of the earth, the separate and equal station to which the Laws of Nature and of Nature's God entitle them, a decent respect to the opinions of mankind requires that they should declare the causes which impel them to the separation—'"

He talks fast. My hand races, but I'm struggling to keep up. I want to say "slow down," but I want to meet his challenge more.

"'We hold these truths to be self-evident, that all men are created equal, that they are endowed by their creator with certain unalienable rights, that among these are life, liberty and the pursuit of happiness.— That to secure these rights, governments are instituted among men, deriving their just powers from the consent of the governed.' Have you got all that?"

"Of course I got it!" I say, like it's been easy. But I'm not sure I really have. I haven't used my shorthand much, lately, and he'd gone so fast.

"Very well then, show me. Copy it all out." He turns to Sally. "I want to see his hand."

"Which?" I ask, holding out both.

"What?" Franklin asks, puzzled.

"Which hand do you want to see?"

"Oh … no," Franklin's face clears. "I mean I wish to see your handwriting: how legible it is. I assume, daughter, that this is where you are leading."

"Me? Lead you? Ha! Wouldn't dream of it."

"Nonsense, you do it all the time. Go on, Marcus, write it all out."

I take up the gold pen, dip it, and make my first stroke. Another blot stains the page.

"Do not press so hard," Franklin instructs. "As with most things in life, a light touch is best. Try again."

I hold the pen lightly. With just the slightest pressure, it glides across the page and the letters flow.

"Excellent!" says Franklin. "Your hand is so clear, anyone can read it. Oh yes, Sally, he'll do. Most handily!"

"Do what?" I ask.

"Why, be my amanuensis."

"Your what?"

"My amanuensis. My scribe? My clerk?"

"I dunno," I say doubtfully. "Sounds kinda boring."

"It certainly would be more interesting for you than sitting idle. You would spend your time with me, which some have found … useful. And you would be paid, of course."

That gets my attention.

"How much?"

"Ah, now *there* is a knotty problem! Money is so uncertain now. We have specie—that's gold and silver coin. And various paper currencies. But you will not be able to tell what any of it is worth. I could offer you a dollar a week, or a pound, or pieces of gold or silver, but you wouldn't know how much any of them would buy. Sometimes, I don't know. In many instances, we barter. A farmer might trade a bushel of apples for a new hat, or a pig for a pitch fork. Why don't we say I will take care of all your needs—"

"Oh, yeah, right! Like that ain't the oldest trick in the book!" I say, thinking: *I ain't from Philly for nothing!*

"Wait! Hear me out! So impetuous! AND give you spending money so you may begin learning the values of the various currencies and the goods you'll want to buy. Assuming I haven't found a way to send you back, once you understand our economy, we will come to a more specific arrangement. Satisfactory?"

"I dunno," I say again.

"What don't you know?"

"This whole thing. Being your amena-thingy—"

"Amanuensis. You heard what I told Temple. I have so much work: correspondence, scientific articles, the blasted autobiography, the convention. I fell and broke my wrist a while ago and now, writing is painful. I need a scribe. Judging from what I see on this page, you have a talent for it."

But did I? Franklin hadn't actually read all that I'd written. I'd really struggled to keep up. It was one thing to take notes for class. Making a record for someone to rely on was a whole other deal.

"You're talking about the Constitutional Convention, right?" I ask to change the subject, but also, to make sure.

"It is a convention of deputies called to investigate how our nation is constituted, yes."

"Like I said, the Constitutional Convention."

"Is that what you call it in your time? WAIT! Don't tell me!" Franklin's holding up both his hands now, like he's motioning an oncoming train to stop. "No discussion of our futures. That must be a condition of your employment—of your continuing to remain in this house. You cannot tell anyone anything about what lies ahead. Just as I cannot tell you your future."

"I haven't agreed to work for you yet."

"No, but will you?" he asks eagerly.

Old man, you are one persistent old man! I'm just about to say. But I don't because downstairs someone is knocking on the front door.

CHAPTER 7

Franklin moves to the other side of the room and looks straight out the window. He doesn't open it or try to look down to the street. He just looks straight out.

"Suffering Jehoshaphat! It's General Washington!"

"You mean George Washington?" I say.

"*General* Washington, yes, and he has quite a retinue: Robert Morris, with whom he stays; James Madison, his neighbor in Virginia, and Alexander Hamilton, his aide-de-camp during the war. Ah, and there is James Wilson. Sally, quickly, greet them. Say I will be right down. Offer refreshment. There's a new cask of porter and some Madeira wine Elise can open. Marcus, please fetch me my coat and cravat from those pegs over there. I must look my best. It isn't every day the General calls."

"How did you know who it was from up here?" I ask. "You never even opened the window."

"My busy-body."

"Busy-body?"

"Yes, attached to the window, outside the house."

He points to a device that reminds me of the side mirror on a big truck. Only it's three mirrors instead of one, all suspended from a metal arm.

"I've arranged the mirrors in such a way that I can tell who is at the front door without going downstairs to answer it, and without anyone knowing that I'm looking. If I don't want to see someone, I simply pretend I'm not home and no one's the wiser."

"Kind of like a low-tech security camera."

"A what?"

"A security camera? You know, a video system? Closed circuit TV?"

"Marcus! Stop! Please! What did I just say about the future?"

"Yeah, but if I tell you about some of the things coming, you could 'invent' them first. Think how much you'd make."

He looks at me and shakes his head, kind of like I'm a disappointment.

"Marcus, I've never profited financially from any of my discoveries or inventions. I hold no patents. Not on lightning rods or stoves or anything else. I believe ideas and progress should be shared freely. More important, I believe humankind must progress and develop naturally. To purloin an invention from the future and introduce it before its time could be disastrous. Would you give a razor to a baby? Again, I must insist, do not tell anyone, including me, anything about what is coming. Understand?"

I nod, but I'm thinking: *What the heck am I gonna be able to talk about?*

"Good. We'll talk more of this later."

He's finished tying his cravat. He holds out his arms for me to slip on the knee-length brown coat that completes his suit.

"For right now, though, I want you to remain here. Perhaps acquaint yourself with my library, since it looks as though you will spend considerable time here. Pick a book. What do you like to read?"

"I don't, much. At least, not usually."

"You don't *read?*" He peers at me like my nose just grew a big, fat wart.

"Well ... books, I mean. I read lots of articles on the web about—"

"Web?"

"Uh ... yeah ... but that's about the future sooo ... never mind. Anyway, I read lots of articles about new inventions and stuff."

"Ah, something we have in common."

"And science fiction! I like science fiction a lot ... which, again, is all about the future sooo ... never mind. Anyhow, Mom and Pop think it's junk. They want me reading more about history. Plus, I got this history paper—"

"Wise of them! One cannot learn from the mistakes of the past if one does not know that past. Or as Shakespeare wrote: "What's past is prologue." Well then, let us confine ourselves to history, shall we? Follow your parents' wishes, since I seem to have been placed *in loco parentis* concerning you."

"In loco-what?" I say, watching him search along the higher bookshelves.

"*In loco parentis.* It is a Latin term meaning 'in the place of the parent.' Seems I am to be your guardian."

"I'm 17. I don't need a guardian."

"I'm not sure you know what you need—*Aha!* There you are, old friend! Marcus, bring me my long arm, please—that rod with the two fingers, by my desk."

Franklin points to a long wood pole with two prongs on one end. A cord runs from one of the prongs or "fingers" down the pole.

"I hold no patent on this either," he says as I hand it to him.

He raises the business end to a high shelf, positions the prongs around a leather volume, and pulls the cord. The "fingers" grasp the book, which Franklin pulls off the shelf and lowers into my hands.

"There. *Plutarch's Lives.* History and biography in one. You can learn about the ancient Greeks and Romans: Alexander the Great, Julius Caesar, Cicero, Marc Antony, Brutus. That should please your parents.

"You're welcome to sit at my desk. There's generally a nice breeze from the garden. Or, if that fails, there's always my fan chair. Here, sit."

He practically pushes me into a heavy wood and leather arm chair with a treadle at its feet. That treadle connects to a pole rising behind the chair to a piece of cloth stretched over a wood frame to make a fan. Franklin steps on the treadle and the fan swings back and forth.

"Whoa! Cool!" I say.

"Yes, cooling. That was the idea when I designed it."

"No, I meant … uh … never mind."

"I will be back as soon as I am able."

I sit at the desk and open *Plutarch's Lives.* Its leather binding creaks. Dust runs up my nose and I sneeze. And the print is so small and uneven. I really miss my iPad, even if it is six years old and I'm its third owner.

I never do start reading about Theseus and Romulus, the founders of ancient Athens and Rome—not then. Franklin has everyone in the garden and I want to get a look at Washington. After all, I'm trying to write a paper about him.

But I can't see anyone. They're all sitting under the mulberry tree. I stick my head out the window and twist this way and that. All I can see are leaves and branches.

I go back to the desk to try reading again, which is when I notice I'm hearing every word they're saying. The *porte-crayon* and paper are right in front of me.

One of the reasons I hadn't immediately said yes to Franklin's job offer was that I really wasn't sure I had the skills. Now, in my head, I hear my father's voice: *This might be your opportunity to find out, hijo.* Then Gus's voice: *Try, Marcus. You'll never know unless you try.* So, I pick up the "pencil" and try copying everything I hear.

I have trouble at first because I can't see anyone, and, except for Franklin's and Scotsman James Wilson's, I don't know whose voice is whose. But, as they exchange greetings, good wishes, and other pleasantries, they call each other by name. Pretty soon, I've got them figured out.

George Washington's voice isn't prissy at all—which I expect from the reading I've done. It's soft and relaxed—a little bit Southern and a little bit English.

James Madison, also from Virginia, has those same tones, but his voice is higher and he talks faster, like he's anxious.

Robert Morris, who Franklin later tells me is the Philadelphia businessman who financed the Revolution, talks fast with the kind of English accent that reminds me of Paul McCartney or Ringo Starr—which makes sense since all three come from Liverpool.

I have the most trouble with Alexander Hamilton. Franklin later explains he's a lawyer who'd been born and raised in the Caribbean, come to New York for college, joined an artillery company to fight the Revolution, and so impressed Washington that he'd served as the general's chief staff aide for most of the war. His voice is clipped and brusque one minute, and relaxed and charming the next.

Just as I start copying, Washington says: "Doctor Franklin, I must thank you for that very fine speech you had Mr. Wilson read, asking the delegates to elect me president. I am humbled by your praise."

"No need, General," Franklin says. "I had an ulterior motive. A little bird told me I was being considered for the job. That speech was my only means of escape!"

As the men chuckle, James Wilson says: "The vote was unanimous—tha's the important point! We've begun our convention in complete agreement. Tha' must continue. Tha's what we were discussing at the Indian Queen: how to forge consensus. We've some ideas, and with yer invitation this afternoon, Doctor, I thought you'd no' be offended if we came for yer opinion."

"Not offended at all. Your company is most welcome. And I must commend you, Mr. Madison. The resolutions you and your fellow Virginians devised are an excellent starting point for the convention's deliberations."

"Oh, we mean them to be more than a starting point," Madison says. "We mean them to be the basis of an entirely new government."

"A strong national government to act with decisiveness and vigor," Hamilton says.

"Aye, instead of the weakling we ha'e now—completely beholden to the states!" James Wilson says.

"I tell you, Doctor Franklin," Washington says, "if something is not done to bring the states to heel, our nation will fail. We are at the edge of chaos, as proved by that "Shays' Rebellion" up in Massachusetts: armed farmers shutting the courts to escape their debts—and our government with no army to stop them!"

"As dangerous as that was," Alexander Hamilton says, "it is not the worst of our problems. Our nation's credit is ruined because millions in war debt remains unpaid. States fight over trade and territory. Foreign powers attack our citizens and commerce, both here and on the high seas."

"Aye," says James Wilson. "The British will no' evacuate their forts on the Great Lakes despite their treaty obligations and they encourage Indians to attack our frontier settlers. The Spanish ha'e closed the Mississippi River to our traffic. Overseas, Barbary pirates take our ships and hold our citizens hostage."

"And our government cannot stop it because it has no power," Hamilton says. "Not to tax the states, or to keep them from warring, or to protect our people and private property."

There's a silence, and as I shake out my aching hand, I wonder: *How come I never knew the country had so many problems getting off the ground? And how are they going to fix it?*

"You are right: the states do have all the power," Franklin agrees. "But how will you change that? Having spent years in state government,

I can tell you the men running them are very jealous of that power. What might they do upon learning you mean to take it from them?"

"I know what I would do," Robert Morris says. "Recall my delegates. Refuse to participate, as Rhode Island is doing right now to keep her independence. Then correspond with other states to do likewise. Shut down the convention."

"Which is why, Doctor, we have been discussing a rule of secrecy for the convention," Hamilton says. "To prevent word from spreading that we are designing an entirely new government."

"Yeah, like that'll work," I mutter to myself.

"I suppose," Franklin says unenthusiastically, "if the delegates will even accept such a rule. But more important, as James Wilson has said, we must find ways to build consensus among the delegates. That will be difficult. Years ago, as the Crown's deputy postmaster, I traveled the whole of what is now our country. Life in Georgia and the Carolinas is very different from life in Massachusetts, as are their people. Even the differences between Pennsylvania and Connecticut are significant. Those differences—each state's particular needs—will have to be accommodated if compromise is to be forged."

"Well, you canno' have consensus without first there being a lot of talk," James Wilson says. "I know of no better device for encouraging the free flow of ideas than having the convention meet first as a 'committee of the whole.'"

"Committee of the whole?" I ask under my breath.

"Oh, I like that idea," Franklin says. "Many fewer rules, which relaxes the atmosphere. And no vote is final. Everything decided has to be voted on again by the delegates sitting as the formal convention."

"Which allows the delegates to ascertain just which way the wind blows on a particular issue, which aids building consensus," Robert Morris says.

"I would add a rule permitting any delegate at any time to request reconsideration of a vote previously taken," Franklin says. "That would give us even more freedom to enter into consensus—vote for something we don't like to resolve an issue temporarily and move on—knowing that if later we still do not like the resolution, we can ask for reconsideration."

"I favor both measures," Washington says. "As I favor a rule of complete secrecy for all convention proceedings. No admitting the public to the Assembly Room, no reports to the press, no correspondence with non-delegates concerning deliberations—nothing. All delegates on their honor to keep mum and not even an open window through which an eavesdropper might spy."

My hand freezes! Isn't eavesdropping exactly what I'm doing?

"Unfortunate since Philadelphia in summer is so beastly hot," Madison says. "But if it means we can debate without pressure from the press, the public, and state government men jealous of their power, I will support it."

"I'm not sure I agree with absolute secrecy," Franklin says. "Don't we risk losing the people's trust? They'll think we're going behind their backs to grab power for ourselves."

"Not if we submit our final product to the people for approval," Madison says. "And not if we make it clear that they are the ones who are sovereign and from whom all power flows."

"I suppose I can go along with that," Franklin says.

"Excellent," Washington says.

"And now, Gentlemen, I must retire," Franklin says. "'Early to bed, early to rise,' and all that. But, as I said to James Wilson earlier, I hope you and all the delegates will treat this house as your own during our convention—as a place of respite where all may come to relax with each other after our labors in the State House. Indeed, if it's consensus and compromise amongst the delegates we seek, this garden may prove a perfect venue."

As Franklin's guests say goodnight, Washington tells them: "You gentlemen go ahead. I wish to speak with Dr. Franklin briefly about a private matter."

"Dr. Franklin," he says, once they're alone, "I know the convention's preferment of Major Jackson over your grandson Temple must be disappointing. I want you to know I am sorry for it and that the delegates meant no disrespect."

"There is nothing to be sorry for, General, although I appreciate your words. Major Jackson has the confidence of the delegates. My grandson does not. It is true his daily attendance would have offered me certain conveniences. But the last thing we are gathered for is my convenience. I can make do without him."

"Nevertheless, if I may provide any assistance, please ask."

"I will be sure to. Good evening."

A few minutes later, Franklin comes to the library.

"What's this?" he asks, picking up one of the pages I'd filled with shorthand.

"I ... I've never actually taken dictation for anyone professionally, so I thought I better practice."

"Practice on what?" he asks.

"Well ... I could hear what you were all saying, so I ... ."

"Wrote down everything we said?" Franklin's eyes are open very wide and his lips pressed together so hard they make a thin, straight line.

"I wasn't trying to spy or anything. I just—"

"Every word?"

"I'm sorry," I say, grabbing up all the papers. "Here, you can have them—"

"Read me what you wrote. Start at the beginning and read out loud what you wrote."

I do.

"Remarkable!" he says when I finish. "It is exactly the conversation as I remember it—word for word! Oh, indeed you are a likely lad!"

"You mean, you're not angry at me eavesdropping?"

"Oh, yes, . . . well." His face goes all stern. "That was wrong. Very wrong. Don't do it again. Ever. Ever. Never. Never!" Then he smiles slyly. "Unless I tell you to."

CHAPTER 8

"Now, to work," Franklin says. "Take your things and sit there." He points to a large table surrounded by chairs in the middle of the room.

"Thought you were going to bed," I say.

"At my age? I'll be asleep soon enough. Permanently!"

We work on Franklin's correspondence for several hours. He dictates. I listen closely and pray my shorthand skills are good enough.

Finally, he lights a candle for Elise and has her take me to where I'm to sleep.

It's a closet-sized room on the top floor, with the steeply sloped roof for its ceiling. The small bed, table, and chair barely fit. And since hot air rises, it's a sweat-box. There are no windows, but there is a trap door in the roof.

"Let's open it up and get some air," I say.

"That is not its purpose," Elise says.

"Then what's it for?"

"If a neighbor's house burns, we open it to pour water on the roof to keep flying embers from causing a fire. Otherwise, it is to remain closed."

"But it's hot! Look at me! I'm all sweat!"

"Yes? And if there is a sudden rain storm, what then? The mattress will be ruined."

"I don't *believe* this!"

"Believe what you like," she says, putting the clothes she's gotten from the "slop chest" on the chair. "My roof also has a door. It was left open. The rain came. The straw in the mattress filled with mold."

After she leaves, I climb onto the bed, open the trap, and poke my head outside.

The cool night breeze is a relief. But it's so dark! No lit-up buildings or blazing signs; no headlights on the streets or spot-lit Franklin Bridge. I can see street lamps on some of the sidewalks, but they hardly give off any light at all—just a little glow.

Then I look straight up.

I've never seen so many stars!

And I've never heard such quiet. Complete silence except for the chirrup of crickets and the whisper of a light breeze.

That star-filled sky and that quiet fill me, not with peace, but with such feelings of fear and "alone-ness." I think: *I'm cut off from everyone and everything I've ever relied on: Mom, Pop, Penny, my grandparents, electricity, plumbing, air-conditioning, cars, computers, cell phones, and everything else in my world. Can I make it here? I already proved I can't chop wood! And what if I can't do what Franklin needs? I don't know the first thing about being a clerk; or how to act like I'm from 1787. What if I screw up? Would they really throw me in jail or the asylum?*

Then I hear Gus's voice in my head: *Marcus, relax, will you? You got this! You can do this! Use your eyes. Use your ears. Study the people—how they walk, how they talk. Copy them. You love acting. Here's your chance. And learn all you can from Franklin. God, what I wouldn't give to be in your shoes!*

God, what I wouldn't give to have Gus back and here with me right now.

And I worry what my family must think. That I really did run away to be an actor in New York? Just because I wasn't getting my way? Or worse, that something awful happened to me? That I'm hurt, or dead? Are Mom and Pop thinking they've lost their only remaining son forever?

A great wave of tiredness washes through me as I realize there's nothing I can do. I climb down and lie on the narrow bed. Through the opening in the roof, I hear a voice call out: "Eleven o'clock and all's well." I fall asleep, hoping it will be true.

***

No one wakes me the next morning. The bed does that. The thin mattress of crackling straw on the narrow frame of wood and rope is the hardest place I've ever slept. No wonder I'm so stiff and sore.

The trap door is still open, so I climb up for another look.

"Definitely not my Philly," I mutter as I turn a complete circle. No tall buildings; just block after block of stumpy wood or brick houses, all with chimneys pouring smoke.

To the west, beyond the houses, green forest stretches for miles, like a rich, emerald carpet. To the east rise the masts and spars of sailing ships on the Delaware River. To the north, the houses along Market Street block my view of the market. But I can hear the low buzz of the crowd and the cries of the sellers. It sounds a little like a block party.

I want coffee. A green Starbuck's sign flashes in my mind's eye.

"Yeah, right!" I say as I close the trap and get down.

I pull on the clothes Elise has left: an itchy and stained beige shirt, canvas britches, baggy stockings with lots of patches, a scuffed-up leather vest, and cracked leather shoes. None of it fits right. All of it smells moldy. Plus, I haven't washed. I need a shower, or bath, something—anything—to clear the fuzziness from my head and get me sharp.

I go downstairs, hoping for breakfast. There's no one in the dining room, and no sign anyone's been there. A tall, ticking grandfather clock shows it's just past nine o'clock.

Hearing voices in the cellar, I go down and find Franklin, Sally, and Elise in the kitchen. While Sally chops vegetables and Elise feeds wood to the fire, Franklin sits at the table, drinking tea and studying several long, broad sheets filled with columns of small print.

"Ah, Master Slug-a-bed!" he says, looking up.

"S'up?" I say through a yawn, and then remember how I need to start acting like I'm from here. "I mean, Good Morning. Whatcha—what are you reading?"

Franklin shoots me a look and then goes back to his paper, a small smile playing at his lips.

"*The Pennsylvania Gazette*. It is the newspaper I once published and that made me my fortune. I sold it long ago. But I still enjoy reading it."

It's not like any newspaper I've ever seen. It's only four pages and it has no pictures.

"You should see the newspapers we have—"

"Marcus?" Franklin warns, holding up a finger, which is when I remember the future.

"Sorry, sorry. Sometimes, I'm not so sharp in the morning. Is there any coffee?"

"There is tea," Elise says. "And you have missed breakfast. Here, everyone rises at dawn and we are done eating by no later than six."

"How come you didn't wake me? I'm right down the hall."

"It is not my job," Elise says.

"After the shock you've had," Franklin says absently, nose back in his paper, "you needed the rest."

"If I can't get coffee, can I at least get a wash?"

"There is the bucket. There is the pump," Elise says, pointing.

"Or there is the river," Franklin says, turning a page.

"Think I'll start by washing my face, if that's okay."

I fill the bucket. The water looks clear, but when I splash it on my face, it doesn't taste very good.

"Use this to dry yourself," Sally says, handing me a rough piece of linen. "That shirt is a disgrace. Look at all those patches. And the staining under the arms!"

"Washington will be pleased," Franklin murmurs as he studies the last page. "Not a word about our convention." With a contented smile, he folds the paper and then looks to his daughter. "Fortunately, it is market day today and the shops are open. You and Elise will buy victuals and Marcus and I will go to Timothy Wimpole's for clothing and then to town hall."

"Why town hall?" I ask.

"I'll explain on the way."

Minutes later, we set out, me in my ratty clothes and an old, broad-brimmed hat; Franklin in his brown suit and three-cornered hat, leaning on his gold-headed walking-stick and my arm; and the women following behind in bonnets and dresses so long that the hems are black with dirt.

"Now remember," Franklin says to me, "you have a throat ailment. So, no talking."

We pass through the arched carriageway connecting Franklin's place with Market Street. Talk about chaos! Hundreds, maybe thousands, crowd the broad, cobblestoned avenue going about their market chores.

The sheds running down the middle of the avenue sell every kind of food: meats, fish, fowl, fruits, vegetables, cheeses, herbs, spices. Soap-makers and knife grinders, wool-spinners and fabric weavers, cobblers and seamstresses, blacksmiths and gunsmiths, and all sorts of sellers of wines, ciders, and beer call out their wares. Sides of beef and whole hogs dripping blood and covered with flies hang from sharp, iron hooks.

Every second brings a new, sharp sound: the ring of a blacksmith's hammer, the crack of a wagoner's whip, the clop of hooves, the rumble of iron-rimmed wheels, a bull's angry bellow, chickens clucking, roosters crowing, geese honking, dogs fighting, and, when we near the river, the clang of ships' bells, and the cries of sailors, dock workers, and gulls.

And every breath brings a new stink: pee and manure from the livestock, old blood and innards from the butcher's stalls, the bloated carcass of a horse rotting in an empty lot, open sewers, garbage in the street, and the river at low tide.

We reach the corner of Third and Market. Franklin stops and pulls from his pocket a large leather wallet resembling a modern envelope.

"You'll need money, daughter." Opening the flap and digging with his fingers, he fishes out several silver coins. "Buy what we need for the week. We'll meet at home later."

Franklin and I watch Sally and Elise wade into the crowd, using their market baskets to clear the way.

"And don't forget peppermints for the children!" Franklin calls after them.

A young woman in a green dress, low-cut and stained and grimy at the collar and cuffs, slips her arm through Franklin's.

"Is it really peppermints you're wanting, dearie? How 'bout somethin' spicier, if you knows what I mean? I'm Katy, Katy Katz."

She meows, then hisses, then swipes her claw-like hand with its broken, dirty nails, and then lets loose a belly laugh through a mouth of black and missing teeth.

"Fancy buyin' Katy a drink? I knows a place over in Helltown. Owner's a friend. Makes a lovely punch. Nice rooms, all private-like."

"Here! You!" a rough voice shouts.

A big-bellied man with a face full of stubble, a tall staff, and a small, wood box hooked to his belt by a crank grabs Katy's upper arm.

"Take your hands off the gentleman 'fore I lock you in the stocks."

"I'm not doin' no harm. Me and the gentleman's just talkin'. Ain't we, dearie?"

"It's quite alright, watchman," Franklin says. "This woman's no bother. No need to trouble yourself."

"I'll be the judge of what I take trouble over. We've entirely too many of these sorts around, 'specially on Market day, along with them pickpockets. Sometimes they work together. They use the girls as a distraction and then pick a man's pocket clean as you please. How do I know you ain't one of 'em?"

"Look at me, watchman," Franklin says. "Am I young or agile enough to pick a pocket and escape? It takes a steady hand. Does this look steady to you?" He shows trembling fingers.

"No, I s'pose not," the watchman says grudgingly. "But you seem familiar. Pretty sure I seen you before. Maybe you're running this girl and using the boy to do your dirty work."

"I assure you, that is not the case. The reason I seem familiar is—"

"Wot's this boy to you anyway? Don't look like he's your kin, not in them duds," the watchman snarls, then grabs me up by the collar. "Wot's your name, ragamuffin?"

I hate being handled. Anger balls my own hands into fists. I'm just about to step into the guy to try rolling him with one of the Green Beret judo throws Gus taught me, when pain explodes in my foot. I look down. The end of Franklin's walking stick mashes my toe.

"Now there's no need for suspicion," he says to soothe the watchman. "As I was about to say, the reason I seem familiar to you is that I am Dr. Benjamin Franklin. This is my servant."

Servant? I shoot him such a look.

"Wot? Franklin? *The* Benjamin Franklin? President of the Executive Council?"

"Aye, sir. At your service."

"Go on witcha! Yer tellin' lies, you is. I'm s'posed to believe Benjamin Franklin would have hisself a servant dressed like he is?"

His large hands grab my shirt and Franklin's coat.

"If he's your servant, where's his indenture papers? Don't have any, do he? Cuz you're lying, just as I suspected. I'm takin' you'se both to the jail on charges of—"

"Dr. Franklin!" a man calls.

James Wilson and another man hurry towards us. Wilson's companion is well-dressed, but short and thin with a foxy face and wispy gray hair combed forward over his forehead.

"James Wilson! How glad I am to see you!" Franklin says. "And you, James Madison!"

"Dr. Franklin, a pleasure to meet again so soon," Madison says. "Allow me to say, I found last evening most instructive."

Now I recognize the high-pitched voice and the genteel, rounded tones; and realize that this is the man who wrote the resolutions they'd talked about in the garden.

"We're just on our way to the London Coffee House. Will ye join us?" Wilson says.

"Nothing would give me more pleasure. But alas, we have business and can't seem to get past this watchman. He doesn't believe I am who I say."

Wilson's eyes open very wide.

"Watchman Emery!" he commands, his Scottish burr thick. "Ye know me, don'tcha!"

"Yessir."

"We've seen each other in and around court many times, ha'e we no'?"

"Yessir."

"And ye know I be well acquainted with the head o' the watch?"

"Yessir."

With every "Yessir," the watchman's head ducks lower.

"And d'ye or d'ye not know this is Dr. Benjamin Franklin?"

"Well ... I s'pose I do now, Mr. Wilson."

"Then d'we ha'e a problem?"

"Nosir, we do not." The watchman turns to Franklin. "Beggin' your pardon, Dr. Franklin. Ain't never seen you before in the flesh."

"Quite all right, constable. We're all good fellows here. And no harm's done. But this lad and I must be on our way. We've business to tend."

Just then, the noise from the crowd swells. Katy Katz cranes for a better view. A black man—barefoot, hand-cuffed, dressed in sand-colored pants and shirt—bolts through the crowd, chased by two men.

One is white, stocky, and well-dressed with ginger hair. The other is black, as massive as any pro linebacker, and wearing a red shirt and fringed, leather leggings.

"Stop him!" cries the white man. "That's my property!"

Watchman Emery unhooks the wooden contraption from his belt and, twirling it by its handle to make a loud, ratcheting sound, runs after them.

"That blackguard!" Franklin says. "Were I younger and thinking faster, I would have tripped him with my stick."

"Who? The watchman?" Wilson asks.

"No. Swinbourne, the merchant."

"Is that him? I know of him, but we ha'e never met."

"Damned slaver!" Franklin says, then shakes his head, then shrugs. "Well, nothing to be done, I suppose. And I see young Katy Katz used the cover of all this commotion to slip away. Good for her, poor wretch! Mr. Wilson, Mr. Madison, thank you for your assistance. And don't forget, tonight the Union Fire Company meets. Bring as many delegates as care to come. There will be plenty of plain-spoken men there, all with political views. You may find it instructive."

As we part, Wilson and Madison shake Franklin's hand. Neither offers his hand to me.

"That settles that!" Franklin says. "I thought we might wait until after the tailor's, but I now see that would be foolish."

"Can I talk now?"

"Quietly. Move your lips as little as possible."

"Wait on what?"

"Getting you indentured."

CHAPTER 9

"Getting me *what?*"

"Indentured."

"What's that?"

"An indenture is a contract between a master and a servant by which the servant agrees to serve the master for a term of years in exchange for … well … it could be any number of things, really: passage on a ship, food and lodging for the term, a parcel of land at the end of the term. It's a quite common arrangement. Many have made their way to this country by agreeing to be indentured. Indeed, when I was a boy I was indentured as a printer's apprentice to my brother.

"Now, I've taken the liberty of having my grandson Benjamin print an indenture for us to sign before the City Clerk—"

"I don't understand. Why are we doing this?" I ask, struggling to say as little as necessary through lips that move as little as possible.

"For two reasons. First, I must be able to explain your presence here, as well as define our relationship, in terms others will understand. Second, and much more important, I must have a way to afford you the protection you may need. This indenture will establish you as my property. I dare say there are few who will seek to harm or interfere with the property of the President of Pennsylvania."

"Wait a minute! You're going to *own* me?"

"Hush! Precisely."

"Oh, I don't like the sound of this—not one bit. What if I don't want to do it?"

"Well … the choice is entirely up to you, of course. I can't force you. But it will make it more difficult to protect you should you fall into difficulties. Suppose, for example, you are stopped again by a watchman.

You would explain you are my indentured servant, produce a pass I will write for you, and, were that not enough to satisfy him, bring him to my house where he would be shown the indenture as proof."

"But if you're going to own me, doesn't that mean I have to do whatever you say?"

"It can, and in most cases it does. But remember, we are doing this only to afford you protection and so that we will have a relationship that I can explain to the rest of the world. How you and I manage that relationship is entirely up to us. Now, I have already promised that I will not exploit you. I now promise that, between you and me, we will treat the indenture as if it does not exist. Satisfactory?"

"I ... guess. Wait—who was the guy being chased?"

Franklin shrugs. "Runaway slave, I suppose."

"And he's owned too. Right?"

"Yes. But it's entirely different. He had no choice. You do."

"What'll they do if they catch him?"

"I don't know. Whatever they like, I imagine."

"Whip him?"

"Probably."

"Which is what you could do me."

"I would never! Besides, that hardly ever happens with an indentured servant, although ... " His voice trails off as he frowns, as if he's remembering something or seeing a picture in his mind's eye. But then he shakes his head and his voice comes back strong. "Marcus, you are just going to have to trust me."

I'm not happy about it, but if it's going to protect me from people like that watchman, then I'm willing to sign whatever Franklin wants me to sign.

"Ah, here we are," he says as we reach the corner of Second and Market. "Our City Hall."

It's a red-brick building with two chimneys and a sloped roof topped by a cupola and a weather vane—small enough so that ten of them could fit inside the enormous Philadelphia City Hall of my day.

Franklin takes me upstairs to a room lined with shelves filled with ledgers. A pale, paunchy, middle-aged man with ink all over his shirt stands writing at a tall desk. The thumb and finger holding the quill are black as tar.

"Ah, Mr. Lowery, good to find you in on a Saturday."

"Dr. Franklin! A pleasure, as always. You know me: work, work, and more work. It's what keeps me going."

"Yes, and keeps your wife out of the little hair you have left." Franklin chuckles.

"You know me too well, Doctor."

"Well, after more than forty years, I should hope so. Marcus, Mr. Lowery worked in my printing office when he was a boy. I helped teach him his letters and his hand."

"And helped get me my position as City Clerk."

"Mr. Lowery, this young man is Marcus Santana. He is my assistant. He is originally from Philadelphia, but has just returned from Paris and has agreed to indenture himself to me for the next six months to repay the funds I advanced for his passage. If you will lend me your quill, I will fill out the contract, the lad and I will sign it, and then you can witness it."

Franklin takes the indenture from his pocket and begins filling it in.

"Only six months, you say?" Lowery asks. "That is a blessedly short indenture."

"Indeed it is. But it is what Marcus and I have agreed."

"Is that true, lad? Are you agreeing to this indenture? To be owned by Dr. Franklin and to do all that he says?"

I'm just about to answer when my other foot explodes in pain. I look down and there's the tip of Franklin's walking stick, mashing my toe again. I grit my teeth as Franklin says: "Unfortunately, Marcus cannot speak right now, due to an injury to his throat. He must remain silent or risk losing his voice permanently."

"Well, he can nod, can't he?" asks Lowery.

Which I do.

Franklin finishes filling in the contract, signs it, and passes it to me with the quill to read and sign. Short enough to fit on half a page, it gives Franklin ownership of me for six months in exchange for the cost of the sea voyage I never made, plus my food and lodging during that period; and promises my freedom at the term's end. I sign and pass the contract to Mr. Lowery who witnesses it and stamps it with his seal.

"There you go young man. You've got yourself the finest master anyone could have. I should know. I was his apprentice for seven years."

We leave City Hall and walk slowly down Market towards the river. The masts and spars of docked ships loom high.

At Front Street, we turn right and walk several blocks along a near-deserted, muddy, garbage-strewn street past shut-up shops, warehouses, and taverns, until we come to a small alley which Franklin guides me into. I can tell he's tired. He leans heavily on my arm.

"Need to rest?" I ask.

"No. We've arrived."

A sign over the door reads: "Timothy Wimpole, Tailor."

A little bell jingles as Franklin opens the door. We step into a small, low-ceilinged shop with a long counter and mostly empty shelves, all of dark wood. Shadowy and smelling of dust and smoke, the shop seems deserted. But then a gaunt, black-haired man steps through a curtained doorway.

"Yes, gentlemen, what will you buy?" he calls, searching through the gloom. His voice is nasal and raspy and sounds like he doesn't want us there. His feet scuff at the wood floor as he comes towards us.

"Good day to thee, Timothy," Franklin says.

Only a few feet away now, the man stops and stiffens. His face is all sharp lines and angles. It cranes forward, as if to peer harder.

"Doctor Franklin," he says flatly, looking like he's swallowed something nasty.

"In the flesh, Timothy."

For what seems like forever, the only sound is a ticking clock. The two men stare at each other. Franklin's face never loses its pleasantness. Wimpole's grows more and more bitter.

"And your purpose?" he finally snaps.

"Your assistance."

The tailor's eyes go wide.

"My assistance? After everything, you come to me—"

"This young man is my clerk. He needs suitable clothing. All his were lost in transit, so he needs them urgently. I remembered you work quickly. We come, not just for a suit, but all the clothes he will need." Franklin produces his wallet. "We will pay cash."

The tailor's eyebrows shoot all the way to his hairline and his hands come together like he's praying.

"If it's quick you need, I'm certainly your man," he says. "What exactly is required?" He rubs his hands like he's washing them.

"Two suits: coat, britches, weskits; black and of plain, middling quality; light in weight for summer. No satin, velvet, or brocade. Plain buckles and buttons at the knees—no silver. White shirts, stockings, undergarments—better have four sets. Linen shirts for the suits. Several of cotton. Stockings to be black, gray, or white. Also, a set of long trousers."

Wimpole writes as Franklin talks.

"Wig? Hat?" the tailor asks eagerly. "Neck stocks and neckerchiefs? And shoes! Those I'd have to get from the cobbler. Or you can—"

"Yes, yes, all that," Franklin answers. "Take care of it. But again, no adornment. Plain metal buckles for the shoes."

"I'll just get my tape and take the lad's measure. As you can see, I don't stock much these days. I'll have to order most of this from my supplier, Mr. Swinbourne. He'll want his money up front."

He motions for me to stand on a short wood box. "Take off that hat and vest, boy" he orders, looking at me with distaste. "I certainly see why you need new clothes. Wherever did you come by these rags?"

Franklin quickly says: "He cannot speak due to an injury to his throat. So, I would ask you not to question him. Is there some information you need him to declare in order to proceed with the fitting?"

"Er … no," Wimpole says, his eyes on the coins Franklin has taken from his wallet.

"I trust this Spanish piece of eight will be more than sufficient for your purchase from Mr. Swinbourne," Franklin says, offering the silver coin. "And then this gold doubloon upon your delivering everything to my house by no later than eight o'clock, Monday evening. Agreed?"

"No, I'll want two gold doubloons, seeing as you want it so fast."

"No, you'll have one doubloon, or I shall go elsewhere."

Wimpole stands there, glowering. "No one will give it to you as fast as you need it. Not for that price!"

"We shall see," Franklin says coolly, turning and heading for the door. "Come along, Marcus."

"WAIT!

Franklin and I turn.

"The silver and the doubloon, then. But I want 'em both now."

Franklin takes a long moment, looking like he's considering carefully. Wimpole's hands clasp tightly, then begin their washing motion.

"Very well," Franklin finally says. "Proceed with the fitting."

I get back on the box and Wimpole starts measuring.

"Heard from son William?" Wimpole asks, like it's a challenge.

Franklin doesn't answer.

"Guess I shouldn't have asked," Wimpole mutters.

"Excellent guess," Franklin says. "Assuming a guess can ever be excellent."

"Shame you two never put aside your differences," Wimpole says.

"More shame for him than me."

"Well, well, ain't you the cold one? Shame for me too. I lost a good friend."

"You lost your connection to wealth and power."

"Maybe, but we were more than that. I shared my boyhood with him. I'd think you'd remember, since it was you who took us on some of our adventures—flying kites, catching fireflies, fishing and swimming in the river."

"I remember," Franklin says softly.

"Those were good days."

"That they were," Franklin agrees, softer still. Then he seems to shake himself. "But my son forsook all that. He chose the power and prestige that came with the royal governorship of New Jersey, instead of doing right by the people and fighting for their independence."

"Sure of that, are you? Sure you and all your rebel friends were right to split us off from England?" Wimpole's tone is bitter and as he works with his measuring tape, I can feel his hands shake with anger.

"He chose allegiance to a tyrant king over loyalty to his family and countrymen," Franklin says. "And to me! His father from whom all his good fortune flowed! I was the one who obtained that governorship for him!"

"Yeah ... well ... God forbid we loyal British subjects should disagree with any of you lot! Enjoying your visit to my shop? Pleased by the reduction of my circumstances, are you?"

"That is not why I am here!" Franklin says through gritted teeth. "We need a job done and you're the best man to do it. And it's no use blaming me for your troubles. You were the one who chose to serve British officers while they occupied Philadelphia during the war. I had nothing to do with what happened to you. I was in Paris."

"Nothing to DO? Who was it went around protesting taxes and holding congresses and writing declarations of independency? Who was it started the damned war? I never asked for that. I never agreed to it. Not any of it! I was an Englishman, loyal to my King, same as all my life! I didn't ask for any independent state of Pennsylvania, nor any United States neither—"

"No, you didn't."

"No, sir, I did NOT!" he roars and I wince. "And when my King's lawfully appointed officers asked for my assistance, I gave it. Like any loyal subject would do!"

There's another long silence, so tense my hands and stomach clench.

"You are right," Franklin finally says. "It was not fair. War is never fair. But, I remind you, you chose to remain and throw in your lot with the King. You even profited from that choice, for a time. I wonder that you remain now. Why not go to England if your allegiance is to the King?"

"Where am I going to go in England? Who do I know? Philadelphia's my home. I was born and raised here. Life was good before you lot started mucking about. Now look. Economy's in a shambles. No one's got money to spend. I can barely afford the rent on this place. And it's been like that for as long as I can remember. Oh, what I wouldn't give to see the English back and in charge and running things right and proper. Lots of others I know, too."

"We are working hard to correct—"

"Oh, of that I am sure! Just like you worked hard on that treaty which promised compensation to Loyalists who lost their property. Where's the compensation for my shop and all the goods you lot destroyed?"

"As I said, we're working—"

"Yeah?" Wimpole interrupts bitterly. "Well, you work at that and I'll work at this. And we'll see who's first to get something useful done. Now, I've got all I need and I'd appreciate it if you would leave me to my work. Good day to you, Dr. Franklin!"

CHAPTER 10

We exit the alley onto a deserted Front Street. I look at Franklin. His face is pale and sweaty. He leans heavily on me and his stick.

"You okay?" I ask.

"It is the stone on my bladder. I will be fine. Just help me back to the house," he says hoarsely.

"Guy's sure got one big chip on his shoulder," I mutter.

"'Chip on his shoulder?' What does that mean?"

"That he resents everything and everybody: you in particular!"

"He has some cause, I suppose. He once had a shop several times the size of what he has now. And employed a number of seamstresses and apprentices. All the finest gentlemen went to him, including my son. Then he chose the wrong side and lost everything."

"If he hates you so much, why go to him?"

"Because he can deliver what we need more quickly and cheaply than anyone else. He has few other customers and works with alacrity, which means he can get the job done now. With any other tailor, we would have to wait for a week or more."

"Oh, okay, I see. We went there so you could squeeze him. Get yourself a little pay-back?"

"Pay back? Squeeze? Whatever do you mean?"

"Come on, Doc. You just said it. He doesn't have a lot of other customers. Which means he's gotta do what you say for the price you want. He wanted two gold pieces. You made him settle for one. You took me there to squeeze him."

"I most certainly did not! I took you there because I need a clerk properly dressed and quickly. You need clothes so you will not stand out. He needs money that may well keep him out of debtor's prison. Everyone's interests are served. And, if he does a good job, when people hear he has worked for me and I am pleased, they may give him their custom."

"And that would make you feel good?"

"Well, it would not make me sad. I want very much to see us mend the fractures our War of Independence caused. We must be one nation, loyal to each other. Not Loyalist or Rebel, or Englishman or Pennsylvanian or Virginian or Massachusetts man, but Americans all. Maybe this forgiveness I am showing can, in a small way, help that along."

"Didn't look like he appreciated it much."

"Also, we were friends in happier times. I hate seeing friends struggle, even if we've fallen out."

I look at Franklin and am surprised by the sadness in his face.

As we come closer to Market, the street becomes more crowded.

"Marcus, you had better stop talking. You never know who sees what."

Together, slowly, we walk up Market Street (called High Street, back then). How primitive everything seems! Not a single task is performed by machine. Horses and oxen draw carts and wagons, human feet operate knife-grinding, spinning, and pottery wheels; carpenters use axes, hand-saws, and chisels to fashion wood. Muscle, both human and animal, seems the only engine of accomplishment. And fire. There are so many open fires—for cooking food, dyeing material, forging metal, boiling soap, washing clothes—that an acrid, throat-biting haze fills the air.

We reach the low, arched carriageway leading to Franklin's printing shop and home.

"Thank you, Marcus," he says, breathing hard. "I am grateful for your strength."

Which makes me feel pretty good—and grateful to Gus for introducing me to the gym. But seconds later, all those good feelings get blown away.

"Make way! Make way!" a man up Market Street cries over the ratcheting of a watchman's noisemaker.

Swinbourne, the red-shirted black man, and the watchman have caught the slave. They've shackled his ankles and chained his manacled wrists to his waist and take turns shoving and kicking him down the street.

The slave doesn't look terrified, now. He looks hopeless. Even when he's pushed so hard he almost falls, his face stays dull and listless, like he's incapable of caring anymore.

"Easy, Lucas," ginger-haired Swinbourne says to the black man. "I paid a good price for this one. I don't need you damaging my investment."

"*Damaging my investment?*" My initial pity for the slave turns into a sudden, rising anger that balls my fists and makes my cheeks burn.

Just as I step forward to tell the men to stop, Franklin grabs me by the shoulder and pulls me into the arched carriageway, out of sight.

"Say nothing, Marcus," he warns. "I know you want to. But you dare not interfere with another man's property. Now, quickly, take me back to the house."

***

As soon as we get back, Franklin has me and Elise fill his bath with water almost boiling, all of which has to be lugged from the kitchen hearth up the stairs. Then, wearing a long, white night-shirt "for modesty's sake," he has me help him in and motions me to a chair.

"I'm sorry you had to see that," he says. "But perhaps it is for the best."

"For the best? How can you say that? How can you even think it? You saw how that man was treated. I can't believe you didn't do anything!"

"I could not. As you must learn, in this time and place, it is perfectly legal to own slaves. What is not legal is interfering between a man and his property. Had you tried to aid that slave in his attempt to escape—especially in front of the watchman—you almost certainly would have been arrested and imprisoned or fined. Which means that I could have been fined, and certainly embarrassed, since I'm responsible for you—"

"You mean, since you own me."

"Well ... yes ... I suppose that is one way to look at it, if you like—"

"I don't like! Not one bit! You never told me that was going to be part of this whole indenture deal: that I'd have to watch everything I do and say so you won't get in trouble."

"No, I did not. I did not think of it. And I am sorry for it."

"Can't wait to find out what else you haven't thought about," I say under my breath. "So, if slavery's legal, what am I supposed to do? Just stand by and do nothing?"

"I'm afraid that is all you can do."

"But that goes against everything I've ever been taught—everything we're supposed to stand for where I come from."

"I know."

"You know? How do you know?"

"Because we have had this conversation previously. That is all I will say—all I can say. Except that I understand your feeling and that I am doing all I can to try and abolish slavery. But until it is abolished, you must not interfere in any matter involving a slave. Do you understand? No matter how cruel and unjust, you must not interfere. Say you understand."

"I understand," I say, thinking to myself: *But I don't agree. And my "understanding" doesn't mean I have to do, or not do, a single thing.*

"Good," Franklin says with a nod, like the subject is closed. "I must say, our small sojourn revealed to me more perils than I had anticipated. I really am not sure I can let you out of my sight, at least until you are better acquainted with our world. But do you know? That may just afford us an opportunity.

"I felt very secure walking with you today. My balance is not what it was. I have grown increasingly concerned about falling, especially after injuring my wrist. But with you, I felt no trepidation.

"I wonder if you might be willing to stay by my side. Not all the time. But when I am out in public and when I may be compelled to walk or stand for a long while and may need someone to support me. We could keep an eye on each other, so to speak. You would keep me from falling. And I would keep you from getting into trouble."

"You gonna crush my toes again with that stick?"

"Possibly, if I see you about to err and I need to."

"How about you just tap my foot instead of putting all your weight on me?"

"We might try that."

"Well then, I'm willing to try hanging out … um … accompanying you."

"Excellent! Now, I believe we've begun to build you a good story. Let us add to it, put flesh on its bones, so to speak.

He thinks for a minute, and then outlines my new identity.

"Originally from Philadelphia, you accompanied your parents to Paris, where your father opened a merchant house to import American goods. He sent you to serve as one of my clerks in Passy until my departure in 1785. Your parents subsequently succumbed to small pox. That will gain you sympathy and discourage people from asking further about them. You wrote and asked for my assistance to return to Philadelphia. I advanced the funds for your passage and you have agreed to repay me by way of the indenture. On board ship, during rough seas, you fell and struck your throat, bruising it severely, which is why you cannot talk. Yes, I think that will do nicely. What do you think?"

"How long am I going to have to keep my mouth shut?"

"That depends on you. The sooner you learn how to sound like one of us, the sooner you can talk. Now, what say we begin our new venture this evening, when the men from the Union Fire Company come for their meeting?"

"What's this Union Fire Company you keep talking about?" I ask.

"It's something I and several other fellows organized years ago to put out house fires. The members come. We call the roll and ascertain our inventory, discuss necessary business, and then enjoy refreshment and fellowship together. There are many who will want to talk with me and I probably will have to stand for quite some time. And there will be persons I don't want to talk with, whom I need help avoiding, such as that odious Swinbourne."

"Why would you let him in?"

"I have no choice. He is a member of the company. He lives nearby. Membership depends on geography, not popularity. When fire comes, we need every available hand to fight it and prevent its spread from house to house to house. But just because he is a member does not mean I must speak to him. So, keep a sharp eye peeled and if he approaches, move us quickly away."

CHAPTER 11

That night, Franklin and I stand at his library window and watch the men of the Union Fire Company arrive in the garden. Sally has found better clothes for me so I can go to the meeting: an old brown suit, stockings, and linen belonging to her husband, Richard, plus a dark brown wig tied back in a queue, or ponytail. Fitting, since it smells like a horse.

The men have brought all their equipment: leather buckets, wooden ladders, coils of rope attached to big metal hooks, axes, canvas bags, rolls of what looks like thick leather strap, and some kind of trough with a see-saw double handle set on carriage wheels.

"That's what you use to put out fires?" I say. "How?"

"Do you see the engine on wheels? That is our water pump. When a house catches fire, the men wheel it over and form a bucket brigade. They use the leather buckets to carry water from a water source—like a well or a pond—to the engine. The rolls of leather are hoses made by sewing the edges of the leather together. Once the trough is filled, the men use that double handle to pump the water through the hose, and onto the fire. The ropes and hooks are for pulling down flaming walls and the canvas bags are for carrying valuables to safety."

"Really? You call that an engine? Doc, you need to come back to my Philadelphia and see what a real fire engine—"

"Oh, they came!" Franklin says, like a kid who'd expected Santa Claus to forget him.

"Who?"

"The delegates. Well, not all of them. But look. Now of course, you know Mr. Wilson and Mr. Madison. But I don't think you've met the others, even though some were at the house last night. There, that stocky, gray-haired man is Philadelphia financier Robert Morris. He was with us to sign our Declaration of Independence, and lent us a great deal of money to fight our War of Independence. General Washington is staying at his home here in Philadelphia.

"And that large, handsome man with the peg leg, that is Gouverneur Morris—"

"What state is he the governor of?"

"He isn't. His name is actually Gouverneur, pronounced Goo-vern-er. He is an excellent lawyer from New York, which he represented in our Continental Congress. When he lost his bid for re-election, he moved to Philadelphia to work in finance with Robert Morris. No relation, by the way. Gouverneur is also a Pennsylvania delegate."

"How did he lose his leg."

"I'm not sure. He says in a carriage accident. But others whisper it was when he jumped from a window to escape a jealous husband. You'll keep that to yourself, of course."

"Seriously? Who am I going to tell?"

Franklin shoots me a sharp look over his glasses, then smiles a thin smile.

"Good point! Now, that red-haired gentlemen is Alexander Hamilton, also an outstanding lawyer from New York. He and Mr. Madison are both very close to General Washington and are responsible for calling this convention together.

"And there is Roger Sherman from Connecticut, the strangest looking man, if I do say so myself—"

"Kind of looks like Frankenstein."

"Who?"

"Never mind," I say, realizing neither the book nor the movie exist yet.

"Mr. Sherman is extremely intelligent and hard-working. He began as a farmer and shoe-maker, taught himself the law, and became a judge and politician so highly respected that his people sent him to our Continental Congress. He and I served on the committee that produced our Declaration of Independence."

"These men, and all the others sent to our convention, are our nation's finest—our most talented. You would do well to study them closely.

"Now, quickly, let us go down. It is rude of me to neglect my guests."

Torches along the gravel paths and candles on the serving table lend the garden a soft, golden light. I stand behind Franklin, out of the way but ready to assist, as he greets the men of the Union Fire Company. I can tell the working men by their gnarled hands and frayed, stained clothes. The richer members wear wigs, clean linen, and gleaming silver shoe buckles. Franklin treats all as old friends, asking after their families or businesses, trading a quip with one or a bit of news with another. Clearly, he is enjoying himself.

Then Swinbourne arrives. He is a stocky, pink-faced man with ginger hair who struts, chest-first, on plump little legs that look like the drumsticks on a Thanksgiving turkey. It's a warm night, but he wears a green velvet coat and a weskit made from heavy, red brocade; and constantly swipes his face with a sweaty handkerchief.

As he approaches, Franklin steps back and loops his arm through mine.

"Let us away!" he says softly and steers us to a table where the delegates sit.

"Welcome, gentlemen," Franklin says. "Welcome all. I am delighted you are here. Now, there is plenty of ale, wine, and cider for refreshment. Elise here will bring whatever you wish. Some of your wonderful lemonade for me, please, Elise."

"Really, Doctor? Where is the fun in that?" Gouverneur Morris teases. "I had heard you to be a lover of the grape."

"I admit, I miss my Madeira. But at my age, and with this stone and gout, best to eat and drink plainly. Otherwise, as with the couple who weds in haste, tonight's joys will become tomorrow's sorrow."

"Oh, well said, sir!" Gouverneur Morris exclaims in the midst of his fellow delegates' laughter. "Well said!"

An elderly man holding a ledger joins us.

"Phillip Syng!" Franklin cries. "Hoorah, you're here! Gentlemen, Mr. Syng is one of my oldest friends, and the finest silversmith in all Philadelphia."

"You flatter me, Doctor. Our city boasts many fine craftsmen."

"Nonsense! That's his inkwell on General Washington's table in the Assembly Room. We used it to sign our Declaration of Independence. Let us hope we put it to more good use soon."

"And who is this?" Syng asks, turning to me. "A new recruit for our company?"

"Gentlemen, my apologies," Franklin says quickly. "This is Marcus Santana, my new clerk. Born and bred in Philadelphia and just home from studying in Paris. Unfortunately, an injury to his throat has left him unable to speak for the next several weeks."

"Clerk to this old lightning rod?" asks Syng. "Good luck to you, m'boy. You'll need it."

"What say, Mr. Syng? Shall we begin?" Franklin asks. "I imagine the members would like to conclude the evening's business and return to socializing."

"Quite right," Syng agrees. "Everyone! Everyone! Your attention, please. First order of business: the calling of the roll and inventory. You, young man," he says, pointing at me. "As you're a clerk, take this book and pencil and mark down who is here and their equipment."

Franklin nods that I should.

I quickly see the names are already written in the ledger. All I have to do is check them off and write what they've brought. Old man Syng peers over my shoulder to read out the names.

James Abbot?" he calls out.

"Present," a voice from the crowd answers. "Two buckets, five bags; all in good order."

I check him off and write down his equipment. Syng pats my shoulder and says: "Fine. That's fine. We can read that nicely. William Carmichael?"

"Present. Two buckets and a hook, two bags; all in good order."

"George Devereaux?"

No one answers.

"George Devereaux," Syng repeats testily.

Still no answer.

"Not here? Then mark him down for a fine," Syng says. Franklin and several others nod or murmur their approvals.

"Benjamin Franklin?"

"Present. Four buckets, a hook, an axe, and a ladder; all in good order."

And so it goes, on through the names of the thirty or so men gathered in the garden. When the last man has answered, Syng takes the book from me to tally the equipment.

"Any new business to discuss while the count is being made?" Franklin calls out.

"Well, it's not new business," says a man. "But last meeting we talked about maybe buying a new engine. I've heard there's some now that pump faster and easier—need less men to pump—and shoot more water."

"Yes, we did," Syng agrees. "And John Swinbourne said he would write to London and ascertain a price."

"Can we not give the business to someone here in the United States?" Franklin asks. "I've heard there is a man in New York City—"

"No!" Swinbourne says. "Now is the perfect time to buy from England. They are selling their goods to us cheaply. Besides, how many duties and tariffs will we have to pay to New York, and then New Jersey, and then Pennsylvania as the new engine travels from there to here?"

"It is true," Franklin says. "England sells us its goods cheaply. But she does so now in the hopes of driving American manufacturers out of business. To ruin us in a way she could not do fighting a war. You watch what happens to those prices once there are no American firms to compete with. They will rise and rise and rise."

"You don't know that," Swinbourne says dismissively. "I say the company should get its equipment at the lowest price. As agent and shipper for one of the London companies making these engines, I can get that price."

"That's if you've got room on any of your ships that ain't taken up by African slaves," someone grumbles.

"Oh, I'm sure I can find space," Swinbourne says. "What I don't know is whether my ships will reach their destinations or be able to off-load their cargoes if they do. This government we've got ourselves is useless. No navy to protect our shipping from piracy; and it has utterly failed to persuade the British to re-open ports throughout their empire to American goods. How much better off we'd be if we were still part of that empire. Perhaps it's time to admit that this experiment with independency is a failure and return to the fold and make some decent money."

"Damned traitor!" someone in the crowd calls out. Several others hiss.

"Traitor is it?" Swinbourne answers. "Who was it gave his two best ships to the confederation's navy for the war? And who was it lost those ships by not arming and maintaining them properly? That same navy!"

"Gentlemen! Gentlemen!" Franklin says quickly. "All this is beside the point! Now, I am the last man to argue against saving money. But at least let us find out from this New York company the engine's cost and the price for shipping, all duties and tariffs included, and then compare it with the price Mr. Swinbourne reports."

"You may embark on that fool's errand, if you wish, Dr. Franklin. But I guarantee, you won't beat my price."

"Time will tell," Phillip Syng says. "Any other business?" he asks the crowd. "No? Then here is the tally: sixty buckets, twelve ladders, twelve hooks, six axes, fifty bags, eighty feet of hose, the pumping engine, and our bell. Aside from a new engine, does anyone think we lack any necessary equipment? No? Then our meeting is adjourned. Let the socializing begin."

Franklin sees Alexander Hamilton standing alone on a pathway and, taking my arm, begins walking towards him.

"Dr. Franklin, a moment if you please," a voice calls after us.

Franklin stiffens, then turns. It is Swinbourne.

"Doctor," Swinbourne says, holding out his hand, "my friends tell me I am sometimes overzealous. I assure you, I meant no offense. I hope we can be friends."

Franklin stares at the hand until Swinbourne takes it back. The smile on the merchant's perspiring face sours.

"Now, this is certainly noteworthy: the celebrated Dr. Franklin refusing an offer of friendship. And from a fellow patriot, no less," he says, running his tongue over his lips. He does that a lot. Maybe it's why his lips look so red.

I feel a presence at my shoulder and see that Alexander Hamilton has joined us. He moves to Franklin's other side, so that he and I now bracket the old man, ready to lend our support.

"You think the loss of two ships entitles you to call yourself a patriot?" Franklin asks.

"It certainly is much more than most of these men gave to our glorious cause."

I hear something between a sigh and a growl come out of Hamilton. But he doesn't say anything. He just stares at Swinbourne, his lips forming a thin, bitter line.

"I don't believe you *gave* anything," Franklin says. "Indeed, if Mr. Adams correctly recounted to me your arrangement with his Naval Committee—and John Adams is nothing if not painstakingly faithful to the truth in such matters—you *leased* your ships to our navy."

"Well, yes. But at a price well below market value—"

"In exchange for which you received privateering rights, which you exercised most profitably with your remaining vessel. You captured a number of merchant ships, which you now use to transport slaves between African, West Indian, and American ports. In short, you make your living from human misery—"

"Doctor, I transport cargo. No more and no less. And I do so well within the bounds of the law. I must say though, your criticism astounds me when you continue to use slaves."

"I do *not*, sir!"

"You do not, sir? Come, come. I see that comely dark wench you have serving—"

"Mr. Swinbourne, what is it you want?"

"Why, to do business, sir," he says, licking his lips again. "I wish to present you with an opportunity for profit. The wench, I can get quite a nice price for her. Either on the auction block at tomorrow's sale in Camden or through private placement. In fact, I know of a quite wealthy gentleman seeking such a woman—he has a weakness for African females, if you get my meaning—and would pay handsomely. Or, I could buy her from you now and take her with me. What say you?"

Anger—rage—rises in me. My hands ball into fists so tight, my fingernails cut into my palms. I'm a heartbeat away from throwing a punch.

But before I can move, for the third time that day, Franklin plants his walking stick—and all his weight—down on my toe. At the same time, Hamilton's hand grips my shoulder. I look to Franklin. His eyes are hooded, his face chalk-white. And when he speaks, his voice is colder than any I've ever heard.

"Sir, I own no one. The young lady you speak of is not a slave. She works for wages and comes and goes as she pleases."

"Tut-tut, sir! I've traded enough black flesh in my time to know a slave when I see one."

"Mr. Swinbourne!" Franklin says. "She is a free individual owned by no one, except herself. In addition, she is a member of my household and under my protection. Leave her be or you will have me to answer to. The presidency of Pennsylvania's Supreme Executive Council may not carry much power, but it carries enough, and I have friends enough, that should you interfere with her in any way, I will see you ruined. Now sir, as the company has concluded its business, you have no reason to remain. Please leave my house."

With that, Franklin turns on his heel. He does not limp or lean on his stick. He walks quickly, like a much younger man, to join the rest of the delegates.

"Oh, bravo," Alexander Hamilton says quietly as he watches Swinbourne retreat. "Bravo indeed."

CHAPTER 12

The next day, Sunday, I return to Franklin's library and write out a complete transcript of his meeting with Washington, Wilson, and the rest in the garden.

"Remarkable," Franklin says as he reads. "It is exactly as I remember it. You have a wonderful talent!"

"I guess," I say, shrugging. Truth is, learning shorthand was never my idea. I only did it because Mom kept bugging me about it, saying it would help a lot in college and law school.

"Marcus, do not belittle your own capabilities."

"I'm not. It's just that ... well ... I don't have much use for it anymore, since I decided more school's not really what I need ... or want."

"Oh? And what is it that you want?"

"To be an actor."

"An actor?" He repeats, like he's never heard of one.

"Yeah, you know, in plays—"

"I know very well what an actor is. Although you won't find many here in Philadelphia since the Quakers who have a very large say in running this city frown on theatricals because they find them contrary to their religion. A pity, for when I lived in London and Paris, I very much enjoyed the theater. But I'm surprised you should want this, since actors are not well regarded."

"They're not?"

"No. They lead itinerant lives, always traveling from one place to the next, forming and then breaking attachments, always on the lookout for ways to earn their daily bread. Some regard them as little better than criminals and vagabonds."

"Well, not where I come from. Where I come from—"

"No! Don't tell me! The future, remember?"

"Sorry! Sorry. I keep forgetting."

"But how does more schooling conflict with your desire to be an actor? I should think that the more education you are able to attain, the better off you will be, no matter what calling you decide to follow. It's why I and some other Philadelphia men started the Academy and College of Philadelphia, to help to ensure that our people are educated."

"You sound just like … Pop," I say; and a sinking feeling of sadness hits me.

"Pop?" Franklin asks, confused.

"My dad. My father."

"Ah. Then I shall regard that as a complement. But, Marcus, why so downcast?"

"I don't know … I guess I just … miss him. Miss all my family. And, right before I came here, him and Mom and me had a pretty big—"

"He, my mother, and I," Franklin corrects.

"He, my mother, and I had a pretty big blow-up—"

"An explosion? A storm?"

"A fight—an argument—"

"Ah—"

"—about my grades. I threatened to quit school to move to New York for acting, and now that I'm not there, they probably think that's what I did—that I just ran away."

"Oh," he says, almost like a long, drawn-out whisper. "I see. … well … as someone who actually did run away from his family and obligations, I can understand how you feel. But I wouldn't worry too much. I am sure you will see them again."

"How would you know?" I say, and immediately hate how rude I'm being. But Franklin seems not to notice. If anything, his voice becomes gentler.

"I know something of your future, remember? You are just going to have to trust me."

Then he gets all brisk and business-like.

"Now, to work! You've proved yourself adept recording conversation, so my dictation should be easy. I'm writing my autobiography, as I have been for years, periodically. I'll start and get so far, tire of it and lay it aside, and then take it up again. Truthfully, I find it tedious. But many have been after me to do it. I hope the result will prove instructive as to the benefits of virtue, thrift, and industry. I would like everyone to have my good fortune. Maybe this will help some to achieve it."

He dictates for several hours, until it's time for supper. When we stop, my hand is a claw and my brain is mush.

Early the next morning, after a breakfast of oatmeal, bacon, bread, and tea, I go back to the library and write out the first several pages of Sunday's dictation, in which Franklin describes *Poor Richard's Almanac*, which he began publishing in 1732.

"This really is quite excellent," Franklin says, looking over the finished work, giving me a warm feeling of accomplishment. "It seems we make a good team. Now, I want you to stay here today and see if you can finish what we did yesterday. Also, look again over the pages from Friday night's meeting with General Washington *et al.* in the garden. Make sure they are the best they can be. I'm off to the convention."

"Need me to walk you over to Independence Hall?" I ask hopefully, it being a sunny day and I not wanting to spend it inside. Also, I want to see more of the city.

"Where?" Franklin asks.

"Independence Hall—I mean the State House."

"I'll pretend I didn't hear that. Although it is good to hear that we will maintain our independence—at least for a while. No, I do not need anyone to walk with me, not today. Today, I shall travel to the convention in style."

"Really, Father!" Sally says when we get downstairs. "Could you not find a more modest means of transport?"

Through the open front door, I see a crowd gathered around what looks like a large, green closet with windows and a bench inside. Four filthy men dressed in grimy rags and chained at the ankles stand to one side. Two of them hold long, wooden poles.

"In Paris, they consider this sedan *très, très chic,*" Franklin says.

"Too bad we can't say the same for the poor devils who must carry it," Sally answers.

"There is nothing wrong with convict labor," Franklin says. "And they'll each make a copper or two and thus have something with which to increase their comfort in the Walnut Street Jail. Help me in, Marcus."

As I pass by one of the men, my nose catches his stench. My stomach turns at the sour-sweet stink of old dirt, body odor, and who knows what else, and I gag and swallow, fighting to keep my breakfast down.

Once Franklin is seated, I close the door. The prisoners thread the wooden poles through metal holders at the sides of the sedan. On Franklin's command, each takes a pole-end and lifts. As the sedan rises off the ground, the poles bow from the weight.

"Much more comfortable than a carriage," Franklin says contentedly. "No jouncing, which will save my bladder considerable discomfort. Watch how the poles flex as the men go. It is like riding a magic carpet."

With that, he taps his walking stick on the front window sill and the prisoners carry him away.

"Absolutely delightful!" I hear him exclaim as his bearers veer to skirt a pile of horse manure in the street.

"My father can be such a little boy," Sally says, shaking her head as she goes back in, leaving me with Elise.

We do not touch as we watch Franklin's sedan. But still, I feel her presence, like a warm, electric kind of force.

I look over at her. Her face isn't cold, now. She has relaxed it, allowing all her strength and prettiness to come through. Her soft Afro accentuates her high forehead and cheekbones and her neck rises swan-like to the clean line of her jaw. Her flared nose points straight and true to lips that are plump and full. And I love her eyes: almond shaped and deep, deep brown. They make me feel warm and good every time she turns them on me.

She catches me looking.

"Boy?" she snaps. "What do you stare at?"

"I ... I ..." I stutter, stung. I hate her thinking I am a boy.

"Have you forgotten how to speak?"

Obviously I have, because nothing comes out.

"The doctor said he gave you work in the library."

I nod.

"Well? What do you wait for like a big oaf? Go inside! Work!"

***

The clock strikes ten and I set to work writing out Franklin's dictation. He's still in the 1730's, but now talking about the "Junto," a club of 12 men he helped form to exchange ideas to benefit society, like how to improve the Philadelphia city watch—the police—and how to light the streets and keep them clean.

Around noon, Elise comes in to sweep and dust. I so want her to like me, and know she doesn't. I think: *Maybe if we go somewhere outside the house, spend some time together, she'll see I'm a good guy.*

My heart races as I ask: "Want to go out and maybe get a coffee?"

She looks at me as if she can't believe what I just said.

"What? You don't drink coffee?" I say. "Okay, how about getting something to eat?"

"Are you a fool?" she asks.

"What do you mean?"

"I am black. You are white. We cannot mix."

"Who says?"

"All … everyone says. Whites and blacks do not mix. Is that not so where you come from?"

"No. It's not. People are free to see who they want. Even to become family. I have an adopted sister who's from Somalia—in Africa," I explain, not knowing whether, right now, there even is such a country.

"I don't believe it."

"It's true."

"Here, it is not. It is forbidden for whites and blacks to go together."

"So … we can't be friends. That's what you're telling me?"

"I have no friends."

"What about Franklin. He said you're friends."

"*Doctor* Franklin is my employer. That is not a friend."

"Well, I'd like to be your friend. I'd like to spend time with you and get to know you."

Again, she looks at me like I'm unbelievable. But then her face takes on a calculating look.

"You want to be my friend? You want to spend time with me? Then you come downstairs and I will teach you to split wood."

With that, she leaves the library. I follow. It might not be lattes at Starbuck's, but it is something.

Chapter 13

I spend the next hour with Elise, learning how to split wood. I'm clumsy, at first, and embarrassed by her impatience. But I get better, good enough to earn a grunting nod of approval. At least, that's what I hope it might be.

I and my blisters return to the library to finish Franklin's pages. When I'm done, I read the rest of his autobiography, thinking that if I'm to help him with it, I should know what's in it.

What I read shows me why Mom, Pop, and Gus have always been such fans—why they've always thought living next to Franklin Court is so "awesome."

Franklin is born into a Boston family without much money—so little that they cannot afford to send him to school for more than a few years. He doesn't even get to begin high school. And while he dreams of going to sea, instead his father indentures him to his brother, James, as a printer's apprentice.

But Franklin refuses to accept that he can't be educated. Gaining access to a neighbor's library, he reads all the books he can, tackling really difficult, demanding subjects like math, navigation, logic, and rhetoric. At the same time, he works hard at his brother's newspaper, even writing satires to help it make money.

How does James repay him? By smacking him around!

So, Franklin takes off—leaves his friends, family, everybody—and lands in Philadelphia, where he spends the next 25 years making his fortune as a printer, writer, publisher, and businessman. Then, when he's only 42, he basically gives it all up to devote himself to "natural philosophy," meaning science, with no formal training whatsoever.

He discovers that lightning is actually electricity—making him world famous—and invents the lightning rod to protect buildings from catching fire. He could have made a fortune by patenting his invention, but he refuses to. Instead, he gives it to the world—as he does all his other inventions, like the Franklin fireplace, the busy-body, bi-focal glasses, swim fins, his "long arm," and others.

A great believer in public service, he helps set up various civic organizations, including Pennsylvania Hospital, the University of Pennsylvania, The Library Company of Philadelphia, and the American Philosophical Society, all of which thrive into the 21st Century. And he holds many, many public offices: Assistant Postmaster General for the colonies; member of the Pennsylvania Assembly; Colonial Agent for Pennsylvania and other colonies in London (a little like an ambassador); Pennsylvania delegate to the Second Continental Congress and one of the drafters of the Declaration of Independence; Postmaster General of the United States; ambassador to France and Sweden; negotiator of the treaty with Britain ending the Revolutionary War; and finally, "President of the Supreme Executive Council of Pennsylvania," otherwise known as President of Pennsylvania.

And those are just the highlights. He doesn't write about all of it in the Autobiography. Some of it I learn as he teaches me chess in the library. But what sticks with me most from the Autobiography is his advice for a happy life: Be industrious, be frugal, be virtuous and, most important: be useful. Mom and Pop have always been big on that last one. So was Gus.

***

Franklin arrives home from the convention in the late afternoon, this time in Washington's carriage. The general himself helps Franklin into the library.

The ride has been hard on him. He shambles in, braced on Washington's arm, out of breath, his face gray, and his lips pursed so tightly they almost disappear.

"Here, you!" Washington commands. "Take the Doctor's other arm. Help me seat him."

"Thank you, General, most kind," Franklin says hoarsely. "I'm sorry to be a burden."

"Not at all, Doctor," Washington says. "It was a long session."

This is my first time seeing Washington. He isn't what I expected; I suppose because he's flesh and blood and not bronze or marble or paint. But there's more to it than that. The man moves with such style and grace. And he has such a force to him, a power. I think it's what Gus meant when he once tried explaining "command presence" to me. Washington's fills the room—and Franklin's library is a very big room.

"General, allow me to introduce the newest member of my household," Franklin says, once he's caught his breath. "Marcus Santana, who has just arrived from Paris. Unfortunately an injury to his throat has left him temporarily unable to speak."

Washington eyes me, like I'm a horse he's thinking of buying. And I try eyeing him right back. But it's hard because I'm pretty intimidated.

He's taller than me, and very powerfully built. His black suit and white stockings are so well tailored I can see the muscles of his legs, back, and shoulders gather and shift. His face looks like his portraits, but much less perfect. Like me, he has a lazy left eye. It wanders while the right one bores into me. Squint lines and pock marks from small pox mar his skin. He doesn't wear a wig, but has his long, white hair powdered and tied back in a queue. I can see the powder along his scalp line.

He finishes inspecting me with a nod of his head. When I nod back, a perplexed expression takes over his face.

Well what do you want me to do, I think, *bow and scrape and act like your servant?*

He turns from me to gaze at the drawing of the snake above Franklin's desk, which, since a picture is worth a thousand words, I reproduce here:

"A fine piece of propaganda, Doctor," Washington says. "I remember it well from our French and Indian War, and of course, our War of Independence."

"I am most flattered, General. Although it is nothing compared to the leadership you provided in both conflicts."

"Remind me, in what year was it first published?"

"In May of 1754, in my *Pennsylvania Gazette*, only days before your troops went into battle against the French near Pittsburgh. As you may remember, I had argued that a single government over all the colonies was necessary to successfully prosecute that war."

"So you have believed in our union for all these years."

"I have always thought it crucial."

The two men are looking at each other now, almost as if they are sizing each other up, testing each other. I'm uncomfortable, standing there, unable to speak. So, I bow and start for the door.

"Just a minute, Marcus," Franklin says. "There's something I want to ask of General Washington, and it concerns you."

Washington looks as surprised as I feel; but Franklin takes no notice.

"General, I have a problem and I am hoping you can help me, as you said you might."

"Doctor Franklin, you need only ask, and if I can grant it, the help is yours," he says warily.

"Good. When the convention decided not to make my grandson Temple its secretary, he left Philadelphia."

"I had heard."

"Which has left me without a clerk."

"I am sorry for that, but I hardly see what I can do to bring him back."

Franklin holds up his hand. "That is not what I am asking. Hear me out. As luck would have it, on the day Temple left, Marcus arrived from Paris. He and I have worked together before and he has proved himself quite excellent taking my dictation."

Washington eyes me again and that same perplexed look reappears.

"Indeed," Franklin continues, "he employs a most ingenious system to write rapidly and accurately. He can produce a verbatim record of, not only what I dictate, but any conversation."

"Can he? How … useful."

"As I had him do just the other evening when we all met in the garden," Franklin adds.

For what seems the longest time, the only sound in that room is the buzz of a fly.

"You … had … this … boy … eavesdrop on our private conversation?" Washington finally says, his voice low and dangerous.

"No, no, no," says Franklin. "I had him conduct an experiment. And it was a success! Show him the pages, Marcus."

I get them from the desk. Washington snatches them from my hand and reads quickly, dropping each to the floor as he finishes.

"Extraordinary," he murmurs. "This is the conversation we had. Just as I remember it. Franklin, to whom have you shown these pages?"

"No one! As I said, this was an experiment. I would never share them with anyone unless I had all the participants' permission. Doing otherwise would breach their trust."

"But how?" Washington asks. "How was he able to copy down everything we said so quickly and legibly?"

"He wasn't. Not without an intermediate step. Marcus knows something called short-hand. Marcus, show him those pages."

Washington examines the pages filled with my squiggles.

"A code," Washington says.

"Allowing Marcus to rapidly record what is said and write it out later in a clear, readable hand. Time-consuming, but effective.

"Now, General, my memory is not what it was. Indeed, I am having trouble recalling what anyone at the convention said today, including me! Of course, were Temple its secretary, I would have access to the daily record. I note Major Jackson makes few notes, limiting himself to recording the votes. And without notes to refresh my recollection, I have little hope of being useful to our cause. If I cannot remember each delegate's position, I cannot help to forge the necessary compromises. And I cannot make my own notes because a fall injured my wrist."

"Doctor, what is it you are proposing?" Washington asks, looking like he really doesn't want to know. I'm not sure I want to either.

"I want you, as President of the convention, to seat Marcus somewhere in the Assembly Room. Not amongst the delegates, certainly, for there's precious little room on that floor. But if you can find a place for him—possibly in the public area between the front door and the rail, well away from the delegates—and let him copy what is said, I could have a record."

My jaw hangs open. The look I get from Washington shuts it tight. He stands there, hands on hips, head tilted back, looking down that big Roman nose. Then he shakes his head.

"I can't allow it," he says.

I think: *What a relief!*

"Oh? Why not, pray tell? Franklin asks coolly.

"Your memory may be failing, Doctor, as is mine. But surely you remember the convention is contemplating a rule of secrecy."

"Yes, and what of it? All the delegates are free to take their own notes. If the rule of secrecy is adopted, that won't change. Delegates can note whatever they please. They just can't publish their notes. James Madison plans to record as much as possible of the convention."

"Yes, but Mr. Madison is a gentleman. This fellow is a mere boy—"

"He is a young man with a very special skill—which I need so that I may be of help to the convention. I would, of course, obey the prohibition against revealing anything."

"Yes, but why should any of the delegates trust that this chap will also obey? –Oh yes, I see, because he can't talk. But you said that is only temporary. When he regains the ability to speak, how can any of us be sure he will not reveal what has been said?"

"First, because he will promise you that he will not. Second, because I am vouching for him."

Washington looks away, out the window, seeming to consider. The fly buzzes. I hold my breath, hoping Washington will stick to his refusal. Franklin's relying on me for an accurate record of the convention is way more than I bargained for.

Finally, Washington looks back at me and asks: "Boy? Do you know what it means to swear an oath?"

I consider shaking my head no, but that would just make me look ridiculous. I nod.

"And if you are permitted to do this, do you swear by almighty God that you will not reveal to anyone what is said or what takes place at the convention and that you will do all in your power to safeguard and keep secret all the notes you make?"

I look to Franklin. His face is eager. He nods his encouragement. I raise my right hand and nod.

"This doesn't mean I've decided anything, Franklin," Washington says. "But it occurs to me you are right to want a record that you can review. And while any delegate has the right to make such a record for his own use, you, because of an injury, cannot. That places you at a disadvantage, especially considering your age. I shall need to consult with several other delegates. Bring the boy to the convention tomorrow and I will let you know my decision."

"Thank you, General. I am in your debt."

"In the meantime, please see about getting him some decent clothes. No one is going to want him in the chamber dressed like that."

I'm wearing the canvas britches and stained work shirt from Franklin's slop chest. I think it lucky Franklin told Wimpole the tailor to have the clothes ready by tonight. Which leads me to wonder: had bringing me to the convention been Franklin's plan all along?

***

Wimpole delivers the clothes on time. But nothing he's made fits. The pre-made clothes are fine: the shirts, shoes, stockings, wig, and hats. But I swim in anything he's made. The britches are too big at the waist and fall to my calves. The weskit might fit Cedric the Entertainer. And the coat sleeves are so long, I can't get my hands through the cuffs.

"Oh no, that won't do at all," Franklin says. "It seems our friend Wimpole has attempted a bit of 'pay-back' of his own. You'd better get Elise."

When we return, he leads us to a high-backed leather and mahogany chair near one of the bookshelves. Bending from his waist, he fiddles at the seat. With a *bang*, it turns from a chair into a step-ladder.

"Whoa! Awesome!"

"What is awesome?"

"This chair-ladder thing."

"I assure you, there is nothing awe-inspiring about it. It is merely a convenience. A clever one, I'll admit, since I'm its designer. But really, it is no more than a whimsy."

I stand on the first step as Elise, her mouth full of straight pins, maps out new hems and seams.

"Ouch! Watch it! I'm not a pin cushion, you know."

"Hold still!" She slaps my ankle.

"Ow!"

"Stop your nonsense! A five year-old is more manly. There. *Finis.* Take them off and I will sew. You shall have them tomorrow morning. Well? What do you wait for? Take them off!"

"I will just as soon as you go, or turn your back, or something. I don't need you watching me undress."

"Why? You have nothing I have not seen, or that interests me."

"Gee, thanks," I say as Franklin chuckles.

"You really sure you want me doing this?" I ask him.

"Is there some reason I should not?"

I really don't want to admit my fear about not being up to the task. So I say: "Well, it's just I don't want any special favors—I mean, I don't want you owing anyone on my account."

"No? Well then, I shall owe them on *my* account. You see, Marcus, in this life I have found that the man who once did you a favor will be much more willing to do you subsequent favors than the man who has received a favor from you. Before this convention is over, I may have to ask for many favors, or compromises, from these delegates. Best to get them in the habit of giving now.

CHAPTER 14

The next morning, Elise helps me dress, fastening the knee buttons on the britches, cinching the weskit in back, and showing me how to tie the cravat. It reminds me of getting into costume for a play; and I hope the clothes will help me to act more like someone from 1787. And they do, I think. The shoes and stockings make me want to walk more gracefully. The weskit—snug around my back, ribs, stomach, and hips—helps me to stand tall and straight and not to slouch.

"There. Now everything fits," Elise says, running her hands along my shoulders to smooth the fabric. I can feel the warmth of her hands through the cloth. "It is good the doctor ordered linen and light cotton. They will help with the heat."

I'd wondered about that. Summers in my Philadelphia are mostly hot and humid. Some days feel like a bathroom full of steam after a hot shower. Was the same true here? How would it be without air-conditioning?

Richard Bache's old, brown wig with the pony tail isn't going to help. It's heavy and itches. With all the sweat that must have been poured into it, no wonder it smells like a horse.

"Do I have to wear this?" I ask Franklin as we're about to leave.

"It is the fashion and thus will help to make you inconspicuous, so that you will not be noticed."

"Oh, that'll feel really good. Thanks. Thanks a heap," I say, fitting my new, black tricorn over it.

"You are most welcome."

Even though summer is coming, the morning is cool enough to be chilly. Franklin's gout and bladder stone still bother him, so he takes the sedan chair. I follow on foot, carrying my notebook and *porte-crayon* in a cloth haversack, or pouch, strapped over my shoulder.

It takes only minutes to walk to the Pennsylvania State House, which looks very much like it does in my Philadelphia: a two-story, rectangular, red-brick building with a central tower and a row of tall, evenly spaced, white windows on each story. An equally tall, equally white door stands at the center of the ground floor.

But there are differences. For one, there's no big, white belfry on top of the tower—just a roof with a small steeple. And it looks so much bigger than in my day: maybe because all the tall buildings, including the Curtis Center where Mom has that expensive office, aren't built yet.

The convicts set the sedan down at the front door, which is guarded by sentries, and I help Franklin into the building.

Immediately to our right as we enter, the lobby expands into a big, high-ceilinged room where the Pennsylvania Supreme Court is in session. Three judges in rich, red robes sit at the high bench underneath a painting of the seal of the Commonwealth of Pennsylvania.

"Do you know what used to be in place of that painting?" Franklin asks softly.

Remembering I'm not supposed to talk, I shake my head.

"The King's coat of arms. Do you know what happened to it?"

Another shake.

"On the day the Declaration of Independence was read publicly for the first time, on July 8, 1776, to be exact, members of the Pennsylvania State Militia took it down and threw it on a bonfire. It was quite a sight. It saddened me, a bit, because I had been a loyal Englishman all my life—right until the day the King's ministers made it clear all my diplomatic efforts would go for naught.

"And yet, I was excited too, to think that we were starting this very new thing called the United States of America, and how the reins of our fate were now firmly in our own hands, and of all the possibilities that would be engendered by the peoples' liberty—quite limitless, really. These days, I have something of that same feeling. While we have won our liberty, and maintained it, we have not yet forged the unity crucial to our survival. That forging must begin at this convention."

We turn to stand before the Pennsylvania Assembly Room's high double doors, also guarded by sentries. At that moment, Washington arrives. As the sentries snap to attention, he and Franklin greet each other and pass through the doors, with me steps behind.

The Assembly Room is a lot like I remember from visits with my family: large, rectangular, with a high, white ceiling, walls of white plaster and gray wood paneling, tall windows, and a plain, plank floor. A simple glass chandelier for candles hangs from the ceiling.

About ten feet inside the door, a low railing with a center gate runs from the north wall to the south. Washington goes through the gate, but Franklin stops and waits for me.

"Usually, this area before the gate is for the public," he explains, "so that they may come and witness our Pennsylvania Assembly. Not so for our convention. The public will not be welcome here; as you will not be welcome beyond this gate. I'm sorry on both counts. Let us just hope you will be allowed to remain in the room. I see a table and chair has been placed in that back corner, so possibly my hope is not in vain."

Franklin goes onto the Assembly floor to join Washington, James Wilson, James Madison, Alexander Hamilton, and several other delegates.

They stand in front of a raised platform, two steps high, at the center of the back wall. A table covered in green cloth and bearing a gleaming silver ink stands on the platform. Next to it sits a high-backed, delicately carved, wood arm chair with a brass-studded leather seat. It's so fancy, it reminds me a little of a throne. The top of the chair-back features a gold-painted carving of a half-sun on the horizon.

A series of tables, also covered in green cloth, and at least fifty spindle-backed chairs—which Franklin calls Windsor chairs—crowd the platform, which is flanked by two matching fireplaces with marble mantles. Wood fires burn in both. They take the chill out of the air, but also make the room smoky.

Delegates pass through the gates to gather in small groups or sit at tables. All of them are white men. Most look prosperous in their knee-length coats and britches, fancy weskits, white stockings, and buckled shoes. Some are hard-eyed with purpose, others jovial and expansive; still others seem tired, or worried, or bored. Some look at me with curiosity. Others ignore me completely. I definitely feel like I don't belong.

Peg-legged Gouverneur Morris joins Washington, Franklin, Madison, Hamilton, and Wilson at the dais. All listen closely as Washington talks to Franklin. Occasionally, one glances in my direction, which only makes the butterflies in my stomach flap their wings harder. I wonder how long it's going to be before Washington has the sentries toss me into the street.

I turn away to look out one of the southern windows to see what's there. In my Philadelphia, it's a park with grass and trees and walkways lined with benches completely open to Walnut Street and the public, and beyond that, tall office buildings. But here, it's a garden surrounded by a high brick wall with a tall set of double doors opening onto Walnut.

Over the wall, I can see another two-story, gray-stone building. It's so massive that it takes up almost the whole block between Fifth and Sixth Streets. I later learn this is the Walnut Street jail, where the bearers of Franklin's sedan are imprisoned.

Behind me, I hear a man say: "What think you of this plan put forward by the Virginians?"

Everything in me clutches, since I think he's talking to me, asking for my opinion. Should I turn around? Try to pantomime I can't talk?

But then another man says: "I think it complete nonsense! Nothing wrong with what we've got now. A simple congress where every state has an equal vote and there's no king or prime minister to be a tyrant and no judges to muck things up in court."

"Yes, but it can't *do* anything," the other man says.

"Exactly my point! It can't do anything and therefore will create no mischief. And the powers-that-be of my state—the people who sent me—very much want it to remain that way."

A hand grasps my elbow and I almost jump out of my skin, thinking it's those sentries.

But it's Franklin.

"I was correct. That is for you," he says, nodding at the small table and chair in the back corner. "Washington has fixed it. Now, remember, not a word. No matter what anyone says, do not answer back. Otherwise, you'll make me a liar and we'll both be done for."

I nod.

"And Marcus?" he says, laying his hand on my shoulder. "I know you are anxious about your capabilities. Don't be. Just remember, you can do anything you set your mind to."

So he knows, I think; and feel grateful for his confidence.

I open my notebook and wait, *porte-crayon* ready.

Washington stands on the central platform, next to that throne-like chair. He doesn't need to say anything. Just standing there is enough to quiet everyone down.

"Before we begin, I wish to discuss a minor matter without there being a record of it."

I see James Madison put down his pencil. I do the same.

"You all know our esteemed colleague, Doctor Franklin. Recently, he injured his wrist, making writing painful. He has brought his clerk to take notes for him. That clerk, who sits at the back of the room, has sworn an oath that he will not reveal anything occurring here.

"I've accepted his oath: first, because presently he is incapable of speaking due to an injury—so I would ask that none address him directly—and second, because Doctor Franklin has vouched for him. The notes he takes will be for the exclusive use of Doctor Franklin. In light of all the Doctor has done in service to this country, I felt this accommodation warranted and that no one here would object. Should anyone wish to do so, speak now."

The room stays silent. All eyes are on Washington. No one even glances at me.

"Thank you, gentlemen," he finally says.

"Yes, gentlemen," Franklin echoes softly, "my sincerest thanks to all of you for extending me this favor. I shall not forget it."

Washington calls everyone to order and the delegates get down to business. My hand races to record everything they say.

They spend the first part of the morning on rules, including the one that prohibits all the delegates from publishing anything about the convention. It's all to be kept secret, so the delegates can freely explore and debate ideas without having to worry about public opinion or outside pressure until after their work is done.

Washington directs the Assembly Room's caretaker, a short, limping, salt-and-pepper-haired black man named Joseph, to close all the windows and draw the curtains so that no one outside can see or hear what's going on. When he finishes, Joseph returns to his place on a stool between the fireplace and the end window facing south.

Washington recognizes Edmond Randolph, the Governor of Virginia, a big, broad-shouldered man with dark, graying hair swept back from his forehead and a face so solemn it seems sad. But his voice is deep and rich and commands everyone's attention.

America is in crisis, he says. Many want her to fail, or predict that she will. The present government is too weak and ineffective. Consisting only of a congress, it cannot run the country, or protect its people and borders, or put down internal rebellions, or settle disputes between the states, or develop whatever needs to be developed for everyone's benefit.

To strengthen the government, the Virginia delegation has developed a fifteen point plan to replace the existing Confederation Congress with a two-house legislature to make the laws, plus an executive branch to run the country, plus a judicial branch to resolve legal disputes.

Of course, he says a lot more than that, and it takes him a couple of hours to say it, including going through the entire plan; but that's the gist of it.

When Randolph finishes, the convention decides to sit as a "Committee of the Whole" to consider his proposals, just like Franklin and everyone had talked about in the garden. No vote or decision taken by that committee will be final, freeing the delegates to fully explore and debate all the proposals and gauge "which way the wind is blowing" on various issues.

Washington then adjourns the convention for the day.

CHAPTER 15

When Franklin and I emerge onto Chestnut Street, the sun is shining and the day is warm.

"Take that back to the house," Franklin says to the prisoners waiting with his sedan chair. "Marcus, you and I shall walk. The exercise and fresh air will do us good."

He grasps my arm with one hand and plants his walking stick with the other and we move slowly down the street. The sun glints richly off the stick's dark, varnished wood.

"Like your stick," I say quietly out the side of my mouth. "Where do I go to get one?"

"Hush now. We are in public, remember? And you don't—since you are not old enough to need one. Nor are you a gentleman, nor a man of property. You are a clerk, an apprentice, a servant. Such a stick would be well beyond your means and station."

I don't like that one bit. Who is Franklin to call me a servant? But the old man doesn't give me even a second to object.

"As for this particular stick, it has no duplicate, I believe," he continues. "It was a gift to me from Madame de Forbach, the Duchess of Deux-Ponts in France, to commemorate our Revolution. It is made from the wood of a crab-tree and has a head of solid gold wrought to resemble a cap of liberty. A most prized possession."

I don't much care. I'm still seething over the whole "servant" thing.

We come to Fourth and Chestnut. As we wait for a team of oxen pulling a large wagon full of planking to pass, Franklin looks down Fourth.

"Looks like there's an informal caucus about to take place at the Indian Queen," he says, pointing to the several delegates gathered at a door. His face saddens. "It would seem there is little place for an old head in the councils of the young."

Good! I think. *See how you like being thought less of and feeling left out.*

Just then a small, closed carriage drawn by two horses pulls up and Gouverneur Morris leans out the window.

"Doctor Franklin! Wondered where you'd got to. I've got Mr. Madison here."

The little Virginian leans forward and nods to Franklin with a wave.

"We're all meeting at the Queen for a confab. Will you join us?" Morris asks.

"Oh my, yes. I would be honored!"

"Come, Marcus," Franklin says with a big smile as the carriage pulls away, "let us see if we can ascertain which way the winds blow."

"Do you know the best feature of this establishment?" Franklin asks as we reach the entrance.

Since a stocky woman in a long dress, apron, and mob cap stands in the door watching us, I shake my head. The whole silence thing is getting real old, real fast.

"The back door is only steps from my home," he says, smiling the smile of a Cheshire cat. "Good day to you, Mrs. House."

"Welcome, Doctor Franklin."

She leads us into a large, dark, smoky room filled with wood tables where well-dressed men talk over food and drink. Some have their clay pipes lit.

"There," Franklin says, pointing to the large table where Virginia Governor Edmund Randolph, James Madison, Alexander Hamilton, James Wilson, and Gouverneur Morris sit with another delegate I'd seen that morning. He wears a white wig, has a prominent nose, and speaks with an English-Irish kind of accent.

"Doctor Franklin," the man says, standing and bowing his head in greeting. "An honor to make your acquaintance. Pierce Butler, sir, from the sovereign state of South Carolina."

"The honor is mine," Franklin says warmly, shaking Butler's hand.

I help Franklin into the empty chair next to Madison's and start to sit in the one between him and Butler.

"No, Marcus. That is for a delegate," Franklin says and then points to a small neighboring table. "Sit there. I will have Mrs. House bring you food. Rabbit stew all right? Good!" He turns away before I can even nod.

Everyone is looking at me as I move. My ears burn. That's how embarrassed I feel. I want to tell Franklin to go shove it. But I can't, not without making a liar out of him. So, I sit and seethe. The conversation soon makes me forget my anger.

"Governor Randolph, I liked your presentation of our fifteen propositions very much," James Madison says.

"I should hope so, Mr. Madison," Randolph answers with a smile and a nod of the head. "Since the entire plan comes from your pen."

"Well ... yes ... " Madison says, clearly embarrassed, "but I never could have imparted the rhetorical force you managed. It's one thing to write an idea. It's quite another to persuade others it has merit. I think your oratory accomplished that. But, do you know? As I listened, I felt something was missing. The plan makes clear our new government should consist of a legislature, an executive, and a judiciary. But it doesn't specifically say what the new government's *place* must be."

"I agree," Alexander Hamilton says. "Although the proposals clearly intend that the national government be superior to the state governments, there is nothing that specifically says that."

"Sma' wonder, since half the delegates would bolt fer home," James Wilson says.

"Even so," Hamilton continues, "the delegates must understand we are designing a government that will have supreme power over the states; that it will be a *national* government, not a confederation government. They must understand and accept it. Otherwise, we might as well go home."

"Oh, surely not before we've had our dinners," Franklin quips, sending a laugh around the table.

"Then why not say it?" Gouverneur Morris says. "Governor Randolph, have you the proposals?"

Randolph takes a sheaf of papers from his satchel and hands them to Morris.

"Look, right here," Morris says, pointing. "Why not say that a national government ought to be established consisting of a *supreme* legislature, executive, and judiciary?"

Just then two familiar-looking men walk by. It is the merchant Swinbourne and Wimpole the tailor. They stop at the delegates' table.

"Dr. Franklin!" Swinbourne says. "How delightful to meet you here!"

Franklin looks up. His eyes widen. I wait for him to tell the two men off: Wimpole for delivering badly made clothes and Swinbourne just for being Swinbourne.

But he does nothing of the kind.

Instead, he smiles and says, "Gentlemen, a pleasant day to you both."

"Might you introduce us to your associates?" Swinbourne asks.

"Certainly," Franklin says and, as I watch in amazement, introduces both men to all the delegates.

"How goes your convention, gentlemen?" Swinbourne asks. "How do you propose to repair our government?"

"Of course, we have only just begun," Franklin says. "But we have confidence that improvements can be made. Do we not, gentlemen?"

As the delegates nod and murmur agreement, Swinbourne says, "Good, good! Just so long as you make no change to the laws regarding the importation of slaves. After all, good business is good business. Speaking of which, Franklin, have you thought any further on my proposal regarding the wench? She'll fetch a pretty price, I tell you."

"Perhaps this is something you and I might discuss in more depth at another time?" Franklin says.

I can't believe what I'm hearing. Only a few nights ago, Franklin kicked Swinbourne out of his house. Now, he's actually going to discuss selling Elise? When he's called her his friend?

Mrs. House walks up to Swinbourne and Wimpole.

"I'm sorry, gentlemen," she says. "I have looked everywhere. There is no table available. It's likely to be at least a half-hour before one is."

"Perhaps I might be of assistance, Mrs. House," Franklin says. "I am sure my clerk won't mind giving up his table to these two gentlemen. Will you see that he is fed in the kitchen?"

"Of course, Doctor Franklin. Very kind of you, I'm sure," Mrs. House says.

"Yes, Doctor Franklin, very kind," Swinbourne agrees.

"Much, much too kind," Wimpole whines.

"Marcus?" Franklin says. "Off with you."

All eyes are on me. I have no choice. I have to leave. But I am furious. I don't wait for Mrs. House or go to the kitchen. I stalk out of the tavern and back to Franklin's house, shaking with anger all the way.

***

When Elise opens the door, I push past her to tear up the stairs and into my tiny room. I throw open the trap door and breathe deep to calm myself.

"*God!* What a freakin' *hypocrite!*" I hiss out loud, thinking no one's there.

"Hey, boy! Why you make all this commotion?"

Elise stands at the door.

"Go away," I say.

"Yes? Go away? So, now the boy who wants to be my friend wants me to go away? Very well, I go."

"No! Wait! Stay. I'm sorry. I'm just angry at Franklin. I didn't mean to take it out on you."

"I don't want to hear that you are angry with the doctor. You have no right."

"You weren't there. I have every right."

"To be angry with the man who gives you food and a bed and the clothes you wear? You foolish boy! What he do to make you so angry, eh?"

"Treated me like a servant."

"What you mean?"

"I mean, he treated me like a servant. First, he actually said I was one. Then, at that tavern, he ordered me to go sit at a table by myself. And then he made me give up the table to that slave-trader Swinbourne and go eat in the kitchen—"

"So? What you think? That you are the doctor's equal? At least you can enter a tavern. I would never be allowed there. Or other places whites go."

"And that's just plain wrong! Oh, that is *so* wrong!"

"Yes? And what of it? It is the way it is."

"Not where I come from. Where I come from, everybody gets to go where they want and nobody's better or has more rights than anyone else—"

"Boy, stop talking about where you come from! You are here now—"

"And stop calling me boy!"

"What else should I call you but what you are? A boy, who demands that things be the way he wants; when he should accept what is there and think how to use it to get what he wants."

"Is that what you do? Bow and scrape and hope for whatever crumbs you can get?"

"No! You stupid! I bow to no one! I use what I have to get what I need. If someone likes my cooking, I cook. If someone needs something sewed, I sew. Whatever is required—so long as I get what I need!"

"Yeah? And what's that? Some food and a closet like this to sleep in?"

"NO! My son and my *Maman*! THEY are what I need!"

She slaps her hand over her mouth.

All my anger drains away.

"What are you talking about?" I ask.

"Nothing. I said nothing. I go."

She turns to leave, but I leap to the door and close it, trapping her. Her head comes only to my shoulder. I can smell her warm, sweet breath.

She puts her hands on my chest and I make room for her to sidestep away. But I still block the door.

"Tell me. Tell me about your son and mother."

"They are in the Carolinas ... somewhere ... I think ... I do not know. My master sold them."

"Your master? You were a slave?"

"Yes, in Saint-Domingue. I was born a slave, on a plantation where my mother was cook."

"So that's who taught you."

"Yes, and I learned more in Paris."

"Whoa, back up! Paris? How did you get from Sant—where was it?—to Paris?"

"Saint-Domingue, the French side of the island of Hispaniola, in the West Indies."

"How did you get from there to Paris?"

"It's a long story and not very nice."

"Tell me. I'm a good listener."

"Maybe sometime, if I come to trust you. But now, I cannot. You are too young, too foolish, too … reck—what is the word?"

"Reckless?"

"Yes, reckless!"

"I'm not trying to make trouble. But I've got my pride, you know?"

"Can you eat pride? Will it clothe you? Will it send you back to where you belong?"

"Guess not."

"And to get back, you must stay alive. Yes?"

"Yes."

"Then you must learn your place and how to govern yourself. Otherwise, you may pay with your life, and even with the lives of others. Do you understand?"

"Yes," I say, nodding. "But look, there's something else you need to know…"

I'm just about to tell her how Franklin agreed to talk to Swinbourne about selling her when the door swings open. Sally stands in the threshold.

"Here, you two, what do you think you're doing behind closed doors? Shouldn't be closed. This is a proper house."

"Just talking," I say. "Elise was explaining to me some of the ways things are done here. The wind came through the trap and blew the door shut."

Sally's eyes shift keenly between Elise and me. Satisfied, she nods curtly.

"Father's downstairs in his library. He wants you, Marcus."

"I'll be right down."

Sally nods and leaves.

"Please," Elise says softly when Sally is out of hearing. "I should not have told you. You must never tell anyone. Otherwise, they may try and take me back." She takes my hand and grips it tightly "Promise me you will say nothing to anyone."

"I promise."

Her eyes search mine, like she's looking to see if I'm telling the truth. Then, she nods.

As I go downstairs, my hand that had been in hers tingles.

CHAPTER 16

"There you are! Where have you been?" Franklin says impatiently. "There is work to be done."

"Up in that closet of a sweat box you call a room, if it's any of your business."

My talk with Elise has done nothing to cool my anger. I still think Franklin has betrayed both of us.

"This is my house," Franklin says. "Of course, it is my business. Whatever is the matter with you?"

"You! *You* are what's the matter with me! God, you are such a hypocrite, talking out of both sides of your mouth, saying one thing and doing another. You lied to me!"

"I most certainly did not. And I would be very careful with my accusations, were I you. In this time and place, calling a man's honesty into question can get you killed. Do they still have dueling where you come from?"

"See? Exactly what I'm talking about! Say one thing, but do another. We're not supposed to talk about the future, but now here you are, asking about it."

"Touché, Marcus. You are correct. And I apologize. But tell me: aside from that one, small lapse, what other proofs have you that I lied or am a hypocrite?"

"You told me that the whole indenture thing was just for show and that you weren't going to treat me like a servant. But that's all you've been doing. No Marcus, servants don't use walking sticks. No Marcus, you can't sit with us, go eat at that table. Marcus, give your table to Swinbourne and go eat in the kitchen with the rest of the servants."

As I speak, Franklin stares at me in disbelief. Now he shakes his head.

"Marcus, you have completely misunderstood what we are about. I have never regarded you as a servant. But yes, I have treated you as one because that is the role I need you to play in order to explain your presence and protect you. I thought you understood that, as you did so well so long ago. Perhaps, that is the problem. I expect you to be who you were. But you are not him yet. Quite possibly, you need this experience in order to become him. Regardless, know this and know it well: I do not regard you as being less than me. To the contrary, I have always thought of you as an equal, indeed, as something akin to a partner."

It's a good speech. And the bit about being Franklin's partner is a really nice touch. But I'm still not buying it, not all the way, not yet.

"And what about Elise?" I say.

"What about her?"

"Well, first you say how she's your great friend, but then you tell Swinbourne you'll talk to him about selling her."

"You are quite correct. I most certainly will talk to Mr. Swinbourne about selling Elise. And I will tell him again what I told him in the garden: that she is a free woman and not for sale and not to be interfered with."

"But at the tavern, you said—"

"At the tavern I said and did nothing, except request that we discuss the matter at another time."

"You should have told him to get the hell out. Why didn't you?"

"Why indeed? Let us review, since it seems I must be your teacher if I am to have a capable assistant.

"You saw me at table with, amongst others, Governor Randolph, James Madison, and Pierce Butler, southerners from slave-owning families and who represent slave-owning citizens. It is a hard fact that many of our delegates—including General Washington—depend on slaves to operate their farms and plantations and thus, for their very livelihoods. They have not yet come to regard slavery as an evil.

"I, having been both an indentured servant and a slave owner, am well acquainted with slavery's evil. The delegates know I favor abolition. And that makes me suspect in their eyes. But they also know of my skills as a diplomat and for fashioning compromise—skills which may be quite valuable in the weeks ahead.

"Swinbourne is well aware of all of this. As a slave trader it is his business to ascertain who supports and who opposes that which makes him rich.

"Now, you saw Swinbourne come to me in front of those delegates and ask again to purchase Elise—to actually trade in human flesh. Several nights ago, you saw me refuse him in the garden in the strongest possible terms. So, why would he ask again? Why repeat the question when, in all likelihood, I will refuse again in even harsher terms? Why risk that embarrassment? Why, Marcus?"

"I ... I don't know."

"To get me to do exactly that in front of those men—to show them that I am a fire-breathing abolitionist incapable of compromise and thereby call my skills as a diplomat and negotiator into question. In essence, to take me off the board, like a rook might take a bishop in a game of chess. Not only does he want to make sure that slavery is not harmed as a result of this convention, I suspect he also wants revenge for my attempt to block him from procuring the new engine for the fire company—and for later demanding he leave my house—for embarrassing him.

"Now, what did I do? Did I rise to his bait? No. Instead, I accommodated him. I made no promises. I simply asked to discuss the matter at a later time. And then, as further proof of my reasonableness, I offered him and Wimpole your table.

"I did that, not to hurt Elise, or you, or to help Swinbourne or Wimpole; but to show all the men at that table that, even though I may oppose slavery, I am a reasonable man who can be dealt with. Do you see?"

"Not really. I mean, why's everything got to be so complicated? If a thing's wrong, it's wrong. And slavery's as wrong as anything can be. If it had been up to me, I would've taken that fancy stick of yours and given him a good beat-down."

Shaking his head, Franklin sighs.

"Marcus, do you understand what we're trying to do?"

"Not when you talk like that, I don't! Not sure I care, either—"

"What we are trying to do," he says in that infuriating, over-patient tone of his, "is fashion a government by which, for the first time in centuries, the people govern themselves. That hasn't happened since the ancient Greeks and Romans. All Europe is governed by monarchs and aristocracies having near absolute power. Citizens have almost no say in how they are governed. Oh, the English have some with their House of Commons, but they also have a powerful monarchy and aristocracy.

"Most people think self-government is a fools' errand—that it can't be done and that this new country called the United States will fail. And it is failing, because we are acting as thirteen independent states rather than as one nation.

"This convention is attempting to fix that: to forge union amongst the states, to find the things that we have in common and ways to solve our differences. Slavery is one of those differences. And it's a crucial one because the southern states believe they depend on it for their economic survival. That doesn't make it right, but it is a fact that has to be acknowledged and somehow dealt with. Somehow, we will have to wean ourselves away from slavery. The question is: how? Now do you understand?"

No, not really, I want to say. But that would only prolong the argument. Since I can tell there is nothing I can say to change Franklin's mind, I nod and we go back to work.

***

The next morning, I return to my small table in the corner of the Assembly Room.

The delegates start off by electing Nathanial Gorham from Massachusetts chairman of the Committee of the Whole, which means that Washington has to give up that throne-like chair and sit with the Virginia delegation. It doesn't matter where Washington sits. He's still the man everyone looks to.

They begin debating the fifteen-point Virginia Plan introduced the day before. Right off the bat, Governor Randolph proposes that all thirteen states place themselves under a supreme national government made up of a legislature, an executive branch, and a judicial branch—just like peg-legged Gouverneur Morris suggested at the Indian Queen.

There's some grumbling that maybe the convention is going outside its authority and that the state governments won't agree to give up their sovereignty, but in the end, because of all the problems the country is having because of the weak Confederation Congress, the delegates vote almost unanimously: "That a national government ought to be established consisting of a supreme Legislative, Executive and Judiciary."

The delegates begin discussing the proposed new legislature and how many votes—or how much say—each state would have in it. Some want every state to have an equal say, or one vote—which is the system they're currently using at the Confederation Congress in New York and here at the convention. But others want each state to have an amount of say that is proportionate to its share of the country's population. For example, if 25% of the U.S. population lives in one particular state, under a system of "proportional representation" it would receive 25% of votes in the new legislature.

They spend the rest of the day going round and round on which was fairest: one-vote-per-state or proportional representation. But they can't agree on anything. In fact, the delegates from Delaware, the smallest state, say that if the convention votes to change from equal voting to proportional representation, they just might have to leave. That's when the delegates decide to put the whole question off until some other day and adjourn.

CHAPTER 17

When we return to Franklin's, Sally, the children, and dinner are waiting in the garden. Elise serves potato soup, a smoked eel from the Delaware River, venison stew, peas and carrots, and lemon pudding. All of it is delicious, even the eel, which I have my doubts about, but which I dig into so Elise won't be offended, even though she still hardly ever looks at me.

Franklin can't have any of it since his digestion is bothering him. He has oatmeal instead, which he takes with cinnamon and lots of milk, which makes it look like mush, which he eats slowly throughout our meal.

"I've had news from Richard up in New York, Father," Sally says.

"Oh? And how is your husband faring in his pursuit of new business opportunities?"

"Apparently, he's found several: land investments in the Northwest Territory and also a new type of river boat powered by steam. He wrote to say they will require him to be away for several months and that I and the children should not wait for him to go to Temple's farm when the summer heat and sickness begin."

As I listen, I wonder what she means. I know about the heat. But sickness?

"How I envy him his pursuits!" Franklin says wistfully. "What I wouldn't give for twenty more years to see all the marvelous things this world, which soon I will leave, has in store."

"How fares the convention?" Sally asks briskly, closing down all talk of Franklin's leaving.

"Splendid! We make great progress."

"Say what?" I say. "You guys—"

Then I remember I'm supposed to be working on sounding like someone from 1787.

"You gentlemen couldn't—could not agree on anything today. And Delaware's delegates said they will walk out if you try to change the way Congress votes."

"Marcus, were you not listening?" Franklin asks. "Before that, the delegates agreed to a *supreme* national government. That means they understand and agree that their state governments will all have to give up sovereignty—power—to the national. And *that* is a very large step indeed."

"I'm surprised," Sally says. "After everything we went through to stop England lording its power over us, I should think a powerful central government is the last thing anyone wants."

"Many feel that way," Franklin says. "But I found what Pierce Butler said today promising. He has always opposed giving the current Congress too many powers because it is the only arm of government. But if we divide power amongst legislative, executive, and judicial branches, he's willing to reconsider—to 'go great lengths' is how he put it. Many delegates indicated agreement.

"Dividing the national government's power amongst branches will be very important. Each branch will have to check and balance the others so that no branch becomes a tyrant, like King George and his ministers and parliament. All in all, I was very encouraged."

"Yes, but what about the delegates threatening to walk out if you switch to proportional voting?" I ask.

"The important thing is that no one did. And that is even more encouraging. People were wise enough to see agreement could not be reached today, and to agree to postpone the issue, which will give everyone time to think how best to resolve it."

"Wouldn't it be easiest not to make any change?" young William Bache asks.

"Possibly, but easiest is not always best," Franklin says. "Of course, the states with small populations, like Delaware and Georgia, would like nothing better. They want to keep equal voting because they fear the large-population states with far greater wealth—Massachusetts, Virginia, and Pennsylvania—will overpower them or swallow them up. But if all states have one vote, the smaller states—of which there are ten—think they'll be able to out-vote the larger.

"Naturally, the large states think that would be terribly unfair since they'll be paying most of the money to run the national government. They want proportional voting so they'll have many more votes than the smaller states. That way the small states won't be able to spend their money recklessly; or interfere in anything the big states want to do."

"Still, father, the two systems seem very different. If the delegates can't agree on which one to use, how will you resolve the impasse?" Sally asks.

"Oh, I have no idea," Franklin says. "I only know it will take much thought, debate, and compromise to find a solution all can live with. Which is why I am encouraged by how the delegates handled today's disagreement. No tempers were lost. No one walked out. They wisely decided to put the issue aside and return to it later. Which I hope will become our *modus operandi* throughout the convention."

Grandpapa, what is a *modus operandi*?" young Sarah Bache asks.

"*Modus operandi*," her brother William says, "from the Latin, meaning mode of operation, or a way of doing something."

"I didn't ask you, did I, William Bache?" Sarah scolds.

"Nonetheless he is correct, Sarah. Excellent, William," Franklin says, smiling with pride. "I see that the money spent on your tutor has not been wasted. And now, I suggest our *modus operandi* be to proceed with Elise's lemon pudding, after which, Marcus, you and I must return to work. There's much to do!"

***

Over the next few weeks, as summer comes on and the days get warmer, the convention pretty much grants Franklin's wish regarding its *modus operandi*. They find the things they can agree upon and set aside the things they can't.

For instance, even though they can't agree how the states will vote in the legislature, they agree that legislature should be divided into two houses, the first to be elected by the people and the second by the state legislatures.

They also agree there will be a chief executive to run the government (although they're not sure whether it should be a single person or a committee, like Pennsylvania's Supreme Executive Council that

Franklin heads); and also a Supreme Court and lesser courts to judge the laws. And they agree the executive should have a veto over the legislature.

"Progress is being made, Marcus. Progress is being made," Franklin sometimes says contentedly on our walks home. Since I'm still supposed to keep my mouth shut in public, I can't argue. But I wonder if the delegates will start disagreeing when they stop sitting as a Committee of the Whole where no decision is final.

Actually, the disagreements begin earlier, on Saturday, June 9th to be exact, when the committee returns to the issue of how the states will vote.

It's hot inside that Assembly Room. It's nice outside, it still being early June. But inside? With the windows nailed shut and the drapes drawn to keep everything secret, the temperature keeps climbing. Most of the delegates take off their long coats and weskits and wave paddle-like hand fans under their chins to cool themselves. I envy them. I don't have a fan, or a free hand to wave it with, since my table is rickety and I have to keep it steady with one and write with the other. Within a half-hour, my coat sleeve is soaked with the sweat I've swiped off my forehead.

Lawyer James Paterson rises to speak for New Jersey, a small state. With his pale skin, long nose, and white, white hair cut very, very short, he reminds me of a porcupine. He is so set against small states losing their equal votes, he's downright hostile.

"There is no reason a wealthy state contributing much should have more votes than a small state contributing little. Rich citizens do not have more votes than poor ones. Mr. Wilson from Pennsylvania suggests the large states will unite amongst themselves if other states reject proportional voting. Let them, if they please. But let them also remember they cannot compel others to unite. New Jersey will *never* join in this plan! She would be swallowed up. I would rather submit to a monarch— a despot!—than such a fate."

That's when Wilson jumps up.

"All authority is derived from the people!" he declares, his face red and his brogue thick. "Equal numbers of people ought to ha'e equal numbers of representatives, and different numbers of people different numbers of representatives."

The Scotsman's voice rises to an angry wail.

"If the small states will no' confederate on this plan, Pennsylvania—and other states, I presume—will no' confederate on any other! If New Jersey will no' part with her sovereignty, then there's no point in talking of government!"

At that, all the fans freeze and the chamber gets very, very quiet. I see surprise and worry, even fear, on the delegates' faces. Paterson must see that he and Wilson have upset everyone because he moves to adjourn until Monday. The delegates agree and rush for the doors.

Walking home, Franklin looks troubled. He keeps mumbling to himself, then frowning, then shaking his head, as if trying something on for size and then rejecting it.

"Are you all right, Father?" Sally asks as we sit down to dinner. "You seem—"

"I am fine!" Franklin says. Then he shakes his head. "I am sorry, daughter, the convention has me ... perplexed. The delegates have reached that impasse over voting we talked about. Neither the big states nor the small will give an inch. Tempers are flaring. I was surprised at James Wilson today. Being a lawyer, he must know this is not a time for passion, but for calm and reason."

"Grandpapa," young William says, "I don't really understand why proportional voting is preferable to each state having a single vote. My tutor asked me to explain it to him, and I couldn't."

"Well ... it has much to do with what Mr. Wilson said today about power residing with the people. He and many others believe that it is not each state that must have an equal say, but each citizen.

"Right now we are considering a proportional voting system in which each congressman, no matter what state he is from, would represent a certain set number of people, say 30,000 citizens per congressman. Under such a system, 30,000 people from Pennsylvania would have the same single vote in Congress as 30,000 people from New Jersey, who would have the same single vote as 30,000 people from Massachusetts. By logical extension, that means that a single individual from Pennsylvania would have just as much voting power as one from any other state.

"Now, William, answer me this: Which do you think the people are more likely to support? A system in which each *state* has an equal say in how the nation is governed? Or a system in which each and every *individual* has an equal say."

"The one in which every individual has an equal say?" young Sarah says.

"Yes! Very good Sarah! The one in which every individual has an equal say. Indeed, some—like Mr. Wilson and Mr. Madison—believe that principle is the very foundation upon which self-government rests."

"My tutor says self-government is an idiotic idea," William says. "He says the people don't know what's best for them and that they need a king and aristocracy to tell them what to do."

"He does, does he? Ha!" Franklin laughs. "Perhaps, daughter, it is time to find a new tutor!"

Then Franklin grows quiet and his face becomes troubled.

"I tell you, however, I did not like the tone of today's debate. Delegates are becoming much too set in their opinions and combative. Finish your pudding, Marcus, quickly. We have a speech to write."

CHAPTER 18

We work on that speech all weekend.

Monday morning, the convention is less tense, but still uneasy.

James Wilson and Rufus King of Massachusetts formally propose proportionate voting in the House of Representatives.

Then Franklin asks to be recognized. His voice is too weak for him to give the speech himself. Wilson gives it for him.

The Scotsman who'd wailed so angrily at Paterson delivers Franklin's words modestly and without drama.

"Mr. Chairman, it has given me great pleasure to observe that until we came to this matter of proportionate representation, our debates were carried out with calmness and reason. If anything to the contrary has occurred, I hope it will not be repeated.

"For we are sent here to confer with each other; not to fight. Declarations of fixed opinions, and refusals to change them, neither enlighten nor persuade. Certainty and anger on one side causes certainty and anger on the other; and will create division and discord in this great endeavor, instead of the harmony and unity we need to be effective in promoting and securing the common good."

I watch the delegates. Wilson may be speaking, but all eyes are on Franklin. He sits proudly still, his eyes moving from delegate to delegate, like he's willing each one to heed his message.

Using himself as an example of the flexibility and conciliation he is urging, he tells how he used to think that each member of Congress should consider himself a representative of the entire nation instead of just their state; and that this would reduce the need for states to have representation in proportion to their populations.

But now, he sees that most delegates do not agree with that. So, he has reconsidered. He now believes that the number of representatives allotted to a state should be proportionate to its population and that decisions should be made by a majority of representatives instead of a majority of states. He understands smaller states fear being swallowed up, but he can't agree since he can't see how any larger state would benefit.

Wilson finishes Franklin's speech and sits beside him as the delegates thump the floor with their walking sticks to applaud. Franklin bows his head a little.

When the delegates vote on the motion for proportional voting in the House of Representatives, it passes by a large margin.

Then things get ugly.

***

It is James Wilson who touches off the fire. He proposes that, when counting a state's population in order to determine how many Congressmen it gets, three-fifths of all black slaves be included in the count.

I'm writing so fast, trying to keep up, that I don't really think about what the proposal means. Not until pinch-faced Elbridge Gerry, a businessman from Massachusetts, starts talking. He doesn't like Wilson's proposal one bit. Southern slaves are property and property shouldn't be used to calculate a state's number of representatives, he insists. If property is to be used, then northern cattle and horses should also be counted.

And that's when it hits me: black slaves are going to be used to increase the number of representatives a slave-holding state gets. Will those slaves also get a vote? No. They aren't even being considered as people. They are strictly property. That's what Gerry means with his talk of cattle and horses.

Which leads me to an even worse realization—one that so disgusts me that I throw down my *porte-crayon* and stand, shoving back my chair so hard it squeals and *brrruuups* across the floor.

Gerry stops talking. Heads turn. Brows furrow. On his corner stool, Joseph the caretaker shakes his head. That's when I remember exactly where I am and who I'm supposed to be and sit back down.

Frowning at me, Franklin brings his finger to his lips. He wants me quiet. Well, I don't care what he wants—not after what I've just heard!

But then, I see Washington staring at me from his place at Virginia's table. "Feel" would be a better way to describe it. He fixes those arctic-blue eyes on me. They are so cold, and his face is so stony, I feel like I can't breathe. Ducking my head, I busy myself fitting a new lead into the brass case.

Gerry starts up again. I bend low over my work.

But as I scribble, I seethe. Who is Washington, or any of these men, to say any other person is their property?

In the end, all those fine gentlemen vote that states are to be represented proportionately according to their white populations and three-fifths of their black slaves. And not just in the House of Representatives, but also in the Senate. It looks like the "three-fifths rule" is going to control both houses of Congress; and that makes me sick.

***

As soon as Franklin signals, I bolt. Usually, I wait for him outside the door. But after that? I need air.

I charge up Chestnut towards Sixth. I'm not sure why I go that way. Maybe it's force of habit, being the way I go whenever I visit Mom in her Curtis Center office. But I'm not thinking about that. I'm thinking about the realization that made me jump up like the jack-in-the-box Penny had when she was a toddler.

The convention has just voted to use black slaves to give slave-holding states a bigger say in Congress, possibly a big enough say to keep slavery from being abolished. Black slaves will be used to perpetuate their own slavery.

I stop at the corner, furious at the unfairness of it.

Convicts from the Walnut Street Jail are at work excavating the cellar for a new courthouse for the City of Philadelphia. The site is muddy because of the rain the night before. Unshaved, unwashed, their hair greasy and matted, the prisoners wear torn, grimy, mud-encrusted rags and balls and chains at their ankles.

A huge, hulking prisoner with rippling biceps and hands as blunt as mallets rolls a wheelbarrow past me. The chain bolted to the shackle around his ankle is long enough to allow the ball to rest inside the barrow. Still, the shackle has raised bloody sores.

That just adds to my outrage. I ball my fists in anger. Which is when his stink overwhelms me and I gag and turn away.

"Here, you!" he growls. "Wot's your problem? Got sumfin' to say?"

"Sorry," I say, but it comes out a whisper. Then I remember I'm not supposed to talk.

"Wot? Wot was that?" he snaps, dropping the handles of his barrow.

I make a cutting motion at my throat to show I can't talk.

"Don't give me that! I heard you say sumfin'. Sounded like 'sorry.' Is that what you said? That you'se sorry? Didja hear, lads? This young whelp says he's sorry."

Picking up their iron balls, other prisoners gather around.

I make the cutting motion again.

"And wot might you be sorry about? Have we offended thee, young gentleman? D'ye not like our style of dress or our perfume?"

Growls of laughter rise from the men. They press in on me. Their rankness hammers at me.

"Betcha he thinks hisself better n' us. Betcha he *knows* he's better n' us."

I shake my head.

"No? Yes? Wot's it to be?"

I shake my head faster. The men crowd closer.

If you want to get out of this, you're going to have to fight, I think. My heart hammers. I've never been in a street fight before. And it's going to be five against one. As I realize I'm about to catch a beating, muscles along the side of my face start to twitch. But I refuse to back down. Gus wouldn't have. And I need to know that I'm just as brave as him.

"Better n' us. That's wot this whelp thinks," the big man urges.

As the men growl their agreement, the big man lifts the iron ball out of the barrow and drops it in the mud, splattering me from head to foot.

"There! Wotcha think now, Mr. Fancy-man?" he says as the other prisoners grab me.

What do I think? Now, I'm so furious, I'm not thinking. I want to smash his face—smash all their faces. I don't care how big they are, or how many, or how bad they can hurt me. But I can't move. Iron hands have pinned my arms behind my back.

"Oh look!" the big man says. "The boy's got hisself all hot! Look at him, lads. You could fry a egg on that face."

"Needs knocking about! Teach him his manners," another man jeers.

More hands seize me. I struggle, but they are too many and too strong. I am powerless to stop them.

Chapter 19

"Stop that, Thomas McAndrews! Stop that, all of you!" a hoarse voice commands.

I don't have to turn to know it's Franklin. All hands drop away and I am free.

"Aren't you in enough trouble, Thomas? How many more weeks to your sentence?"

"Two," the big man answers gruffly, looking embarrassed.

"If you don't want to make it ten, leave my clerk alone."

"Clerk? I … I didn't know—"

"You never do! That's why you're here instead of helping my grandson at the printing office and taking care of your family. Jesu, man, you look awful. And you stink of rum. How many times have you been told to stay away from spirits? You have no head for 'em."

"They're a comfort."

"A home, food on the table, a fire in the hearth, and a bed warmed by a good woman, those are true comforts, wouldn't you say? Comforts that your drinking has put at risk. Am I right?"

McAndrews stares at the ground.

"Hopeless!" Franklin sighs. "Well, no matter." Fishing some coins from his pocket, he says: "Thomas, here are five pennies: two for you and one each for the men you will gather to bring the sedan from my house and convey me to the home of Robert Morris at Sixth and High Streets. Send me the jailor and I'll square it with him. The rest of you, go back to work."

As the men disperse, Franklin puts his hand on my shoulder for support.

"The gout and stone are bad today, Marcus. Come into the garden and wait with me."

I help him through the State House into the walled garden where we sit on a stone bench. Entirely deserted, it is so quiet there, so peaceful. There is a gentle wind. Mourning doves coo.

"I am very cross with you," Franklin says after a while. "Don't speak, in case someone is watching from a window. But nod if you understand."

Turning my back to the State House and its windows, I shake my head instead.

"Just what did you think you would accomplish with that display?" he asks.

I shrug.

"Ah, I see. You didn't think."

"Oh I thought, alright," I hiss through gritted teeth. "You guys! Using slaves to give the Southern states more votes in Congress so slavery will always be legal!"

Franklin raises an eyebrow at that.

"Very astute," he says.

"Astute, my ass! How can anyone even think that way?"

Franklin sighs unhappily.

"It's an imperfect world, Marcus. Right now, southern states believe they need black slaves if their farms and plantations are to survive. If they have no guarantee that slavery will not be abolished, they will separate from the United States and form their own country; or turn to a foreign power like England, France, or Spain for protection; or both. Once again, we will have foreign armies on our soil and our revolution—all those deaths, all that destruction—will have been for nothing."

"Maybe England, France, or Spain would be better. Maybe they'd abolish slavery."

"Hah!" Franklin scoffs, slapping his thigh. "Who do you think began this monstrous trade in the first place? Europe! Why, there are more slaves in South America and the Caribbean than in all our thirteen states! Europe's hands are much bloodier than ours."

"Didn't know it was a competition."

"Marcus, why is this so important to you? These are not your people."

"Yes, they are!"

"They are? Who says so?"

"Mom and Pop. They taught me and Gus that all people are part of the same human family, no matter where they come from or what they look like, and that you have to be kind to everyone and cruel to no one if that's the way you want the world to be and how you want to be treated."

"Can this be true? Has our Enlightenment progressed this far? Tell me, do all people believe this?" Franklin asks excitedly.

"No … not everyone … not even most," I answer; and his face falls. "But a lot of people. Including me and Gus. Like he always said, "You've got to *be* the change you want to see in the world."

"Refresh my recollection. Gus is?"

"My brother—"

"Ah yes, I remember now. He was the soldier killed in battle—"

"I don't want to talk about that," I just about bark, but then rein myself in. "I mean, since it's the future."

"His death makes you angry?"

"Like I said, I don't want to talk about that."

"No … quite right." He lays his hand on my arm. "What were we saying? Oh yes, slavery. Marcus, believe me when I say there are men in that room just as opposed to slavery as I am. Men like James Wilson and Alexander Hamilton and Gouverneur Morris. Even Washington and Madison from Virginia—even though they own slaves—are beginning to recognize how harmful it is. But each state has different needs and if we are to forge a nation—a true United States—everyone will have to compromise—"

A coughing fit doubles him over. I slap his back, trying to help him get rid of whatever is choking him. He motions for me to stop and I help him sit upright.

"Jesu, that hurts!" he says as one hand goes to his lower belly and the other wipes thick, yellow phlegm from his chin with a handkerchief.

"Are you alright?" I ask.

"Fine. I'm fine. Just need to catch my breath."

I watch Franklin carefully as he recovers and the color comes back to his face.

"I am impressed that you so quickly grasped the cruel irony of the 'three-fifths rule.' You are learning. Of course, you are correct. Black slaves may well be used to increase population numbers to strengthen the South's legislative power, and that power may well be used to perpetuate slavery.

"But things are not as grim as they seem. I can't promise this will happen, but some delegates want to completely end slavery by a certain date. I don't know what that date will be. It will have to give everyone time to prepare for complete emancipation, as we have done in Pennsylvania with our Act for the Gradual Abolition of Slavery.

"And preparation will be needed. States relying on slaves will have to find a new source of labor or pay Negroes for work and provide decent conditions. All citizens will have to accustom themselves to the idea that blacks will walk amongst us free. And blacks will have to learn how to be free—not an easy task when you've been told what to do all your life and had all your decisions made for you."

Franklin plants his walking stick and I help him stand.

"Let us go back out to Chestnut Street. The jailor and McAndrews and his men should be arriving."

"Where are you going?" I ask softly as we pass through the deserted State House.

"To Robert Morris's home, to see General Washington, who is residing there."

"Why?"

"Why is Washington residing there?"

"No, why are you going to see him?"

"Because I have been summoned."

"Summoned? How come—why?"

"I assure you, I don't know, but I would wager all the money in my pocket it has something to do with your … protest … this afternoon. Marcus, your head may well be on the chopping block. Fortunately, you do fine work—work I desperately need. So I will do everything I can to keep you in that chamber. But you can never react like that again. No matter what you hear. Agreed?"

I don't want to agree to anything, not if there is something I can do to make the delegates see that how they are treating slavery is just plain wrong. So I deflect.

"You could always tell him my leg cramped up and I stood to work it out."

"Agreed?" he repeats, staring at me hard. "Don't speak, just nod."

Which I do.

"Good. Now help me to my chair. Then go home and change. You're a mess! … Cramp indeed," I hear him mutter. "Although …"

CHAPTER 20

I arrive at Franklin's house to find Elise on her way out.

"*Mon Dieu!* What happened?" she asks, staring at my clothes. Then she giggles.

"A carriage splashed me," I lie. I don't need her knowing I've been bested by a gang of convicts.

"You look like *un bouffon.*" Now she is laughing. "What do you say in English? A buffoon? Like in the circus?"

"Clown?"

"Yes! Exactly! A clown!"

"Thanks. Thanks very much."

But I can't be angry with her for laughing. It gives her the most beautiful smile.

"Well? What do you wait for? Take them off and put them in the kitchen. I will clean them tonight when I return."

"Where are you going?"

Her smile fades.

"Joseph Carver has invited me for a supper, if it is any of your concern."

"Oh," I say, feeling my heart sink. "Didn't know you had a boyfriend."

"Boyfriend? What is that? I know a man. What of it?"

"I just didn't know you were seeing anyone ... like romantically—"

"Romance? I have no time! I go to see a man and his family: his wife, his children, his *maman*. They offer supper to people and I am invited. Preachers are to speak about being Negro and free."

"Can I come?"

"No, you cannot come. It is for Negroes."

"Please? Franklin's off visiting and I don't want to stay cooped up in that library by myself. I won't be any trouble."

"No."

"Why?"

"Because you are white. You will make people … how do you say? … uncomfortable."

"No I won't. I'll be so quiet no one'll even notice me."

"Well, I cannot stop you from coming. But I will not walk with you. Blacks and whites do not walk together. I leave in five minutes. What you do is up to you."

I race to my room. Looking in the small mirror I'd bought at the market, I see that the mud on my face has dried white. I really do look like a clown. Pouring water from a pitcher into a wash bowl, I quickly scrub it off, dress in the cotton shirt, long pants, and broad-brimmed straw hat Wimpole provided, and hurry downstairs.

She's already left.

I rush out the front door and spy her some fifty yards away, just turning onto Chestnut.

I follow, letting her keep a good half-block ahead. She walks west, until reaching Fifth and then turns south, passing the State House and the fortress-like Walnut Street Jail. Several blocks later, the brick sidewalks and cobblestone paving end and the streets turn to dirt. Empty lots alternate with shabby brick or wood homes, nothing like the rich Society Hill townhouses in my Philadelphia. The day is hot and still. No breeze rustles the leaves. The stink of garbage, chamber pots, and animal manure dumped in the now deserted street turns my stomach.

There's no one around. I quicken my pace to gain on her. When I'm only several steps behind, I call to her.

She whirls around, her face full of fear. "Do you always sneak onto people like that?"

"It's sneak *up* to people. And no, not usually. But you said you'd wait and didn't."

"I gave you five minutes. You did not come. I left."

"Where are we going again?"

"As I said, to the home of Joseph Carver."

"Who's he?"

"You do not know? Dr. Franklin did not tell you?"

"No."

Suddenly, she stops and side-steps and I narrowly miss stepping into a gutted dead cat crawling with maggots.

"Oh man! That is *so* gross!"

"He is caretaker at the State House," Elise says, unfazed by the cat. "Dr. Franklin got him the position to reward his service in the war. He fought in many sea battles and took a ball in his hip."

"Oh, him," I say, connecting the name to the short, limping black man with the salt-and-pepper hair who'd shaken his head when I'd stood in protest.

A mosquito whines in my ear and I slap. My palm comes away bloody.

"So, who are the two preachers?" I ask.

"Men who try to help Negroes."

"Help? Help how?"

"I don't know!" she snaps. "This is why I am going. To learn! You ask too many questions!"

"Sorry. I just want to know what to expect. Besides, I don't get to talk much. So this is kind of my chance."

"Chance?"

"Yeah, to talk. Maybe to get to know you better?"

"Why do you want to do that?" she asks with a puzzled look.

"Well … I don't really know anything about you. I mean I know you're from that island and you were a slave and that you're looking for your Mom and little boy—"

"I said forget that!" she hisses back at me over her shoulder. "I should not have told you. Did you tell someone?"

"No! I promised I wouldn't and I didn't. But that doesn't mean I don't want to learn more about you."

"Why?"

"Well, for one thing, I bet you've got a good story to tell. I mean, you got all the way to Paris and then back here. And because I like you and when you like someone, you want to know more about them."

"Oh, you mean you are a nose."

"A what?"

"A nose. Like a bear with the bees' hive. You put your nose where it does not belong."

"Oh! You mean nosy. We say nosy. Not trying to be. Just trying to get to know you. To be friends. I don't have any here. It looks like you don't either."

"I have no time for friends. Only work. To earn money. To get my *Maman* and son."

"Maybe I could help."

"You? What help can you give? You cannot walk the street without being covered in mud!"

"Franklin seems to think I'm okay. Maybe you could trust his judgment."

She stops and turns. I join her. She peers at me, as though trying to see me in a different light. I stand there. She can inspect me all she wants.

"This is it," she says.

"What?"

"The home of Joseph Carver."

My heart sinks with disappointment. She hasn't been looking at me at all. She's been looking over my shoulder at the house behind me.

It's a short, narrow, two-story home of uneven brick with a sagging roof and lop-sided chimney. The door is unpainted. The windows have no shutters. Inside, thin, ragged cloth covers them, like curtains, so I can't see in. But I hear fiddle music and clapping.

Elise knocks. The unlatched door swings open. I start in, but Elise stops me.

"I will go first. And remember, no talking."

We enter a dark, smoky room, deserted except for a young boy turning chickens on a spit over the hearth. He points to another door and says: "They's outside."

We walk into a small backyard of mostly bare earth and weeds, and a little vegetable garden, surrounded by an old wood fence. Chipped, cracked, and half-filled plates of food sit on a rough plank table. Some fifteen or twenty blacks are gathered around a fiddler. They look like working men and women: no long coats or silk vests for the men or fancy, frilly dresses for the women; just plain linen or cotton, or osnaburg that looks like burlap, all faded and frayed and salt-stained from sweat.

The only person I recognize is Joseph Carver. But he isn't anything like the caretaker at the State House. That man keeps his eyes down, his shoulders slumped, and his mouth shut as he limps through his chores and does everyone's bidding. This man stands upright and broad-shouldered. His eyes are bright and his face full of fun as he claps to the music and watches everyone dance. I stand at the back of the crowd, my hat pulled low. Everyone is so involved in the dance that no one notices me … at least, at first.

The young boy brings the spitted chickens out and gives them to a large, fierce-faced woman with coal-black skin and cloud-white hair springing every which-way from under a dark-blue kerchief. Grasping each carcass with a fleshy hand, she takes them off the spit and chops them into parts with a cleaver.

When the fiddler ends his tune to cheers and clapping, Carver holds up his hands and calls: "Gather round, folks! Now, we all know why we're here."

"Yessuh! For this fine feast!" a man says, getting a laugh from the crowd.

That "feast" doesn't look so very fine. Just the chicken, some yams and squash, some plates of cornbread, whatever is in the bubbling pot hanging over a fire from a tripod, and some pitchers of funky-smelling water, the only drink offered.

"Quiet, Peter Wayne!" Carver laughs. "You'll get your fill soon enough. Now, we're here today to …"

His voice falters at the sight of me. He stares at me in disbelief, as if I'm a ghost or some other apparition he can't fathom. A second later, his face clears, the smile is back, and his voice is as strong as ever.

"We're here because these two gentlemen, Reverend Absalom Jones and Reverend Richard Allen—you fellas come over so everyone can see you—we're here because these men are starting The Free African Society and they need our help."

Two men dressed in black suits and white linen wilting in the heat join Carver. One, looks about forty, and is of medium height and solid build. Round-faced, with mahogany skin, he wears a black wig with side curls and a queue tied back with a ribbon. The other man is younger, taller, and slimmer with clean-shaven, caramel-colored skin stretched tight over high cheekbones and a full head of curly gray hair that starts at his forehead in a widow's peak.

"Thank you, Joseph," the shorter, round-faced man says. "As many of you know from our time at St. George's Methodist Episcopal Church, I am the Reverend Absalom Jones and this is the Reverend Richard Allen.

"Everyone's heard that St. George's has asked us Africans to remove ourselves from the whites downstairs and sit in the upstairs gallery. As a result, both I and Reverend Allen feel we can no longer minister there. We hope to establish our own church soon. But that is not what I want to talk about today. I want to talk about what the recent events at St. George's mean.

"They mean we are not liked in Philadelphia. We ... are ... not ... liked! We may have gained our freedom. We may have sweated our very blood to earn the money to buy it, or fought, even died for it in the War of Independence. But we are not liked. There is no one we can rely on in troubled times. NO ONE! Except God, and maybe each other.

"That is what Reverend Allen and I have been discussing: how we Africans can come together to assist one another. Some call it forming a mutual aid society. We are calling it the Free African Society.

"Brothers and sisters, so many of our people are in need: women who have lost husbands; children who have lost parents; men and women who need employment to earn their daily bread.

"And we are at the very bottom here in Philadelphia. We must change that. We must learn how to change that: how to find work and save money and buy homes; how to build our own banks and businesses and schools and how to run them.

"For these purposes, Reverend Allen and I urge you to join our Free African Society. We ask for dues of only a shilling a month—to be used to relieve those in need—and that you attend meetings and share information to benefit other members. Perhaps you know of a job, or available housing, or goods going for a good price. Perhaps you will share that information in the hopes of learning something from another member that may benefit you.

"This is a time of great possibility for everyone in this country; and so can it be for all the African citizens of Philadelphia, but only if we work together. That is why we are creating this society, so that all free Africans can advance by working together.

"And now I invite you to partake of this meal the Lord has provided and you all have brought to table—a fine example of what can be accomplished if we work together. The Reverend Allen and I will answer any questions you have. For those wishing to pay their shilling to join us, we stand ready to enter your names into our ledger."

I don't know how successful Reverend Jones's speech is. Most people make a beeline for the food. But not Elise.

"Lend me a shilling," she says. "I want to join."

I fish out the small leather pouch holding my wages from Franklin and pour the unfamiliar coins into my hand. Elise plucks one up and hurries over to the clergymen and Joseph Carver. As I follow, Carver and the two preachers watch me carefully.

"Reverend?" Elise asks. "Can your society find family who are slaves and set them free?"

I've just taken off my hat to wipe the sweat from my forehead. Before the Reverend Allen can answer, Joseph Carver says: "Say, I know you. You're the young man who's clerk to Dr. Franklin. The one who can't talk."

"Yes, that's right," Elise says. "I hope you don't mind. But he believes in the work you are doing and wanted to meet you, so I …"

"Oh no, it's fine, it's fine," Carver says quickly, although I can tell it really isn't. A lot of people are staring at me now. Elise had been right: I'm making everyone uncomfortable. "Any friend of Dr. Franklin's is most … welcome."

"Reverend?" Elise asks again. "Can you find family who are slaves?"

Reverend Allen shakes his head. "In truth, that is not something we do."

"No, it is not," says Reverend Jones. "Perhaps, in time, but now, we are just beginning."

Elise nods and then holds the shilling out to me.

"They can't help," she says without expression. "Thank you anyway."

"Wait!" Reverend Allen calls as we start to walk away. "Tell us what the matter is."

"What is the use?" she answers. "If you cannot help, you cannot help."

"Why, it is just as I was explaining. Mutual assistance. Establishing relationships within and outside our African community. We might not be able to help, directly. But maybe we know someone who can."

"Or someone who knows someone who can," Reverend Jones adds. "Tell us, sister."

Elise looks at the men doubtfully and then at me. I shrug, as if to say: what have you got to lose? She motions for them to come closer and talks softly but urgently.

"My mother and son. We were slaves in Saint-Domingue. The master sold them to a man who said he would sell them in the Carolinas. And that is all I know."

"It isn't much," Allen says doubtfully.

"No, it isn't," Jones agrees. "But I do know there are men who make their living finding people."

"Yes," Allen says. "I have heard of one in particular, over in that abominable Helltown, north of the market. A man named Lucas Rush. I know little about him. Only that he demands a very high price, and that he's the devil to deal with. But if he puts his mind to finding someone, they are found."

"I know a Lucas Rush!" Joseph Carver says. "Or I did. Sailed with him on the privateer *Diana* in the war. I wouldn't be here at all if it wasn't for him. When I took that ball in my hip in our battle with the *Lively,* he slung me over his shoulder and got me below to the sawbones. Don't know what happened to him. Last I heard, he'd quit being a sailor to hunt and trap to get enough money to start a farm. Probably ain't the same fella. But if it is, well ... Reverend ... you may think him a hard man, but I knows him to be a good'un."

"Then perhaps this is something you should pursue," Reverend Jones says to Elise.

"But I have no money," Elise says. "Almost everything I earn goes to Dr. Franklin to pay him back for my passage to America."

"I'm acquainted with Dr. Franklin," Reverend Allen says. "A most excellent man. Perhaps he might lend you additional funds? Or possibly, his abolition society might provide assistance?"

"No, he has done so much. I cannot ask for more."

"Then perhaps Mr. Carver here can help you work something out with Mr. Rush, if indeed it is the same man."

"Perhaps," she says, her face full of doubt. "Thank you." She starts to turn away. "No, wait! Marcus, give me the shilling. I will join."

"Well, that's fine," Reverend Jones says. "We will enter your name. Don't forget now, it's not just a shilling. It's a shilling every month."

"Yes, I know. It is a good thing you are doing. I want to be part."

"And we welcome you. Now, how about you, young man? Of course, our society is for Africans, but we willingly accept contributions."

I hand him another shilling.

CHAPTER 21

By the time we finish with the preachers, almost everyone has gone. I wonder if I've driven them all away. But when Elise says we should eat, I see another explanation. There's almost no food left: no chicken, bread, or potatoes; just a couple of lonely yams on a greasy plate—well, lonely except for the flies. I haven't eaten since breakfast. I'm starving.

Our hunger must be obvious because a voice that's low and hoarse, but somehow sweetly musical says to Elise: "Try my pepper pot, gal. It's good and it's hot. But be quick, 'cuz this be the last of it!"

The voice belongs to the white-haired woman who'd hacked the chicken into parts. Now she tends the bubbling iron pot.

"They's ain't nothin' else. Anyways, my pepper pot's best in the city, least that's what all the ladies and gentlemens that comes see me says. Here, try some. Leastways, here, it be free."

She ladles portions into small bowls and gives them to us without spoons. Carrots, celery, onions, peppers, and meat swim in a broth full of cloves and peppercorns.

I watch Elise bring the bowl to her lips, drink some of the broth, and then eat the meat and vegetables with her fingers. I follow her lead.

What a wonderful soup! The best I've ever eaten. It starts out sweet and savory. Then the heat builds, opening my sinuses and setting my tongue and throat to prickling. And when it hits my stomach, that heat fills me with such comfort.

"So good, *Maman,*" Elise says. "What meat you use?"

"Tryin' t'steal my recipe?" The old woman's eyes narrow with suspicion.

"*Mon dieu, non!* I would never do such a thing?" Elise says, offended.

"Dey's lots of peoples sellin' pepper pot over to the market," the old woman says. "But none's good as mine. Everyone says so. Which be why I makes more money than all the rest. Tell my secret to a pretty thing like you? You'll take my customers. Times is hard. This family needs the money I make."

"I am no thief!" Elsie insists; then raises her chin to look down her nose. "And I don't need to sell soup on the street. I work for Dr. Franklin."

"I know who he is. You too!" the old woman says. "M'boy Joseph tole me. You that gal cooks for Franklin, who come all the way from Paris. Well, Paris or no Paris, Franklin or no Franklin, jes remember, Frenchie, y'ain't no better n' me. Too good to sell soup on the street, is you? Girl, I bet I make more money'n you. So don't go put'n on airs!"

"I'm not!" Elise says, setting her bowl down hard on the table. "I asked what was in your soup to compliment you. Because the soup is very good! And you dare call me a thief?"

"Here, here! What's all this?" calls Joseph Carver, limping over. "Mama why you fussin'? We's all supposed to be friends here and helping each other, jes like the reverends said. Not fight'n between us."

"Mind yore business, Joseph! Don't need you fight'n my battles, nor settling 'em neither."

The old woman looks Elise up and down.

"Child?" she asks, her eyes again narrowed. "Was you really complimenting my soup? Not trying to steal it?"

"Madame, I swear by the Virgin."

"Tripe!" the old woman says. "Oh, there's some bacon for flavor. But mostly, it's tripe. Some of the butchers gives it to me free and I gives 'em back lunch."

"Ahhhh, *Je comprends* ... I see ... very clever, and so well done. Tripe is difficult," Elise says, nodding sagely.

I tap her on the shoulder and shrug.

"You don't know tripe?" Elise asks.

I shake my head.

"*L'estomac de vache.* How do you say? The stomach of the cow?"

I grimace.

"No, no! It's fine. This tripe has been very well washed and boiled. I can tell. I've had tripe that wasn't and it tastes nasty, like ... well ... never mind. But you can eat this. It's good."

"Better eat quick while it's still hot. And if'n you want more? Come see me any time over to one of them empty market stalls 'tween Fourth and Fifth, 'ceptin market days when I gots to sell from the corner. Can't miss me. But brings your money. Over there, I don't give nuthin' away—not even to your Dr. Franklin, who likes my soup much as anyone."

"Dr. Franklin comes to you?" Elise asks.

"Used to. No more. Says his innards ain't up to it. But time was, he'd come a couple times a week, pay me his two pence just like everybody else."

"That is how much you charge?" Elise asks. "Only two cents? You cannot make much."

"She don't," says Joseph Carver.

"Two shillings a day, maybe three, if I'm stingy with my portions. But no matter how stingy I am, always seems there ain't enough left for all that wants it. Cain't carry enough all that way to satisfy everyone."

"I keep telling her to quit," Carver says. "They's nights she comes home so tired, she cain't hardly start the next batch. I've seen her fall asleep cuttin' up them carrots. But every morning, she's up before the sun and carrying made-soup over to that market."

"How'm I gonna quit?" the old woman asks her son. "Even with your Lucy takin' in sewing and both young'uns apprenticed out, and lettin' that sailor-man board his wife and kids upstairs, we barely got enough for rent and food. And I won't go to the work house, or the alms house neither. Anyways, I don't work half as hard as you. How many jobs you got? Caretakin' over to the State House. Diggin' graves over to the Stranger's Ground and ditches and cellars. And chopping wood and white-washing and fixin' up them nasty streets with cobblestones."

"Mama, you know all that work's irregular. Assembly only sits over to the State House for a part of every year. This convention they's got is a one-time thing. And the rest hires me when they needs me—with no guarantees after I finish they's ever gonna hire me again, specially not with this hip."

"Fine thing too! You with that English ball still in you and we's all got to worry about where the next penny's comin' from. Well, if you can't quit, neither can I."

"How long does it take to prepare the ingredients for your soup?" Elise asks.

"How long? Sometimes seems like the whole night. But I guess that's just cuz I's tired. Good day? Like a Sunday, when I gots time? Two hour or three, I guess. Why you askin'?" That look of suspicion is back.

"No reason," Elise says. "I am just curious. And what vegetables do you cut?"

"I knew it!" The old woman slaps the heavy thigh under her skirts. "You is tryin' to steal my business!" She rises and charges Elise, her face full of fury. "Gal, for that I'se gonna give them ears a boxin they ain't never gonna fergit!"

"STOP!" I cry, rushing between them.

"*Mon dieu!*" I hear Elise whisper.

Carver stares at me wide-eyed.

Which is when I remember.

"Well, the good Lord be praised!" Carver says, "You can talk, after all!"

"Yeah … I guess I … recovered," I say lamely, looking to see who else has heard. But everyone is gone.

"Don't sound to me like there ever was anything wrong."

He's got me. And he knows it from my face.

"So why's you pretendin' you cain't talk?"

"Dr. Franklin thought it'd be better if everyone at the convention thought I couldn't. That way, no one would worry I might leak what was going on."

"Leak?" asks Carter, frowning. "Whatcha mean leak?"

"Telling secrets you're not supposed to," I say, before realizing that "leak" is a term from the future. *Which is exactly why Franklin doesn't want me talking,* I think.

"Leak," Carver repeats, then smiles. "I like that. And you surely is right about them gentlemens want'n to keep everything secret. Made me swear on the Bible I won't say nothin'. Like I can't keep a secret! Boy, I was in the war! We had plenty secrets!"

"I'll bet you did."

"Where we was goin' next, what we was gonna do when we got there. Never could be sure whose side anyone was on. So jest best to keep yore mouth shut. Anyways what do I care for their secrets? I cain't rightly understand what they're talking about. Don't care to neither, s'long as they pays me. But your secret? That I'll keep. Been watching you. You a little hot-headed. But you keeps your head down and works hard. I like a man who works hard. And I like a man who's on our side. You didn't have to give that money to the preachers."

"I want to help."

I hold out my hand and he takes it.

"Thanks, Mr. Carver. Means a lot," I say, keeping hold of his hand.

Dusk is coming on, and with it, more mosquitos. They're evil little suckers, biting right through my clothes. I'm not the only one slapping and scratching.

"We must go," Elise says, "before it is too dark. And I am gone longer than I said."

We say goodbye and soon are walking that foul-smelling dirt road. In the distance, I can just make out the weak glow of the whale-oil lamps that light the streets in the better parts of town. Franklin had designed a special glass globe for them so they wouldn't blacken with smoke. But here, there aren't any. Just the slow-fading light of dusk. And the mosquitoes. And the flies. And the maggoty dead cat I almost step in again.

"Nice folks," I say, hoping to take my mind off it. "Old Mrs. Carver's a real pistol."

When Elise doesn't answer, I glance over. She counts on her fingers while whispering to herself.

"What are you doing?" I ask.

"Shh!"

"Well, excuse the heck out of me!"

With an exasperated groan, she drops her hands.

"Counting, if you must know, Mr. Nosy."

"I got *that* already. What I mean is: why?"

But she'd gone back to her whispering finger-calculations. I can't make out much. But I do hear the word "tuppence." And that's enough.

"Mrs. Carver was right! You are going to —"

"Idiot! Again, I lose count!"

"I don't believe it! After everything you said. You're going to steal her business."

"No! Not steal. Help it!"

"Help it? How?"

"Well … I am not sure. She makes a good soup. And she works hard. But she makes only two pennies a bowl. For that, she must rise early, cook, carry her pot and bowls to the market, sell all the soup, pack and carry everything home, then prepare the next soup. Now, she says she makes two or three shillings each day. A shilling has twenty pennies. So, she must sell twenty or thirty bowls a day. And she said on many days, she runs out before many customers have eaten."

"So? What can you do about it?"

"What if I make the soup for her? She teach me and I make it. But I make more, which I can do because I am closer to the market. Instead of one pot, maybe two or three. And if she charges more? Three pennies, instead of two? If she sells twice the bowls, that would be forty to sixty bowls at three pennies a piece, or 120 to 180 pennies, or six to nine shillings a day. If she gave me a third, that would be two to three shillings for me and four to six for her. She would do better than now. I would begin making money for my mother and my son."

"Yeah, but you've already got a job."

"So? I have time that is my own. Also, I don't think Dr. Franklin or Mrs. Bache would refuse me to use their kitchen."

"Instead of going to all that trouble, why don't you just borrow the money from Franklin?"

"*Non! Absolument!* I already owe too much—the money he paid the captain for me—"

"Whoa! Franklin paid for you? You mean he bought you?"

"No! No, no. That is not what I mean. Not at all."

"Well then, what do you mean?"

"Never mind. I told you before, it is a bad story."

"About how you got here from France?"

"No, how I went to France."

"And?"

"Oh! You are so annoying with your questions!"

"It's true," I say, borrowing one of Franklin's self-satisfied smiles. "And you know what's really annoying? I never give up. I just keep asking until I learn what I want to know."

She half-growls, half-groans in frustration.

"All right! All right!" she says. "If absolutely you must know …"

CHAPTER 22

"I was born on a sugar plantation on Saint-Domingue. I grew up in the big house where *Maman* was cook. I was not chained or beaten, like those who worked in the fields. I learned my mother's recipes and to sew and keep the house. I grew to fifteen and knew everything so well the master, Claude, made me keeper of the house.

"He had a wife, but she did not like the plantation, although it belonged to her family. They owned a bank in Port-au-Prince and she spent most of her time there.

"Soon, Claude came to my bed. He said he loved me and gave me a baby.

"When *mon fils*...my son, little Adam, was born, Claude promised the child would stay with us and not go to the fields and one day have a tutor and go to France for school and be free.

"But then storms came to ruin the sugar. Claude could not pay money he owed. He tried the gambling, but he lost and his debt grew. He sold all he owned: horses for racing, jewelry, furniture, books. Then he had nothing except for the house servants he owned when he married, including *Maman.*"

"Sounds like a real prince," I say bitterly.

But my sarcasm is lost on her.

"Prince?" she asks dreamily. "Yes, I thought so. Such a strong, handsome man. So sure of himself and his future."

I've never seen a face go from dreamy to bitter so fast.

"I was such a foolish, foolish little girl! A man came, from Charleston I think. Claude was so happy. He said the man would take his problems away. He gave me money to go to the general store some miles away to pay the debt. It was an hour, maybe two, to ride there. But on the way, the horse went lame and I came back. When I arrived, I saw *Maman* and little Adam, chained, in the man's wagon.

"I ran to Claude. 'What is this?' I said.

"'They are sold,' Claude told me.

"I said, 'No! You cannot!'

"Claude said he must or be jailed for debt.

"I said, 'Sell me too! I cannot be away from my mother and son. Sell me with them!'

"He said no, I must stay to make more babies to replace what was sold. No one has ever made me so angry! I ran at him to beat him or kick him or—I don't know what—I hated him so! But his foreman took hold of me and with one hit to my head I was … I lost … how do you say? Conscience?"

"Consciousness?"

"Yes. When I woke I was in the foreman's hut in the cane field, tied with ropes. It was night. He was asleep. Drunk, I think, from rum. I got free and ran to the forest.

"I thought the buyer would take *Maman* and Adam to Port-au-Prince, so I went, hoping he would take me too. I walked three days to get there. I hid in woods and swamp if anyone came. My only food was wild mangoes. I waited for rain to drink because swamp water kills.

"Only one ship was there. I thought it must be taking *Maman* and Adam to America. Very late at night, I sneaked up to the ship—"

"It's sneaked *onto*—"

"*Mon dieu!* Up to, into, onto! Make up your mind! So, I went down. But there were no slaves, only barrels. I heard someone and hid among them. I was so tired, I fell asleep. When I woke, we were at sea. I stayed behind those barrels for days. I came out only very late to steal food from the galley. Then I was caught and taken to the captain.

"He wanted to throw me to the sea, since it was illegal to bring blacks to France. But I said his cook gave him and his crew food fit only for pigs, and I could give better. I would make them the best meal ever and he could throw me over if it was not.

"As you can see, I did not drown. The captain liked my food so much he smuggled me through Le Havre to his home in Passy, just outside Paris, to cook for his family. But his wife was jealous and did not want me.

"They fought. She wanted to send me to the camps they have in France for illegal blacks. Then one night, Doctor Franklin came with his friend John Paul Jones. Doctor loved my cooking and came several more times and talked to me and the captain and his wife, and it was arranged: I would work for Doctor and the captain and his wife would get money for their trouble.

"When Doctor left for Philadelphia, I came with him. Now I work to pay back the money he paid the captain and for my passage here. When that is finished, I can begin saving to find my mother and my son.

"So, that is my story. Are you satisfied now, Mr. Nosy?"

I'm speechless. I'm awestruck. She is so brave and strong, but also so alone. I can't help my heart from going out to her. I want to help her and make everything alright for her.

"I could give you the money Franklin pays me," I say after a silence that seems like forever. "I'm not really using it—"

"Are you crazy? Why would you do that?"

"Maybe because I like you?"

"You are silly! A silly boy!" There is nothing affectionate about the way she says that. "I would never do that for you. Money is too dear. And I will not owe you."

I keep my eyes to the ground. I can't have her seeing how badly she's wounded me. We walk in silence until just before reaching where the street is paved and lit.

"Hey boy," she says, putting her hand out to stop me. "I am not for you. Do you understand?"

"No," I say, stung and sullen.

"I am saying: there can be nothing between us."

"Who says—"

"I see how you look at me. But I am Negro and you are white and the law says there can be nothing between us. Besides, I am too old for you."

"No you're not."

"Very well. Then you are too young. I need either a man, or to be alone."

"I'm a man."

"Are you? I don't know. But even if you were black, I know you are not for me."

"How can you know that?"

"I know. You do not make me feel safe."

No one has ever said anything like that to me before. It makes me feel sick, like I've just been punched in the stomach.

Putting up her hand like a cop halting traffic, she motions for me to stay where I am, hidden in the dark. I watch as she steps into the lamplight provided by Franklin's globes, determined to do whatever I can to change her feelings.

***

We arrive home to a thoroughly annoyed Sally Bache.

"Where have you been, Elise? I said I could spare you for an hour. It's been almost three. There's bread that needs baking and linens to wash. Marcus, you're to go straight to the library. He's been calling for you every ten minutes, seems like."

I found Franklin at his desk reading the transcripts I'd finished.

"Finally! Where were you? There's work!"

"I went with Elise over to Mr. Carver's."

"Carver?"

"You know, the caretaker at the State House—"

"I know who Carver is," Franklin says. "I hired him."

"That's what he said."

"Did he now? And what else did you talk about?"

"Nothing. You shouldn't be mad at him. He seemed grateful."

"Why would I be angry with a man such as him? Wounded serving our cause? Employing him was the least I should do. Why were you at his home?"

"I went with Elise to hear the Reverend Jones and the Reverend Allen. They're starting—"

"The Free African Society. Yes, I know," he says brusquely.

"You don't approve?"

"To the contrary: I think mutual aid societies excellent. What I don't approve is you attending such a gathering, not in that part of town, not with you being white, and not with your knowledge of the future. I thought we agreed you weren't to talk to anyone outside this house."

"I didn't," I lie. "I just went with Elise to listen."

Franklin searches my face with a sharp, appraising look.

"How did it go with Washington?" I ask.

"My meeting with *General* Washington was uncomfortable. You were the topic. Fortunately, the general is my friend and knows I need you. But as I said earlier, you must never again make such a demonstration; otherwise, I daresay you and I *both* will be forcibly removed from that Assembly Room. Do I have your promise?"

I have no other choice, unless it's to spend my days cooped up in the house waiting for Franklin to figure out how to get me home.

"I promise," I say.

"Good. Now, to work."

"Wait a minute," I say. "Not until you tell me how you're going to get me back home."

"I am working on it, Marcus."

"That's what you always say."

"Yes, because it's true."

CHAPTER 23

The next day, nervous about the kind of reception I'll get after my outburst, I re-take my seat. Everyone seems calmer—perhaps because they've gotten past the issue of proportional voting. No one even glances at me.

Over the next few days, the delegates finish considering the Virginia Plan as a Committee of the Whole. Now, it's time to vote on whether to keep working on that plan as the full convention or scrap it and start all over again.

I'm certain I know how the vote will go. They've just spent three weeks deciding to have a national government supreme over the states, with power divided among three branches, all checking and balancing each other. Are they just going to throw that away? And for what instead? There's no other plan.

That's when I learn that nothing is certain in politics. Just as the Committee of the Whole is about to vote, New Jersey's William Paterson, the delegate who looks like a porcupine, asks for a recess to prepare one, which he comes in with the next day, which provides for a much weaker national government more beholden to the states.

The delegates spend the next few days debating his plan, and then another day listening to yet another plan from Alexander Hamilton, who wants to elect the president and senators for life—like the British monarchy and aristocracy—and to eliminate all the state governments. Hamilton's proposals aren't even discussed.

Finally, the delegates vote. And when they do, they reject the New Jersey Plan and decide to keep working on the Virginia Plan. They also dissolve the Committee of the Whole, returning George Washington to that throne-like chair on the dais.

Now the delegates' votes will really begin to count.

***

Full-on summer hits and that Assembly Room gets really uncomfortable. Secrecy requires that all the windows remain nailed shut. That may keep the flies and eavesdroppers away, but not the heat or the racket from Chestnut Street: iron horseshoes and wagon wheels crashing against cobblestones, whip cracks and drovers' cries, the moans of unhappy livestock, and all the shouting and banging from the court house construction next door. I have to really fight to hear. And with the heat? Usually by noon, I'm a sopping mess with one heck of a headache. All for the rule of secrecy.

Washington is a demon for that rule. One day, one of the delegates accidently drops his copy of the Virginia Plan somewhere on the State House grounds. The General is furious!

"Gentlemen!" he says icily, standing on the dais and glaring at everyone just before adjournment. "I am sorry to find that a member of this body has been so neglectful of the secrets of the convention as to drop this outside. I must entreat you to be more careful, lest our dealings get into the newspapers and disturb the public with premature speculations. I know not whose paper it is, but there it is," he says, tossing it on the table. "Let him who owns it take it!"

Amid stunned silence, Washington bows, picks up his hat, and stalks out ram-rod straight, leaving the delegates pop-eyed or open-mouthed. No one ever does pick up that paper.

The delegates spend the next two weeks debating the Virginia Plan all over again. They quickly agree the government "ought to consist of a supreme Legislative, Executive and Judiciary," much like they'd done as a Committee of the Whole. Only this time, instead of calling it the national government, they call it "the government of the United States."

And, after lots of back and forth, they agree again that the legislature will consist of two houses. Members of the House of Representatives will be elected by the people every two years and senators will be elected by the state legislatures to serve six year terms, with one third of the Senate elected every two years.

And when they return to the issue of proportional voting? They get stuck again! And again, it's big states (Massachusetts, Pennsylvania, and Virginia) versus the small states (all the rest). The small states don't want the big states swallowing them up, and the big states don't want the small states squandering their money. For days, the delegates argue, neither side giving an inch.

The Connecticut delegation proposes a compromise first suggested weeks ago by the odd-looking, one-time cobbler Roger Sherman: proportional voting in the House and equal voting in the Senate.

But that proposal seems only to make matters worse. Delegates start talking about the country breaking up and states going their own way or forming alliances with each other or foreign powers and the possibility of war.

On Friday, June 29, the delegates narrowly vote that the House of Representatives will be governed by proportional representation.

When the delegates turn to the Senate, Connecticut again proposes one vote for each state. The debate carries into the next day, a very hot and muggy Saturday, and a very bad one for the convention.

James Wilson says again how unfair it would be for the smaller states—whose combined populations make up less than a third of the country's total population—to be able to dictate to the larger states. "Can we forget for whom we are forming a government?" the Scotsman cries. "Is it for men, or for the imaginary beings called states?"

James Madison, his ally, follows. The small, thin, sometimes sickly-looking Virginian carefully lays down his quill and rises. Yes, there is a division between the states, he says. But it is not based on size. It is based somewhat on climate, but mostly on slavery. Therefore, the division is between North and South.

It's the first time I've actually heard anyone say that. It sends a chill through me because—as I read in the Lincoln biography Pop brought home for me to do my paper—he's just put his finger on what causes the Civil War.

But the point quickly dies. Franklin kills it when he rises and re-focuses everyone on the big state versus small state dispute, telling both sides that they must "part with something" in order to find a solution.

But they won't. In fact, Rufus King from the "large state" of Massachusetts and Gunning Bedford from the "small state" of Delaware really get into it. When Bedford warns that if the small states aren't treated fairly they'll turn to a foreign power for protection, King goes ballistic, accusing Bedford of being dictatorial.

With that exchange, the mood turns so dark and ugly that all I want to do is get out of there. Washington too, I guess, because he quickly adjourns the session, giving the delegates a day and a half to cool off.

On Monday, July 2nd, with the Fourth of July recess approaching, before anyone has a chance to say anything to make things worse, Washington has everyone vote on Connecticut's proposal to give each state one vote in the Senate. If a majority vote aye, the country will have a compromise Congress in which the House represents the people and the Senate represents the states.

Convention Secretary Major William Jackson calls the roll of states. As each votes, I keep score. By the end of the vote, there are as many Ayes as Nos. The convention is deadlocked!

One after another, delegates urge the formation of a committee to find a compromise and for the appointment of one delegate from each state; which is exactly what the convention votes to do. And who do they appoint to represent Pennsylvania on this "Grand Committee?" None other than that great advocate of compromise, my host and employer, Dr. Benjamin Franklin.

So much for my Fourth of July!

***

Out on Chestnut Street, I wait for Franklin for what seems like forever. When he finally comes, he walks and talks like a man twenty years younger.

"Come, Marcus! Lots to do if we are to be ready for this evening!"

As we're in public, my lips are sealed, but that doesn't stop me from frowning and shrugging to pose the obvious question.

"I have offered dinner to the entire committee tonight at the house. All will come at seven. It is now four. So, not much time. Run and tell Sally and Elise and say I said to order whatever they need from the Indian Queen. Some oysters, I should think, and crabs if we can get 'em; a mutton joint, a turkey or guinea hens, and a ham, and whatever else they've got. And drink! There must be plenty: porter, Madeira, claret, cider, ale, and rum. Nothing else predisposes the soul so well to compromise. Tell Sally to spare no expense. I'll want you upstairs, listening and making notes. Not verbatim, mind you; just note each man's position. I must be able to remember where everyone stands if we're to find a solution through conciliation."

It is hot and humid that night. But the mood in Franklin's garden is festive. The ale, wine, and rum flow. Elise passes amongst the committee members, offering oysters and clams, and drawing more than one appreciative look, which makes me jealous.

Franklin has me bring down his glass 'armonica, the musical instrument he invented. He's threaded a metal rod through a series of glass discs, each a different size; then cradled it in a wood box and connected it to a foot pedal that spins the discs. Each produces its own distinct tone when rubbed with a wet finger, just like with the rim of a glass. The sounds the 'armonica makes are beautiful, crystal-like and eerie, as if from another world. Franklin tells me that Mozart so loves the 'armonica that he wrote a piece especially for it.

Franklin doesn't play any Mozart that night. But he does end with "Yankee Doodle," which everyone cheers. Franklin rises and takes a very deep bow and I begin to suspect he can be a very large ham.

"Doctor, what is the recipe for this punch?" Luther Martin from Maryland asks, slurring his words. "I believe it is the finest I've ever tasted."

"High praise, indeed, Luther, coming from you," the normally cranky Elbridge Gerry from Massachusetts says. "Rumor has it you've just about reached the bottom of the Pennsylvania Assembly's store of rum."

"Yes, it is true, I have been known to enjoy a libation or two, from time to time."

"As have we all. As have we all," Franklin says soothingly and with a chuckle. "It is a concoction of Elise's. I will ask her to give you the recipe. Only take care not to drink too deep, otherwise like me, you'll come to know the dregs—like this blasted gout.

"Now, Gentlemen, a treat is in store. With this infernal heat, I thought dining indoors would be unpleasant. And so, this evening, we shall have what the French call *"un pique-nique."*

At his gesture, the door to the house opens and Sally and Elise and several serving girls from the Indian Queen come bearing platters and plates filled with food: a tureen of soup, a large turkey, a leg of mutton, a huge ham, hot and cold vegetables, several sorts of potatoes, and loaves of fresh baked bread. Torches are lit in the gathering dusk. The men serve themselves, heaping their plates high. Elise fills their glasses full of Franklin's cherished Madeira wine. Everyone eats off their laps on benches arranged in a loose semi-circle.

"What is this soup, Doctor Franklin?" Luther Martin asks. "Delicious. I love a good hot soup."

"Again, something Elise prepared. Quite the culinary magician!"

"Too much spice for this New Englander," Elbridge Gerry crabs.

"I know of no better way to combat the heat," Virginia's George Mason says.

The talk turns to personal matters: wives and children, crops and businesses in a disappointing economy, war experiences, how expensive Philadelphia is, and the hope for an end to the convention so everyone can go home.

"Gentlemen," Franklin says, seeing his opening, "if any of us are to return to our favored pursuits in the near future, we must find a solution. The small states want equality of voting, and the large states want proportional. How do we reconcile the difference?"

"Give each state one vote and be done with it!" Luther Martin snaps. "Every state entered into this confederation independent and expects to remain so. Maryland will not give up her sovereignty to be swallowed by Virginia. That I can assure you."

"My dear Mr. Martin," says George Mason. "Virginia has no designs on Maryland. *That* I can assure *you*."

"Can you say the same about Pennsylvania vis-à-vis my Delaware?" Gunning Bedford asks.

"Or my New Jersey?" William Paterson asks.

"Oh, you so-called small states!" cries Elbridge Gerry. "You are so intoxicated with your sovereignty! It will be the ruin of us! Listen, I was a member of the Continental Congress when those Articles of Confederation were drafted. I'll admit, I voted to allot a single vote to each state, even though I thought it was a bad idea. But the peril we were all in—what with the war and everything—demanded it. And so did you small states!

"But those Articles are defective. Look where they've brought us! In debt with no ability to repay! Neither trusted nor respected by anyone in Europe! No military to protect us! Fighting amongst each other! We must do something! Otherwise, we will disappoint not only America, but the whole world. If our Union fails, if we have no government, who will there be to settle the controversies between the states? What will become of our treaties? Who will pay the debts owed to our people and to Europe? We *all* must make concessions. After all, concessions were made when each one of our states adopted its own constitution. So must we in creating our national constitution."

"Yes. We must make concessions," George Mason agrees. "Too many people are talking about what will happen if this convention fails. States threatening to form combinations or to call on England or Spain for assistance is a bad business—a very bad business! Does anyone really want again to be under England's yoke?"

"Yes, but why should my Delaware give up the equal vote she has always been entitled to?" Gunning Bedford asks. "You still haven't explained that."

"And why should tiny Delaware, with less than 2% of the population, dictate to Massachusetts or any other state what it can and cannot do?" Gerry argues back. "Especially when the rest of the states pay 98% of the nation's expenses, including for Delaware's protection, should she need it."

"Gentlemen," says Connecticut's Oliver Ellsworth, "despite our difficulties, I still believe we can devise a good plan of government. The answer, I am convinced, still lies in having proportional voting in one chamber, and equal voting in the other. Our system is partly national, and partly confederated. Yes, we are one country, but a country made up of states. If we have proportional voting in the House, the big states will be protected from the possibly unreasonable demands of the small states. And if there is equality of voting in the Senate, the small states will be able to protect themselves against encroachment by the large."

"Depending on what powers you give to each chamber," George Mason says.

The delegates fall quiet then, so quiet I can hear the chirp of a cricket. Staying well back from the window, I look down into the garden. The torches have burned out. Fireflies dance in the dark, winking and twinkling like the nighttime lights on the Benjamin Franklin Bridge that won't be built for another 140 years.

"Say what you said again, George," Franklin says.

"I said, 'Depending on what powers you give to each chamber.'"

"That's what I thought you said. I think you may just have hit upon a very good idea."

CHAPTER 24

Franklin spends all the next day meeting with the committee at the State House while I stay behind transcribing. The delegates have a lot to say and I've fallen several days behind, which worries Franklin.

"You must keep me current, Marcus. Otherwise, I'll seem a dodderer and no one will listen to me," he says more than once.

It's clear, to me at least, that the delegates do listen to Franklin. They don't always follow his advice, but they listen. And sometimes, they even cool their tempers because of what he says. If my transcripts help him maintain his stature with the delegates, then I'll do everything I can to keep up-to-date. It looks like I'll need the rest of that day and the next—the Fourth of July—to catch up.

The coming Fourth stirs my own memories. It's always been an important holiday for my family, especially since Gus loved it so much. Some years, we'd go down to Penn's Landing to listen to the Philadelphia Orchestra as fireworks spangled the night sky over the Delaware River. And on the Independence Day before his deployment to Afghanistan, Gus had come home and we'd all gone to the big party along Franklin Parkway with its music and dancing and street food. Before the fireworks over the Philadelphia Museum of Art, just Gus and I took a walk along Boathouse Row. He told me that one of the reasons he'd gone into the Army was to get his college paid for so that there'd be enough money for me to go.

I'd never told Mom and Pop about that talk. I'd never told anyone. But it weighed on me. How many times had I blamed myself for his death? How many times had I thought: *if Gus had just gone to college and not worried about my future, he'd still be with us?* My 232 year distance from home had done nothing to lessen the pain or guilt I felt over Gus. But I had started to wonder whether it was part of the reason I'd stopped wanting to go to college.

The morning of the Fourth, Franklin and his family go to a special thanksgiving service at the Reformed Calvinist Church with Washington and other delegates. Elise goes to the Carvers. She doesn't invite me. In fact, since telling me I wasn't for her, she's pretty much ignored me. I keep looking for ways to do things for her—to be her hero, I guess. But there aren't any. She won't even take my wages. And money is what she wants most!

With everyone gone, I work quickly and actually finish around noon, which leaves me with nothing to do. It's too hot to stay inside, or even in the garden. The coolest place I can think of is down by the Delaware. I decide to go—maybe find a meal and also cool off and clean myself up with a swim (man, what I would give for a bar of Dial Soap and a stick of Right Guard). As for Franklin's not wanting me out alone? I'm pretty sure I've been around long enough to know enough to be okay.

Dressed in light cotton britches, linen shirt, and my straw hat, carrying money and the pass Franklin has given me, I leave the house. The heat hits me like I've opened an oven door.

Market Street is crowded. Fourth of July or not, it is also Wednesday—Market Day—and there are farmers, fisherman, butchers, and bakers with all kinds of goods. They call out their wares, eager to sell before the flies, hot sun, and stink of offal and manure rotting on the streets ruin what they'd worked so hard to harvest.

The day is cloudless. As the strong sun beats down, salty sweat pours off me. Along with shoppers, holiday merry-makers crowd the street, some weaving and rowdy, obviously drunk. One lurches into me, hard, knocking me off the sidewalk. As I stumble, my hat falls off and rolls into a gutter of filthy water.

"That'll teach ya' ta' get immy way, ya' great bloody donkey!" The man who'd pushed me cries.

I stare up into his leering, drunken face and suddenly see red. I bunch my hands into fists and am just about to launch myself at him when the rumble of wheels and the cry "make way!" makes me turn. Four fast-moving horses drawing a wagon bear down on me. I quickly back-pedal, slipping in horse manure, and just barely keeping upright. By the time the wagon passes, the drunk is gone.

My hat is ruined. After cleaning my shoes off in the very same gutter, I leave it there and head down Market for the river. I pass two women locked in the stocks, both with signs hanging around their necks. One reads "Perjurer," the other "Thief." A gang of youths throw all kinds of dirt and garbage at them while a watchman looks on and leers. He is the same watchman who'd stopped me and Franklin several weeks before.

The women are filthy with mud and who knows what else. A dead rat lies on the ground, directly in front of one. The watchman looks at me. His leer turns to a look of recognition. I quickly move on, starting to question whether this walk is a good idea.

At the City Hall in the center of Market Street, a large crowd has gathered under the wrought iron balcony, above which a large American flag with thirteen stars lazily furls and unfurls in the light breeze off the river. I look up with everyone else, wondering what we're all waiting for.

A long drum roll silences the crowd. A man steps out onto the balcony. He is dressed somberly in a black suit with white stockings, stock, and wig and carries a large paper.

"Here ye! Here ye!" he cries. "All persons seeking to know the contents of that certain declaration which did proclaim our separation from the kingdom of Great Britain and our independence from same, draw near and give your attention."

Holding the paper by its top and bottom, he reads out in a strong and steady voice:

IN CONGRESS, July 4, 1776.

The unanimous Declaration of the thirteen united States of America,

When in the Course of human events, it becomes necessary for one people to dissolve the political bands which have connected them with another, and to assume among the powers of the earth, the separate and equal station to which the Laws of Nature and of Nature's God entitle them, a decent respect to the opinions of mankind requires that they should declare the causes which impel them to the separation.

We hold these truths to be self-evident, that all men are created equal, that they are endowed by their Creator with certain unalienable Rights, that among these are Life, Liberty and the pursuit of Happiness.—That to secure these rights, Governments are instituted among Men, deriving their just powers from the consent of the governed …

I'd tried reading the Declaration of Independence a couple of times, for school. But I'd never gotten much out of it. All that old-time language made it such a chore. Now, though, the pride, the *passion*, in this man's voice commands me to really focus on the story that Thomas Jefferson and the Continental Congress had sought to tell the world: how the King of England had abused his power and established an absolute tyranny over citizens having a God-given right to live freely and pursue happiness, and who had repeatedly and respectfully asked for relief, only to be answered with more abuse.

And then comes that final paragraph:

We, therefore, the Representatives of the united States of America, in General Congress, Assembled, appealing to the Supreme Judge of the world for the rectitude of our intentions, do, in the Name, and by Authority of the good People of these Colonies, solemnly publish and declare, That these United Colonies are, and of Right ought to be Free and Independent States; that they are Absolved from all Allegiance to the British Crown, and that all political connection between them and the State of Great Britain, is and ought to be totally dissolved; and that as Free and Independent States, they have full Power to levy War, conclude Peace, contract Alliances, establish Commerce, and to do all other Acts and Things which Independent States may of right do. And for the support of this Declaration, with a firm reliance on the protection of divine Providence, we mutually pledge to each other our Lives, our Fortunes and our sacred Honor.

By the time he's finished, my arms are prickled into gooseflesh, despite the heat of the day. A great cheer rises as a uniformed rifle company fires volleys in salute.

Slowly, the crowd disperses. My stomach growls. I haven't eaten since breakfast. I continue towards the river, looking for someplace to eat.

I come to the London Coffee House at the corner of Front and Market. Franklin has said that this is where some Philadelphia merchants and traders come to eat, drink, and do business.

A wood awning supported by columns shades the front of the coffee house. A black man dressed in a sweat-darkened osnaburg shirt stands at one of the columns, swaying from side to side. At first, I think he's drunk. But as I come closer, I see that his wrists are manacled around the column. Blurry, red-brown lines crisscross the back of his wet shirt. His eye is bruised so badly it's almost closed and his bottom lip is swollen and split. His bare feet leave bloody tracks on the veranda's dusty, raw-wood boards.

"What happened to you? Who did this?" I say.

The man doesn't answer. He won't even look at me.

"Hey," I say. "I want to help you. What can I do to help?"

Just as I reach for the manacles to see how they might be unlocked, the door to the coffee house opens and Johnathon Swinbourne steps out. He does not see me because he is talking to the large black man who'd helped chase the slave up Market Street several weeks ago. Now, that man has a short-handled cat o' nine tails shoved in his belt.

"Right, Lucas, take this one back across the river," Swinbourne says. "If he makes any trouble, give him another couple of stripes with that cat, or its butt end in his other eye. Can't run if he can't see. No need to be gentle. He'll have plenty of time to heal on the voyage south."

"Money," Lucas says.

Swinbourne hands over a leather pouch. Lucas unties it to look inside.

"Here, don't stop to count it now!" Swinbourne says. "It's all there. Have I ever shorted you?"

Lucas tips all the coins into his hand and carefully counts. Apparently satisfied, he frees the slave from the column, ties him with a long rope to the saddle on a waiting gray mare, mounts the horse, and leads the slave into Market Street, heading for the river.

With mounting fury, I watch the slave struggle to keep up with the fast-walking horse. The cobblestones must be torturing his already bloody feet. Several times he trips and almost falls. Lucas never slows. The slave can walk or be dragged; it is all the same to the slave catcher.

Slowly, I become aware of Swinbourne watching me. He's staring at me pop-eyed and red-faced, as though outraged by my outrage.

"Here, you! What are you looking at?"

Remembering above all to keep silent, I press my lips together, grit my teeth, and shrug.

"I know you. You're Franklin's servant. The one he sent to eat in the kitchen at the Indian Queen."

Rage wells up in me.

"Well? Answer me, you bloody great fool! Whatcha' looking at?"

Fool? My hands ball into fists again, just like when I'd been pushed into the street, and I step towards him.

He shrinks back.

"What? You threatening me? Raising your hand? For that, you'll get a bloody good whipping. Constable!" he yells.

That brings me back to my senses. I quickly turn away to walk up Market.

"No use running away!" he calls. "I know just where to find you. Tell your Mr. Franklin, I and the constable will attend him shortly."

CHAPTER 25

I don't stop running until I reach Franklin's. By the time I get there, I'm soaked in sweat—as much from fear as from the heat. I look down the alley to the carriageway to see if Swinbourne and a constable are following. I wait in the open doorway, but no one comes.

"Marcus, close that door!" Sally Bache cries. "You're letting in all the flies."

I turn to see her and Franklin coming down the stairs. He is in a bathing shirt and dressing gown and has his arm around her shoulders. She struggles under his weight, even though she is large-framed and strong. Franklin's face is gray and sweaty.

"What happened?" I ask, going to help them.

"I might ask the same of you," Franklin says hoarsely. "You look a wreck—"

"Nothing happened," Sally says crossly, cutting off her father, "except that the service and oration were so long in that heat that father's stone decided to have its own revolution."

"There's that humor I so adore," Franklin says, "sour as lemons. Perhaps grandson Benjy should hire you as his almanac writer."

"Hush, Father! Save your strength."

"I'm not dying, for pity's sake. All I need is a cooling bath."

"Marcus, with Elise not here, I need you to fill father's tub," Sally says.

"And I'll need you to help me into it, I'm afraid," Franklin says. "Once you have me settled, retrieve your notebook. I have dictation."

"Father, no!" Sally protests. "No work!"

"It isn't much, daughter. Before the service, the committee found a solution. My memory being what it is, I need to get it on paper before I muddle the terms."

As quickly as I can, I make the ten trips to the pump to fill the bath, get Franklin situated, and fetch my notebook.

"How do you feel? Better?" I ask.

"Most refreshed," he says, no longer gray but still looking tired. "Use that to write on." He points to the broad plank he sometimes lays across the tub as a desk. "All right, here is the compromise the committee will suggest:

"First, in the Senate, every state will have one senator and one vote. As such, small states will have just as much say as the large states, and will be able to protect themselves from encroachments.

"Second, in the House, voting will be proportional. Each state will have one representative for every 40,000 of its citizens. That means large states will have more votes and shouldn't have to worry about small states telling them what to do.

"Third, all money bills — all taxation and spending — will be limited to the House and will not be subject to change by the Senate. Since large states will have more votes, small states should not be able to waste their tax dollars.

"There, that's it. That's all of it. Well? What do you think?"

"What do I think? I ... I... don't know."

"Marcus, you have been in that chamber for five weeks. You must have some opinion."

"Oh, I have an opinion. But not about how Congress votes. You need to abolish slavery."

He looks at me unhappily.

"I don't believe we will. Not here, not now. The southern states believe that slavery is indispensable—that their economies depend on it. I've already had the abolition society ask me to present a petition to the convention. I had to refuse them. And I'm their President."

"Why? Why would you refuse?"

"Why? Marcus, you've seen how contentious things are. Most delegates thought they were coming here simply to revise the Articles of Confederation—to make adjustments to the present government so that it would run more smoothly—not design a new government to take substantial amounts of power away from the states they've sworn to serve.

"If we now tell the southerners they must also give up their slaves, I daresay they will walk out and we will be left without even a confederation. I truly believe abolition will come, but now is not the time. Understand?"

"Yes, I understand. But I don't agree. You'd stop a lot of suffering if you outlawed slavery now."

His look becomes even unhappier. But then he peers at me.

"I still don't understand why you take this so personally."

"I dunno," I say, shrugging.

"That's no answer. How do you expect anyone to respect your opinion if you are not willing to defend and explain it?"

I don't want to talk about my reasons because I'm embarrassed.

"Now, why is this so important to you?" he presses.

"Because I hate seeing what's being done: the beatings, the cruel treatment, the complete lack of respect for them as people, as human beings. They're treated like animals because they're considered animals and it makes me sick. It goes against everything I've ever been taught. And I hate the way it makes bullies out of the people who own and trade in slaves. It makes them cruel."

"Aha, now we're getting to it! So, it is personal with you. Because you have been bullied?"

I don't want to answer that. Yes, I'd been bullied as a freshman in high school, for being a geeky, nerdy, straight-A student with a name that pegged me as coming from an immigrant family. Gus, a senior, had put a stop to it and I was embarrassed by that—by both the bullying and Gus's stepping in. Also, I've seen the way Penny is sometimes treated because she's black; and I hate that too. I don't want to admit to Franklin that my reasons are personal. It sounds selfish; and I want Franklin to think I'm noble. But I'm also curious to find out how he knows.

"What makes you think so? Did I tell you that the last time I was here?"

"No, no. I just thought I recognized a fellow sufferer. You see, I was bullied by my brother when I was his apprentice. There was nothing I could do about it because he was also my master. Since then, I have always hated the very idea of arbitrary power—of being under someone else's control. I wondered if that was something we have in common."

"Maybe," I concede.

He looks at me sharply again.

"Will this be a problem for you at the convention? We're not done with the slavery question yet. Not by any means. Must I worry about you making another unseemly display?"

"No," I say.

"You promise? I have your word?"

"You have my word."

"Good. Now, help me out of this and upstairs so that I may dress and visit with my grandchildren in the garden."

As we go upstairs, his arm over my shoulders and my arm around his waist, he wrinkles his nose.

"I suggest you wash. Like last month's strawberries, you are overripe. Where did you go this afternoon that you have returned in such a state?"

Even in his eighties, Franklin doesn't miss much.

"I went to the market looking for something to eat."

"Alone? Hmm … " he says, tilting back his head and looking at me through the bottoms of his bi-focals. "So? Tell me. What did you find?"

Trouble, I want to say. But I'm not sure I should tell him about Swinbourne. On the one hand, I'm worried about what might happen if the trader and constable come. On the other, if they haven't shown by now, they probably won't; and I really don't need a lecture about staying out of trouble.

Forewarned is forearmed, Pop's voice whispers in my head, *and better safe than sorry.*

"Yeah, I was meaning to talk to you about that."

"What?" Franklin asks warily as we reach the top step.

Below, the front door opens and an excited Elise hurries in, looking directly up at us. I've never seen her smile like that: joyful; her face glowing. It makes me a little afraid. Something has happened to make her very happy; and I'm not part of it.

"Dr. Franklin!" she calls, running up the stairs. "Dr. Franklin, I have a favor to ask."

"Help Marcus help me to my dressing room so I can change and you may ask anything you like. I don't promise my answer will be yes. But I promise to listen."

We get Franklin to his dressing room and, at his direction, fetch him a linen shirt, stockings, buckled shoes, and the britches to his lightweight, plain brown suit. He steps behind a screen to dress.

"What is the favor, Elise?"

She takes a deep breath.

"Doctor, you know I wish to find my son and my mother who went with a trader from the Carolinas. I have learned of a man who might help. But he would have to travel to search and wants money. Also, if he finds them, he will need money to buy them."

"Oh yes, quite a lot, I should think," Franklin says. "Are you asking for a loan?"

"*Non!* You have done too much already. I cannot be so much in your debt."

"An admirable position. So, what do you propose?"

"You know the Carvers."

"Quite well."

"Mrs. Carver would like me to help her business."

Now in his stockings, shirt, and britches, Franklin steps from behind the screen.

"Aha! That's where that pepper pot came from several nights ago. I thought I recognized it. But what kind of help does she want?"

"You know, she is old and she lives so far from the market. There is only so much soup she can bring. Every day, it is gone before all her customers have been fed. But we are right here. If I make the soup downstairs and help sell, we could feed everyone and make two or three times as much—maybe several pounds for me every week. This money I would use, first to pay my debt to you, and then to find my family."

"Well, I'm certainly not going to turn up my nose at a chance of repayment. But have you talked to Sally about this?"

"*Non.* I thought it better to talk with you. You are the head of the house and it is you I owe the money to—"

"And because you know Sally will not be happy since it is she who will be most inconvenienced," Franklin says, his eyes twinkling.

"I would work hard to prevent that."

"I know you would. And I applaud you wanting to do this. It reminds me of me when I was young. Are you sure I can't persuade you to take the loan? It would make my life much easier with Sally."

"Really, I would prefer not."

"Then you have my permission. Use our kitchen. Help Mrs. Carver. But only in your spare time. If you are going to continue to live and work here, your first commitment must be to this house. Agreed?"

"*D'accord.*"

"Good … and maybe you ought to let me talk to Sally."

"*D'accord.*"

"Talk to me about what?" Sally asks as she bustles into Franklin's dressing room.

"Er …" Franklin begins. But Sally cuts him off with a chop of her hand.

"There's men for you at the front door, Father."

"Men? What men?"

"The Chief Constable for one. And he's brought that fellow Swinbourne. And also the tailor, Mr. Wimpole."

"And? What do they want?"

"However should I know? To talk to the great Benjamin Franklin, I should suppose."

"Saucy girl!"

***

"I think I know what this is about," I whisper in his ear as we come to the stairs.

He shoots me a sharp look.

"Hush! Not another word!" he whispers back.

The three men look up at us. My mouth goes dry.

"Welcome gentlemen," Franklin calls down. "What may I do for you on this most patriotic of days? A contribution to some civic endeavor perhaps?"

"Hardly, Franklin," Swinbourne says.

"We've come to take your clerk," the Chief Constable says.

"That young devil propping you up," Swinbourne says.

"Whatever for?" Franklin asks.

"He raised his hands to me," Swinbourne says.

"Did he? That's quite serious. Well, now I understand your reason for being here. And yours, Chief Constable. But what about you, Timothy Wimpole? Why are you here? What's a tailor want with a set of shackles?"

162

"Tailor Wimpole is the newest member of the constabulary," the Chief Constable says. "I'm instructing him in our ways."

"Ah. Is tailoring no longer to your liking, Timothy?"

"Man's got to do something to earn a living when times is hard."

"Yes, and when the tailor's forgotten how to measure," Franklin quips.

I almost laugh over that one. But a scowling Wimpole doesn't think it's funny.

"Now, what happened?" Franklin says. "Mr. Swinbourne, you say my clerk raised his hands to you. Why ever would he do such a thing?"

"I called him out for staring at me and he raised his hands, threatening me."

"Is this true, Marcus? Did you raise your hands to him?"

I shake my head.

"He's a liar," Swinbourne growls.

"Is he now? Are you, Marcus? Are you a liar?"

I shake my head again, emphatically. Now I'm so offended, my hands are balled up.

"There!" Swinbourne cries, pointing. "Look how he makes his fists!"

"Is that what he did when you called him out for staring at you?" Franklin asks Swinbourne.

"Exactly so!"

"I hardly call that raising his hands," Franklin says. "Indeed, they are down by his sides."

"But look at the way he's made them fists!" Swinbourne splutters.

"Yes? And what of it? A man may clench his hands for many reasons: pain, fright, joy, fear, or maybe because his palms itch. Perhaps you misunderstood."

"I didn't misunderstand anything!"

"We ain't going to be able to sort this out standing here," the Chief Constable says. "Best I take him over to the jail and he can wait for the magistrate to decide what's what. Mr. Wimpole, put the shackles on him."

I take several steps back. I'm not about to let anyone haul me off.

"Just a minute!" Franklin's voice, now deep and strong, makes us all go still.

"Constable, you are arresting an innocent man upon no evidence whatsoever. And you are doing it in the home of the President of Pennsylvania. Now, I admit, I have little authority over city matters, or the workings of the constabulary, but I assure you I have many friends who do: friends who determine who the City of Philadelphia will and will not employ. If you continue with this, there will be serious consequences.

"And Mr. Swinbourne, your ability to do business as a merchant-trader depends much upon your reputation, both here in this country and in London and Paris. I am well known and I am listened to. You can imprison this young man unjustly, if you like, but I assure you there will be the direst repercussions, for you, personally, and your business interests."

"What?" Swinbourne laughs incredulously. "You'd do that for him? A mere lad?"

"I'd like to say I would do that for any innocent man wrongly accused. But the truth is you aren't doing this because Marcus threatened you, but because of your personal dislike of me over my stance on slavery and for embarrassing you at the Union Fire Company meeting and because you want to brag you've bested me. In other words, you are trying to hurt someone having nothing to do with our feud in order to get at me. That I cannot allow.

"It's up to you, gentlemen, either persist in this business or leave my house. But do one or the other quickly for my grandchildren and our dinner await."

The constable runs his hand over his mouth and looks to Swinbourne.

"Y'ain't got any more'n the ball'n of his hands? Careful now, you was out on the street and there's sure to be witnesses. Man like you—successful and all—don't need a perjury charge."

Swinbourne is red-faced with anger.

"Franklin, you haven't heard the last of this," he barks. Shouldering his way past the constable, he yanks open the front door. "Well, Wimpole, come if you're coming!"

Dragging the shackles meant for me, Wimpole follows Swinbourne.

With a raised eyebrow, Franklin looks to the constable.

164

"Aye, Wimpole is Swinbourne's man," he says. "I'd be careful if I was you, Dr. Franklin. Swinbourne's got powerful friends too. That's how Wimpole got this position."

"How interesting, constable! How very, very interesting," Franklin says as he goes to the man, puts a hand on his shoulder, and begins guiding him towards the garden. "Anything else I should know? Perhaps you would like to stay for dinner and a very fine Madeira?"

CHAPTER 26

We return to the State House the next morning, July 5th. My solemn promise to Franklin that I'll hold my temper is still fresh in my heart. I feel very grateful towards him for saving me the night before. That gratitude makes me even more determined to keep my promise.

The Grand Committee recommends its compromise: proportional voting in the House, which would have one representative for every 40,000 citizens; one vote per state in the Senate; and the House having exclusive control over taxing and spending.

Despite everyone's hope for quick approval, they wrangle for the next ten days: mostly over how many representatives each state will get in the House and how to ensure that each state's share of representatives keeps current with shifts of population between states.

It is Virginia's Governor, Edmond Randolph, who proposes that a census be taken periodically to count each state's population. I'm familiar with the census because I'd sat with Pop as he filled out the required form back in 2010. But I never knew it was required by the Constitution—or that it helped slavery find its way into the Constitution.

Southern delegates insist slaves be fully counted to increase population numbers and increase southern votes in the House. Northern delegates don't want slaves counted at all.

The debate itself really tests my resolve to keep my promise to Franklin.

"The labor of a South Carolina slave is just as productive and valuable as that of a Massachusetts freeman," Pierce Butler proclaims. "Since wealth provides great defense and utility to the nation, slaves are as equally valuable to the nation as are freemen. Consequently, equal representation should be allowed for slaves in a government which is being instituted principally for the protection of property; and is itself supported by that property."

Virginia's George Mason disagrees.

"Even though this would benefit my state, it would be unjust," he says. "Yes, slaves are valuable. They raise the value of land, increase exports and imports and thereby generate revenue for the government to feed and support an army. In cases of emergency, they can even become soldiers themselves. Since they are useful to the community, they shouldn't be excluded when calculating representation. But I can't regard them as equal to freemen; and could not vote for that calculation."

Nor can Pennsylvania's Gouverneur Morris.

"I don't agree that blacks should be admitted into the census. The people of Pennsylvania would revolt at the idea of being put on a footing with slaves. They would reject any plan that would have such an effect."

Referring to blacks as wealth? Calling them useful? Warning of revolt amongst whites if they were compared to blacks? What kind of world was I living in?

And I don't know what to make of Gouverneur Morris. Later that afternoon, it seems like he's on our side when he says: "If I am forced to the choice of doing injustice to the Southern states or to human nature, I must do it to the Southern states. I could never agree to encourage the slave trade by allowing the South representation for their Negroes."

But then the next morning, he proposes that states and their citizens be taxed in the same proportion as their share of congressional representation. In other words, if a state has 20% of the population, it should have 20% of the seats in the House and pay 20% of the national taxes. It's clever—I have to give Morris that—because it means that the more representatives a state has the more tax it will have to pay. If slaves are counted in the census, slave states will have more House seats, but also higher taxes.

Clever or not, it just about sends North Carolina's William Davie into orbit.

"It is high time to speak out!" he thunders. "I can see that some gentlemen mean to deprive the Southern states of any representation for their blacks. North Carolina will never confederate on any terms that do not rate them at least as three-fifths. If the Eastern states mean to exclude them altogether, our business is at an end!"

Good! Walk on out! I want to shout.

Then Gouverneur Morris rises again.

"It's been said that it's high time to speak out, and I will do so candidly," he says, his peg leg thumping as he paces. "I came here to form an agreement for the good of America. I'm ready to do so with all the states. I hope and believe that all will enter into that agreement. But if they will not, I am ready to join with any states that will. It is useless for the Eastern states to insist on what the Southern states will never agree to. It is equally useless for the Southern states to require that which the other states will not agree to. The people of Pennsylvania will never agree to the inclusion of Negroes."

A tense silence takes over that hot, muggy room where delegates have cast off wigs, removed coats, unbuttoned collars, and wave fans under sweaty chins.

But then, delegates from Connecticut, Virginia, and Pennsylvania suggest a new compromise: that all white inhabitants and three-fifths of black inhabitants be counted when calculating each state's share of representation in the House and of the nation's taxes.

The "three-fifths of black inhabitants" was the compromise between the South's demand to count blacks fully and the North's refusal to count black's at all. A census would take place within six years of the first meeting of the new Congress and every ten years after that.

That motion passes: six states in favor, two against, and two divided.

Now that they've settled how to determine each state's representation in the House, it's time to vote on the Grand Committee's entire compromise. Including all the changes made since July 5th, that compromise proposes:

1. that Congress consist of the House of Representatives and the Senate;

2. that the House initially consist of sixty-five seats parceled out amongst the states according to estimated percentages of population;

3. that a census be taken within six years of Congress's first meeting, and every ten years after that, to determine the population of each state, counting all whites and three-fifths of blacks, and that both taxes and House seats be reapportioned according to each census;

4. that all taxing and government spending bills originate in the House; and that the Senate have no power to change them; and

5. that every state have an equal vote in the Senate.

First thing Monday morning, July 16th, before anyone can raise another objection or suggest another change, the delegates vote. By the slimmest of margins—one vote—they agree to accept the "Connecticut Compromise."

CHAPTER 27

The day is rainy and sullen. Maybe that's why no one cheers the "Connecticut Compromise." Or maybe it's because a lot of people don't like it. I, for one, think the whole "three-fifths" thing stinks.

After adjournment, prisoners from the jail carry Franklin home in his sedan so he won't get wet. I walk and get soaked.

We have a late afternoon supper of cold chicken for me and mush for Franklin up in the library. Franklin reaches over and filches my drumstick, leaving me only a thigh.

"You can't have that!" I say.

"Oh, bother," he says crankily. "I paid for it. I'll eat it if I like. Have Elise bring you the other. Or cook another chicken and I'll help you eat that too."

"I mean because of your health. Not with all the butter and salt and pepper she uses."

"My health! I have given up quite enough for my health! Wine, spirits, oysters, beef and all the other foods I like. I work every day with the dumbbell. A tiny drumstick will cause no harm."

He is tired. I can tell from the dark patches under his eyes and the whispery hoarseness in his voice. I am too. The late evenings, the early mornings chopping wood for Elise, the days spent racing to copy the debates in that tense hot-house of an Assembly Room, the nights sweating in that garret, airless even with the trap open—they've all taken their toll.

I suggest we take a break.

"Nonsense!" Franklin says, scowling behind his heavy bi-focals. "'Never leave that 'til tomorrow which you can do today.' People have kindly written. I would be churlish not to respond. Here! Here's one from my old friend John Paul Jones. Do you know? I helped get him his ship from the French. He named it *Bonhomme Richard* after my 'Poor Richard' of the Almanac. He asks how the convention goes."

"What will you tell him?" I ask, curious to know what Franklin really thinks. We've been so busy we've had no time to talk.

"I shall tell him it goes well. We will need the support of men like him—our war heroes—if our new government is to succeed."

"But you don't think so."

"Oh, but I do! I think it is going very well, despite all the tumult."

"How can you say that?"

"The delegates were confronted with a very fractious issue, one that easily could have caused them to throw up their hands, go home, and say these thirteen states can never be united. But they persisted in trying to find an agreement; and they succeeded! Is this compromise to everyone's liking? Most definitely, no. Are there some, even many, who are more than a little unhappy? Most definitely, yes. But, it is a compromise all can live with."

He's proud of himself. I can tell from his smile and the way he leans back in his chair with his hands folded over his mound of a stomach. And that makes me angry.

"A compromise everyone can live with? Really? Seriously? How about black slaves? You think they can live with slavery? With being regarded as three-fifths human?"

"I know, Marcus. I know. I am doing all I can. But, as I've said, this is neither the time nor the place to fight for abolition."

"If not now, then when?" I ask, borrowing an expression of Pop's that Gus had adopted for his own.

"Soon."

"Oh yes, soon. Same thing you say about getting me home."

Franklin sighs, like a locomotive bleeding off the last of its steam. As he does, he seems to shrink. A mournful expression molds his features.

"I'm sorry," I say. "That was out of line—uncalled for."

"No, no," he whispers. "You are quite right. But, do you know, Marcus? Suddenly, I am quite tired. Let us take your suggestion and put all this off until tomorrow."

***

I help Franklin to his room and into his nightshirt and bed.

Even though I'm tired, it's only 7:00 p.m. and still light out. Plus, I'm hungry again, made even more so by the aromas coming from the dining room as Sally and the children have an evening tea for their supper.

I find Elise and Mrs. Carver in a kitchen full of meats, vegetables, and spices, slicing and dicing as fast as anyone on *Top Chef.* And I hear wood being split in the wood room.

"What are you all doing?" I ask.

Elise looks at me sharply.

"What does it look like? Cooking! Working! Making the pepper pot! We start tomorrow."

Her voice is impatient, but she looks so beautiful, working hard like that. Purpose and perspiration set her face aglow in the light from the kitchen's hearth fire and candle lanterns.

"Anything to eat?" I ask quickly, to hide my mooning.

"You have already had supper," Elise says.

"I know, but Franklin ate most of it. Don't I get tea?"

"When we have ours, if you must."

"Maybe you should make him work for his tea," Mrs. Carver half-whispers to Elise with a wicked, teasing gleam in her eye.

I know she doesn't mean it, since I'm white and, in this time and place, whites don't work for blacks. But I leap at the chance, finally, to be able to do something for Elise.

"Sure, I'll help. What do you need?"

"Here," Mrs. Carver says, holding out two wooden buckets. "Fill these with water for boiling … please."

When I present her with two full buckets, she trades them for empty ones. After my sixth bucket, she says: "That's fine, fine. Thank ye kindly. Now, if you're still of a mind to work, Mr. Carver needs help with that wood. He ain't as young nor as strong as he thinks."

I go to the wood room. Mr. Carver, shining with sweat, gratefully hands me the axe and begins stacking the wood he's split. The copper "electrical water heater" Franklin had been testing when I arrived still stands in the corner. Franklin has done nothing with it since that day.

An hour later, wood stacked, four pots of soup simmering, and all the Bache family's dishes washed and put away, we sit down to our own tea. Elise gives us each a bowl of the pepper pot, a square of buttered corn bread, and a large mug of strong, dark tea.

"You'se a hard-worker," Mr. Carver says. "Same as you is down to the convention. You should see him," he says to Elise and his mother. "All day long, he jes writes and writes and writes. All them men talk and he copies it all down."

"Where be the good in all that?" Elise asks. "Of what use?"

"Well, I don't know. But Doctor Franklin, he finds it useful. Some of them gentlemens was meeting upstairs over to the State House. I brung 'em the ale they asked fer and there's Franklin showing one of t'others what he done said ten days before."

A warm prickle of pride goes through me when I hear that.

"Don't understand what they all meeting fer anyways," Mrs. Carver grumbles.

"Tryin' to build us all a new govmint," Mr. Carver answers.

"What they want to do that fer?"

"Cuz the one they got ain't no good, I guess."

"Doctor Franklin, he says we must have a government that is chosen by the people and that is for the people," Elise says. "No more kings or princes or English or French or Spanish saying what to do. America is to be for Americans to say what is right and it must have a government everyone can be proud of."

"Everyone? I surely don't know about everyone," Mrs. Carver says. "Matter of fact, I knows people who want them Britishers back!"

"What people?" Elise asks hotly.

"They was two fellows jawing over to my stall just yesterday—one of 'em that new constable. Said to that Swinbourne fella' he wanted to fight the war all over again, and this time things'd be different. And that your Mr. Franklin'd get what's coming to him."

"Doctor Franklin," Elise corrects. "He said that?"

"Sure did. That and how Doctor Franklin and the rest of all them at the convention was traitors that oughta be hung—them and anyone else who won't swear they's loyal to the King. And t'other one, he agrees, saying they'd all go to hell or get blown to hell or some such thing and that the British was just waiting to swoop down from Canada to take back all they lost."

"Yeah, like that's really gonna happen," I blurt; and then kick myself because I've said it relying on my knowledge of the future.

"Whatchew know about it?" Mrs. Carver snaps, her bottom lip curled.

"Mama? Why you got to be so harsh?" Mr. Carver says.

"Did I ask his opinion? No, I did not!"

"I didn't mean to—" I start, but she cuts me off.

"I's treated bad enough at the market! Don't need it here. Fat pumpkin-head slave-trader telling me get out his sight while he eats my soup? Shoulda spit in it!"

"Oh Lord, don't do that," Mr. Carver says. "They'll put you in the stocks, if you's lucky."

We fall silent; and stay that way a long time.

But then Mr. Carver gets to his feet, all forced enthusiasm.

"What time you ladies plan start'n tomorrow?"

"What time I start every morning?" Mrs. Carver answers. "Five o'clock. Something different about tomorrow?"

"Well, sure! Two of you'se gonna be selling from two different places. I got to get here and load up the handcart in time. I done brung it tonight, by the way, Missy 'Lise. So's I don't have to drag it all that way in the dark tomorrow morning. It be right outside the side door, all waiting fer loading. I'll be here at 4:30, then. Give me plenty of time to get you all situated and be over to the State House by 6:00."

"Since you got the cart here," Mrs. Carver says, "maybe you kin stay home. Sleep late."

"What you mean?"

"Well, you been tellin' us what a good worker the boy is. Let him do it."

All three faces turn to me. I really don't want to get up at 4:00 a.m. Or lug whatever I have to lug over to Market Street. Then again, maybe this is another chance to do something for Elise.

"Okay," I say. "Happy to do it."

A stony look from Elise is the only answer I get.

CHAPTER 28

The rain clears out, taking all the humidity with it, and the next day breaks bright and clear. I'm up to see it. I help Mrs. Carver set up near Second and Market and then meet Elise on the south side of Market at Fourth, where her stand will be. When I get back to Franklin's, I go straight to the cellar to split the day's wood.

I'm finished by six and working in the library with Franklin by six-thirty. We work hard through the morning, catching up, and then walk together through sunny, rain-washed streets to the convention.

"I saw you from my window, loading up the cart. Are you to become part of this business?" Franklin asks as we wait on a corner for a carriage to pass. You can answer, by the way. I think you've made enough progress learning our ways that you may begin to talk in public."

Finally! I think. Indeed, I've been working hard to learn to walk, talk and move like a man from 1787. I've picked Washington and Hamilton as my models, trying to move as gracefully as the General and to speak with as much straightforwardness as Hamilton.

I say to Franklin, "I'm just giving whatever assistance I can. Do you disapprove?"

"Not the work itself. Possibly your motives. Although 'disapprove' is not the word I would choose. 'Worry' puts a better name to it."

"Worry?"

"Yes. I see how you look at Elise. We all do: Elise, Sally, even the children. A romance would be most unwise."

"Really?" I say, my temper starting to rise. "And why, pray tell, would that be?"

"Well … aside from the fact that such a romance would contravene the law and outrage society, there is also the fact that you will be leaving.

I know that as surely as I know the names of my children. If Elise grows to have feelings for you, to depend on you, what will she be left with when you are gone?"

Despite my new-found permission to speak, I can only fume. Mostly because I know he's right.

***

No matter how tired we might get, the pace never lets up, especially not at the convention. It seems like "The Connecticut Compromise" has put the delegates in a mood to get things done. Over the next two weeks they make a number of decisions as they hurry to set the basic framework of the government.

For instance, they agree the executive will be a single person instead of a committee; and that there will be a Supreme Court and lesser courts to decide cases involving the laws passed by Congress.

They also decide that federal law will supercede conflicting state laws.

There's a great deal of debate over how to elect the president, and who should elect him. Some want the people to vote. Others argue the people will never know enough to select the best man, or that they'll be so prejudiced for candidates from their own states that no one will ever gain a majority. Those folks want Congress to elect the president.

But others say that will make the president too eager to curry Congress's favor, especially when he wants to get re-elected; and that the way to make sure no branch of government ever becomes too powerful is to make each branch as independent of the others as possible.

Still others want the selection process to take the differences in population amongst the states into account, much like proportional voting in the House.

As a compromise, they agree to have the president chosen by electors selected by the people, with each state receiving the number of electors equal to its total of congressmen and senators. And since a state's total number of House seats depends, in part, on its slave population, slavery will also affect presidential elections.

I have to work really hard to keep myself from shaking my head in disgust. I still remember my promise to Franklin.

When it comes to selecting the Supreme Court, the delegates decide the president will appoint the various justices with the Senate's "advice and consent," or approval.

The delegates then debate how their finished product—the Constitution—should be ratified. Some want to submit it to the state legislatures, since the Articles of Confederation require the legislatures to consent to any changes to it. Others want the citizens of each state to elect delegates to special ratifying conventions so that the Constitution will derive its authority directly from the people.

By an overwhelming majority, the convention decides to do some of both: submit the Constitution first to the existing Congress up in New York—whose members were chosen by the state legislatures—and then to the people by means of conventions.

On July 26, the delegates finish debating the Virginia Plan. It is now time to actually write down what they have decided. In other words, it is time to produce a first draft of the Constitution.

To do this, they create the Committee of Detail and appoint to it lawyers John Rutledge from South Carolina, Governor Edmond Randolph of Virginia, Oliver Ellsworth from Connecticut, James Wilson from Pennsylvania, and merchant and legislator Nathaniel Gorham of Massachusetts. The convention recesses until August 6 to allow the committee to do its work.

***

Suddenly, my days are mostly my own. Franklin still has work for me: letters and the autobiography, but that takes up only a few hours every day. And that autobiography is not his favorite activity. He'll stop in a second to talk to Sally or play with one of his grandchildren, or even to re-read a book that catches his eye from the shelves. I soon learn that all I have to do to get him to stop work is offer a game of chess.

Despite Franklin's warning, I use some of my time to help Elise and Mrs. Carver. I almost have to. That first morning caused all sorts of commotion because Elise, in her excitement, completely forgot everyone's breakfast. And didn't she hear about it from Sally when she got home after selling all her soup!

The result? Elise has to agree to take care of breakfast and all her morning chores before going to the market.

That leaves Mr. Carver and me to take up the slack: opening every morning and serving until Elise gets there. Fortunately, Mr. Carver is also on break from the State House. When the convention resumes, he won't have to be there until 9:00 a.m. and I won't have to be there until even later. We decide to split the work 50-50, him taking one day and me the next.

On one of my mornings, I've got my back turned to the counter as I feed the fire to keep the soup hot. I hear three sharp raps and turn. Lucas, the black who works for Swinbourne, stands before me, massive in his red shirt and fringed leather leggings.

"Gimme one," he orders, staring at me, perfectly still, like a tiger lying in wait. His very presence fills me with such unease that I feel unable to talk.

I fix a bowl, hand it to him, and point to the sign I'd made that says "3 cents a bowl, every bowl, no filling again!" I hold out my hand to collect, praying he won't notice the tremble.

He ignores it and digs into the soup, finishing it in about four slurps.

"Elise," he says, wiping his mouth with the back of his hand. "Where she at?"

My unease spikes to full-on alarm. I'm certain he's there to drag Elise back to the master she escaped in Saint-Domingue. I also know there is nothing I can say to help the situation. All I can do is shrug.

"Elise," he repeats.

I shrug again. His stare never leaves my face.

"Tell her Lucas Rush was here. Mrs. Carver sent me to see about her family. She can find me at Mrs. Carver's stall."

He tosses thee pennies on the counter and leaves.

Elise arrives a little later. When I tell her about Lucas, she cries: "Where? Where is he? I must see him immediately!"

"Wait!" I say. "Elise, you should not deal with him. He's a bounty hunter. He catches slaves and takes them back."

"What? Are you crazy? He is Mr. Carver's friend. The one who saved him in the war. Now he makes his living hunting and trapping. I heard Mr. Carver say so."

"And I am telling you that I have seen him handling run-away slaves ... *twice!*"

"You? You are just a boy! You do not know what you see!"

That hurts.

"Fine! Have it your way. But maybe you should think about this. What if he's looking for you? What if he is working for the man who owned you on Saint-Domingue?"

"How would Claude know where to look? Or who to look for? No one knows I went to France. Or that I came to Philadelphia with Doctor Franklin. And my name is not what it was."

"Still—"

"No! I must find my mother and my son. If Mr. and Mrs. Carver think this is the best way for me to do that, then meeting this man is what I must do. Stay here while I go."

"Please?"

"Please? Please what?" she asks impatiently.

"It would be nice if you asked 'please,' instead of ordering me around, especially since I'm not being paid."

"Yes, you are right. I am sorry," she says, and then walks off to meet Rush. I never did get my "please."

She is back a half an hour later.

"He says he can find them!" she says excitedly. "He knows people in the Carolinas, many people, since that is where he is from."

"Did you talk to him about if he's a bounty hunter?"

"No! Why would I do that? Should I insult the man who can find my family? Or the Carvers? All because of something you thought you saw?"

I can see arguing won't change her mind. So, I think up a new "impediment," as Franklin might say.

"How much does he want?"

"Nothing! Since I am a friend of the Carvers, he has said he will do it for nothing."

"You know what nothing's worth?"

"Quoi?" she asks, looking at me as if I'm a stranger.

"Nothing."

***

When I get back to Franklin's, I find him in the library, reading the first draft of the Constitution a messenger has just delivered. Recess is over. The convention resumes tomorrow.

CHAPTER 29

It is hot and steamy again, just like every August in Philadelphia.

And just like every August in Philadelphia, a lot of people leave town. However, they aren't going to "the Jersey Shore" for beaches, boardwalks, and the cooling ocean. These Philadelphians—the ones who can afford it, like Sally and her children—go to farms and country homes to escape diseases like yellow fever, malaria, and typhus caused by filthy streets, raw sewage, bad water, and swarms of flies and mosquitos.

But the delegates are stuck. They've already been in Philadelphia for two months, away from their families, homes, and businesses; lodging at inns and boarding houses, mostly at their own expense, some sharing rooms, others piling up debt. No one has much patience left. Most everyone just wants to go home. (*At least they know how to get there,* I think more than once.) So, they have an incentive to work quickly through the first draft of the Constitution.

The Committee of Detail has transformed the amended Virginia Plan's 19 resolutions into 23 Articles. In debating those articles, the delegates cover some ground they've covered before, but make important decisions.

For example, some think only landowners should vote. Most citizens now own land, they argue, and need to be protected from being outvoted by those who don't. That proposal fails.

And they reconsider the Senate not being able to tax and spend, which was a key provision of the Connecticut Compromise. Ultimately, they reverse themselves and give the Senate the power to vote on money bills.

They also spell out the House of Representatives' specific powers, including: regulating foreign and interstate commerce; laying and collecting taxes; borrowing to finance the government; issuing money;

declaring war; raising an army and navy; and fixing standards for weights and measures, just to name a few.

It seems like the Committee of Detail went out of its way to protect slavery—which causes a pretty big fight. Its draft Constitution prohibits Congress from taxing imported slaves or exported goods, including goods produced by slaves, which will save the southern states a lot of money.

When Maryland's Luther Martin insists on banning or taxing slave importation because it is "inconsistent with the principles of the revolution and dishonorable to the American character," South Carolina's delegates fire back with both barrels.

"South Carolina can *never* accept this plan if it prohibits the slave trade," Charles Pinkney says. "Every time there has been a proposal to extend Congress's power, South Carolina has moved to prevent it from meddling with the importation of Negroes. Now, if you leave South Carolina free to do as she wishes on this subject, she might, gradually, cease importation."

Yeah, there's a promise if I've ever heard one, I think bitterly as Washington adjourns the convention and I rush out of there before anyone can see how disgusted I am.

The next day—August 22nd—is a very bad day for me. It starts in the morning. Franklin and I come to the State House early. He goes inside. I stand on Chestnut, waiting for all the delegates to go in.

As a group of them pass, I hear one say: "I refuse to vote for those articles until they require the return of runaway Negroes escaping outside the state. Congress just did that in the new Northwest Territory ordinance. So must we. They're our property. We paid good money for 'em. There must be a law saying if one runs off, it gets dragged back, from no matter where!"

"Eff'n like to drag you someplace, eff'n *pendejo!*" I whisper.

Things are no better inside the Assembly Room.

Oh, there's talk about how evil slavery is. Even Virginian George Mason says, "Every master of slaves is born a petty tyrant." But he isn't advocating abolition, only banning more imports, which, as another delegate points out, will increase the value of Virginia's existing slaves.

Delegates from Georgia and the Carolinas insist they can't do without slavery; that it is one of their "favorite prerogatives;" and even that slavery benefits the whole country. Slaves increase production, they argue, which makes more goods available for internal consumption and foreign export, which increases tax revenues. Besides, they say, one half of mankind has been enslaving the other half since ancient times.

Then South Carolina's John Rutledge warns: "If the convention thinks that North Carolina, South Carolina, and Georgia will ever agree to a Constitution that interferes with their right to import slaves, it had better think again. The people of those states would be fools to give up so important an interest."

"Their right to import slaves," that's what did it. How dare he call that a right! How dare he think himself and his fellow citizens entitled to snatch men and women from their homeland, cram them into ships, auction them off, and then subject them to the worst deprivations: forced labor under the lash; food and shelter barely fit for livestock; and the complete deprivation of liberty, any sort of happiness, and life itself! How dare he call that a right!

The anger rises in me like puke. I'm so furious, I want to charge onto the floor, grab Franklin's gold-headed "liberty" stick, and give Rutledge a beating he'll never forget.

Franklin must sense something because he turns and glares at me. I know he's warning me, that he wants me to be still. But I just can't, not with all that rage in me. Still, I keep control. I carefully place my *porte-crayon* on the desk, rise, and stalk for the door.

The room stirs. I can feel everyone's eyes on me. Their disapproval washes over me in waves. But I don't care. As far as I'm concerned, all of them can go jump! I walk out and slam the door behind me.

***

I don't go back to Franklin's, not right away. I'm pretty proud of what I've done and want to tell Elise about it. I set out for the market.

When I get there, she's ladling out the last of the soup; and has a lot of disappointed customers at her stall. And Lucas Rush. Only he isn't a customer. He's helping her, washing bowls and sending folks to Mrs. Carver's. It's a strange sight, him in an apron, and I wonder why he's doing it.

The reason soon becomes clear. He and Elise are sweet on each other. I can see it in how protective he is of her, and in the way they banter, and in her radiant smile. She looks at him the way Mom sometimes looks at Pop—the way I want her to look at me.

All my pride and excitement from walking out on the convention leaks away, like air from a punctured tire. There isn't anyone to share it with. As I walk back to Franklin's, I even wonder if I've done the right thing.

But someone has to tell these people that what they're doing is as wrong as it can be, I insist to myself. *Don't they?*

The house is empty. I drag myself into the library to start work. Which is when I remember: I'd left the day's notes on my desk in the Assembly Room. Franklin is going to be really happy about that!

I sit at my table and stare out the window to the place my family's small house will someday be. I just want to go home. I miss my mother and father and Penny, and as always, Gus. I wonder what they'd say if they knew what I'd done. Would Mom and Pop be proud? Would Gus admire my courage? I lay my arms and head on the table, just for a little rest; and fall sound asleep.

***

"Just what was the meaning of that?"

My eyes fly open. There Franklin stands, in his plain brown suit, leaning on his walking stick.

"Just what did you think you would accomplish with that display?"

"Well someone has to tell them they're wrong!" I say, rubbing my eyes.

"And you thought that someone would be you."

Elise comes in with our suppers on a tray. *Good!* I think. *Now, at least someone else will know what I was trying to do—how I was standing up for her people.*

"That's right!" I say proudly. "And I wouldn't have had to if you'd stood up. But you just sat there, saying nothing."

"Correct! Have I not said repeatedly that this is not the time to press for abolition? That the Southern states will not stand for it? What about that did you not understand?"

"Oh, I understand. I just don't agree."

184

"And what of your promise to me? Am I now to regard you as a man who does not honor his word? Or are you nothing but a boy who does not know what honor means?"

That hits me hard. I had been so caught up in trying to do what I thought was right that I'd completely forgotten my promise.

"I … I'm sorry—"

"Well, you've done it now. You have been banished from the Assembly Room. Washington himself told me after the adjournment. You cannot imagine his disappointment and disapproval. I may well have lost his good opinion. And not only his, but that of every other delegate! You may just have destroyed any effectiveness I hoped to have."

"I … I didn't think about that."

"No, I'm quite sure you did not!"

"Hey, I said I was sorry."

"Oh, of that I am sure! But sorry does not sop up the spilt milk!" he says, waving dismissively.

Over his shoulder, I can see Elise watching me, her face like stone.

"Now, I shall have to take notes myself and dictate all I can recall as soon as I get home. What inconvenience! What a waste of time! Just when we are making such progress."

"Progress!" I say in disbelief. I might be sorry, but I'm still furious over slavery being called a "right." "You call that progress? Looks to me like you "gentlemen" are writing a Constitution that will keep slavery going for years to come."

"We may very well," Franklin admits.

"And you approve of that?"

"No. But I can't do anything about it. Charles Pinckney was right when he said one half of the world has been enslaving the other half since ancient times. That is not going to change with a snap of a finger, or a bolt of lightning from on high, or even with the signing of a Constitution. Slavery is a condition, like an illness, and it will take time to cure. Strides have been made and are being made. Many are calling for abolition. But this country needs a unifying Constitution now, or we may just fall apart, and the great potential of the United States will be squandered."

"So you're willing to sign a Constitution that promotes slavery."

185

"No, I'm willing to sign a Constitution that unifies us and gives us a method and a framework for compromising with each other so that we may govern ourselves and so that there are no tyrants over us, foreign or domestic."

"But slavery is tyranny!"

"Yes it is. But tell me: which would you rather have? A Constitution and slavery for a little while? Or no Constitution and no unified country? Think carefully now."

"How do you know it will only be for a little while?"

"I have faith."

My look must tell him it isn't justified.

"What? Do you know otherwise?" he asks, peering at me sharply over his bifocals.

"I'm not supposed to tell you about the future, remember?"

But oh, how I want to tell him exactly what is going to happen over the next two and a quarter centuries, including about the Civil War he and other delegates seem so anxious to avoid.

But I don't, not with "the future" at stake. All I can think to say is: "I'd rather have the Constitution plus no slavery."

"That you cannot have, not right now. And there's an end to it!" He chops the air with his hand. "Now, no more talking. I'm tired and I still have all my notes to dictate. Once we have finished, I will need you to write it all out. After that, I will need you to write out your notes from today, which I managed to retrieve. Elise, please bring Marcus a pot of tea. He has a very long night ahead."

CHAPTER 30

And so, I am banned from the convention.

With Franklin at the State House all day, and Sally and her children off at Temple's farm, and Lucas helping Elise, I have lots of time on my hands—time to realize I'm very disappointed in me. I hate that I broke my promise to Franklin. I'm not like that. I don't break promises. Except, I did; and that makes me feel somehow ... untrue.

And as I think about that, I realize it's the way I've felt ever since Gus's death.

I used to be a straight A student. Everyone expected great things from me. Mom and Gus said I'd make a great lawyer. Pop's parents— award winning researchers in neurobiology—hoped someday I'd join them in science. All that made me feel good about myself.

But when Gus died, everything seemed pretty pointless. I mean, if someone that strong and capable could be wiped out in a nanosecond, then so can anyone. So really, what was the point?

Which is why I quit—which wasn't like me either since I've never been a quitter—and then did only what *I* wanted to do, which was theater where I could be someone else and make the rest of the world go away.

Then in a flash, I'm here spending my days less than 40 feet away from men like Washington, Hamilton, Madison, and Wilson, not to mention Franklin. Yes, I hate how they're handling slavery, but I also admire them tremendously. They're all educated men. Some, like Franklin, Washington and Connecticut's Roger Sherman, are almost completely self-taught. They're all accomplished in their fields, well-spoken, and have the kind of definiteness and confidence I've seen in Mom and some of her professional friends, and that Pop said we were just beginning to see in Gus. According to Pop, it's the kind of confidence that comes from being responsible for people's lives and futures—what Mom calls "knowing what you're about." And the more I'm around that quality, the more I want it; and the further I think I am from getting it.

Now, acting and theater seem frivolous. And I hate what I said to Mom and Pop that morning—how angry and disrespectful I'd been about college. I realize a big part of that came from the guilt I feel over Gus—how he'd gone into the Army so that it would pay for his college and there'd be money for me to go. Although I've never said it, there've been lots of times I've thought: *he's dead because of me.* But now, I also realize that, if that's true, turning my back on my education dishonors his life—and his death.

That morning, Mom said that I was running away from my responsibility to be the best Marcus I could be. I finally understand what she meant. I promise myself that, if I ever do get back, I will finish my education.

In the meantime, I spend all the free time I have prowling Franklin's library, reading everything I can: *Plutarch's Lives,* Thomas Paine's *Common Sense* and *The American Crisis,* Franklin's *The Way to Wealth* and *Experiments and Observations on Electricity.* I even make a start on Adam Smith's *The Wealth of Nations,* reading by candlelight in my attic room before sleep. And I think a lot about that paper on Washington and Lincoln—another self-taught president—I'd now give anything to have the chance to write.

Still, there's work to be done. Franklin usually comes home around four o'clock. Elise brings supper and we labor over convention notes and letters. Some are to other scientists—or "natural philosophers," as Franklin calls them—and cover many topics: ocean currents and temperatures, electricity, manned flight, even the two-headed snake preserved in a glass jar an admirer sent him, which he keeps on a library shelf. But he never once mentions travel through time or between parallel universes; and I'm pretty sure I'm not going home any time soon.

Then one day, Elise comes to the library and asks me to help her and Mrs. Carver again.

"Isn't that what Lucas is for?" I say, focusing on my book, playing hard to get.

"He is on a trip for Mr. Swinbourne."

"Oh, so now you're admitting he works for Swinbourne!"

"*Non!* Lucas is his own man! He works for himself. But … he does … jobs for Mr. Swinbourne."

"Jobs!" I say, snapping the book shut. "How can you even stand being around him? Don't you get it? He catches your people to make them slaves again!"

"*Non!* That is only part! He also brings families together, like mine, who have been sold from each other. And for free, many times. He does what he does for Swinbourne so he will have money to do the other."

"He told you that?" I ask sourly.

"Of course. Who else?"

"And you believe him?"

"Yes! He is a good man. The Carvers would not have sent me to him if he was not."

"That's what you're basing your opinion on? Someone else's opinion? When the proof he's not good is staring you right in the face?"

"I know he is good because I have spent time with him."

My jealousy rises. I've seen them together when he's brought her and her things home from the market. I hate the way she looks at him, and I can't stand the way he struts and preens in order to get her to do it.

"He is good and strong and reliable—a good man who must do hard things to make the money to find my mother and son and take us away from here."

That last part hits hardest.

"You're going away with him? You're in love with him?"

"Love? Love is for children. I told you before. I need someone who is strong, who will provide for me and them."

"But you have Franklin to look out for you."

"Yes? And for how long? He is old. Even he says he will die soon. And what then? Rely on the Baches? They owe me nothing."

"But he makes people slaves again!" I say, slamming my hand on the table. "And he beats them to do it! You of all people should understand—"

"Yes, I do! Because I lived through that!" she cries. "Now, all I want is my family free and to go away from here, maybe to the new land in the northwest, maybe Nova Scotia in Canada. Somewhere to have a farm and take care of each other and be left in peace. That is what he wants too and what we work for."

"Even if it means hurting other people?"

"Them I cannot help. All I can help is my family. Besides, he does nothing illegal. People own people and can do as they please. That is the law. All I can do is take myself and my family to a place where that is not so. To do that, I need money. You have said you care for me and want to be my friend. I am asking you for help to earn it. Give it, or do not."

Of course, I give it.

So my days are hectic again: up at 4:30 a.m. to have both places stocked and selling by 5:00; back to the house by 8:00 for work with Franklin before the convention; splitting wood and then working alone in the library until 3:00 when I go back to the market to bring everything home; and then back up to the library for more work with Franklin, and then to my room to read.

I like being busy like that. The busier I get, the more cheerful I become and the less irritated Franklin and Elise are with me. Our relationships seem to be mending. Elise and I actually joke with each other. I still want her. But she's made the decision for Lucas and somehow I know that fighting it won't change her mind—that it will just drive her further away from me.

It is on Wednesday, August 29th—a market day—that trouble finds us.

The weather has cooled. Sally has returned to check on Franklin, leaving the kids with her husband Richard, who has finished his business and is now at Temple's farm.

I go to pick up Elise's equipment. Sally isn't the only one who's returned; so has Lucas. As soon as I get to her stand, he and Elise take off to walk down Market, leaving me to clean up everything and then get Mrs. Carver's things.

When I get back to the library, the first note Franklin dictates is on the Fugitive Slave Clause the delegates have approved for the Constitution. Slaves escaping over state borders are to be "delivered up to the person justly claiming their service or labor."

"Justly?" I sputter. "JUSTLY!"

"All RIGHT, Marcus!" Franklin says. "I understand your umbrage. And I agree. But I have no time to talk about it now. I'm expected at the Indian Queen. Besides, I've already made my position clear to you. Further discussion is pointless."

Just then, Sally knocks at the door.

"Have either of you seen Elise?" she asks. "It is well past time she started supper."

"Not since this morning," Franklin says.

"She went off with Lucas," I say.

"Who?" Franklin asks.

"A fellow she's been seeing," I say.

"Good for her! High time, too. I wouldn't worry, Sally. Elise is a responsible young woman. I'm sure she will be here soon."

But she isn't. I help Sally prepare supper. As dusk gathers, Franklin walks the few steps over to the Indian Queen. Night falls. Franklin returns around 10:00 p.m. Elise still is gone. I wait up all night. She never comes home.

***

A very angry Mrs. Carver shows up at Franklin's a little after 5:00 a.m.

"Where's my pepper pot? Daylight's wasting, customers complaining, and no money's coming in!"

"There is none," I say. "Elise didn't come home last night."

"Of all the—where she gone?"

"I don't know. Last time I saw her, she was with Lucas."

She glowers. "What's she doing with him? I told her to stay away from him!"

"That's not what she told me. She said one of the reasons she's with him is because you introduced them."

"That was before I knew he was Swinbourne's man."

"Great! That's just great!" I snap. But then, because I know losing my temper will do no good, I rein myself in and ask: "Where do you think she could be?"

"I dunno, boy. But you best start looking, 'cuz there ain't no one else to look."

***

I start on Market Street, the last place I'd seen them. It isn't a market day and many stalls are deserted. Still, there are tradesmen who open every day—butchers, barbers, tanners, soap and candle makers—and even buy our soup for lunch. I go from stall to stall, describing the couple and asking if anyone has seen them. No luck.

I head down Market, in the direction I'd last seen them walking. I cross Front Street and then Water Street to finally arrive at the river with its busy wharfs and warehouses. Masts, spars, and rigging loom. As luck would have it, I spy Lucas walking north. Tall as he is, in that red shirt and with that rolling gait, he's tough to miss. Elise isn't with him.

But Swinbourne is. I don't need him seeing me, not after our last encounter when he tried to have me jailed.

Pulling my hat low over my forehead so they won't recognize me if they look back, I follow them north towards Arch Street and the ferry there.

They stop at a warehouse. Timothy Wimpole, the tailor turned constable, is waiting for them. Swinbourne unlocks the front door and they go inside.

I go to the front door. The sign above it reads *Swinbourne & Company, Merchants*. Obviously, I can't just walk in.

An alley borders the warehouse. I decide to wait there until Lucas leaves. Hopefully, he'll be alone and I can ask about Elise. But then I see an open window. As I near it, I hear voices.

"When she sail?" Lucas asks.

"At dawn with the tide," Swinbourne says. "We'll finish unloading by four this afternoon, I should think. Plan to load after that. Make sure everything is chained tightly. Wimpole, I'll need you to take care of delivering those hogsheads."

"Me? You're the one who knows all the carters and draymen."

"Oh yes, certainly! And have them come back on me?"

"Well, I don't want 'em coming back on me!"

"Perhaps you want to lose your watchman's wages? And the lease on the building I've let you? Trade your shop and home for a debtor's cell?"

"But where'm I going to find someone who can't be connected to me?" Wimpole whines.

"Bloody fool, go out of the city. To Germantown or Darby or Chester. But do it quick! Lots of valuable goods here. Don't want to lose 'em to a spark."

"I best get along to the other side, if'n I'm gonna have everthing ready," I hear Lucas say.

"Go on then," Swinbourne says. "Wimpole and I have more to discuss. I'll see you for the final count."

"Needs my money—"

192

"I paid you already."

"Not for the extra you wanted."

"Oh, you got that bit of business? That's fine, very fine! Fifty, weren't it?"

"Hundred. You knows that."

"A hundred! I'll be lucky to make any profit at all. Ah well, never say Johnathan Swinbourne ever welshed on a bargain. You'll have it tonight, once I've seen all's in order."

"I better," Lucas says. A door opens and closes hard.

I move to the front of the building and peer around the corner. Lucas continues north. I follow.

When he gets to the corner of Arch, he crosses onto the wharf, just ahead of a long line of wagons coming off. By the time those pass, I've lost him.

I run onto the wharf. There is a ferry service to Camden—flat-bottomed boats propelled by men standing to long, sweeping oars—and I think Lucas must be on the one just boarding. I look into the boat. He isn't there.

"Where the heck did you go, Lucas?" I ask out loud.

"Where be my soup?" asks a voice behind me. A stream of brown goo splatters at my feet.

I turn to find a short, wiry, steel-haired black man in dirty canvas pants and a blue, salt-stained shirt. His unshaven face is wrinkled, but his eyes are keen. A clay pipe juts from his mouth. He spits a lot and doesn't seem to care what he hits.

He seems familiar, but I can't place him.

"You know me?" I ask.

"No, but I seen you with Mary Carver and that pretty Missy 'Lise. They makes good soup."

That answers that, I think, as my eyes search for Lucas.

"Where they at today?" he asks. "Done walked all that way to come back hongry!"

I don't answer. I'm barely listening.

"Likes takin' my midday meal there. They's nice to me and only charges a penny."

"Where in heck did he go?" I fume.

"Who?"

"I'm looking for that bounty hunter, Lucas."

"Oh, him. He gone."

"Where did he go?"

"Over the side, down to his dory. Whatchew want with him?"

"I'm looking for him so I can find Elise."

"Yeah, I seen 'em yesterday, out on the river. I works the ferry. Afternoon run, we was halfway 'cross and Lucas was rowin' 'em towards Camden. They both was laughin'. I thought, what's she doin' with him?"

A disgusted look twists the man's features as he shakes his head.

"Looks like you don't think much of him."

"I don't. He works with that Swinbourne fella, snatchin' peoples up and sellin''em south. Snatched me once. But t'were a mistake. When they got me in the light and sees I's too old to fetch a price, they ran me out that place they got 'cross the river."

"What place?"

"Place they buys and sells slaves," he says, like I'm a fool. "Cain't buy or sell 'em in Pennsy no more. So they use Camden, where they loads 'em on ships goin' south."

"You think that happened to Elise?" I ask. All of a sudden, it's hard to breathe.

"Mebbe. Ship leaves tomorrow."

"You know what ship?"

"Course I knows! I's a riverman. I knows everything 'bout my river!"

"Take me," I blurt, surprising myself.

"Huh?"

"Take me out to the ship," I say.

"When?"

"Now."

"Uh uh. Cain't. Workin' the next ferry. If'n I ain't aboard, I lose my place and I needs the money. 'Sides, what you think you can do out there in daylight, 'cept get thrown overboard? And get me me kilt in the bargain!"

"Okay … so … what do I do?"

"Why you askin' me? This ain't none of my business."

"A lady's nice to you—gives you soup for a penny when everyone else pays three—and what happens to her is none of your business? Fine, tell me where to rent a boat and point out the ship. I'll row myself."

"You got money?" he asks, like it's a revelation.

"Never mind what I have! Just tell me where to get the boat."

"Betchyain't never rowed no boat on that river."

That's a bet you'd win, I think.

"Tell you what," he says. "Since it's Missy 'Lise, I'll row you out and back. But you'll wait 'til tonight and you'll pay."

"How much?"

"Got three dollars?"

"Yes."

"Well, if'n you got three, I knows you got five. Anyways, that's what I want. I got two more trips over and back. Meet me here at eight. When it's dark, I'll take you over. Make sure you gots my money or y'ain't going nowhere. Name's Solomon, by the way, Solomon Yates."

"I'm Marcus."

CHAPTER 31

Walking back to Franklin's, I have a chance to think again about my plan; and realize: I don't have any plan at all! Cross the Delaware in a row boat? Board a slave ship to see if Elise is even there and somehow rescue her if she is? It's ridiculous, not to mention stupid—and scary, which I'm really not happy about. I definitely need Franklin's help.

But when I get back to the house, I meet Sally coming down the stairs carrying a chamber pot.

"Where's Dr. Franklin?" I ask, taking the steps two at a time, meeting her halfway. The reek of puke coming from the pot almost knocks me over the bannister.

"Father is ill," Sally says. "Dr. Rush is with him."

"But I have to see him! Right away!"

Her eyebrows shoot up and her face reddens with anger.

"Marcus, did you not hear what I said? He is *ill*. He is not able to keep his food down. Dr. Rush is worried that it is one of the fevers, or the flux. He could …"

"What?"

She shakes her head and pushes past me. "Whatever you need from Father will have to wait."

"But Elise—"

"Elise! Do not speak to me of Elise! Not when she is supposed to be here and is not! I have no time for her! When I think what might have happened had I not come home! Father all alone with no one to fetch the doctor or look after him. After all that has been done for her?"

"But she may be in trouble!"

"Yes? And who put her there? Did Father? Did I? Did you? This house has troubles enough right now. Whatever the matter is, Elise will

196

have to fend for herself. Or you can, I suppose, since I doubt you'd make a very good nurse."

With that, she pushes past me, heading for the kitchen downstairs. I stand there, trying to think of who else might help. The only other people I know are Joseph Carver and his mother and she's too old and he's too lame. I'm on my own.

***

That night, I follow Solomon to the end of the wharf and down a ladder into a rowboat. The old ferryman might be slight, but he's strong and the boat goes fast. I'm scared. Sweat trickles from my armpits and slicks my hands and my stomach keeps tumbling like a washing machine.

"Think she's on the ship or over at the auction place?" I ask. I definitely don't like how high and tremble-y my voice is.

"Ship," Solomon says. "Wouldn't try to auction her off here, not when someone might come claim her or prove she's free. Anyways, that's where I'm taking you."

By the time we're half-way across, it's pitch dark. A low ceiling of cloud hides the moon and stars. I smell the slaver before I see it. It's an awful smell, worse than the foulest street in Philadelphia.

I turn to get a look at what I'm up against. Where the ship should be, all I can make out is a great, dark mass. For a moment, I think Solomon is rowing us right into nothingness. But then I see wood and rigging and the stern cabin's glass windows. It isn't a shadow anymore. The stench and the smack of water against the hull make the ship all too real.

"Don't get too close," I whisper. "Circle around so I can see how to get aboard."

"I ain't doing that! Take hold of her anchor chain and climb up."

"And what if there's a look-out in the bow? Circle around. I need to see what's what."

"Cost you extra."

"Fine! Row!"

It is a stubby wooden ship with two masts and a short bowsprit. The gunwales are high at both the bow and stern, but lower at the center where the entry port is. A rope ladder hangs from that entry port all the way down to the water. Two row boats are tied to the rope ladder. They knock against each other and the side of the ship, sounding like axes biting into wood.

For a second, I think that rope ladder is my answer. But then, just to the right of the entry port, I see a man leaning over the gunwale staring into the water.

"Keep going," I whisper.

It looks like I'll have to climb that anchor chain after all. But then I notice square ports with raised wooden flaps running along the side. I've seen enough movies to suspect what they are.

"Does it have cannon?" I ask Solomon.

"She's a slaver, ain't she? Course she's got cannon."

At the middle of the ship, the cannon are on the main deck, where I'd be seen. But sternwards, the guns are below the raised afterdeck—where they steer the ship—and forward of the stern cabin.

"Think I could crawl through that end port without being seen?"

"Mebbe. Hot night like tonight, any crew's gonna be up top. 'Sides, last night in port? I'll wager most everyone's ashore lappin' up rum."

He rows to the gun port. It's an easy reach. I plant my arms and elbows on the sill and launch myself up and halfway through, only to slam right into the cannon.

Stunned, I lose my grip and slide back, out through the port. My feet scrabble along the side, but the wood hull is wet and slippery. Blood pours from my nose, slicking the sill. I feel myself losing way. I look down to step back into the rowboat. It's gone.

I slip and slide until I hang by the four fingers of each hand, arms fully extended. The only thing between me and dark water is air. I curse Solomon, certain he's abandoned me.

My arms are on fire. Gathering every last bit of strength, I hoist myself far enough up to brace my arms along the sill. But I start slipping again. I know I'm going in the river.

A hand like a claw grabs my butt and shoves me through the gun port. This time, I duck and miss the cannon.

I stick my head back out the gun port to see Solomon. I wave in a way I hope says thanks and take my last breath of fresh air.

I creep past the gun carriage into a small passageway. Oil lamps cast dim, yellow light and flickering shadows, making it hard to see. To my right, sternward, I can just make out a closed cabin door. To my left, stairs run to the main deck. Next to them, a doorway leads forward to the rest of the ship.

Putting my ear to the cabin door, I hear voices but can't make out what they're saying. I'll have to be quiet, and quick!

First, find Elise—if she's even aboard.

I make for the doorway forward. Three steps later, I trip and fall with a *clank*. By the dim light, I see I'm lying on a pile of chains and manacles. Something hard pokes into my stomach. I reach under me and come up with a rusty iron mallet.

Footsteps sound from the cabin. Leaving the mallet, I dive for the cannon and squeeze into the cramped space between it and the hull.

The door opens.

"Who's out here?" It sounds like Swinbourne. "Lucas, see who's out there."

More footsteps. I wait to get grabbed by the collar.

But they pass.

"Where were we?" I hear Swinbourne say.

"Them hogsheads," a voice whines. Was that Wimpole? "You said find someone from out of town. I'll need to show 'em hard cash."

I hear a frustrated kind of half-sigh, half-growl and then the jingle and clink of coins.

"There, that should do you," Swinbourne says. "Only be quick about it. I want that stuff out of my warehouse. And we don't want everything over before giving the guy his chance. This is too good an opportunity. My people in London are counting on that guy."

I wonder what "guy" they are talking about.

"I'm doin' my best," says Wimpole. "With how I feel about that old farter, I'm wanting this just as much as you. Thinks he so fine! Tosses his own overboard like trash. And me! Ruined me! Any more rum?"

I hear Lucas's returning footsteps and make myself as small as I can.

"Ain't no one," he says. "Just these manacles and such, and this hammer I had on top. Must've shifted when the wind swung the ship."

He tosses the hammer back on the pile.

"Need you to row me back," Wimpole says. "Got the watch."

"Don't care what you got," Lucas says. "Ain't leavin' fore I gets paid for that little missy, Elise."

"You'll get it," I hear Swinbourne say as the door closes.

Okay, so she's here, I think, relieved. *Now I just need to go get her without getting caught. Just? Yeah, right.*

As quietly as I can, I creep from my hiding place. When I reach the doorway forward, the awful sounds stop me cold. The low moaning, the groans, terrify me. And the smell! I want to jump back into Solomon's row boat, head for shore, and never look back. But I just can't. I'd never be able to forgive myself.

I move into a low-ceilinged hold lit dimly by lanterns. Black men, mostly naked and sweating, lie with their backs against the hull. Shackles chafe their ankles. A heavy chain runs through the shackles, binding them all together. In the center of the hold, more men sit in two sections of rows four across with an aisle running down the middle. The rows are as straight as in a theater. Iron rods threaded through the ankle cuffs and padlocked at the ends are what make them so straight.

In one row, several men are fully clothed. I stop at one with a swollen eye and jaw. He shrinks from me.

"Please, don't hit me again. I didn't—"

"Shhhh! I'm not here to hurt you and I'm not a part of this. I'm looking for a woman: small, pretty, in a brown dress, white collar, apron and cap."

"Help me! Let me loose!"

"Have you seen her?" I insist.

"All the women and kids is up front."

"Thanks," I say squeezing his shoulder. "I'll try to come back for you."

I start forward, then stop and go back.

"Where are the keys?" I ask.

"Big fella's got 'em, I think."

Terrific! I think. *How the heck am I going to get anyone unlocked?*

Then I remember what we do when one of us forgets the combination to the padlock on our school locker. I go back, get the iron mallet, and hurry into the forward hold up by the bow.

Naked women and children pour sweat in the dim, sickly, yellow light; stowed like the men and so miserable they never lift their heads to see who I am. I can barely make out anyone's face. *How am I going to find her?* I think frantically.

"Elise!" I whisper hoarsely.

No answer.

I walk crab-like along the hull, trying to look into the faces, rasping Elise's name.

"Here! I'm here!"

There's no mistaking her voice. Through the gloom, I can just make her out.

I kneel and fumble to find the padlock securing the iron bar. If I'm to hammer it open, I'll need more light. A small lantern hangs near stairs leading to a closed hatch towards the bow. I grab it and go back. The women stir and whisper as I pass.

"Elise," I call again, having lost my place.

"Here! … Here!"

Women are murmuring now. A baby cries.

I set the lantern down, find the lock, take careful aim, and swing hard.

Several women in Elise's row cry as the shock of the blow shudders along the bar. I hadn't thought about that.

"Hey, boy! Be careful!" Elise hisses.

But the lock is open.

I pull at the bar. It won't budge.

"The other lock, there!" Elise says, pointing to the other end of the bar.

I grab the lantern and cross the row, trying not to trample feet. The clamor from the women and children grows louder.

I find the other padlock, break it open, and pull the bar through the women's shackles to free them.

Elise removes the cuffs from her ankles and steps out to me. The other women look on, amazed, and then begin removing their own shackles, talking to each other in an African language, making lots of noise. We have to get out of there.

I grab her hand. "Come on! I've got someone waiting for us," I say, pulling her sternwards.

"No!" she says. "The front stairs are faster."

We race to them and climb. But when we reach the hatch, it won't budge.

More children are crying now. The women in Elise's row are all standing.

"STOP!" a voice roars.

I turn. Lucas stands in the door. He holds a lantern in one hand and a pistol in the other.

CHAPTER 32

Lucas moves quickly into the hold.

"Come down!" he orders.

"Just what is going on?" Swinbourne calls from somewhere behind him.

"Nothing I can't handle," Lucas answers. "Go back and finish your business. Woman, come down here to me!"

Elise doesn't cower and she doesn't budge. But all the other women who'd stood sit right back down.

"Get down here, I said," Lucas growls. "You too, boy!"

"We're not going anywhere with you," I say, made brave by Elise's courage. "You're really sick, you know that? Treating your own people this way."

"Ain't my people. Don't have people. All I got is me and I need money."

"There's other ways to make money."

"What? Work as a field hand? Or one of them scavengers picking up everyone's slop off the streets? Ha! Now, girl, you come on and I'll put you back and we'll not say no more. Won't get whupped or nothing. But come now. Otherwise, it'll go hard—"

Above our heads, the deck hatch flies open. A barefoot white guy charges down the stairs. Elise has almost no time to think, but that doesn't stop her. Graceful as a dancer, she moves to the side of the stairway, sticks out her foot, and trips him; sending him flying to crash into Lucas.

Powder flashes and the pistol barks. The ball buzzes by me like an angry wasp before thudding into the hull.

"Marcus! *Allez! Vite! Vite!*" Elise calls from the open hatch. I run up the stairs into a cold rain that slicks the deck.

"This way," I pant, heading for the side to look for Solomon.

He's gone. But the entry port and the rope ladder down to those two row boats is unguarded.

"Can you climb down?" I ask.

"*Oui!*"

She sits on the deck, maneuvering to find the first rung of the ladder with her foot.

I look back at the hatch, expecting to see Lucas or the white guy, but there's no one—not yet.

I look down. Elise is moving so slowly.

"Hurry!" I say.

"I go as fast as I can!"

"What's the matter?"

"You wear these skirts and see how you do!"

Now she's half-way down, with maybe another five feet to go. I sit in the entry port, feeling for the first rung of the ladder with my foot.

I look back—still no one; then look down. Elise has made it into the first of the two boats.

"Climb over to the next boat," I say, starting down the ladder, watching the forward hatch for Lucas.

But it's from the stern that I hear men running. Turning, I see Lucas and the barefoot guy, both carrying rifles. They haven't seen me yet. I duck my head below the deck and scramble down the ladder and into the first boat. Untying it from the ladder, I push off, freeing both dinghies from the slave ship. I scramble into the second boat, untie it, and push off from the first. Luckily, the oars are resting in their oarlocks. Fast as I can, I push them into the water and start rowing.

Or try to. The Delaware is rough. My first pull, I dig the oars in too deep and almost lose them. My second, I barely fan the water. Three pulls later, I've made maybe ten yards.

By the light of the slaver's deck lanterns, I see Lucas and the white guy at the rail taking aim with their rifles.

"Over the side!" I shout to Elise. We both tumble overboard. Just as I hit that cold, black water, I hear the shots. I just know one is going to hit me. But I get lucky.

The current is strong and my clothes and shoes, heavy with water, drag me under. I kick for the surface, in the direction I think our row boat is. But when my head breaks water, all I can see are the dim lights of Philadelphia. Or is it Camden? I'm not sure because I've completely lost my bearings. Struggling to stay afloat, I swivel in the water. The rain comes harder; big, pelting, marble-sized drops that make it hard to see.

About ten yards away, I see the gray hull of one of the dinghies. I swim to it, grab its gunwale, and twist this way and that, looking for Elise. I can just make out the slaver. The current has carried me and the boat pretty far. But there is no sign of Elise.

I call out to her. No answer.

Shivering, all I can think is: *Oh God, please don't let her be shot!*

I call again. The hiss of rain on the river's surface is the only response.

But then, behind me, I hear the water stir. A hand covers my mouth as a warm body presses against my back.

"Shhhhh," Elise whispers in my ear. "Someone comes."

She points. A white hull with quick-moving oars heads straight for us—fast! Whoever is rowing has to be strong. I figure it must be Lucas. The bottom drops out of my stomach. I can't think what to do.

"Whatchy'all doin' down there?" Solomon rasps. "Boats is for being into, not out of."

It's a struggle, scrambling into that little dinghy. But we make it.

It takes Solomon a half-hour of hard pulling to get us to the Market Street wharf. It's late and very quiet in the now gentle rain.

We climb quickly up the ladder and hurry for Market Street.

"That sure was some excitement," Solomon says. "Boy, you's a sight! Look at you! Fat lip, blood still leakin' out your nose—!"

"Where the heck did you go?" I ask angrily, swiping at my face with my sleeve and getting a jolt of pain as my reward.

"Stood off when I heard that first shot. You's paid me to row, not get kilt."

"I know you, don't I?" Elise asks Solomon.

"Come eat your soup ever' day I can, ma'am."

"Ah, you are one of the ones we charge a penny because you cannot afford more. Yes?"

"Yes'm."

"You came all that way for me?"

"Yes'm."

"You are very brave, to do that for someone you know so little."

"No'm," he says with an embarrassed duck of his head.

"You like our soup, yes?"

"Yes'm."

"From now on, every day, for you it is free."

***

As Elise and I walk back to Franklin's, she starts to shiver. I try putting my arm around her.

"*Non!*" she says, stepping away.

"Just trying to get you warm."

"That I do not deserve! I am such a fool! I know better."

"Hey, we all make mistakes."

"Not me. Not with men. Not anymore."

"Don't say that," I plead.

"You are a good fellow, Marcus. Thank you for this. But still, you are not for me."

"Because I'm not strong enough?"

"*Non.* About that, I think I was wrong. It is because Franklin says you will leave."

Thanks, Doc!

***

We get back to the house after midnight.

"We must be quiet," I say. "While you were gone, Franklin became very ill."

"No! *Mon Dieu!* What is the matter?"

"Absolutely nothing," Franklin calls down from the top of the stairs. "Honestly, a man eats one bad oyster and the world stops turning."

"You aren't supposed to be eating oysters," I say.

"Spare me! I've already been scolded by both Sally and Dr. Rush. Washington, Hamilton, Wilson, and Madison were all making a meal of them over at the Indian Queen. I couldn't let them have all the fun."

"Everyone else get sick too? I ask.

"No. It seems I got the only bad one in the bunch. Either that or it did not like the Madeira," he says and then grimaces, like he's just spilled a convention secret.

"But you are not supposed to drink—"

"I'll thank you to keep that revelation to yourselves. I've had quite enough of Sally's upbraiding. Now, where have the two of you been? You look drowned and you are dripping all over the floor. Sally said something about your being in trouble Elise? Go change and come to the library. I must hear everything."

In the library, we take turns telling what happened. Elise tells how Lucas invited her to go for a cooling row over to Camden, only to detour to Swinbourne's ship.

"I knew from the smell something was wrong, as we came up to that ship—and also, because Lucas would not answer my questions. When we got there, he said go up the ladder and I said no, that he must take me back. A very heavy net fell on me. It knocked me down to the bottom. I hit my head. Next, I remember waking up with my feet locked, in that awful place. Then Marcus came."

"Yes, that!" Franklin says. "Tell me about that."

So I do, beginning with my hunt along Market Street.

"One thing is certain, Marcus. No one can doubt your bravery," Franklin says when I'm finished. A warm feeling runs through me and, for just a second, I wish Gus could be here.

"What are you going to do?" I ask him.

"Why, I should think that would be obvious. Go to bed."

"No! I mean, what are you going to do about what happened?"

Franklin blinks that slow, owlish blink of his.

"Nothing. There's nothing I can do. The ship was on the New Jersey side of the river. It may be illegal to import and to buy and sell slaves in Pennsylvania, but in New Jersey, it is still quite legal."

"But he kidnapped her!"

"Did he? It sounded as though she willingly accompanied him—at least at first, while still here in Philadelphia. Best to forget it."

"Forget it? Suppose he tries again? Suppose he goes to the market and drags her off?"

"The market?" Franklin repeats, eyebrows raised high. "Elise, you don't mean to say you're continuing with that business."

"Yes, of course I must," she answers. "I need money to find my family."

"No!" Franklin says. "I cannot have that! Things are at such a delicate stage with the convention right now. For you, the market is finished. I cannot risk calling attention to myself, not in a fight with Swinbourne, not concerning the issue of slavery."

"But—"

"My word on this is final. Elise, you are finished at the market."

"And if I disobey?"

"It isn't a question of disobeying me. I am not your master. But I must make it a condition of your continued association with this house. You must choose: either remain here, under my protection, and forsake the market; or return to the market, but find yourself other accommodations and employment."

He softens the sternness in his voice.

"I realize I am forcing a harsh choice upon you. And I really don't want you to leave. So here is what I propose. I will do everything in my power to find your mother and son. I will pay whatever it takes to have them found and I will buy them and pay to bring them here and then I will set them free."

"You can never find them," Elise says forlornly.

"My dear, have you no faith? I spent years running our postal system, first as the Crown's deputy postmaster for the colonies, and then as Postmaster General of the United States, in which office Sally's husband, Richard, succeeded me. We have friends in every post office in the country. And who is it in every town that knows everyone? Why, the postmaster. If our friends cannot find your family, your family cannot be found."

"But I do not have the money for that, for any of it,"

"It will cost you nothing. Let it be my gift to you."

"I could never accept such a gift."

"Think carefully now," Franklin says, raising a warning finger. "Do not let pride lead you astray."

"May I take time to think?"

"Wisely said. Of course you may. However, while you consider, there can be no going back to the market. In fact, it would be best if you both confined yourselves to the house and garden—at least for the next few days. Lay low, so to speak, while we see what consequences this evening's commotion brings. Although I doubt there will be any, considering the parties involved. Both Swinbourne and Wimpole know that you are under my protection and that I can make life very unpleasant for them both."

I have the nagging feeling there is something I should be telling Franklin. But I can't think what. I'm more tired than I've ever been. Elise looks just as exhausted.

But she's not too exhausted to ask Franklin: "May I at least continue to cook the soup for Mrs. Carver. She has been depending on me—"

"As long as you remain here at the house, it should be alright. But when you see Mrs. Carver, tell her that if she hears anything about you or what happened tonight, she's to come tell you immediately. Clear?"

"Yes, Doctor."

"Good. And now, get me to bed. You two may be able to laze about tomorrow; I still have a convention to attend."

CHAPTER 33

We move into September. The convention is winding down, Franklin says. The delegates are exhausted. Everyone wants to go home. But they keep working through the Committee of Detail's draft and make or reaffirm a number of important decisions, including:

That the President will be chosen by an electoral college;

That the Vice President will serve as President of the Senate;

The process by which the Constitution will be ratified by the states; and

The process by which the Constitution can be amended in the future.

"This question of amendment is vital," Franklin says to me one night. "No one knows if what we've designed will work; or what events may occur to require future changes. Still, we can't have something changeable on a whim. That would lead to an unstable government. So, the Constitution must be amendable, but difficult to amend.

"Thus, it will take two-thirds of both the House and the Senate, or a convention called for by two-thirds of the state legislatures, just to propose an amendment. For the amendment to pass, it must be approved by three-fourths of the states, acting through either their legislatures or specially called conventions."

"Except in the case of slavery," I say, slapping the note Franklin has dictated. "You've made it so that no amendment can be made about slavery until 1808! That means no abolition for at least 20 years!"

Franklin looks to the heavens, as if asking for patience.

"We've already agreed to allow the importation of slaves until 1808," he says. "This is merely the logical extension of that agreement. There'd be no agreement at all if the non-slave states could suddenly turn around and force abolition on the slave states by an amendment. It's only twenty years. By 1808, I daresay slavery will have become economically unfeasible and died of its own accord. It is already happening. Have you any idea how expensive it is to keep a slave—to house and feed and clothe one? Much more expensive than paying for labor—"

"Only twenty years?" I say angrily. "Is that what you think? You have no idea what you're setting the country up for. Eighty more years —"

"Marcus! The future! STOP!" he says hoarsely, clapping his hands over his ears.

"—of slavery, a bloody Civil War with over 700,000 dead, followed by another *century* of racism and poverty and blacks never having a chance!" I might not know as much history as Mom and Pop and Gus, but I know that much.

Slowly, Franklin lowers his hands. I can't tell if he's heard anything I said.

"The southern states will not unify with us unless slavery is protected," he says doggedly.

"That's all you can say? That same old tired line?"

His face woeful, he shakes his head, as if he's a professor faced with the most hopeless of pupils. Then he looks up at the drawing of the snake separated into eight pieces and captioned "JOIN, or DIE." and seems to gain strength.

"Very well, Marcus, you tell me: which would more effectively promote Negro welfare: No union at all, leaving each state free to practice slavery if and as it wishes, for as long as it wishes, since there will be no superior power to stop them? Or a union that allows slaves to be imported for a limited time, during which the government may well acquire the moral authority, and the power, to abolish, not just slave importation, but slavery itself throughout the land?

"Under which alternative do blacks fare better? Under which do they have the greatest chance for liberty and happiness?"

I can't answer. I've never thought of it that way. Even though I know that "the North" will defeat "the South" in the Civil War, and that slavery will end, I've never thought about the fact that "the North" will actually be the federal government, also known as "The Union." It will take the United States Government, sitting supreme above all the state governments, to completely do away with slavery.

"Now, you've been in that Assembly Room most of the summer," Franklin continues. "Have you a better alternative?"

"No," I admit.

"I'm not surprised. But never mind, you're in good company. No one else, including me, has one either. Now, might we please resume work?"

***

On September 10th, the convention finishes debating the Committee of Detail's draft Constitution and submits it to something called "the Committee of Style and Arrangement" for a final polish.

"I believe we are almost done," Franklin says. "The five men on that committee are all fine lawyers, renowned for their drafting skills. If James Madison, Alexander Hamilton, Gouverneur Morris, Rufus King, and Samuel Johnson can't make that document glow, no one can."

The next evening, Madison, Morris, and Hamilton bring their draft to Franklin in his garden. Once again, I'm in the library with the window open, writing everything down.

"The light is fading, and even with my glasses, I'm not sure I can read all this," Franklin says. "Mr. Morris, you have a pleasing voice. Read it aloud so we can see how it sounds."

I've read prior drafts so many times I expect him to begin with the dull, dry recitation: "we the people of the states of New Hampshire, Massachusetts, Rhode Island, etc., do hereby order, declare, etc., the following Constitution, etc."

But that's not what comes out of Gouverneur Morris's mouth.

"'We the People of the United States,'" he begins in his deep, clear voice, "'in Order to form a more perfect Union, establish Justice, insure domestic Tranquility, provide for the common defense, promote the general Welfare, and secure the Blessings of Liberty to ourselves and our Posterity, do ordain and establish this Constitution for the United States of America.'"

"Bravo!" Franklin cheers. "A masterful preamble! Mr. Jefferson in Paris could not have written better. Is that your work, Mr. Madison?"

"I must give credit where credit is due," Madison answers. "Those are Mr. Morris's words. In fact, he has done most of the work on what we all hope will be the final draft."

"Well, they are fine words—the finest!" Franklin says. "Pray, continue."

It takes the peg-legged Morris a good half hour to read the entire Constitution. No one interrupts or comments.

"Remarkable!" Franklin says. "This is nothing like the Virginia Plan or the Committee of Detail's draft. In their place, Mr. Morris, you have written a clear, concise plan of government incorporating what we've agreed to over these past weeks: a Congress composed of a House of Representatives and Senate; an executive consisting of a president, vice president, and various departments; and a judiciary made up of the Supreme Court and lesser federal courts.

"Each branch has its own method of selection, satisfying various constituencies: the public, the state governments, and so forth. Each has its own duties, separating power amongst the branches. Government should be able to act quickly and vigorously when it has to. But when it does not, it will be required to act with deliberation to safeguard the people's best interests. Most important, this separation and delegation of powers should prevent any individual or branch of government from gaining too much power over the people."

"That's what I take from it," Hamilton says. "You can see it in the treatment of war powers. The president is the commander-in-chief of the military, which means he's to conduct any war we fight. But only Congress can declare war and only Congress can decide to pay or not pay for it. Thus, the choice to go to war, and to continue it, will be made deliberately after full debate. But battlefield decisions can be made relatively quickly."

"At least, that's the theory," Madison says. "I must say, I'm not entirely happy. We should do more to restrain power. Congress should be able to veto bad laws passed by the states; and the executive and judiciary, together, should be able to veto bad laws passed by Congress."

"I, too, have objections," Alexander Hamilton says. "I've said we should abolish the state governments and give the federal government all their powers. But no one agrees; and I must compromise. If this is the very best we can do, and I think it may be, then I will work hard to support it. It certainly is infinitely preferable to what we have now, which is little better than nothing."

"Mr. Hamilton is right," Franklin says, "compromises must be made. I wanted only one chamber in the Congress, elected every year, as we have here in Pennsylvania. No one listens more closely to his constituents than a representative up for frequent election. But many very talented men in that chamber think differently. Honestly, I cannot say my ideas are better than theirs. As such, I will support this Constitution with everything I have."

"As will I," Gouverneur Morris says, "even though I hate that slavery has been made part of the bargain. Would that we could have abolished it."

"Here, here!" Madison says.

"Yes," says Franklin. "But while we may be living in times they call in France *les Lumières*, or "the Enlightenment," that does not mean everyone is enlightened. Slavery has existed for thousands of years. It will take much time and effort to abolish it in all its forms, and we are only just beginning. For now, it must be union first, and then abolition."

"I agree," Morris says.

"And I," Madison says. "Let us not forget: what we have written here is not a declaration of social justice. It is a plan of government. Hopefully, it will bring about justice and protect the rights of citizens by preventing any person or government branch from gaining too much power. Speaking of which, I saw George Mason and Elbridge Gerry at the Indian Queen this afternoon. Both want to add an enumeration of citizens' rights. Gerry fears that if he returns to Massachusetts without one, he'll be hoisted over a bonfire like "the Guy.""

"I hope you told them no," Hamilton says. "We cannot protract the debate. The agreements we've managed are fragile enough. Add any more conflict and everything may collapse."

"I said it was unnecessary," Madison says. "First, because all power flows from the people. Nothing we've written in the Constitution changes that. Therefore, any power the government has not been given, still resides in the people. Second, all the states have Declarations of Rights. That should be protection enough. Mr. Hamilton is correct. We need to end this before the entire venture falls apart."

"Hear, hear!" Franklin says.

"Yes, hear, hear," Gouverneur Morris echoes.

"So we are agreed," Madison says. "There's to be no bill of rights."

Since I'm not supposed to be listening, I can't lean out the window and yell: "Yo! Guys! Huge mistake!"

CHAPTER 34

"What's a guy?" I ask Franklin the next morning over breakfast in the kitchen.

He peers at me through his specs like I'm an idiot.

"I mean, I know what a guy is, as opposed to a gal. It's just, last night is the second time I've heard someone talk about burning a guy; and I just wondered if there's a special meaning."

"Gal?" asks Elise. "What is gal?"

"You know, a girl, a woman, a lady. A guy's a boy and a gal's a girl and—"

"Guy Fawkes," Franklin says.

"Who?"

"Guy Fawkes. Guido Fawkes, to be more exact: a Catholic rebel who tried to blow up Parliament in 1605 in order to assassinate King James. He was caught just as he was lighting the fuse to a stockpile of gunpowder, tortured for the names of his co-conspirators, and then sentenced to be hanged, drawn, and quartered. He escaped that most unpleasant punishment—which includes being hanged until almost dead, and then castrated, disemboweled, and decapitated—by jumping off the scaffold to his death."

"What is quartered?" Elise asks.

"Having your bodily remains chopped into four pieces," Franklin says matter-of-factly. "It's the old penalty for high treason. Quite gruesome. I had some reason to fear it not so long ago. Although, I have a feeling that had the British captured me or Messieurs Adams, Jefferson, or Hancock, or any of us in the Continental Congress, they simply would have hanged us and then spent every July 4th burning us in effigy, just as they do 'the Guy' every November 5th, 'Guy Fawkes Day.'"

"What does it mean, in effigy?" Elise asks.

"They fill old clothes with straw to make a man, just like a scarecrow. They build a bonfire, light it, and throw 'the Guy' on top to burn. Then they let off fireworks. It's quite a celebration. Children love it. But Marcus, I'm curious, aside from Gouverneur Morris last night, who else has been talking about 'the Guy?'"

"Swinbourne and Wimpole, on the ship."

"I wonder why. It's not something we celebrate here, obviously. Used to, in colonial times, but no longer. Now we have our Fourth of July."

"I don't know, but I heard Swinbourne say he has friends in London counting on it."

"Really? The logic escapes me. But then logic was never Swinbourne's strength," Franklin says, his eyes twinkling. "I shan't worry over it, not today. The Committee of Style is presenting its draft and that will bring more debate—but hopefully not too much more. We really do need to make an end and present our work to the country."

***

An exhausted Franklin comes home that afternoon. He leans heavily on me and the banister to climb the stairs.

"Will we never be done? All day on whether it should take two-thirds or three-quarters of the Congress to overrule a president's veto. It was three-quarters, now it's two thirds. At least we quashed George Mason's and Elbridge Gerry's motion for a declaration of rights—unanimously, after practically no debate."

"That's a mistake," I say flatly.

"No, it's not!" he says petulantly. But then he masters himself and his tone turns patient. "While I agree such a bill would have advantages, this is not the time. We need this Constitution passed by the convention and ratified by the states, now. If the people want a bill of rights, the Constitution can be amended to include one. But right now, more argument is the last—"

There is a loud, rapid knocking at the door downstairs. It stops, then starts again, stops, and starts again.

"Quite insistent, whoever they are," Franklin says, peering at his busy-body through the window.

"His hat is so large, I can't really see—Oh how marvelous! Marcus, quick! Help me downstairs!"

Franklin doesn't need my help. He's so eager to get to the first floor he practically pulls me down the stairs.

A short, slight man in white wig and stockings and a sky-blue suit stands just inside the door gesturing emphatically and spraying a machine-gun kind of French at Elise.

"Jean-Pierre, *mon ami*," Franklin cries.

The Frenchman beams as he comes to Franklin and embraces him.

French is the only language spoken for the next few minutes. Sally joins us. From the look on her face, it's clear her French isn't any better than mine.

"Father, just what is going on?" she finally interrupts.

"Sally, this is my dear friend Jean-Pierre Blanchard, from Paris. He and another man were the first to fly across the English Channel. They did it in a balloon filled with hydrogen gas and brought me the first letter by air from friends in London."

"Does that mean we have another guest?" she asks flatly. "Richard and the children will be home any day."

"So?" Franklin says. "What else is this big house for?"

As Sally stands with her hands on her hips and a frown on her face, Franklin and Blanchard jabber at each other. The more Blanchard talks, the more excited Franklin becomes.

"Most excellent news!" he says. "Jean-Pierre is here to demonstrate balloon flight. He wants our help—and quickly, since we'll want to have the demonstration no later than Sunday. First, Sally, you must go to the printing office and bring young Benjamin here. Second—"

"What? Just like that?" Sally says. "He comes a-knocking without even a letter to say he's coming; and we're supposed to—"

"He did write," Franklin says. "Months ago from Paris. But it never arrived. Who knows? Maybe the ship foundered or the mail was left aboard to sail the Caribbean. It makes no difference. What Jean-Pierre will show us is one of the most exciting developments of the age. I was pleased to be part of it in Paris. I saw the Montgolfiers' fly their hot air balloon, powered by burning straw. And I put some money into Jacques Charles's hydrogen filled balloon—which is how I met Jean-Pierre, who follows the hydrogen method.

"Now, Sally, once you've told young Benjamin to come, go to Doctor Rush and tell him it is urgent that he attend me here. If he is not at home, then seek him out. Once you've done that, go to the ironmongers and tell Mister Sawyer to come.

"And you Marcus, do you think I can trust you to go to the Walnut Street jail and tell the jailer to come immediately?"

"Yes, Dr. Franklin," I say, pleased to have regained some measure of his trust.

"Good. I'd better give you a note. He can be disagreeable. Be as quick as you can."

Minutes later, I hurry up Chestnut Street towards the State House. The convention and the Pennsylvania Supreme Court are adjourned, so the place is deserted. I cut through the building and its large back garden and cross Walnut Street to enter the jail.

A guard at the front asks me what my business is. I tell him I carry a message from Franklin for the jailer. With a jerk of his head, he orders me to follow.

The prison is a U-shaped compound with a large courtyard in the middle. The guard directs me to the wood door at the far end of the west wing. As I cross the courtyard, I pass a tall, thick post.

I reach the door and knock. A large, bearded man yanks it open and towers over me.

"Who're you?" he snarls.

"I … I come from Doctor Franklin," I answer. "This is his note. He asks that you come to him immediately."

"Is that so? I'm s'posed to drop everything and come runnin' just because the great Benjamin—"

"Here, you! Jailer!" a voice behind us calls.

I turn to see the guard escorting a young white man—well dressed in blue coat, tan breeches, and polished riding boots—leading a slave by a chain attached to a metal collar. The slave's hands are shackled behind his back.

"Jailer, I'm on my way from Camden back to Virginia," the young man says. "This new slave I bought is giving me trouble. Talks back, looks me in the eye—that sort of thing. A man on the ferry said you'd teach him his manners."

"Can't right now," says the jailer. "I'm wanted elsewhere."

"Well, how long until you're back?" The young man whines. "I'm in a hurry."

"Don't know. Could be a hour. Could be two," the jailer says slyly.

"Look, we're talking five swift licks. Shouldn't take more than two minutes."

"Here! Who d'you think you is, wanting me to drop everything and hop to it when it's Benjamin Franklin who needs me urgent? You want me to keep him waiting, it'll cost you."

"How much?"

The jailer looks the young man up and down.

"Five silver dollars."

The young man laughs a haughty laugh.

"You're lucky to get a shilling. But as I'm in a hurry and have no time to dicker, I'll pay you one silver dollar."

"You'll pay me four, and like it."

"Two silver dollars. Final offer."

The jailer says nothing. He just stands there, arms crossed over his chest, looking down at the smaller man.

"Oh fine! Four it is," the young man huffs.

Disappearing into his room, the jailer comes back carrying a short-handled cat, a lot like the one I'd seen Lucas Rush carry.

"Right, you," the jailer says, pointing the whip at me, "go tell Doctor Franklin I'll be along presently, as soon as I finish this here chore."

I start to leave. But the clank of the chain behind me makes me stop and turn. The jailer has dragged the slave to the post in the middle of the yard. I can almost feel the iron collar knocking at his jaw and collarbones and chafing his skin.

The jailer frees his hands.

"Shirt!" The owner calls to the jailer. "And don't go ripping it off him. He'll need it for the journey home."

With the butt of his whip, the jailer taps the buttons on the slave's shirt. The slave's hands tremble as he undoes them, but his face is like stone as the jailer re-shackles his hands around the post.

His back is to me now. He's been whipped before. Long, crusted scars crisscross his mahogany skin.

"Not too hard, jailer," the young man cautions. "I can't be nursing a sick slave all the way to Richmond. Just enough to remind him to keep his eyes out of mine and that the only words I want to hear are 'Yes, massa'."

I want to turn and go. But I can't. Something—I'll never understand what—has me rooted me to that spot.

The jailer takes a wide stance and strikes. The knotted strands whistle, then bite into the man's back with the sound of a mallet pounding meat. I flinch. My muscles jerk. But the slave does not scream. He takes the lash with a grunt. His back muscles bunch as he braces himself for another. Old cuts weep.

The young man stands in front of his slave, hands on his hips. He nods and the jailer lays on another stroke. Blood, bright red against his brown skin, wells and oozes down his back.

I want to stop it, but know I cannot. After three months in the world of 1787, if I know anything, it is that I am absolutely powerless to help. For once, anger does not rise in me. I have not cried in a very long time, not even when Gus died. But now, as I watch and hear that damned cat's talons rip into flesh, tears well, then pour down my cheeks.

CHAPTER 35

I hurry from the jail, my eyes swollen and streaming. I use the walk home to try and pull myself together. By the time I reach Franklin's, I think I'm fine.

But I must look like I'm not. When I enter the library, Franklin—who's meeting with Dr. Benjamin Rush, whom I'd met briefly the night of Franklin's illness—immediately asks: "Marcus, whatever is the matter?"

"Nothing," I say.

"Clearly, it is not nothing," Franklin says. "Something has upset you. I cannot help if you won't tell me what it is."

"I saw the jailer whip a slave."

"Abominable!" Rush cries. "Exactly why slavery must be abolished, Franklin!"

"My dear Doctor Rush, you know I am working diligently towards that end." Franklin says; then asks me: "What was his transgression?"

"If anything," Doctor Rush says. "And who says it was a he? Slave women are also whipped."

"Yes, Doctor, I'm well aware," Franklin says patiently. "I repeat, Marcus, what did the slave do wrong?"

"The owner said he was disrespectful, that the slave talked back and looked him in the eye. For that, the jailer tied him to a post and whipped him until he bled."

"Monstrous!" Doctor Rush says.

"But not illegal," Franklin says, "and until it is made so, there is nothing to be done.

"Now, Doctor Rush, the oil of vitriol to make hydrogen, we shall need quite a lot of it. Monsieur Blanchard says at least thirty bottles. Do you know where we can lay hands on such an amount?"

"I do. John Pennington, a student of mine, has developed a process to convert sulfur into the acid you want. He should be able to supply you. But Doctor Franklin, this business in the prison yard, really, it must be stopped! That there is a whipping post is bad enough. Public floggings have no place in civilized society, no matter the crime. But that one man can drag another to be whipped for nothing more than a look is barbaric. It goes against everything you and I have fought for all these years, including the Declaration of Independence we were so proud to sign."

"I couldn't agree more, Doctor Rush," Franklin says. "But I am powerless to do anything and frankly, I need the jailer. Monsieur Blanchard requires a protected area in which to fill his balloon with the hydrogen created from the reaction between the oil of vitriol and the iron filings I've been promised. Where better than the prison yard? It is large and will accommodate hundreds of spectators, each of whom will tender a small admission price so that Blanchard can pay his expenses. It will provide refuge from the wind during inflating and the initial ascent. And, it is across the street from the State House. All our delegates must see this new mode of travel. It has tremendous implications for the country—for exploration, militarily, and most important, for our commerce."

"Papa?" Sally appears at the library door with the jailer.

"Mister Kyle," Franklin calls, "good of you to come. Take a seat."

The jailer slowly walks the length of the room, his head tilted back, his mouth open, and his eyes darting like flies as he takes in the stacks of shelving. Threads and droplets of blood from the whipping stain the front of his shirt.

"Sure do have lots of books," he says. "What do you do with 'em all?"

"Read 'em," Franklin says dryly. But then his tone becomes solicitous. "Mister Kyle, I need your assistance."

"Always happy to help, Doctor Franklin, you know that. Came as soon as I got your note," he lies.

"Doctor Franklin," Doctor Rush says, rising, his face and voice angry. "I'll take my leave now, if I'm to see young Pennington and get him started on your vitriol."

"Thank you, Doctor."

Without a glance in the jailer's direction, Rush walks quickly from the room.

"Marcus? You may also go," Franklin says. "Mister Kyle, I have a proposition that just might make you some money."

"A bit of coin is always welcome!" I hear Kyle say as I leave.

***

The next several days are busy. Franklin puts Elise and me at Blanchard's disposal: Elise because she speaks French and me to do the donkey work—lifting, hauling, fetching, carrying, and also posting and handing out handbills announcing the balloon's flight on Sunday.

I don't mind the physical labor. Franklin and Blanchard are so excited, their enthusiasm is infectious. And this is science! It will be the first demonstration of manned flight in the United States. Forget the Wright Brothers and Kitty Hawk, this is where it really all begins. To me, this is as exciting as any launch from Cape Canaveral.

Also, Franklin is very optimistic about the convention. The delegates are moving quickly through the Committee of Style's final draft, rejecting most of the suggestions for further changes. Even Franklin's idea that Congress have the power to dig canals to improve transportation is voted down.

But Gouverneur Morris is successful in having a change made to the Fugitive Slave Clause. He inserts a bit of legal mumbo jumbo that stops the Constitution from acknowledging the legality of slavery. Franklin is very proud to tell me about it.

"You see, Marcus?" Franklin says. "We are making progress."

"Let me ask you something," I say. "Is there anyone today who is a slave who will not be a slave as the result of that change?"

"Well … No … But—"

"But? But nothing. It means nothing, practically. It's all just smoke. Just like Pennsylvania's "gradual abolition" law you always talk about. I read the copy on your desk. It does nothing to free existing slaves, only children born after the date of the act, and them only after they reach twenty-eight."

"Your points are valid," he concedes, his shoulders slumping. But then he fixes me with one of his appraising looks. "You are such an intelligent young man, Marcus. You have a keen mind and a sense of right and wrong that will serve you well in many instances. But you want to guard against that certain inflexibility I have noticed in you. It can lead to priggishness, and no one likes a prig. Just ask John Adams. There isn't a finer man, or a more exasperating one because of his unwillingness to bend. But you don't need me to tell you that. You'll be finding …"

His voice trails off and he frowns.

"What?" I ask. "What will I be finding?"

"Mmm?" Franklin's eyes are wide and innocent. "Who can say? Certainly not I. But the point I'm trying to make—we have prevented the Constitution from declaring slavery to be legal. That leaves the ground free for one day having it declared illegal and that is a step in the proper direction. A small step, mind you, but a step nonetheless.

"Now, tell me all about Monsieur Blanchard and how our balloon project is faring."

***

"It is done!" Franklin crows when he comes home from the convention on Saturday. "Debate has concluded. The final changes are made. All the states have voted yea, even if some of their delegates have not. The Constitution has been sent to the printer and will be ready for signing Monday morning.

"Oh, there were some croakers! Randolph and Mason from Virginia, and Elbridge Gerry, of course. They want the Constitution submitted to the states for further amendment and then debated again at another national convention. Can you imagine? Nothing would get done until the end of time! All three refuse to sign. General Washington is not happy with his friend George Mason. You should have seen him glare as Mr. Mason rose to explain why he will not sign.

"So, it is out of our hands, or will be on Monday. Now, it will be up to the people, and the state conventions they choose, to ratify it. I only hope that those who favor this Constitution will be able to persuade the people that it really is in their best interests.

"Now, what of Monsieur Blanchard and his balloon? Will he fly tomorrow?"

"He has everything he needs," I say. "We've assembled the basket the balloon will carry. The hydrogen maker—the iron filings, the sulfuric acid—they're all ready to go."

"Is that what you call oil of vitriol in your time, sulfuric acid?"

"Thought I wasn't supposed to tell you about the future."

"No matter. It makes sense, since sulfur is the prime ingredient."

"Anyway," I say, "Blanchard will start filling the balloon tomorrow morning and should be ready to go by no later than 4 o'clock."

"Excellent! And the handbills I had young Benjy print? Have they all been distributed?"

"I've pretty well covered the city. I put them up at any tavern or business that let me. Plus, I've been handing them out around the State House and at the market.

How many are left?"

"50, maybe 100."

"Let's not waste a one! Go to the waterfront. Pass them out to the passengers getting off the ferries. The more people who know about this, the more excitement there will be."

"Yes, and the more money Monsieur Blanchard and Mister Kyle will make."

"Is that wrong?"

"For Monsieur Blanchard, no; for Mister Kyle, absolutely!"

"But Marcus, it is not who makes money that is important. It's that the people get a chance to see the future; and I'll wager this will be a very big part of that future. Am I right or wrong?"

"Who can say?" I ask, smiling enigmatically. "Certainly, not I."

"I do wish you would stop throwing my words back at me. It really is most annoying."

***

I head down Market to distribute the last of the handbills along the waterfront. Even though it is mid-September, summer's heat has returned and my shirt sticks to my skin. It being market day, the street is teeming with buyers and sellers, which only makes things hotter. I pass Mrs. Carver's stall and wave, but she has so many customers crowded around, she doesn't see me.

I catch sight of Wimpole at the back of the crowd, looking very unhappy to be there. Like the runt of a litter, he scurries back and forth trying to find a spot to worm his way through. When he can't, he whines,

"Make way! Make way! Constable coming through!" When no one pays attention, he throws up his hands and stamps down Market.

I follow, not to follow him, but because we're both headed for the river. When he reaches the wharf at Market, he turns north, towards the Arch Street ferry. Swinbourne's warehouse lies dead ahead. The owner himself stands right outside the front door.

"Here! You! Wimpole!" he calls roughly. "I mean to speak with you."

Wimpole stops. Afraid one of them will recognize me, I turn my back and study a display of china and glassware in a shop window.

"Wimpole! Come here, now!"

The next time I look, the two men are gone and the warehouse front door is just closing.

I go to the alley running along the side of the warehouse and see the window I'd listened through before is still open. So, I listen at it again.

"— And I'm telling you, I want them hogsheads gone by the end of the day," Swinbourne says.

"Had trouble finding anyone," Wimpole says. "You want someone from out of town; that's been the trouble. I had a man, but he couldn't come on account of his wife's got the pox. So, I found another; only he can't come 'til tomorrow."

"Tomorrow! And what of the heat today? I've got all sorts of combustibles: rum, flower, flax, wood, bolts and bolts of cloth. Them hogsheads go up and there'll be nothing left."

"But there's nothing I can do!" Wimpole cries. "Besides, I told that old caretaker to be there tomorrow. I don't know where he's at today. Certainly not there."

"Not my concern," Swinbourne snaps. "Get them out! Now!"

"And I'm telling you, I can't today. I've no wagon and no one to deliver to. Tomorrow. And then on Monday, what a celebration there'll be."

"If I'm still alive Monday. Go on then. Go your way, if you can't do better."

CHAPTER 36

Fat and jolly with hydrogen, Blanchard's balloon of red, white, and blue varnished silk towers over the prison yard and the crowd of spectators. I've gotten up at four in the morning to help him inflate it, tie it down, and attach the wicker basket underneath. I hate that we use that whipping post as the central tethering point.

By noon, the balloon is ready. The jailer opens the prison doors. Over 1,000 people pay the five-cent admission price to see it close-up before it flies.

Washington and most of the rest of the delegates arrive around 4:00 p.m. Franklin is one of the last to arrive, riding in his sedan and followed by Sally and also her husband Richard and all the children who've come back from the farm in New Jersey.

The prisoners carry Franklin through the crowd to the basket, where he and Blanchard go back and forth in French. It seems like Blanchard wants Franklin to do something and that Franklin is tempted, but feels like he can't. But Blanchard keeps insisting until finally, with a shrug and embarrassed smile, Franklin nods and says, *"D'accord!"*

"Bon! Bon! Formidable!" says an excited Blanchard.

"Marcus," Franklin says, motioning to me. "Help me in. I'm going to fly."

"Oh Father, no!" Sally cries.

"Oh Father, yes!" Franklin says. "How can I refuse such an adventure? All my life, I've wondered what it would be like to fly like the birds."

"And what if there is a mishap and you are badly injured, or killed?" Sally asks as Franklin braces himself on my shoulder to climb into the basket.

"My dear, Monsieur Blanchard has flown his balloon many times and has yet to suffer anything more than a few bruises. And those only on windy days. A day like today? A day so calm and clear? I am sure we will go up, float for a while, and come down."

"But suppose you do not?" asks George Washington, who has joined us. "Suppose the wind carries you far away? How will you return? You must be here to sign our work."

"And I will be, I assure you. That is why I am taking young Marcus here. To bring me back should anything go awry." Franklin favors me with a smile. "Close your mouth, Marcus, before you catch a fly."

"Well young man? Why do you wait? Your employer needs you," Washington says. As always, when talking to me, he seems troubled. But then enthusiasm transforms him. "Let us not stand in the way of our greatest natural philosopher's next great experiment!"

I climb in, Blanchard signals, and men untie the ropes that tether us. The balloon ascends. A great "Ahhhh" rises from the crowd, only to become a disappointed "Ohhhh" as the balloon stops and hangs ten feet off the ground.

Franklin gives Blanchard a questioning look. The Frenchman looks me up and down, as though measuring me for a suit.

"*Bon!*" he says. "*Alors!*"

Lifting one of the ten large sacks he'd had me fill with sand, he pours half of it over the side. Slowly, we rise—too slowly for Monsieur Blanchard, who pours out the rest and half another bag after that.

That does it. Gravity places its hands on my shoulders, lightly pushing me down and coaxing my knees to bend. The people below grow smaller, their cheers dimmer.

"Ohhh," Franklin says. "Oh, how delightful!"

He'd been right about the wind. The air is very still. We float above the prison with all of Philadelphia stretched before us, its tree-lined streets intersecting each other to form William Penn's grid of city blocks filled with houses and commercial buildings of red brick or gray stone or wood. Smoke from cooking fires rises out of chimneys and makes the air hazy. But it does not obscure the bright, white steeples and cupolas topping the city's churches or the sparkle of sunlight on the Delaware.

The walled back garden of the Pennsylvania State House lies in front of us. It has been closed to prevent crowds hoping to see this flight from trampling it. But it isn't completely deserted. As Joseph Carver watches, several men unload large barrels from a horse-drawn wagon into an open hatch leading to the cellar.

"I feel sorry for Carver and those draymen, having to unload those hogsheads on a Sunday," Franklin says. "Wonder what's in them. Probably the Assembly's winter ration of rum and ale. Replacement for all that Luther Martin's drunk." He winks mischievously. "How wondrous this is, Marcus. Such a gentle means of locomotion. So peaceful."

A light puff of breeze ruffles the white hair at Franklin's shoulders.

"Doctor?" I ask. "Is that what a hogshead is? A barrel?"

"Yes, of course."

At the warehouse and aboard the ship, I'd heard Swinbourne and Wimpole talking about hogsheads. But I hadn't known what they meant. Now, seeing those barrels, and recalling exactly what they'd said, I feel a jolt of alarm in the pit of my stomach.

"Doctor, tell Blanchard we have to go down. Now!"

Franklin looks at me like I've lost my mind.

"I most certainly will not! What nonsense is this?"

"Doctor! Those barrels are gunpowder. Swinbourne and Wimpole mean to blow up the State House!"

Franklin's eyes open wide and his lips press together in a thin, grim line.

"Just what leads you to believe that?" His voice is cold with disbelief.

"I heard them talking. Swinbourne's been keeping a load of barrels for Wimpole. He wanted them out of his warehouse—and I mean he *really* wanted them out, like they were dangerous. And they talked about "the Guy" and getting back at you and having a "final celebration" before the convention was over and how people in London are depending on it."

"Why are you just telling me this now?"

"Because I didn't put it together until just now. I didn't know what a hogshead was or who they wanted paid back. All they ever called him was an "old farter" and someone who threw 'his own' away. But then, yesterday, I heard them again at the warehouse. Swinbourne was really

230

mad. He wanted those hogsheads gone, immediately, because of the heat. But Wimpole said it couldn't be until today because that's when the old caretaker would be there to accept delivery. And now, today, there those hogsheads are, being delivered to Mr. Carver."

"Almost certainly a different delivery," he says dismissively.

"On a Sunday?"

"That still doesn't mean—"

I'm not convincing him. In my head, I scramble, looking for another way.

"Okay," I say, "you tell me. What'd happen if someone did blow up the State House with all the delegates in it?"

"We'd ... lose all the work we've done."

"So, no Constitution and no new government. Plus, you'd lose all the delegates: Washington, Madison, Hamilton, Wilson, the Morrises, you. The most talented men in the country, that's what you keep calling them."

"Yes, to all that."

"So, things would stay the way they are. Like you said, the states would stay independent, free to practice slavery forever and there'd be no central authority to stop them."

"Yes."

"And Swinbourne makes all his money slaving."

"Most of it, I believe."

"And Wimpole wants the British back and blames you that your son William, once Governor of New Jersey, is no longer here to be his friend and help him in his business which is failing so badly he has to work as a constable. In other words, or his words, you ruined him."

All the impatience and skepticism are gone from Franklin's face, replaced by worry.

"You make creditable points, Marcus. Creditable enough to warrant an inspection of those barrels."

We've been so absorbed, I haven't noticed the wind has strengthened and changed direction. But when a gust rocks the basket, I see that, instead of moving slowly northwards, we are rapidly approaching the Delaware—and losing height! Blanchard looks worried. He talks urgently to Franklin.

"What?" I ask.

"He says the balloon is leaking," Franklin says.

"Leaking," I repeat dumbly.

"And he hopes we won't land in the river."

Blanchard picks up a sack of sand and throws it overboard. The balloon rises some, but continues for the river; and then, again, begins to drop.

"I hope so too," Franklin says. "I fear I could not swim to shore."

The wind is strong and steady, now. Almost before we know it, we are over water. And still dropping.

Blanchard points to the remaining bags. Together, he and I toss them all over the side. The balloon rises so fast the bottom drops out of my stomach.

"Marvelous!" Franklin cries. "I haven't felt anything like this since my last storm at sea."

"You're one crazy old man," I mutter as the wind gusts again, rocking us from side to side. We all grab the top edge of the basket to hang on.

Flying high now, we cross the Delaware's east bank and rush into New Jersey. Below, Camden's houses pour smoke. To the east lie acres of rich farmland: fields tilled in rows, orchards heavy with fruit, pastures where sheep or cattle graze—all unmarred by highways or developments. No wonder they'd one day call New Jersey "The Garden State."

Soon, our lack of ballast no longer compensates for our loss of gas and we begin dropping. A forest approaches. My heart hammers as I imagine us crashing into treetops and tumbling through branches to smash into hard ground. But again the wind helps us, carrying us over and into an already harvested cornfield. A flock of geese scavenging leavings explodes into the air. We're five feet off the ground. The forest cuts most of the wind. We slow to what seems like walking speed.

We'll land smoothly, I think, and loosen my aching death-grip. That's when the basket's leading edge hits one of the furrows and we go over. I fly out of the basket and slam into the ground so hard I have the wind knocked out of me, which is probably a good thing since my face is planted in the dirt.

When I can, I roll over to see blue sky. A head and shoulders appear.

"Next time, hold fast," Franklin scolds sagely.

I sit up and study him. He looks perfectly fine. Not even his clothes are mussed. Behind him, the balloon lies in the field, collapsing slowly. Blanchard looks like he's lost his best friend.

Franklin helps me up. I'm surprised by the strength of his grasp.

As I brush myself off, Franklin asks: "How do you suppose we might go about getting back? Certainly a return flight is out of the question."

"Ya think?" I crack as I turn 360 degrees, searching the horizon. Towards the east, a thin line of smoke rises in the air.

"Wonder if that's a house," I say, pointing.

"Possible. Only one way to find out."

He plants his walking stick and steps, only to cry: "Blast this gout!"

"Stay here and rest," I say. "I'll go see if there's any help for us."

"Nonsense! I'll be fine. I must just manage the pain."

"And how are you going to do that?"

"Simply by telling myself it doesn't hurt," he lectures. "Then it won't."

"Yeah, like that'll work."

"It will have to. We must return to Philadelphia as quickly as possible. I fear you are right: the delegates are in great danger. Now, I shall put my arm across your shoulders; and you shall put your arm around my back; and I will use my stick; and together we shall walk … one … two … ooh, that smarts … one … two—"

Monsieur Blanchard catches up to us, taking Franklin's walking stick and draping the old man's other arm over his shoulders, just as I am doing. Together, the three of us set out, matching our steps like marching soldiers.

Minutes later, a man comes in a wagon. He is older, stocky, and strong, with a seamed face and a head as bald and blunt as a bullet. He carries a flintlock rifle and looks mad enough to use it.

"Who are you people?" he barks. "What was that in the sky?"

"Sir, I am Doctor Benjamin Franklin. Perhaps you have heard of me. I and my companions were conducting a scientific experiment. What you saw was a balloon filled with a gas lighter than the air we breathe, which allows the balloon to float in the sky. Very simply, we flew here."

The man's eyes go wide; then become very small as he squints suspiciously.

"Franklin is you? The same Franklin as sired that bastard of a governor who used to do the King's bidding?"

"Alas, the same. Although I hope you will not hold that against my friends and me. I see you carry a rifle of the type procured for the American army. You served in our Revolution?"

"Was with Washington the morning after Christmas when we beat them Hessians at Trenton."

"I honor your service. I too was of service to the nation and I'm hoping—"

"I know what you done," the man says grudgingly. Then he sticks out his hand. "Name's George Parsons. This be my farm."

"We must return to Philadelphia, urgently. Lives depend on it."

"Don't know as I can help you with that. I only got this wagon. Me and my boys need it to get our crops in."

"As I said, lives are at stake," Franklin insists.

"I heard you. But this be my only horse. What if she pulls up lame or an axle breaks? Those roads are rough and if I don't have me wagon, I ain't gonna have—"

"I have gold," Franklin says.

Parsons's mouth snaps shut.

"Shall we say one gold doubloon?" Franklin asks.

A sly look takes over the farmer's face. Franklin matches it and they start dickering. Minutes later, the deal is done. The farmer will take Franklin and me immediately back to Camden and the ferry for Philadelphia and then return for Blanchard and his balloon, all for two gold doubloons.

CHAPTER 37

"Franklin, you ride up here with me," Parsons says. "Your servant can ride in back."

"His name is Marcus Santana," Franklin says. "And as he is a friend, it will please me to ride with him—in the back."

As we set off, the bottom of a sickly, grayish-yellow sun is just beginning to sink below the horizon. We bump and bounce over rough farmland. It is painful for Franklin. His jaw bulges as he grits his teeth. But he never complains.

Things don't improve when we reach the road. It is wash-board in places and rocky or pot-holed in others. Plus, the horse is balky. The sway-backed nag keeps stopping to blow and heave.

"Increase the pace, Parsons," Franklin says. "Our business is most urgent."

"She goes how she goes," the farmer says. "Rather walk?"

"Might be faster," Franklin answers sourly, putting a voice to what I'm thinking.

Parsons stops the wagon.

"You're both welcome to get out and go your own way."

"We could," Franklin says. "But then you'll never get your gold."

With an ugly look at Franklin, Parsons snaps the reins across the horse's back. She walks on. A second snap and Parsons's "hyaaah!" send her into a trot.

It starts raining. Not hard, but steady, soaking through my clothes which grow heavy and itch. I'm grateful the nights are still warm.

We get to Camden. The ferry is closed and there's no one to tell us when the next one leaves. In fact, everything's closed: inns, taverns, boarding houses—which means no place to eat or sleep. I haven't eaten since breakfast. But if Franklin isn't complaining, then neither am I.

The rain never lets up. Parsons finds a place under a tree where the ground is dryer and crawls under the wagon to stretch out. He doesn't invite Franklin or me to join him. We stay in the back of the wagon. Soon, Parsons's snoring tells us he's asleep.

"Thank you," I say to Franklin.

"Mmm?"

"For riding in back with me. You didn't have to do that."

"You're a fine young man, Marcus. It will be my pleasure—I will be proud—to have you as a traveling companion—anytime."

The wind picks up and with it comes more rain, the hard, lashing, soaking kind. It is impossible to sleep. We cross our arms, duck under our hats, and ride it out.

But Farmer Parsons doesn't. The ground under the wagon becomes soaked. When daylight breaks, I am pleased to see he is as wet as us and filthy with mud.

I look across the Delaware to Philadelphia and can just make out the red brick tower of the State House.

"Good," Franklin says. "It's still there. I've had my fears it wouldn't be."

"Look at that river," I say.

The Delaware is a mass of waves and whitecaps whipped up by gusting winds.

"Do you think we'll be able to cross?" I ask.

Franklin looks doubtful.

The owner of the ferry arrives, looks at how rough the water is, and shakes his head.

"Ain't going out in that," he says. "Boat'll get swept downriver, or founder."

"But we have urgent business in Philadelphia," says Franklin. "It is imperative we get across."

"Just have to wait until she calms down. Don't want to drown, do you? Or me to lose my boat? Then where would I be?"

"No, you're right of course," Franklin says. But I can tell he's very worried.

"I could try swimming it," I say. "Get across and get word to General Washington."

Franklin shakes his head. "No, it's too dangerous. When I was young and strong like you, I was a very good swimmer. But I never would have tried to cross under these conditions. We'll just have to wait and hope for the best."

Behind us, a voice cries: "Whatchew mean, ain't goin' out? How's I'm gonna makes my money?"

I know that voice. I turn to see Solomon, the ferryman. I go over and get him and introduce him to Franklin as the man who helped me rescue Elise.

"You are a brave man," Franklin says. "My family is in your debt."

"Family? Missy 'Lise kin to you?"

"Anyone who lives in my house, I consider family. So, you know the river, do you? When will it be safe to cross?"

"Go now, if'n you got the right price."

"How?" Franklin asks.

"Got my rowin' boat, which I use to catch me eels. Fix up my mast and sail for it. Wind's good and strong. We'll get across right fast."

"Bah!" Farmer Parsons scoffs. "Don't pay him no mind, nor any coin neither. He don't know nothin'. You'll drown if you go with him, if the eels don't getcha'."

"I'm willing to risk it," Franklin says. "Solomon, how much?"

"To go out in that? Twenty dollars."

"Fine, let's get started," Franklin agrees.

"Not you," Solomon says. "Boat'll barely take two. You'se too heavy. I'll take the young'un. He can do your bidding."

"And you ain't goin' anywhere, not without paying me my money," Parsons says. "And I still have your friend and his contraption to go back and get."

His face full of worry, Franklin says: "Marcus, attend me."

We step away from the others for privacy.

"Listen closely, Marcus. I am not much in favor of this plan. It is dangerous."

"You were willing to go."

"It is one thing to gamble my life, especially when so near the end. It is quite another to gamble yours, when you don't belong here and your death may cause—"

237

"Who says I'm not supposed to be here?"

Franklin's eyebrows rise. "What do you mean?"

"You keep saying I'm not supposed to be here, that I might ruin the future or cause some kind of cosmic imbalance. How do you know? How do you know that my traveling through time or between worlds isn't exactly what is supposed to be happening? That it isn't part of the plan of "The Great Creator," or whoever or whatever it is that's running things?"

Franklin looks at me and smiles.

"I don't. But I am heartened to hear you ask such an astute question, one I have considered carefully and for which I have no answer. Except to say that, clearly, you have not wasted your time with me. Now, this man taking you across the river, what do you really think of him?"

"We were in a pretty bad situation together, out on that ship. He could've left, but he didn't. And he got me and Elise back safe."

"Sounds a good man. Sure you want to risk this? After all, we don't really know what's in those barrels. Could be nails for a building project I haven't heard about, or any number of things."

"Could be. But what if it is gunpowder? What if they really do mean to blow up the State House? What if they succeed? You won't lose just the Constitution. You'll lose everyone who made it. And then things really will be different for the world I know."

"Then here's what we will do. I will take the first ferry across. Meanwhile, I will pay off Parsons and make arrangements with the ferry owner to bring Blanchard and his balloon across the river. I'll just have to trust Parsons to keep to our deal about getting Blanchard here. You will cross with Solomon. When you get to Philadelphia, go to General Washington. He is staying at the home of Robert Morris—"

"At Sixth and Market. I know," I say, impatient to be away but nervous to be going.

"Tell him our suspicions. Tell him exactly what we think is going on and exactly why we think it. Tell him all that you've seen and heard."

I join Solomon at his small boat and help him put up the mast.

CHAPTER 38

"Wind's against us, so's we gonna have to zig and zag our way across," Solomon says.

I know nothing about sailing, so I have no idea what he's saying.

"Means we gonna have to go first one way and then t'other. That sail's gonna jerk side to side. Last thing we need is you in the way. Lie in the bottom and keep your head down. Be good ballast. Keep us from gettin' blowed over and takin' a swim, mebbe."

The wind is so strong Solomon almost can't get up the sail. I help him hoist and then lie in the row boat's bottom in a cold quarter-inch of dirty water. The boat's hard ribs dig into mine.

The wind stretches the sail tight and we run fast. I can hear the rush of water under the hull. Every time the bow cuts into a wave, it's like getting a cold bath. When a gust of wind heels us over, the river pours over the gunwale.

"Bail!" Solomon yells. "Use your hat."

My tricorn is a leaky bucket, but better than nothing. We take on a lot of water: at least two inches.

I look across the river to Philadelphia. It seems just as far off as when we started.

"Duck, ya fool!" Solomon yells as the boat slews around and the sail whips across the hull. "Told ya, keep your head down if'n you don't want to lose it."

Another gust hits and we heel over again. More water pours in over the side. Then the bow digs deep into another wave and there's a good four inches.

"Bail! Bail!" Solomon shouts in a voice that makes me afraid.

I look back to see him fighting for control, and losing. Over his shoulder, Camden seems as far away as Philadelphia had been only minutes before.

As we turn, an enormous wave hits. It flips us and throws me down deep into the river. My coat, weskit, and heavy shoes weigh me down and, for a couple of terrifying seconds, I think I'm going to drown. I struggle to shuck off everything except my britches, shirt and stockings, and that helps some. Rising now, I make for the surface, reaching it just as the lack of oxygen forces me to open my mouth and breathe. Gulping air, I try raising myself up to look for Solomon, but waves and whitecaps are all I can see.

I call out his name, but hear nothing back.

I swim for shore, changing strokes every time I tire: crawl to breaststroke to side stroke back to crawl. Finally, I drag myself onto a muddy bank. I'm way down river from Philadelphia, soaked, shivering, and shoeless. But I'm alive. Then I remember Solomon. I stand at river's edge, calling his name. No answer. My eyes sweep the river, searching for him or his boat. Nothing.

He's got to be a better swimmer than me, I tell myself. *He's up river, probably. We'll meet along the way.*

I set off for Philadelphia, keeping to the soft sand and mud of the river's beaches and shallows. The low, gray ceiling gives way to sun and blue sky.

As I walk, I call for Solomon. I never get an answer.

I'll see him at Mrs. Carver's, I think. *He'll be there, slurping up a big bowl of pepper pot.*

But when I reach the city, I can't go to the market. The church bells strike 10:00 o'clock. The convention begins in an hour. I have no time to lose. At what is now South Street, I take a diagonal line and zig and zag north and west to get to Robert Morris's house.

I pound on the door with its great brass knocker; and keep pounding until a black servant in white wig and footman's livery opens it. He takes one look at me and starts to close it, but I push it back open.

"I must see General Washington. Doctor Franklin sent me."

The servant laughs.

"Doctor Franklin?" The man's voice is rich and cultured. "Oh, I hardly think so. Doctor Franklin would never send such a rabble. Leave, now, or I shall call the watch."

I know I look awful: no shoes, clothes all torn and stained and stinking of the river.

"Please, I know how it looks. But it's true. Doctor Franklin sent me. I almost drowned crossing the river to get here, which is why I look this way. But the General knows me. He approved my clerking for Doctor Franklin at the convention."

"You, at the convention? Do you think I am a fool? I am no fool! And you are no clerk. Be gone!"

"I'm telling you, General Washington knows me. I just saw him yesterday. Go tell him Doctor Franklin's clerk is here with a message for him. Tell him it's urgent! Go on! There are lives at stake!"

"I will not disturb people at table. Mr. Morris would boil me alive if I interrupted him and his guests for the likes of you. Touch this door again and I shall call the watch."

The door slams shut in my face.

I stand there, weighing my options. I can try again; and probably get arrested. And even if I do get to see Washington, there is no guarantee he'll believe me.

Franklin hadn't given me the right instructions. I can see that now. He should have sent me to the State House first, to find out what was in those barrels. If they are innocent, I won't have to say a thing. Only if they are dangerous will I need to sound an alarm.

Church bells strike the half-hour: ten-thirty. I haven't a second to waste.

I walk-jog as fast as my shoe-less feet will let me to the State House. Sentries guard the entrance. They aren't going to let me in, not with me having been banned, and certainly not the way I look. So I walk down to Walnut, hoping the great wooden doors to the back garden are open.

I'm in luck. Not only are they open, but Joseph Carver is there, cleaning up fallen branches from the storm. I jog over to him.

"What in tarnation happened to you?" he asks, looking me up and down.

"No time to explain," I say, breathing hard. "Listen, yesterday, some barrels were delivered here. You know what was in them?"

"Yeah. Fine porter ale. From General Washington. His gift to the Assembly for letting the convention use its hall."

"How do you know it's really ale?"

"'Cuz that's what the man said."

"Did you check?"

"Now why would I do that? Ain't my barrels. Ain't got no business fool'n with 'em."

"What if they aren't from Washington? What if it isn't porter?"

"Who says it ain't?"

"Doctor Franklin," I say, knowing his word carries more weight than mine. "He thinks they could be gunpowder—enough to blow this building and everyone in it to kingdom come."

"What kinda trick you tryin to play on me? G'wan now! Don't have time to be listening to your foolishness."

"It's no trick. Doctor Franklin sent me here to check it out. I've come all the way from New Jersey and I've gone through a lot to get here, which is why I look the way I do."

"Was you with him in that balloon? Saw it fly over yesterday, but didn't know who was in it 'til I heard some people say it was Doctor Franklin. He okay? Everyone been wondering where exactly he got blown to."

"It's a long story and I don't have time to explain. I need to check those barrels."

"What you need and what I can let you do is two different things."

"I won't hurt anything, I promise. Come watch me. I just want to open one to make sure there isn't any danger."

"Can't be opened, not without spilling what's inside."

"Then how—"

"I could tap one. See what runs out. But if I do and its ale, folks'll say I was stealing."

"No, they won't, not if Franklin's right."

"And if he ain't?"

"Then he'll take the blame and make sure you don't get in trouble."

"I don't know ..."

"Please, Mr. Carver! You could be saving so many lives. And costing so many, if you don't!"

"Okay. Let's go. But make it quick."

He leads me to the two wooden doors with iron hinges that are the hatchway to the cellar under the Assembly Room.

"Where's the lock?" Carver asks. "I know I locked up when them boys got done their delivery."

Pulling open the doors, he goes down the stairs, stopping to light a lantern hanging on the wall. From it, he lights a candle which he uses to light several other lanterns as we proceed into the cellar. By their dim glow, I can just make out old tables, chairs, benches, and boxes. Firewood is stacked along a wall running lengthwise under the Assembly Room. Twelve barrels stand in front of that wood.

We don't need to tap any of them. Someone has already smashed through the end of one. Black powder lies in a mound on the floor and a solid line of powder leads away from the mound. We'd missed it on the way in. Now, I follow it all the way back to the rough, wooden stairs.

It is a fuse. All someone has to do to set it off is open the cellar door, throw in something lit, and run.

Carver still holds his lit candle. Above us, I hear the thud of feet and the creak of floorboards. The delegates are arriving.

"Mister Carver," I say, as calmly as I can so as not to startle him. "Very carefully, I want you to put out that candle. Don't blow. Wet your fingers and snuff it. Don't let anything hot touch the floor. You're standing in gunpowder."

"That's right, don't move, either of you," says another voice, jolting me. "I got my guns on you and I ain't afraid to use 'em."

From behind the stairs, a dark mass rises and then steps out into the cellar holding two flintlock pistols, both cocked.

"Lucas!" Carver says. "What you doin' down here?"

"Nothing I ain't been paid for, old man—and a nice bit of coin too. Enough to get me out of here and slaving and have my own place, and a woman, mebbe, and live in peace. Ain't you nor no one else gonna get in the way of that."

"Okay, take it easy," I say. Lucas is big and powerful, but he's also frightened. He talks fast and keeps licking his lips.

"Both of you, go to the back there and sit against the wall. Sit on your hands," he says.

Carver and I do what he says, except I don't sit on my hands. I tuck them behind my back, trying to make it look like I'm sitting on them.

That costs me Lucas's boot in my stomach.

"Better listen, boy," he rasps. "Old man, take that rope holding up your pants. Tie the boy's hands behind him. Tight! If it ain't, I'll know and give you what I gave him."

Lucas's kick hasn't hurt as much as I'm making it seem. He missed my solar plexus. And I'd learned from Gus how to take a punch. But I act like I've had the wind knocked out of me.

Just as Carver pulls my arm behind my back, I launch myself at Lucas. Aiming as low as I can, I get my shoulder into his knees, wrap my arms around his calves and drive with everything I have.

The pistols explode with a deafening BAM! BAM! and I freeze, certain the gunpowder is going to blow, which gives Lucas time to regain his balance. He hammers at my back with the butts of both guns, driving me to the floor.

As he turns for the cellar door, I reach out to grab his foot, but I miss. A weight like an anvil crashes into my back as Carver uses me to springboard onto Lucas. The slave catcher pushes him off, then sends him tumbling with an open-handed slap that sounds like the crack of a whip.

Lucas makes for the stairs, but Carver is on him again, this time grabbing him by his belt to pull him back. Lucas lashes out with his foot and I hear Carver's cry of pain. Lucas is free now. He takes the stairs two at a time and disappears.

"STOP!" a voice commands.

"Halt or we'll fire!" orders another.

A shot rings out.

I go to Mr. Carver. He is on his hands and knees, shaking his head to clear it.

I help him up and start for the door just as a group of sentries rush down the hatch, flintlocks at the ready. Carver and I both raise our hands. The sentries grab both of us and hustle us up the stairs.

"You boys be careful with them guns," Carver says. "There's gunpowder all over the floor, and in them barrels too."

Lucas lies sprawled on the ground several feet from the hatch, clutching his leg. Blood wells from between his fingers.

A crowd of delegates gathers: Roger Sherman, Gouverneur Morris, and James Madison among them. Others stream out the door, including Washington and Hamilton who'd lent their arms to an exhausted looking Benjamin Franklin.

The crowd makes way for them.

"Sergeant of the guard, report!" Washington orders.

"Well, sir, not really sure I can say what happened. Me and my men heard shots coming from what sounded like below. So we came round to this here cellar door and up popped this fella' at a run with them two pistols in his hands. We told him to stop, but he didn't. Corporal Anderson here brought him down."

"Yes? And what have you to say for yourself?" Washington asks Lucas.

He spits in the dirt at the General's feet.

"I believe I may be able to shed some light on this, General," Franklin says. "It seems there has been a plot to destroy our convention. Downstairs, in the cellar, I think you'll find a number of hogsheads filled with gunpowder. Those will need to be removed. And I think it best we discuss the rest of this privately, inside."

"What is he doing here?" Washington asks, pointing at me. "Doctor, I thought we'd agreed he was no longer to come here."

"We did. And yes, I sent him here despite that agreement. We learned of these barrels on our balloon flight yesterday afternoon. Unfortunately, the wind took us over into New Jersey—just as you feared, General. We returned as quickly as we could, but when we reached the river, it was too rough for the ferry to cross. Marcus volunteered to sail across in a small boat. Judging from his appearance, I daresay he's risked his life to warn us of the danger—a danger which he uncovered and brought to my attention. All of us owe him our lives and our thanks."

Washington looks me up and down with that same perplexed, disconcerted expression I so often seemed to draw from him.

"Franklin, it's extraordinary!" he says in a low voice so no one else can hear, "Every time I see this boy, I'm reminded of someone I knew long ago."

Hamilton looks at him sharply. "General, I have had the very same thought," he murmurs. "But really, it simply could not be."

"General," Franklin breaks in quickly, "may I suggest we adjourn the convention for several hours, say until 2:00 o'clock this afternoon, so that the danger can be removed? Then we may proceed with the signing."

"Excellent plan of action!"

"May I also ask that before we sign, I be allowed to speak? I have something to say I feel the delegates should hear."

"I'm sure we will all listen most attentively."

"And finally, in light of all that Marcus has done, might you now lift your ban and allow him to witness the signing of our work?"

"To allow any less would make all of us delegates seem ungrateful," Washington says to Franklin and then turns to me. "Which, I assure you, young Marcus Santana, we are most decidedly not."

CHAPTER 39

On the way back to Franklin's, I make a detour to Mrs. Carver's at the market, hoping to see Solomon or hear that he'd been there. But he isn't and hasn't been. The thought that he has drowned ties a hard, aching knot in my chest and blurs my vision with tears.

When I get back to the house, I tell Franklin what I think has happened. He sends Sally to fetch the constable to organize a search and me to wash up, change, and meet him in the library. He has one more speech to dictate for this last session, and there isn't a moment to lose.

When I get to the library, I find him slumped in his chair. His face is pale and it looks like someone has smudged coal under his eyes.

"The hero of the hour!" he cries hoarsely. "Or the day! Possibly the century! Although no one can ever know what those curs Swinbourne and Wimpole tried to do. We would look much too weak and vulnerable. And who knows what ideas it might give others? Can you live with that? Unsung heroism?"

I nod. "Pop likes to say 'As long as good's getting done, it doesn't matter who gets the credit.'"

"Wise man, your father."

Again I nod, thinking how I wished Mom and Pop and Gus could have been here to see what I'd done.

"Quickly, take up your *porte-crayon*," Franklin says.

He spends the next 15 minutes dictating in a raspy, quavering voice. I write it all out in my best hand.

The sedan chair arrives just before two. I help Franklin in. His skin is hot and I'm glad he'll be carried. I keep pace with the sedan and my eye on him.

"Oh, Marcus, I've grown so soft," he just about whispers. "One night sleeping rough, and look what it's done. When I was the crown's Deputy Postmaster for the colonies, I traveled the countryside and thought nothing of nights in the open."

We arrive at the State House. Word has traveled that the Constitution is to be signed and a crowd of citizens waits just outside the front door. As I help Franklin from the sedan they applaud, then cheer. A smile, and color, rises in his cheeks and he lifts his tan tricorn in acknowledgment.

Washington's carriage arrives next and the cheering swells. Washington has brought Robert Morris, James Madison, and Alexander Hamilton with him. They, I, and the crowd watch as Washington links his arm through Franklin's and walks with him into the Assembly Room.

Most of the delegates are already seated. Joseph Carver has moved my desk right up against the gated railing separating the public area from the Assembly Room floor. I'll be able to get to Franklin quickly if he needs me. I sit and, as the few stragglers file in, ready my copy book and *porte-crayon*.

Washington calls the convention to order and recognizes my employer. But Franklin has decided his voice is not up to it. As he's done several times, he gives his speech to James Wilson and stands while the Scotsman in heavy, owlish spectacles reads it out:

> Mister President, I confess that there are several parts of this Constitution which I do not at present approve, but I am not sure I shall never approve them, for having lived long, I have experienced many instances of being obliged by better information or fuller consideration to change opinions, even on important subjects, which I once thought right but found to be otherwise. It is, therefore, that the older I grow, the more apt I am to doubt my own judgment and to pay more respect to the judgment of others.
>
> In these sentiments, sir, I agree to this Constitution with all its faults, if they are such, because I think a general government necessary for us, and there is no form of government but what may be a blessing to the people if well administered, and believe farther that this is likely to be well administered for a course of years, and

can only end in despotism, as other forms have done before it, when the people shall become so corrupted as to need despotic government, being incapable of any other.

I doubt too whether any other convention we can obtain may be able to make a better Constitution. For when you assemble a number of men to have the advantage of their joint wisdom, you inevitably assemble with those men all their prejudices, their passions, their errors of opinion, their local interests, and their selfish views. From such an assembly can a perfect production be expected?

It therefore astonishes me, sir, to find this system approaching so near to perfection as it does; and I think it will astonish our enemies, who are waiting with confidence to hear that our councils are confounded like those of the builders of Babel and that our states are on the point of separation, only to meet hereafter for the purpose of cutting one another's throats.

He goes on to promise that he will keep any remaining doubts he might have about the Constitution to himself; and asks his fellow delegates to do the same. Indeed, he encourages all of them to act unanimously in recommending the Constitution to the country; and to demonstrate that unanimity now with every delegate's signature.

As he and James Wilson sit down, the delegates thump their walking sticks in approval. It is a good speech, calling for humility and the sacrifice of egos in order to build unity through compromise and mount a government that will be strong and efficient enough to secure the people's happiness.

But it leaves me feeling hollow. Why? Because when Franklin talks about the happiness of the people, he isn't talking about all the people. If he had been, that Constitution never, ever would have tolerated slavery.

I still haven't found a good, pragmatic argument to refute the logic of "union first, then abolition," especially in light of what comes later. Ultimately, it will require a strong central government—the Union, otherwise known as the federal government—to abolish slavery throughout the country. But the Constitutional Convention's decision to accommodate slavery is one that will help to cause immeasurable suffering for decades, even centuries, to come. At least, that's the way I see it.

When the applause finishes, General Washington calls up each state's delegation to sign the Constitution. Franklin's call for all to sign persuades every delegate present, except three: Governor Edmond Randolph and George Mason from Virginia and Elbridge Gerry from Massachusetts. They believe the Constitution gives the federal government too much power and the citizens and the individual states not enough; and that a Bill of Rights is absolutely necessary. It occurs to me that Randolph's refusal to sign is pretty ironic since the Constitution is based on the Virginia Plan he introduced at the very beginning of the convention.

When it's time for the Pennsylvania delegation to sign, its members come to the dais. Beginning with Franklin, each man mounts the two steps, dips his quill in the silver inkstand made by Philip Syng—the old gentleman who'd asked me to keep the ledger at the Union Fire Company meeting—and scratches his name.

As Franklin watches James Wilson sign, he looks to the gold-painted carving of a half-sun at the very top of the president's chair and says:

"I've heard it said that painters find it difficult in their art to distinguish a rising sun from one that is setting. Often in the course of these sessions, and the vicissitudes of my hopes and fears as to its issue, I have looked at that sun behind the president without being able to tell whether it was rising or setting. But now, at length, I have the happiness to know that it is a rising and not a setting sun."

We leave the chamber and State House a short time later. Franklin's sedan chair is waiting. Carver stands by it, almost at attention, holding open the door. A smile comes to Franklin's face. I have told him all that Carver had done to save the State House and everyone in it. Franklin had wanted the chance to thank him personally and to see if there was anything he wanted or needed. Now, he would have that chance.

Halfway between the front door and the sedan chair, a well-dressed, older woman steps from the crowd, lays her hand on Franklin's arm, and regally asks: "Well, Franklin, what sort of government have you given us?"

Franklin's face turns as grave as I'd ever seen it.

"A republic, Madam, if you can keep it."

And then that sunny smile breaks out again and Franklin walks on to Mr. Carver.

***

Unfortunately, the sunniness of Franklin's smile leaves the weather completely unmoved. By the time we get back to his house, the sky is a low, gray ceiling again.

"I must have a bath and a nap," Franklin says. "There's to be a farewell dinner for the delegates at the City Tavern tonight. I want to be well rested. Our job is far from finished, of course. Now we must turn our attention to ratification by the states. The delegates will have to do much of the work convincing their fellow citizens of the rightness of this new Constitution. We must send them off with feelings of accomplishment and good fellowship so that they will enthusiastically promote it.

"Marcus, tell Elise I shall require extra hot water if I am to soothe these aching muscles. Help her, if you please. Then sit with me. There is much we must discuss."

I go downstairs and find Elise rolling out dough for a pie.

"Do you like apple or berries?" she asks.

Before I can say apple, a voice behind me says. "Oh apple, please. I do so love my apple pie!"

"Solomon!" I shout.

The grizzled older man sits on a stool in the corner by the fire. Naked, except for the blanket he's wrapped himself in, he cradles a bowl of soup in his hands.

"What happened?" I say. "I looked all over for you. I thought you drowned."

"Boy, I told you, I'm a river man. Ain't no way I'm gonna drown. Ain't no way I was gonna lose my boat, neither. When she rolled over like that, her mast and sail broke off. But the boat, she kept float'n right good, even if her downside was up. I grabbed hold and started kicking for shore. That's when the current snatched us up and sent us downriver, and all I could think was how much paddling I was gonna have to do to get back—and with no oars! But then that current put us right in the way of a schooner. She picked us up and sailed us directly to the Market Street Wharf. I went to Mrs. Carver's for something to eat. She was all out of soup and just going home. So, she brought me here. Now, Missy 'Lise is washing my clothes in that big pot, and making me a pie whilst I eat this here soup."

"His clothes, your clothes, they all stink the same," Elise said, laughing. "So they all go in the same pot."

There is something different about her. She is smiling, and there is a lightness in her step and voice.

"You seem happy," I say.

"Happy? I am joyful! Doctor Franklin has found my mother and son. They were sold to a farmer in Virginia. Mr. Madison is making arrangements to purchase them for Doctor Franklin and send them here. Soon, we shall all be together and we will be free. *Maman* and I will work to earn money and save enough to buy a house and my son will go to school and we will be free."

I am happy for her, but also … disappointed. I still have feelings for her. I still think doing something really big for her—like helping her find her mother and son—will be the way into her heart. I haven't yet learned that's not how love works.

"That's great!" I say, hiding my disappointment behind the happiest smile I can muster; and then tell her Franklin wants his bath.

***

Franklin likes having me read to him as he bathes. We are halfway through *Gulliver's Travel's*. Once he's settled, I pick up the book.

"Not today, Marcus," Franklin says. "We must talk.

"I have given much thought to getting you home, as I promised. But now, I must confess, I don't know how. I have no understanding of what happened that day, or how to make it happen again. I believe it must have something to do with the Leyden jars and the electrical water heater I was experimenting with, but I don't know what to do to reopen the portal.

"And yet, I know you will leave here and that we will meet again at another time. You do not know this because it hasn't happened in your life, yet. But it has happened in mine. The question is when, and how, your departure will occur and what to do with you in the meantime.

"You will need to remain here, I think, in case you are meant to leave the same way you came. That being the case, I was hoping you might continue as my clerk. There is still so much left for me to do: my work as President of Pennsylvania and with the hospital and university, scientific papers, the blasted autobiography, correspondence, and most important, the abolition society. I very much want to concentrate a good deal of my remaining energies on that.

"And we do seem to get along tolerably well, that's when you're not baying at the moon about things not changing quickly enough to suit you."

"Is that what you called the Declaration of Independence? Baying at the moon?"

"No, but I'm sure King George did—not to mention his Royal Governor, son William," he says bitterly. But then he relents. "Your point is well taken. Change is hard and often disliked, feared, hated. There's always some old croaker, like me, to scoff and say something that should be done can't be. That is why I need someone like you around—to remind me that it can be.

"So I want you to continue to help me. But if you do, you must control your temper. Can you do that?

"I … I'm not sure. I'm not sure how to do that. I'm not even sure where the anger comes from."

He fixes me with that appraising look of his; and then asks: "Shall I tell you a secret?"

"What?"

"Your brother Augustus's death was not your fault."

A lump swells in my throat, and for the second time that day, my eyes well. I struggle to master myself.

"How do you know that's what I think?" I ask, resenting his intrusiveness, but dying to know.

"Don't ask. Just believe me when I tell you that I know. Your brother died serving his country, which was something he very much wanted to do. He did not enlist in the Army simply to have his education paid for so that there would also be money for your education. He enlisted because soldiering was his calling. I daresay he would have been a soldier—and that he would have died as he did—even had you never been born. So, you have no cause for guilt, no reason to blame yourself. Absolve yourself of it. Place as much distance as you can between you and his death. That may well go a long way to resolving your anger.

"Now, what do you say? Will you help me?"

"I'd like to. I'd like to very much," I say, knowing what he's just said has given me a lot to think about and that, with no way home, I'll have lots of time on my hands to do just that.

"Good! Then you can begin by getting me out of this tub. I am so tired. I really must nap."

I help him dry off and get into a clean nightshirt and climb the stairs to his bedchamber. On the staircase just across from his door his "lightning signal" tinkles softly. I'd first heard it only minutes after my arrival and then all through the summer, whenever lightning was close.

It was another of Franklin's inventions. He'd run a wire from the lightning rod bolted to his chimney down the staircase. Then he'd split that wire in half and attached a small bell to each end. Between the two bells, he'd suspended a small brass ball by a piece of silk thread. Electricity from passing clouds would be drawn down into the lightning rod and run down the wire to each bell, which would then create a current that made the small brass ball swing from bell to bell like a clapper.

"Such a cunning little device, if I may say," he says, smiling wistfully. "My wife, Deborah, hated it. It scared her, I think. More than once I wrote her from Europe with instructions for severing its connection. And yet, each time I came home, it was as I had left it."

He sinks down onto his bed with a sigh of great relief, if not pleasure.

"Wake me at seven, Marcus," he says as I pull the covers up around his shoulders. "That's a good lad. You are, you know, a very good ..."

He can say no more because he is fast asleep.

CHAPTER 40

Outside Franklin's bed chamber, the lightning signal isn't just tinkling anymore. The little brass ball beats the two bells hard and fast, like the striker on an old-fashioned alarm clock. But unlike an alarm clock, the ringing doesn't slow. It speeds up, sounding louder and louder. Suddenly, the little ball freezes midway between the two bells. Seconds later, white electricity sparks and a great, ripping explosion of thunder shakes the house.

I duck my head into Franklin's room to see if he's okay. He's still fast asleep, his face as content as a well-fed baby's.

Through the window on the landing of the stairs, I see the sky has turned the color of black smoke. Torrents of rain lash the house as wind hurls leaves through the air. It whistles through loose panes, chilling me all over.

I hurry down the stairs, eager for the warmth of the kitchen. I find Elise just putting the finishing touches on her pie.

"Marcus, I need more wood for the oven if I'm to bake this pie. Would you get it for me, please? And then, maybe we have some tea and you tell Solomon and me what it was like to fly in that balloon."

"Fly? What is you, boy, a bird?" Solomon cackles.

I go to the wood room and set to work. The faster I finish, the faster I'll get back to Elise. I swing the axe with power and precision, cleanly splitting each log. Above, outside, thunder cracks and roars, making me feel warm and safe in the belly of Franklin's home.

Until Franklin's electric water heater starts acting up. The Leyden jars fill with white light and the copper tank hums, then vibrates, then rattles. Seconds later, the light turns blue. Only, it isn't just the light from the jars, it's the whole room. The source is behind me. I turn. The back wall of stone has again turned to "blue ocean" with a bright, bright sun in the distance.

That brightness hurts my eyes. Without thinking, I hold up my hand to block it. Suddenly, I'm caught in a magnetic pull. I have no chance to decide whether I want to go, no chance to consult with Franklin or to say goodbye to anyone.

That ocean sucks me in and everything goes yellow. As I rush along, paralyzed and feeling all those ants run through my veins, I have no idea where I'll be taken. Back to my own 21st century? Further forward to the end of time or back to the beginning? Philadelphia, PA in the good old USA? Or some planet where the atmosphere is ammonia and the temperature 3000°?

I'm terrified and completely forget what Franklin has said about seeing each other again.

Just like the last time, I land hard. It takes a while for those ants to stop racing and for my senses to start working again. Smell is the first thing to come back: the sour odor of the musty concrete my nose is mashed up against. I sneeze; and that brings back my vision. All the lights are on. An ornate old trunk with brass fittings stands in front of me. Pop's trunk from his parents, where he keeps all his "silly stuff:" knickknacks and memorabilia and souvenirs. Gus's green footlocker stands next to it.

I'm home, in our basement. But when?

As I raise myself to my hands and knees, I hear my mother call: "Marcus? Are you down here? *Marcus?*"

"Here, Mom," I croak. My throat feels like it's full of sand.

"Where?"

"Right here."

I step into the pool of light at the bottom of the stairs and look up. She stands at the top, with Penny. Their coats and hats stream water from the storm outside. Mom peers down at me.

"So ... you're still here," she says. "Decide maybe New York wasn't such a good idea?"

I can't answer. I'm still trying to get a handle on where and when I am.

Mom starts down the stairs. Penny stays behind, but lets out a giggle.

"Whatcha wearin', Marcus? You look so funny!"

I don't know how to answer that either.

Mom's down the stairs now. "Is that your father's old costume from the historical society ball? We didn't send you down here to play dress-up, you know. You're supposed to be writing that paper." She looks at the computer I never turned on. "You still haven't written a word, have you?"

"Uh … no."

"It's noon! What have you been doing all this time?"

Noon? Had I only been gone for four hours? Almost four months in 1787 crammed into some 240 minutes?

"Well? Answer me!"

I scramble for an explanation. She's never going to believe a story about time-travel. I'm not even sure I believe it. But I am dressed in these clothes—the second suit Franklin had bought me from Wigmore and that I'd changed into to go to the State House for the signing.

"Um … research?" I say lamely.

"When we tell you to do something, young man, we expect it done! No questions. No excuses. Just you doing what you're told …"

I could kiss her for going on like that, because it's giving me time to think.

" … when you're told and how you're told. *Claro?*

I'm still thinking and scrambling.

"*Marcus!* Are we *clear?*"

"See, Mom. That's the thing. I was having trouble getting started. So, I … I got up and … I started snooping around … and I came across this in Pop's trunk and I thought it might give me a little inspiration. You know, like any time I put a character's costume on for the first time, I find out all sorts of things about him. So I put this on and I went back upstairs to the books and my notes and …"

She's not buying it.

"And it worked!" I say. "Swear to God. I know exactly who the more important president is and exactly what to write."

"Oh, really?" She's arched her eyebrow and her tone drips sarcasm. "Enlighten me."

"Yes, Marcus. Enlighten all of us!"

I look up to see my father standing at the top of the stairs.

"Poppa!" Penny cries.

"Hello, you," my mother says, looking at him the way I once wanted Elise to look at me.

"I thought we weren't going to see you this weekend, what with your big trial," Pop says.

Reaching the bottom of the stairs, he takes Mom in his arms in a hug that I hope will last forever, to give me more time to think.

"We settled," Mom says. "Opposing counsel called this morning. Seems he and his client didn't want to spend their weekend in the office any more than I did. So, they made a very good offer. My client accepted, and I am free for the weekend. And with the fee I just made, we're looking forward to some financial stability. For once. Seems like forever since I've been able to say that. Anyway, I thought I'd come home and maybe see if you and I could give Marcus a little help on that paper of his."

"Don't need it," I say. "At least not right now. Because I really do know what to write."

"Which is?" she asks, doubt all over her face.

"That it's not a question of who was the more important president. That Washington and Lincoln were equally important to the times in which they lived and therefore to who we are today. Washington led us to victory in the Revolution and then helped fashion the Constitution and served as the country's first president. He was a charismatic, commanding leader who the people rallied around and who helped to liberate the colonies and then unite those 13 separate states into one nation called the United States. Twice, he was the most powerful man in the country, once as commander-in-chief of the Continental Army, and once as President. He could have retained that power for as long as he liked. But each time, he voluntarily gave it up, showing the people that, perpetually, they would have to choose their leaders and that, ultimately, the power to govern resides in them.

"Lincoln was a very different man and a very different president. Where Washington was handsome and graceful and actually part of the Virginia aristocracy, Lincoln came from a struggling farm family, had little formal schooling, was thought by many to be ugly and awkward—some compared him to an ape—and struggled with depression. Despite those handicaps, he was determined to succeed. He educated himself reading, taught himself the law, counteracted his ugliness with a great sense of humor, and became a successful lawyer and politician—so successful that he was nominated the Republican party's second presidential candidate.

"That determination carried through into his presidency, where he insisted that no state had the right to rebel or secede and that slavery was a moral wrong that had to be abolished. Both of those objectives were accomplished. He issued the Emancipation Proclamation, freeing all the slaves in the seceding states and then fought hard for passage of the 13th Amendment which completely abolished slavery throughout the country. And he led the Union to victory over those states, which re-united the country.

"So, each was vitally important to the nation in his own way and in his own time; and each was crucial in making the nation what it is today. The United States probably never would have been constituted had it not been for Washington. And the United States never would have been re-united, and slavery abolished, had it not been for Lincoln."

Mom and Pop stare at me. I want to tell them both to close their mouths or they'll catch a fly, but I don't. Franklin might be able to say it to me. But me get away with saying it to my parents? Ha! as both Mom and Sally Bache would say.

"Anyway, that's the rough outline of what I'm going to write—all with appropriate examples and evidence, of course."

"Well, it looks like you certainly don't need our help," Mom says. "It's a good thesis."

"It's excellent, Marcus, really excellent," Pop says. And that's when I know I just might have this paper aced. After all, he's the librarian with a Ph.D. in American History."

"And how about, before you begin," Mom says, "I whip up a lunch of *patatas fritas con huevos y jamon*? After all, it is your birthday."

"I have a better idea," my father says. "How about we all go to lunch at the City Tavern?"

"Marcus is certainly dressed for it!" Mom cracks.

"We haven't been there in I don't know how long," Pop says.

Not since Gus, I want to say, but don't.

"And I've missed those lunches," he says.

"So have I," my mother says.

"Me too," I say, thinking how, in just a few hours, some 230 years ago, Franklin will also be dining there.

"Oh, and Marcus?" my mother says. "Before you change, you might want to take a shower? You really kind of … stink!"

"Thanks, Mom. Thanks, very much."

As I climb the stairs to the third floor, I look out the window to the steel skeleton representing what had been Franklin's home—and my home too, for a little while. Next to it stands a mulberry tree, smaller than the one I'd known, its leaves shining in the new sunshine after the storm.

There are no laughing children there, now. No important men knocking on the door to ask an old sage's advice. No torches to light their way as they plan a government for the nation. No Franklin, or Sally, or Elise, whom I already miss. But they had been there once. And I had known them. And learned from them, I think: about meanness and cruelty, and growth and enlightenment, and trying to do what's right, even if other things have to be done first and compromises have to be made.

According to Franklin and Sally, I would know them again. Who can say what I will learn the next time around? Certainly, not I.

At least, not yet.

EPILOGUE

Having spent four months at and around the Constitutional Convention and its delegates, I was curious to know what happened with the Constitution, not to mention George Washington, James Madison, Alexander Hamilton, James Wilson, Robert Morris, Gouverneur Morris, and, most of all, my friend and mentor, Dr. Benjamin Franklin. Mom and Pop were kind of puzzled by my new-found interest in history, but they helped guide me to various on-line and historical society resources; and this is what I learned.

Several days after I left 1787, the Confederation Congress sitting in New York debated whether to censure the Constitutional Convention delegates for overstepping their authority and designing a completely new government. That debate ended, not with Congress's censure, but with its approving the new Constitution, which it sent to the states for ratification at special conventions where representatives chosen by the people considered what the delegates had designed.

Men like Wilson, Hamilton, and Madison, actively lobbied for ratification. In fact, several days after I left, James Wilson gave a speech in the back yard of the Pennsylvania State House that was widely reported in newspapers throughout the country. And Hamilton and Madison, along with New York lawyer John Jay, wrote a series of essays arguing the merits of the new Constitution. These were published in newspapers nationwide and are now collectively referred to, and still published and sold, as *The Federalist Papers.*

But there were others like George Mason and Elbridge Gerry, who thought the new Constitution gave the federal government too much power and individual citizens not enough. And many attending the ratifying conventions agreed. They were particularly concerned that the Constitution did not include any statement of individual rights.

In order to insure ratification, those supporting the Constitution had to promise that upon ratification, it quickly would be amended to include a "bill of rights."

It took about a year and a half for the states to complete ratification; and for the people to elect their new congressmen, senators, and president. On March 4, 1789, Congress held its first session, signaling that the federal government was open for business. Virginia Congressman James Madison immediately set to work drafting a set of amendments that guaranteed, among other things:

1) Freedom of speech;

2) Freedom of religion;

3) Freedom to assemble peacefully;

4) Freedom to petition the government for the redress of grievances;

5) The right to bear arms;

6) The right to be secure from unreasonable searches and seizures by the government;

7) The rights to trial by jury, due process, legal counsel, and not to be a witness against oneself in a criminal trial; and

8) The right to bail and not to be subjected to cruel and unusual punishment.

Those rights, and others, were set forth in the first ten amendments to the Constitution, or the Bill of Rights, which the Congress passed on September 25, 1789 and which the states finished ratifying, two years later, on December 15, 1791.

As to the "founding fathers" I'd spent time with: Of course, George Washington was elected our first president, taking office in New York City on April 30, 1789. John Adams was elected his Vice President; and Washington appointed Thomas Jefferson his Secretary of State. Washington had intended to appoint his friend, financer Robert Morris, his first Secretary of the Treasury. After all, Morris had been the "money man" behind the Revolution. But Morris had been elected to represent Pennsylvania in the United States Senate.

Following Morris's advice, Washington instead appointed his former aide-de-camp during the Revolution, Alexander Hamilton. Under Washington's watchful eye, Hamilton repaired the nation's credit by devising ways to pay off the war debts owed by the nation and all its states. He also established a National Bank, a mint for coining money, and a naval revenue service, a forerunner of our present-day Navy and Coast Guard. And he designed a Department of the Treasury that would both collect and disburse government revenues and help create economic conditions beneficial to American commerce.

When war broke out between Britain and France in 1793, Washington refused both Hamilton's advice to side with the British and Thomas Jefferson's advice to side with the French. Instead, in order to give the United States as much time and opportunity as possible to strengthen itself, Washington kept the nation neutral and out of war.

Hamilton was not the only individual from the Constitutional Convention that Washington placed in office. He appointed Virginian Edmond Randolph (the solemn-looking governor who'd introduced the Virginia Plan to the convention) his first Attorney General and later, his second Secretary of State. He nominated Scotsman James Wilson to be one of the first Supreme Court Justices. And, several years into his administration, he named Gouverneur Morris Ambassador to France.

Washington won re-election in 1794, but refused to stand for election to a third term. As he did when he voluntarily resigned as commander-in-chief of the Continental Army in 1783, Washington wanted to return to private life and his beloved plantation, Mount Vernon, in Virginia. He also didn't want anyone getting the idea that the Presidency might become a lifetime or hereditary job, like a monarchy.

Thus, Washington twice voluntarily gave up the most powerful position the nation had to offer, the first military, the second political. For this, Britain's King George III—whose armies Washington had defeated and who lost a significant piece of his empire as a result—called his former nemesis "the greatest character of the age."

Washington died at Mount Vernon on December 14, 1799 after contracting an upper respiratory infection while riding horseback through wet, icy weather to supervise work being done on the estate. He was less than two years into his retirement and only 67 years old. He was buried in the family crypt at Mount Vernon. In his will, the life-time slave owner who had concluded that slavery was bad for the nation, provided for the emancipation of the slaves he personally owned.

Congressman James Madison, Washington's friend and neighbor, and the man partially responsible for calling the Constitutional convention together, drafting the Virginia Plan, authoring *The Federalist Papers*, and drafting and passing the Bill of Rights, became the fourth President of the United States. He presided over the War of 1812, and was burned out of the White House by the British Army. His wife, Dolley Madison, is credited with saving the life-sized portrait of George Washington that still hangs in the East Room of the White House today.

Alexander Hamilton gave up his position as Secretary of the Treasury in 1794 and returned to the practice of law in New York. He continued to advise Washington and to involve himself in New York and national politics. In 1804, a long running dispute between him and Vice President Aaron Burr climaxed in an "affair of honor," or duel. On the morning of July 11th, the combatants and their seconds met at Weehawken, New Jersey. Both duelists fired their single-shot, flintlock pistols. Hamilton's ball missed. Burr's ball hit Hamilton in the abdomen, hip, liver, and spine. The former Secretary of the Treasury died the next day. He was buried in Manhattan, in the Trinity Church graveyard, at the head of Wall Street. Gouverneur Morris gave his eulogy and provided financial support to his family.

After serving one term in the U.S. Senate, financier Robert Morris returned to his business pursuits in Philadelphia. Unfortunately, the success that he had known for most of his life deserted him, and as the result of risky real estate investments and the financial panic of 1797, he went bankrupt, spending three long years in debtors' prison. He died, in poverty, in Philadelphia in 1806 and is buried in the North Garden, or churchyard, at Christ Church near 2nd and Market Streets. Gouverneur Morris, who once worked for him, provided financial support to his family.

That same financial panic also ruined James Wilson. He might have been a Supreme Court justice, but that didn't stop him from investing in risky real estate ventures or from going broke. He, also, was incarcerated—briefly—in debtors' prisons in New Jersey and North Carolina. He, also, is buried in Christ Church's North Garden.

As for Benjamin Franklin—already 81 at the time I knew him—he continued his life of service. He was elected to a third, consecutive, one-year term as President of Pennsylvania. In the hopes that others might find the example of his life useful and instructive, he kept writing his autobiography, managing to double its length, and stopping only when the pain from his stones became so great that he had to resort to laudanum (a mixture of opium and alcohol) for relief. His autobiography ends at 1758, with him living and working in London as Pennsylvania's agent.

And, true to his word, Franklin concentrated a lot of his remaining energies on the abolition of slavery. Continuing as president of Pennsylvania's abolition society, he submitted an abolition petition to the United States Congress. That body, in its infinite wisdom, declined to act, claiming it did not have the power to interfere in states' internal affairs.

Franklin refused to allow that to be the final word. In response, only a month before his death, the creator of *Poor Richard's Almanac* and so many witty, satirical pieces, authored one final piece, published in *The Federal Gazette*, skewering slavery and anyone who would argue for its continuation.

One day in April, 1790, Franklin felt a pain in his chest and then developed a high fever. Having twice suffered pleurisy, one of his lungs now developed an abscess. When that abscess burst, Franklin slipped into a coma. Attended by his daughter and son-in-law, Sally and Richard Bache, and his grandsons Benjamin and Temple, he died peacefully on April 17th. He was buried next to his wife Deborah in Christ Church's Burial Ground at 5th and Arch Streets, only a few blocks from Franklin Court. The couple still rest there today, alongside their daughter Sally, grandson Benjamin, their friend and fellow abolitionist (and signer of the Declaration of Independence) Dr. Benjamin Rush, and, in an ironic twist, Major William Jackson, the man who beat out Temple Franklin for the job of Secretary to the Constitutional Convention; and without whose victory, I never would have become Benjamin Franklin's "amanuensis."

AUTHOR'S NOTES AND ACKNOWLEDGEMENTS

The Quest to Unite Us is a novel, a work of historical fiction. I wrote it hoping to entertain. It is not a comprehensive history of the Constitutional Convention or a complete biography of any of the delegates. My aim was to write an engaging story that would invite you, the reader, to learn more about the history of the United States and some of the people and events that helped to make it what it is today. I thank you for reading and I hope you enjoyed it.

Along the way, you may have wondered: what's real and what's not? What actually happened in history and what are figments of the author's imagination?

Marcus Santana, his family, his home, and his travels through time are all fiction.

Benjamin Franklin, George Washington, James Wilson, James Madison, Alexander Hamilton, and all the delegates to the Constitutional Convention of 1787 are historical figures. Relying on histories and biographies too numerous to list here, I tried to be as accurate as possible relating biographical details about the delegates. Concerning the convention itself, I relied on the contemporaneous notes taken by James Madison, and numerous other sources, in attempting to recreate actual sessions, speeches, and debates. While I took some liberties in order to modernize the language so as to enhance readability, my aim was to report the substance of what the delegates said.

All the scenes that *do not* take place on the floor of the convention are fictional, even though they may involve actual historical figures, organizations, or places; or be similar to events that happened at some other time. For example, the meetings of the Union Fire Company and the Free Africa Society and of delegates in Franklin's garden and at the Indian Queen, the scenes on Market Street and on and around the Delaware River, the plot to destroy the Pennsylvania State House (now "Independence Hall"), and Franklin's balloon ride are completely fictional; as are Elise, Katy Katz, Watchman Emery, Timothy Wimpole, Johnathon Swinbourne, Lucas Rush, Joseph Carver, Mrs. Carver, Jailer Kyle, Solomon Yates, and other minor characters.

With the exception of the hot water heater, all of Benjamin Franklin's inventions, writings, drawings, and publications actually existed; as did the Franklin children and grandchildren appearing in the story, including Sally Bache, William Franklin, and Temple Franklin; as did Franklin's friends Doctor Benjamin Rush (a fellow signer of the Declaration of Independence and abolitionist) and silversmith Phillip Syng (designer and crafter of the inkwell used to sign both the Declaration and the Constitution).

However, the Franklin home at Franklin Court was torn down in 1812 and our knowledge of what was actually there is incomplete. Therefore, much of what is described about the layout and interior is the product of my imagination, based on reading and a trip to Franklin Court and the Benjamin Franklin Museum located there. However, Franklin's garden and mulberry tree were real. The white steel skeleton that stands there today, and the new mulberry tree, are real.

Reverend Absalom Jones and Reverend Richard Allen are historical figures. The story of their departure from St. George's Methodist Episcopal Church and subsequent formation of the Free African Society is true.

Balloonist Jean Pierre Blanchard is a historical figure. And he really did make an ascent from the yard of the Walnut Street Jail. But he didn't do it until 1793, some three years after Franklin's death. President George Washington and future presidents John Adams, Thomas Jefferson, James Madison, and James Monroe all witnessed America's first manned flight. To the best of my knowledge, although Franklin did financially support the development of hot-air balloons while serving as our Minister to France during the Revolutionary War, he never actually flew in one.

My heartfelt thanks and appreciation go to the following who have supported me with their time, interest, effort, and encouragement.

To historian Keith Arbour for reading and commenting on the manuscript and for his insights into Franklin, the times in which he lived, and the publishing industry; and for his friendship and encouragement.

To his wife, Nancy Arbour, for reading and commenting on the manuscript.

To Anne A. Verplanck, Ph.D., Associate Professor of American Studies and Heritage Studies at Penn State, Harrisburg, for reading and commenting on the manuscript and for her insights into 18th Century Philadelphia.

To educator and author Nicholas Noble for his friendship over the years and for reading and commenting on the manuscript.

To Ursula G. Lowerre for reading and commenting on this manuscript (as well as others) and for her always on-point insights; and for her long-time, steadfast friendship.

To Paul C. Lowerre for keeping the financial ship afloat, allowing me to engage in this and other projects, and for his steadfast friendship for over 50 years.

To actress, director, musician and college pal Catherine Lyon, and to Karen Kleppe Lembo, for reading the manuscript and urging me to keep going with the publication process.

To Rachel Woods, for reading and commenting on the manuscript.

To bookseller Barbara J. Kelley for reading an early version and telling me I still had lots more work to do.

To editor Carrie Cantor for telling me where an early version of the manuscript made sense and where it didn't.

And most important of all, to Eugenie, my wife of 35 years, and my best friend for 36, who read so many drafts, listened to ideas, found errors, suggested changes, and was oh-so kind and patient throughout. I could not have done this without you.

Of course, the responsibility for any error or omission found in *The Quest to Unite Us: Book I of the Marcus Santana Time Travel Chronicles* rests solely with me and not with any of the individuals named above.

About the Author

William de Rham once practiced law in Philadelphia, right across the street from Independence Hall, which is where he learned that travel through time really is possible. He lives in Maine where he is at work on Book II of *The Marcus Santana Time Travel Chronicles*.

www.ingramcontent.com/pod-product-compliance
Lightning Source LLC
Chambersburg PA
CBHW071550110726
47908CB00007B/2057